MER

JOELLE SELLNER
&
ABBY BOEH

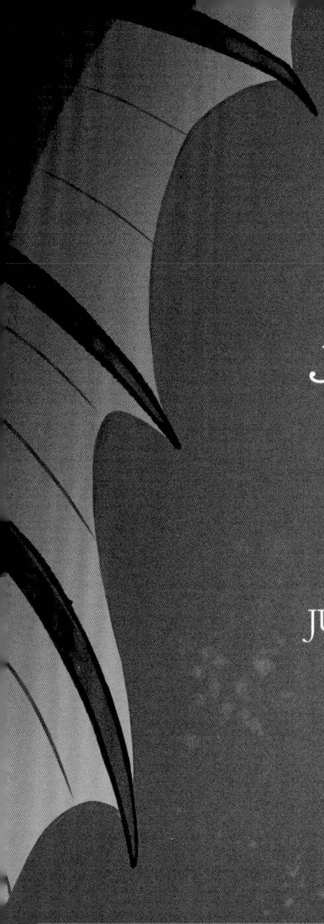

Writer

JOELLE SELLNER

Artist

ABBY BOEH

Colorist
JULIA SCOTT

Letterer
STEVE WANDS

Editor ADAM STAFFARONI
Assistant Editor HAZEL NEWLEVANT

Publisher's Cataloging-In-Publication Data

(Prepared by The Donohue Group, Inc.)

Names: Sellner, Joelle, author. | Boeh, Abby, illustrator. | Scott, Julia, colorist. | Wands, Steve, letterer. | Staffaroni, Adam, editor. | Newlevant, Hazel, editor.

Title: Mer. Vol.1 / writer: Joelle Sellner ; artist: Abby Boeh ; colorist: Julia Scott ; letterer: Steve Wands ; editor: Adam Staffaroni ; assistant editor: Hazel Newlevant.

Description: [St. Louis, Missouri] : The Lion Forge, LLC, 2017. | Interest age level: 12 and up. | "Roar." | Summary: "After the death of her beloved mother, Aryn's father has moved her family to a new town hoping for a fresh start. At first things seem to be going well - Aryn is making friends and has even caught the eye of one of the hottest guys in school. But there are dark forces moving under the surface that Aryn cannot see; and her new crush may not be human."-- Provided by publisher.

Identifiers: ISBN 978-1-941302-28-6

Subjects: LCSH: Teenage girls--Comic books, strips, etc. | Mermen--Comic books, strips, etc. | Good and evil--Comic books, strips, etc. | LCGFT: Graphic novels.

Classification: LCC PN6728 .M47 2017 | DDC 741.5973 [Fic]--dc23

MER

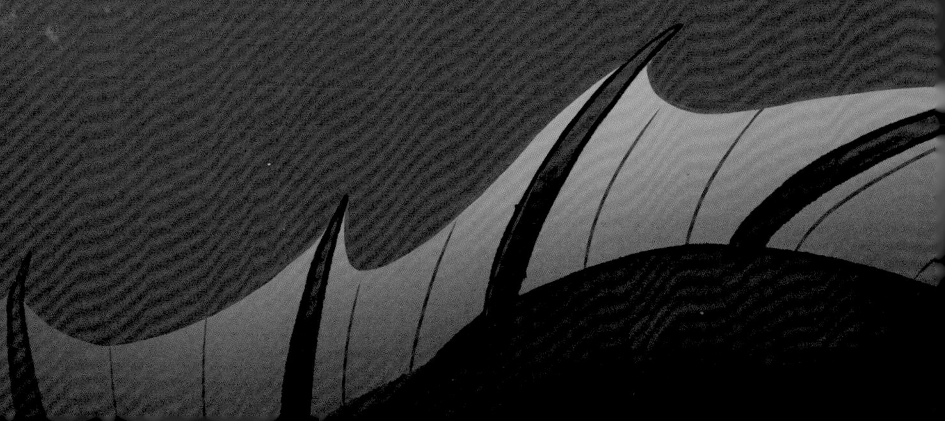

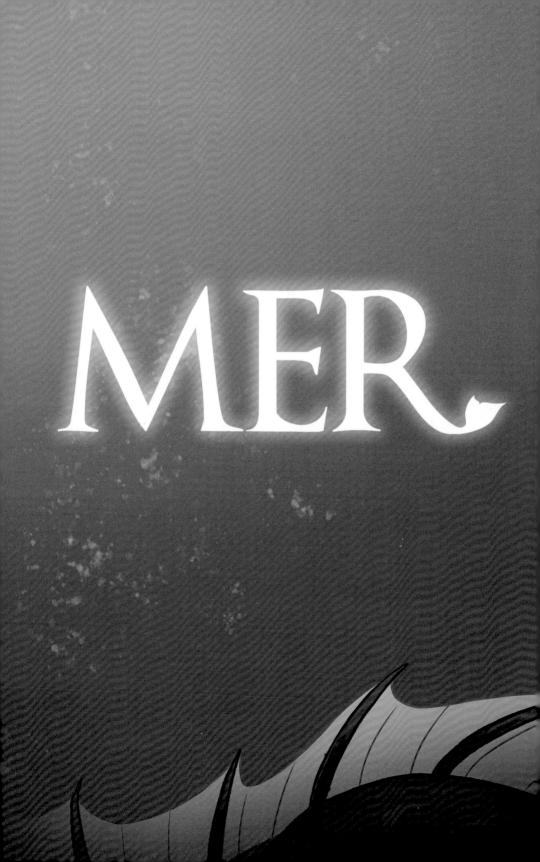

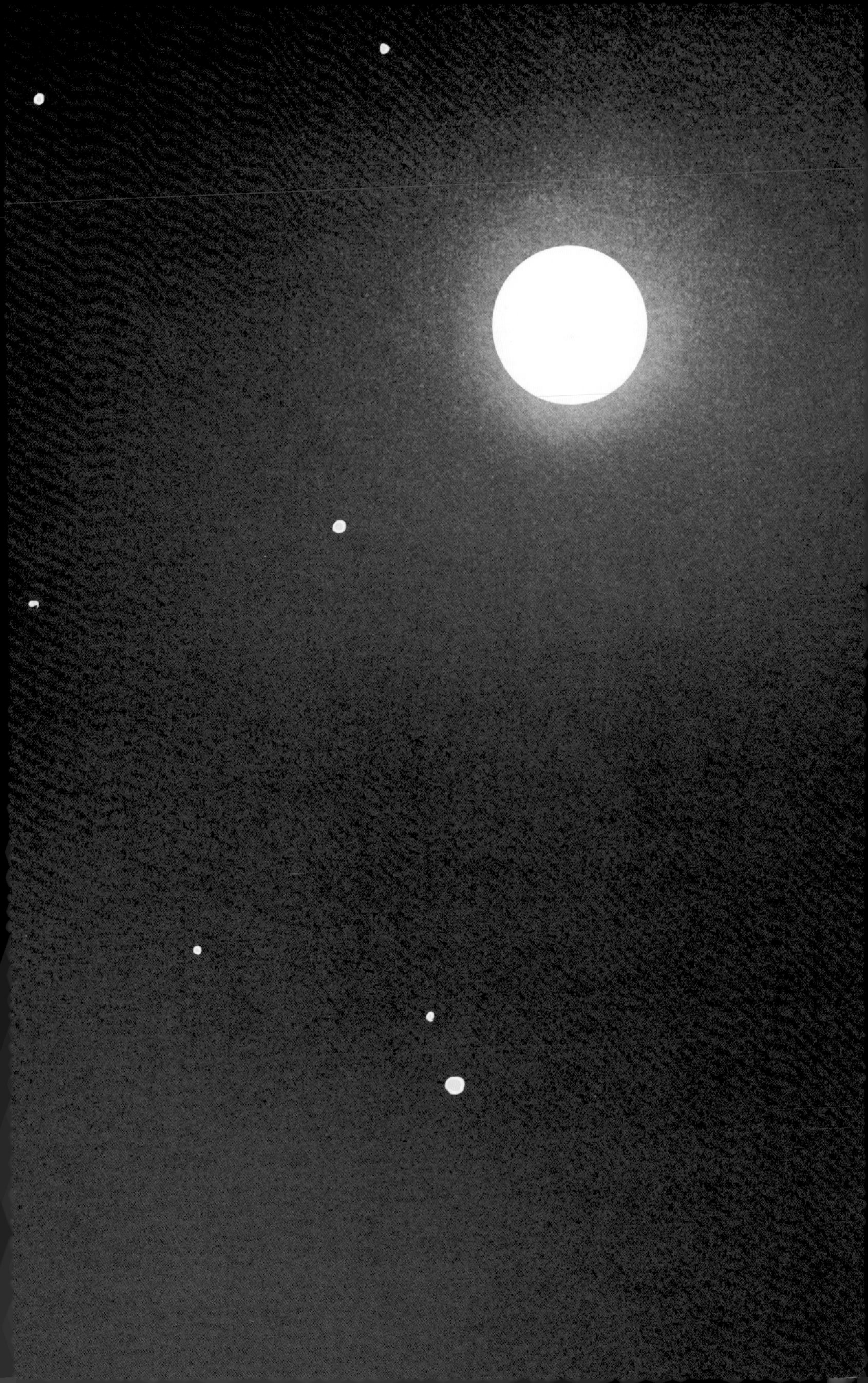

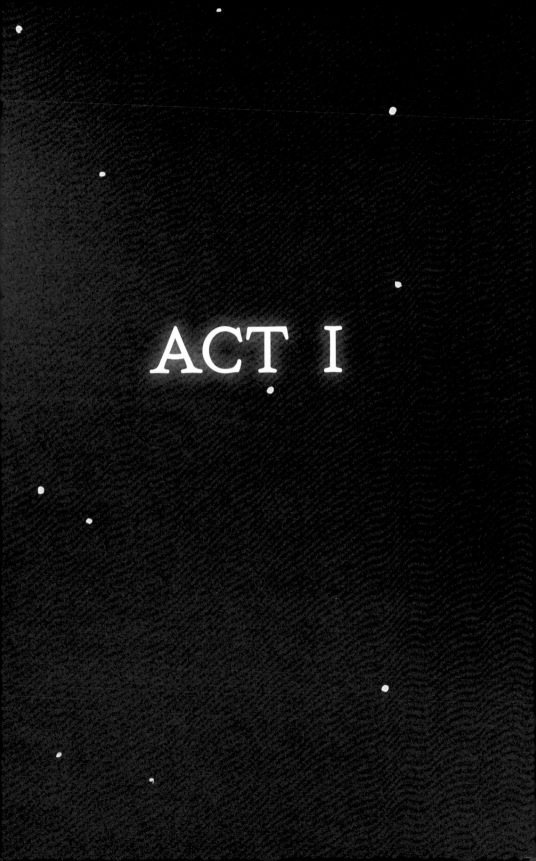

ACT I

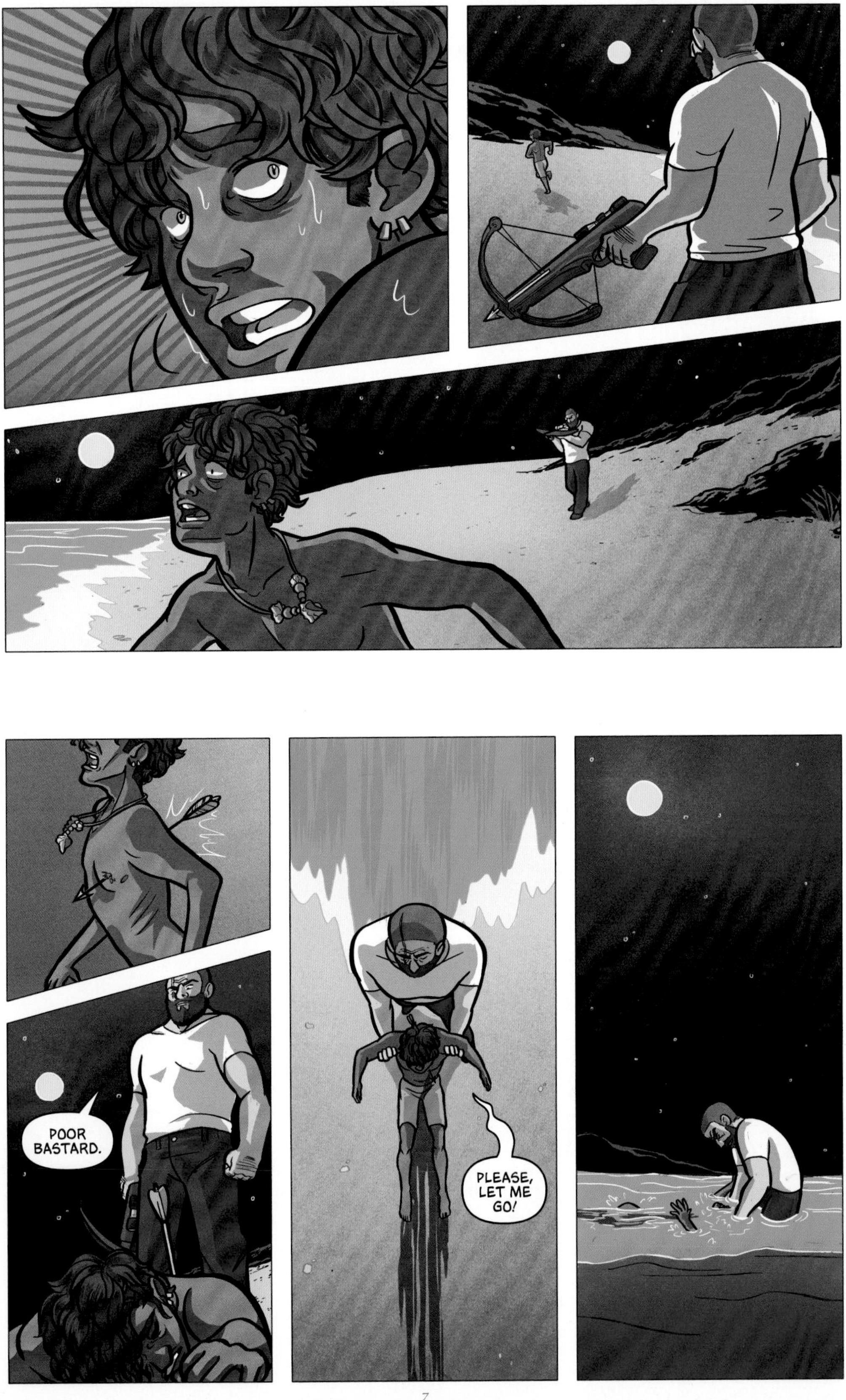
POOR BASTARD.
PLEASE, LET ME GO!

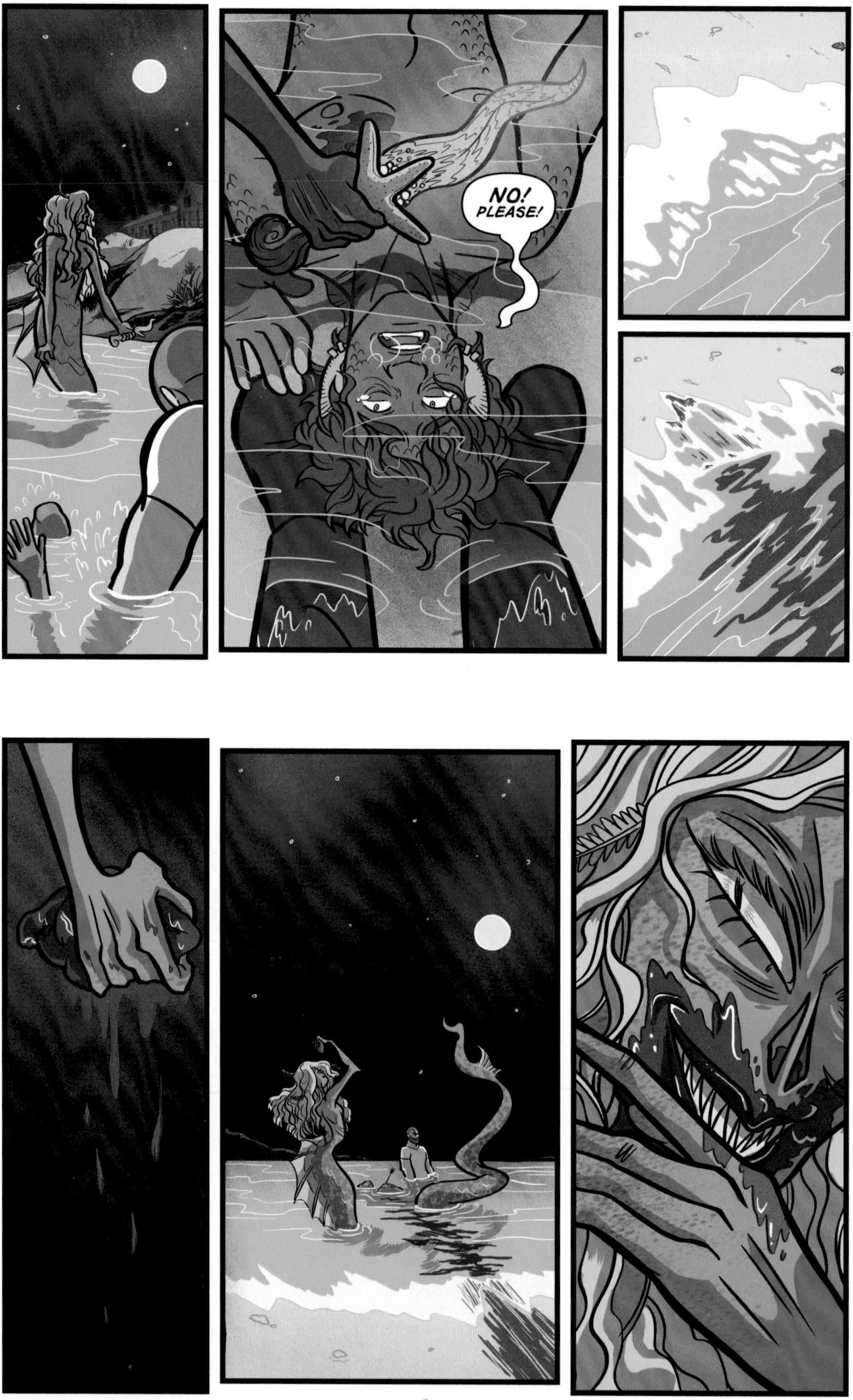
NO! PLEASE!

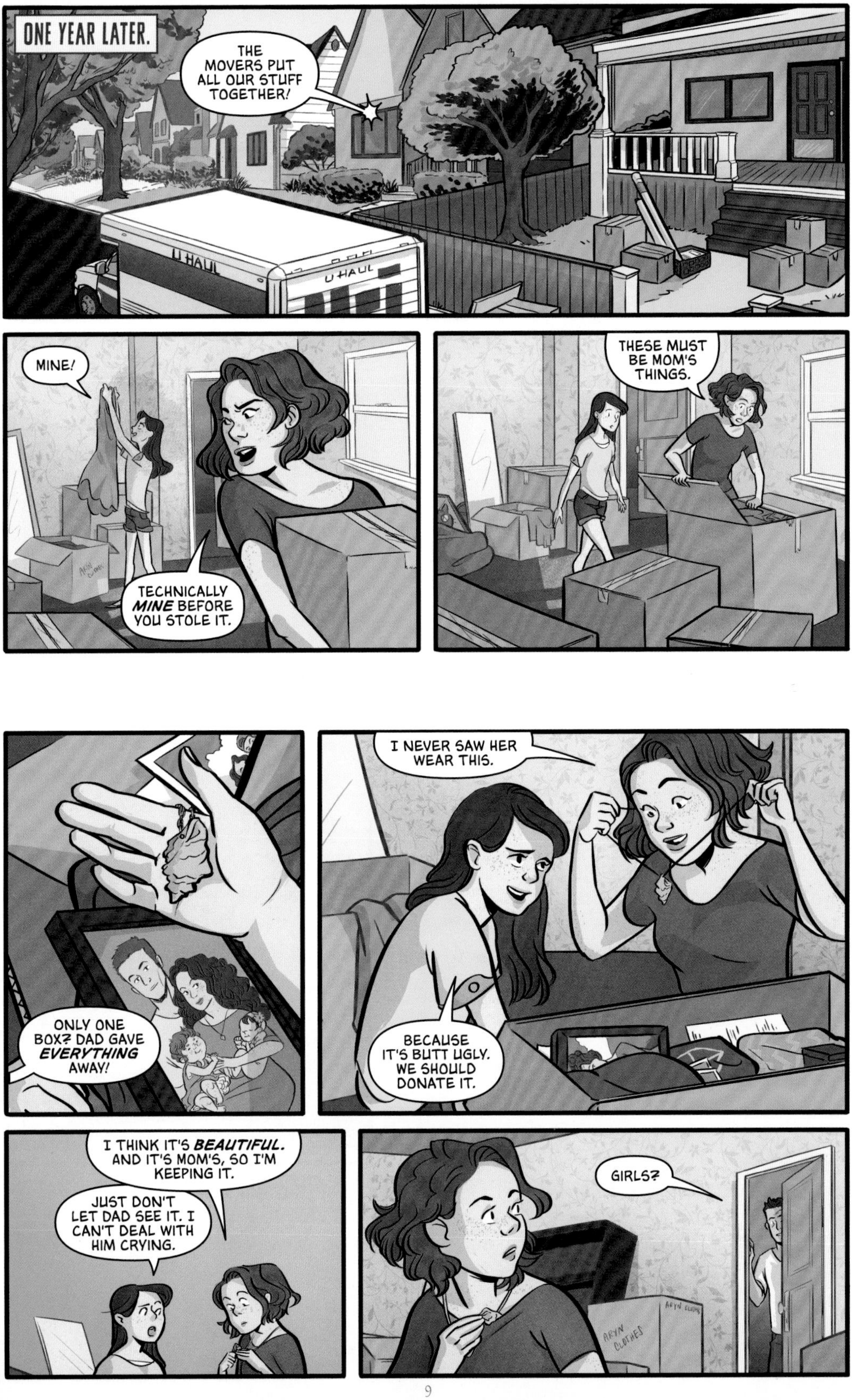
ONE YEAR LATER.
THE MOVERS PUT ALL OUR STUFF TOGETHER!
MINE!
TECHNICALLY *MINE* BEFORE YOU STOLE IT.
THESE MUST BE MOM'S THINGS.
U-HAUL
ONLY ONE BOX? DAD GAVE *EVERYTHING* AWAY!
I NEVER SAW HER WEAR THIS.
BECAUSE IT'S BUTT UGLY. WE SHOULD DONATE IT.
I THINK IT'S *BEAUTIFUL.* AND IT'S MOM'S, SO I'M KEEPING IT.
JUST DON'T LET DAD SEE IT. I CAN'T DEAL WITH HIM CRYING.
GIRLS?
ARYN CLOTHES

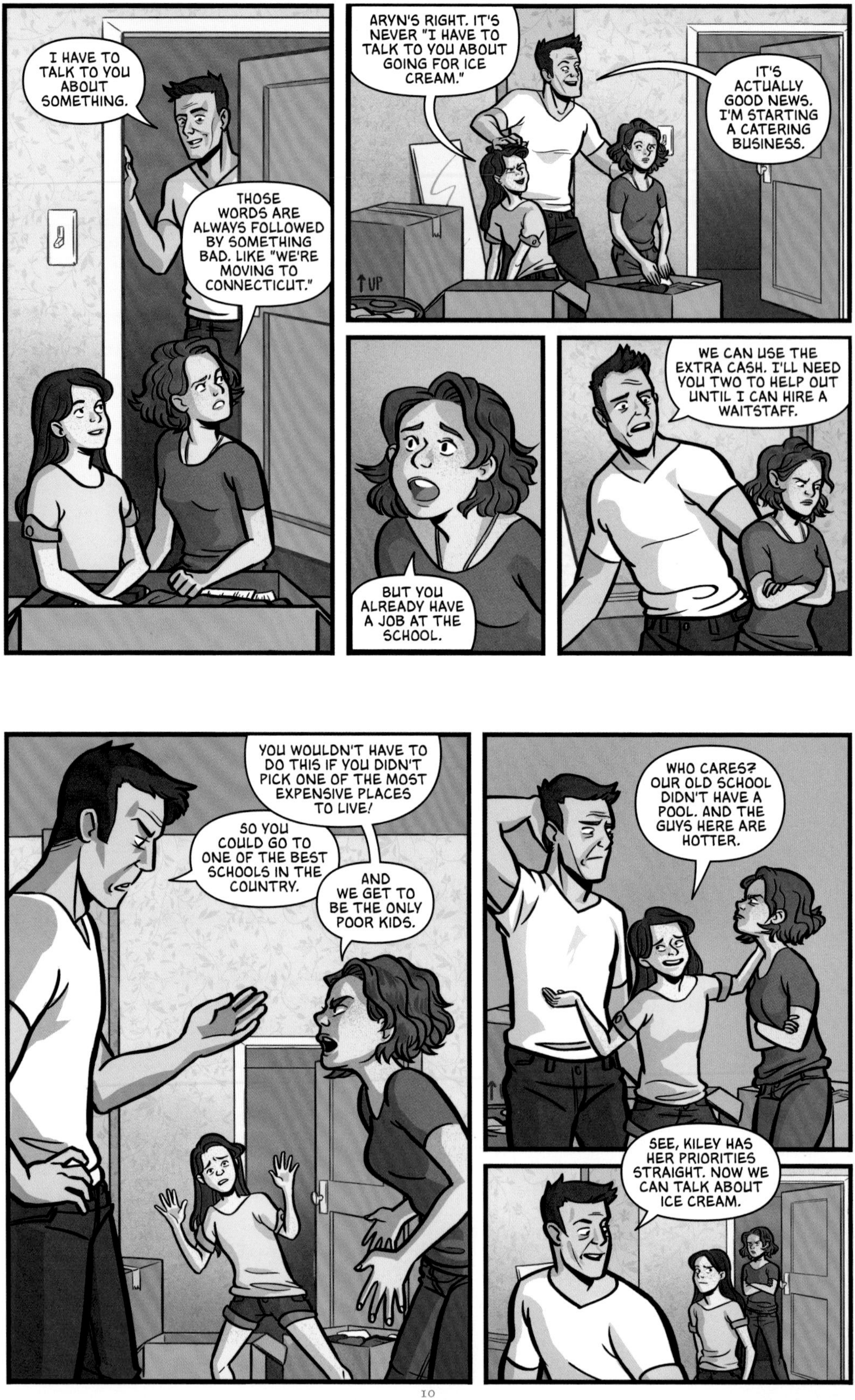
I HAVE TO TALK TO YOU ABOUT SOMETHING.
THOSE WORDS ARE ALWAYS FOLLOWED BY SOMETHING BAD. LIKE "WE'RE MOVING TO CONNECTICUT."
ARYN'S RIGHT. IT'S NEVER "I HAVE TO TALK TO YOU ABOUT GOING FOR ICE CREAM."
IT'S ACTUALLY GOOD NEWS. I'M STARTING A CATERING BUSINESS.
↑UP
BUT YOU ALREADY HAVE A JOB AT THE SCHOOL.
WE CAN USE THE EXTRA CASH. I'LL NEED YOU TWO TO HELP OUT UNTIL I CAN HIRE A WAITSTAFF.
YOU WOULDN'T HAVE TO DO THIS IF YOU DIDN'T PICK ONE OF THE MOST EXPENSIVE PLACES TO LIVE!
SO YOU COULD GO TO ONE OF THE BEST SCHOOLS IN THE COUNTRY.
AND WE GET TO BE THE ONLY POOR KIDS.
WHO CARES? OUR OLD SCHOOL DIDN'T HAVE A POOL. AND THE GUYS HERE ARE HOTTER.
SEE, KILEY HAS HER PRIORITIES STRAIGHT. NOW WE CAN TALK ABOUT ICE CREAM.

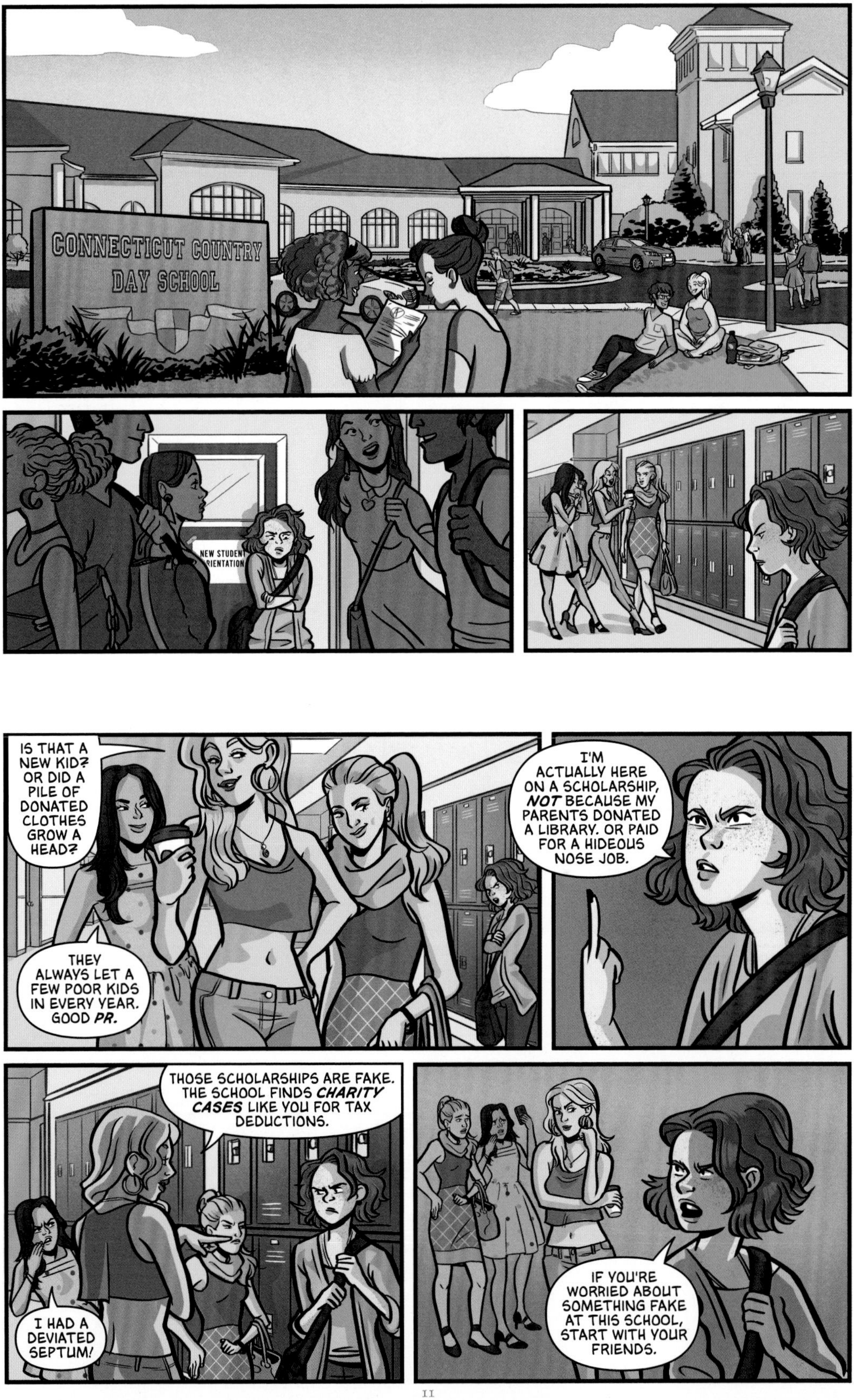
CONNECTICUT COUNTRY DAY SCHOOL
NEW STUDENT ORIENTATION
IS THAT A NEW KID? OR DID A PILE OF DONATED CLOTHES GROW A HEAD?
THEY ALWAYS LET A FEW POOR KIDS IN EVERY YEAR. GOOD PR.
I'M ACTUALLY HERE ON A SCHOLARSHIP, NOT BECAUSE MY PARENTS DONATED A LIBRARY. OR PAID FOR A HIDEOUS NOSE JOB.
THOSE SCHOLARSHIPS ARE FAKE. THE SCHOOL FINDS CHARITY CASES LIKE YOU FOR TAX DEDUCTIONS.
I HAD A DEVIATED SEPTUM!
IF YOU'RE WORRIED ABOUT SOMETHING FAKE AT THIS SCHOOL, START WITH YOUR FRIENDS.

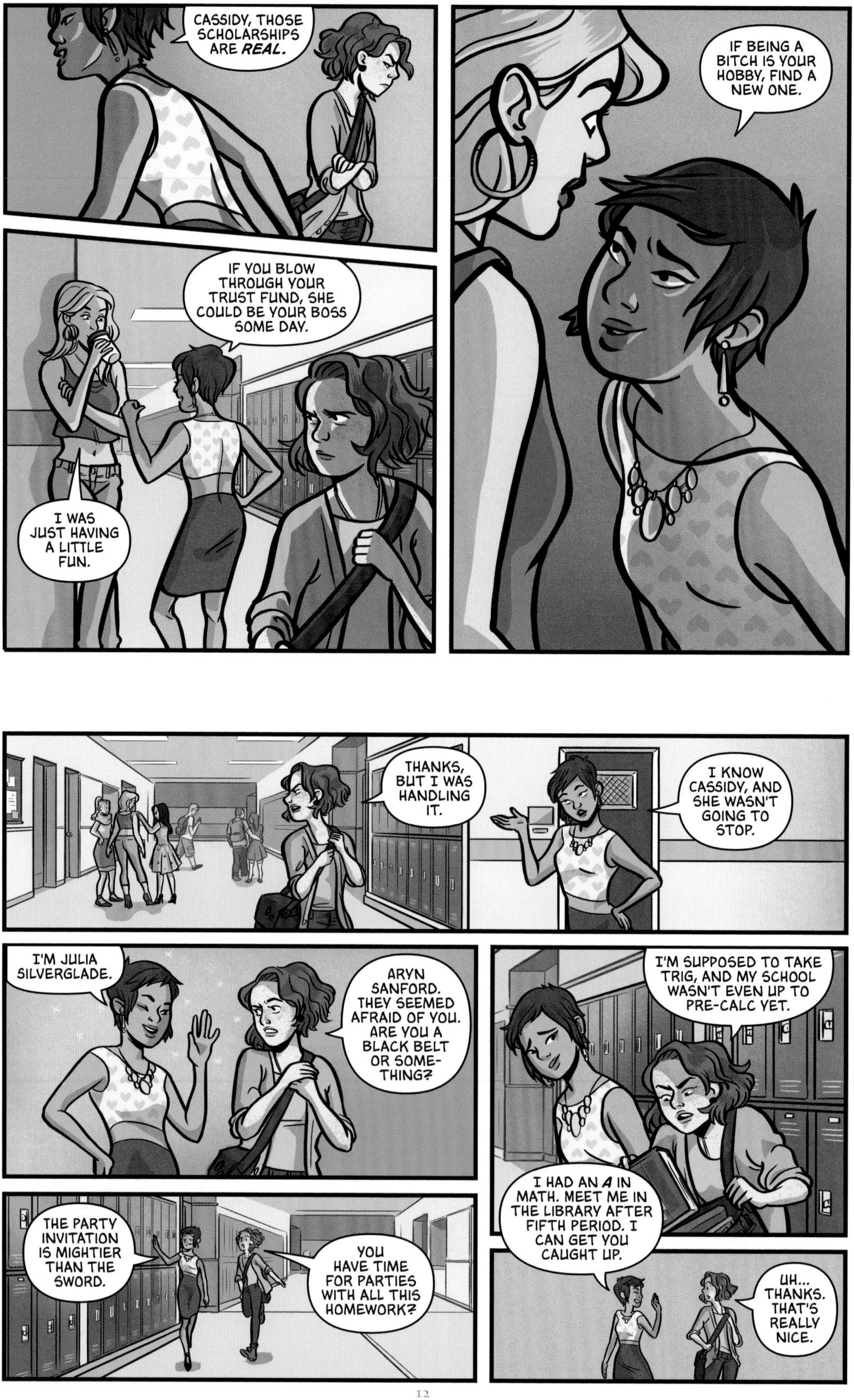
CASSIDY, THOSE SCHOLARSHIPS ARE *REAL.*
IF YOU BLOW THROUGH YOUR TRUST FUND, SHE COULD BE YOUR BOSS SOME DAY.
I WAS JUST HAVING A LITTLE FUN.
IF BEING A BITCH IS YOUR HOBBY, FIND A NEW ONE.
THANKS, BUT I WAS HANDLING IT.
I KNOW CASSIDY, AND SHE WASN'T GOING TO STOP.
I'M JULIA SILVERGLADE.
ARYN SANFORD. THEY SEEMED AFRAID OF YOU. ARE YOU A BLACK BELT OR SOME-THING?
THE PARTY INVITATION IS MIGHTIER THAN THE SWORD.
YOU HAVE TIME FOR PARTIES WITH ALL THIS HOMEWORK?
I'M SUPPOSED TO TAKE TRIG, AND MY SCHOOL WASN'T EVEN UP TO PRE-CALC YET.
I HAD AN *A* IN MATH. MEET ME IN THE LIBRARY AFTER FIFTH PERIOD. I CAN GET YOU CAUGHT UP.
UH... THANKS. THAT'S REALLY NICE.

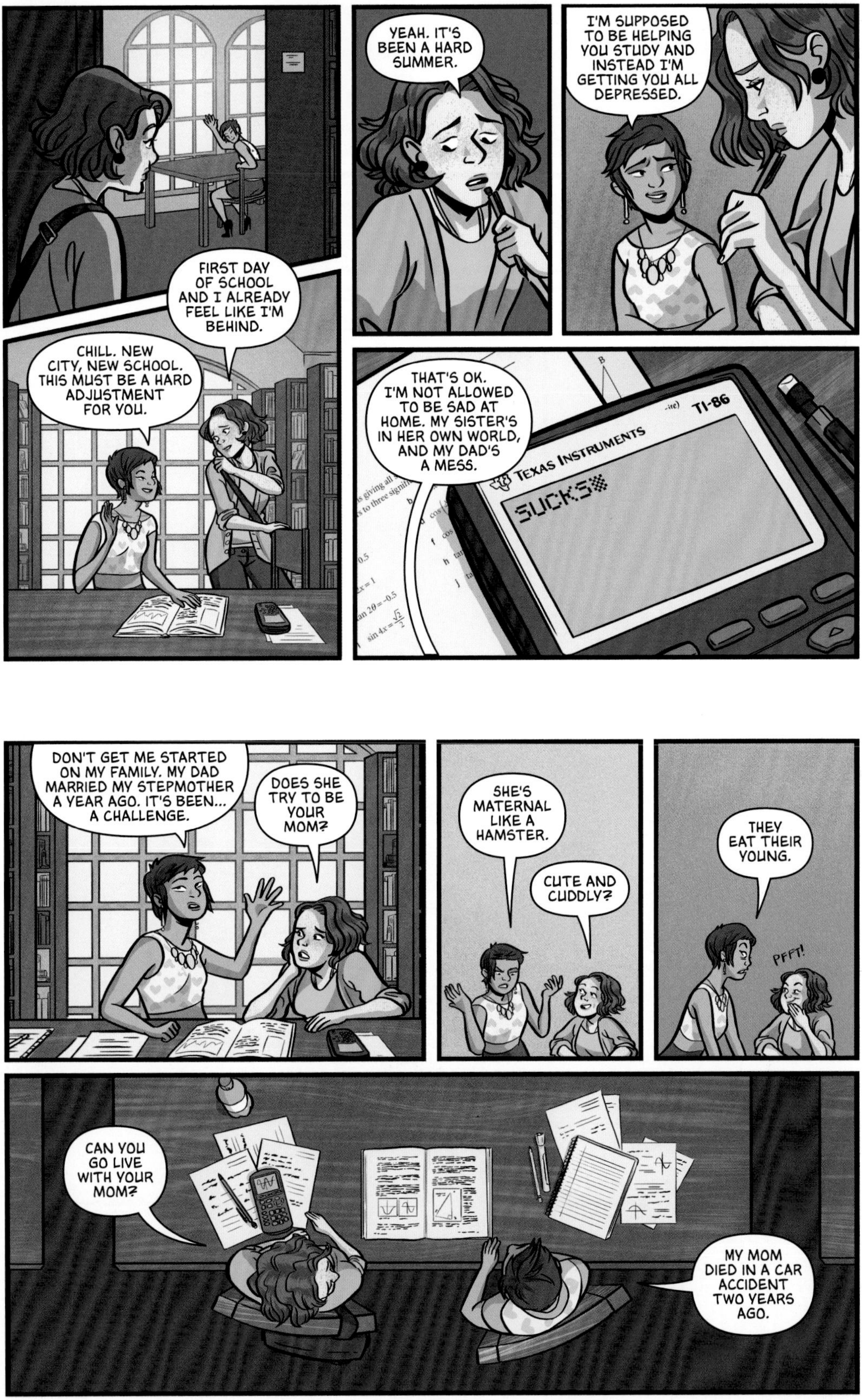
FIRST DAY OF SCHOOL AND I ALREADY FEEL LIKE I'M BEHIND.
CHILL. NEW CITY, NEW SCHOOL. THIS MUST BE A HARD ADJUSTMENT FOR YOU.
YEAH. IT'S BEEN A HARD SUMMER.
I'M SUPPOSED TO BE HELPING YOU STUDY AND INSTEAD I'M GETTING YOU ALL DEPRESSED.
THAT'S OK. I'M NOT ALLOWED TO BE SAD AT HOME. MY SISTER'S IN HER OWN WORLD, AND MY DAD'S A MESS.
TI-86
TEXAS INSTRUMENTS
SUCKS
DON'T GET ME STARTED ON MY FAMILY. MY DAD MARRIED MY STEPMOTHER A YEAR AGO. IT'S BEEN... A CHALLENGE.
DOES SHE TRY TO BE YOUR MOM?
SHE'S MATERNAL LIKE A HAMSTER.
CUTE AND CUDDLY?
THEY EAT THEIR YOUNG.
PFFT!
CAN YOU GO LIVE WITH YOUR MOM?
MY MOM DIED IN A CAR ACCIDENT TWO YEARS AGO.

I'M SO SORRY. MY MOM DIED A FEW MONTHS AGO. LUNG CANCER.

IT'S NICE TO HAVE SOMEONE TO TALK TO BESIDES MY CREEPY SHRINK.

MY FRIENDS DON'T UNDERSTAND. THEY BITCH ABOUT THEIR MOMS AND I BAWL MY EYES OUT EVERY MOTHER'S DAY.

GREAT. I HAVE THAT TO LOOK FORWARD TO.

HER BIRTHDAY WILL BE TOUGH. AND THE HOLIDAYS. BUT AFTER TIME IT GETS BETTER.

I PROMISE.

I HOPE SO.

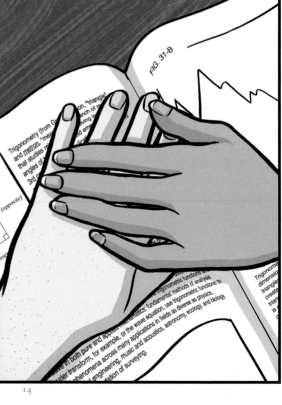

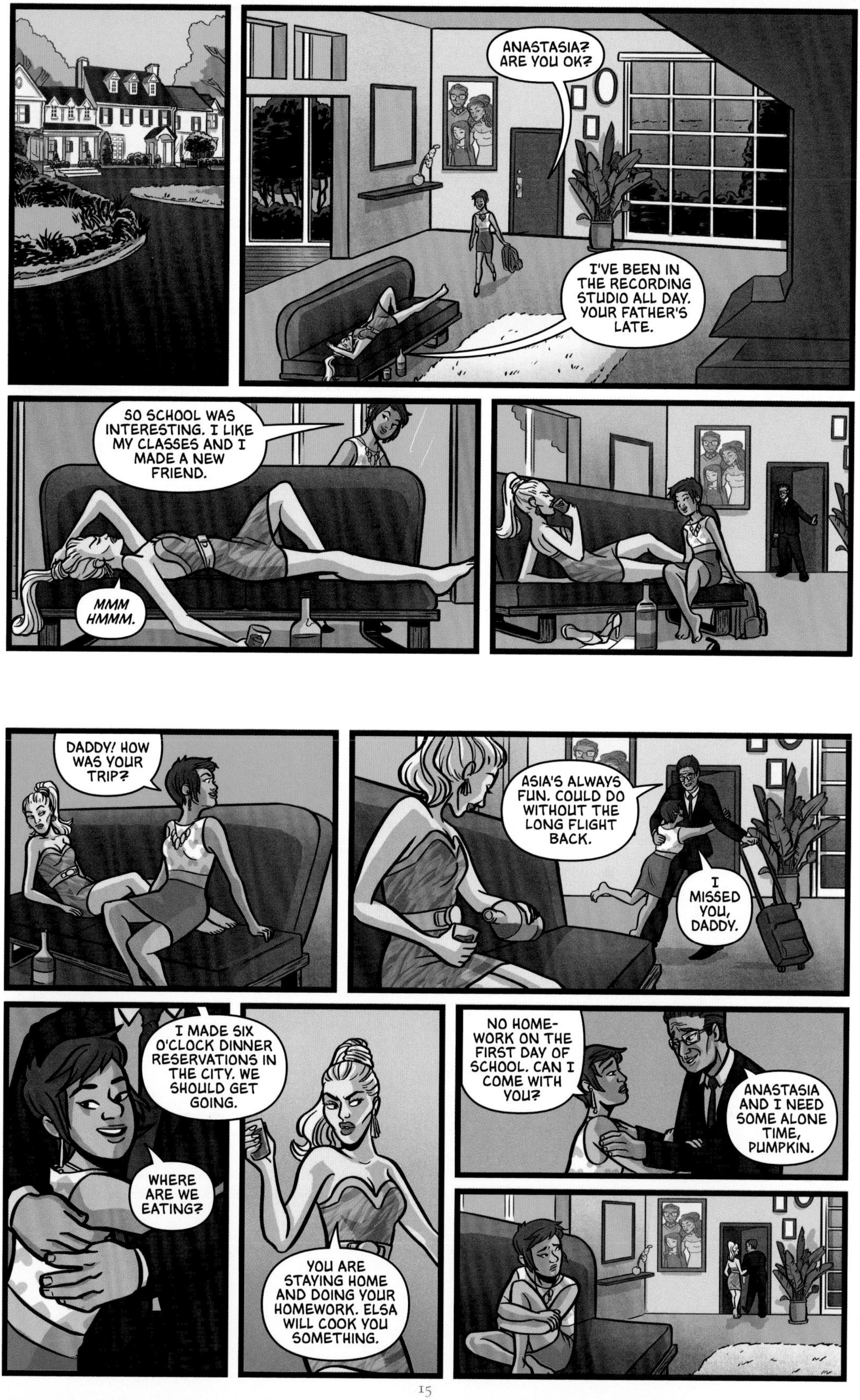
ANASTASIA? ARE YOU OK?
I'VE BEEN IN THE RECORDING STUDIO ALL DAY. YOUR FATHER'S LATE.
SO SCHOOL WAS INTERESTING. I LIKE MY CLASSES AND I MADE A NEW FRIEND.
MMM HMMM.
DADDY! HOW WAS YOUR TRIP?
ASIA'S ALWAYS FUN. COULD DO WITHOUT THE LONG FLIGHT BACK.
I MISSED YOU, DADDY.
I MADE SIX O'CLOCK DINNER RESERVATIONS IN THE CITY. WE SHOULD GET GOING.
WHERE ARE WE EATING?
YOU ARE STAYING HOME AND DOING YOUR HOMEWORK. ELSA WILL COOK YOU SOMETHING.
NO HOME-WORK ON THE FIRST DAY OF SCHOOL. CAN I COME WITH YOU?
ANASTASIA AND I NEED SOME ALONE TIME, PUMPKIN.

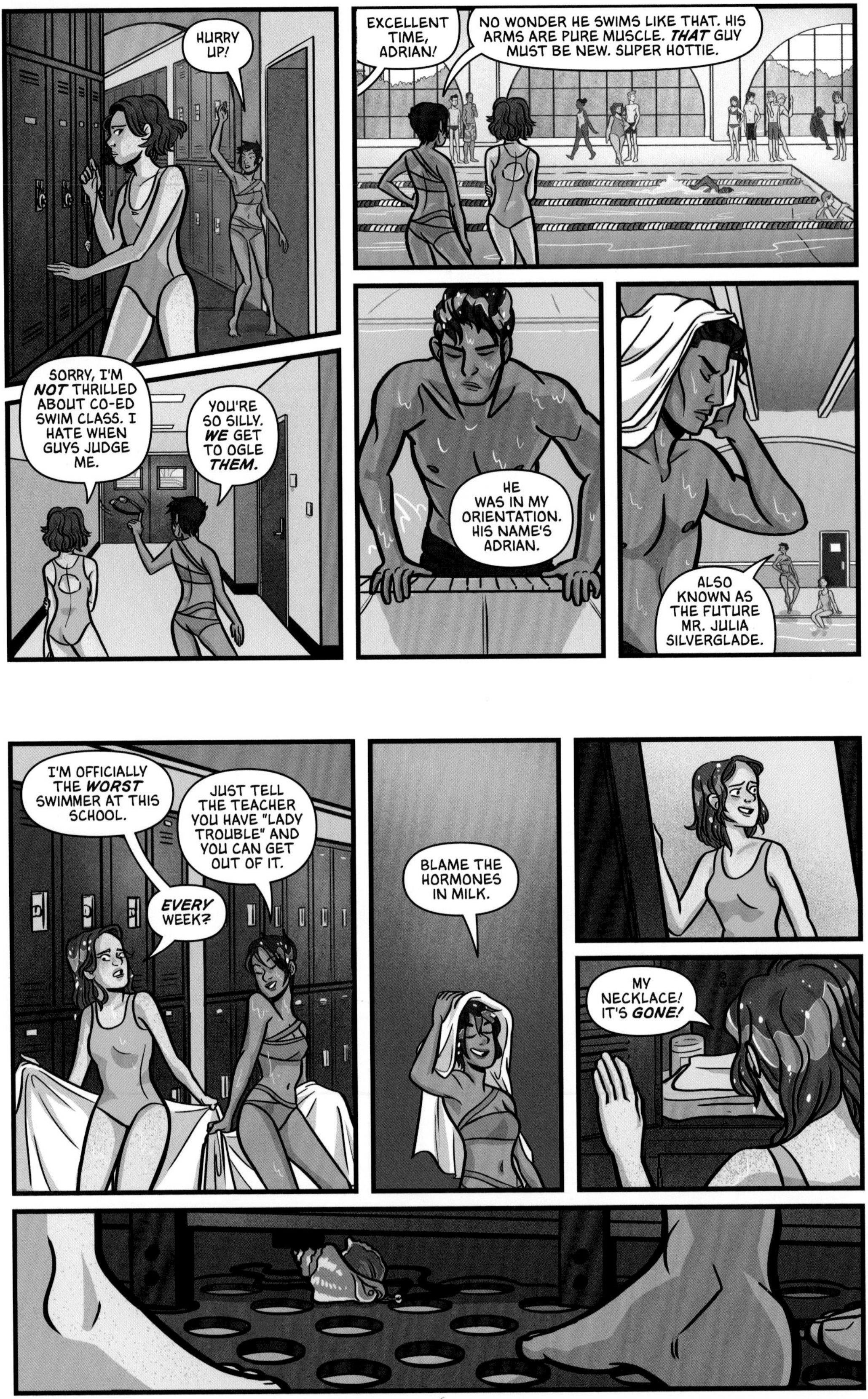
HURRY UP!
EXCELLENT TIME, ADRIAN!
NO WONDER HE SWIMS LIKE THAT. HIS ARMS ARE PURE MUSCLE. *THAT* GUY MUST BE NEW. SUPER HOTTIE.
SORRY, I'M *NOT* THRILLED ABOUT CO-ED SWIM CLASS. I HATE WHEN GUYS JUDGE ME.
YOU'RE SO SILLY. *WE* GET TO OGLE *THEM.*
HE WAS IN MY ORIENTATION. HIS NAME'S ADRIAN.
ALSO KNOWN AS THE FUTURE MR. JULIA SILVERGLADE.
I'M OFFICIALLY THE *WORST* SWIMMER AT THIS SCHOOL.
JUST TELL THE TEACHER YOU HAVE "LADY TROUBLE" AND YOU CAN GET OUT OF IT.
EVERY WEEK?
BLAME THE HORMONES IN MILK.
MY NECKLACE! IT'S *GONE!*

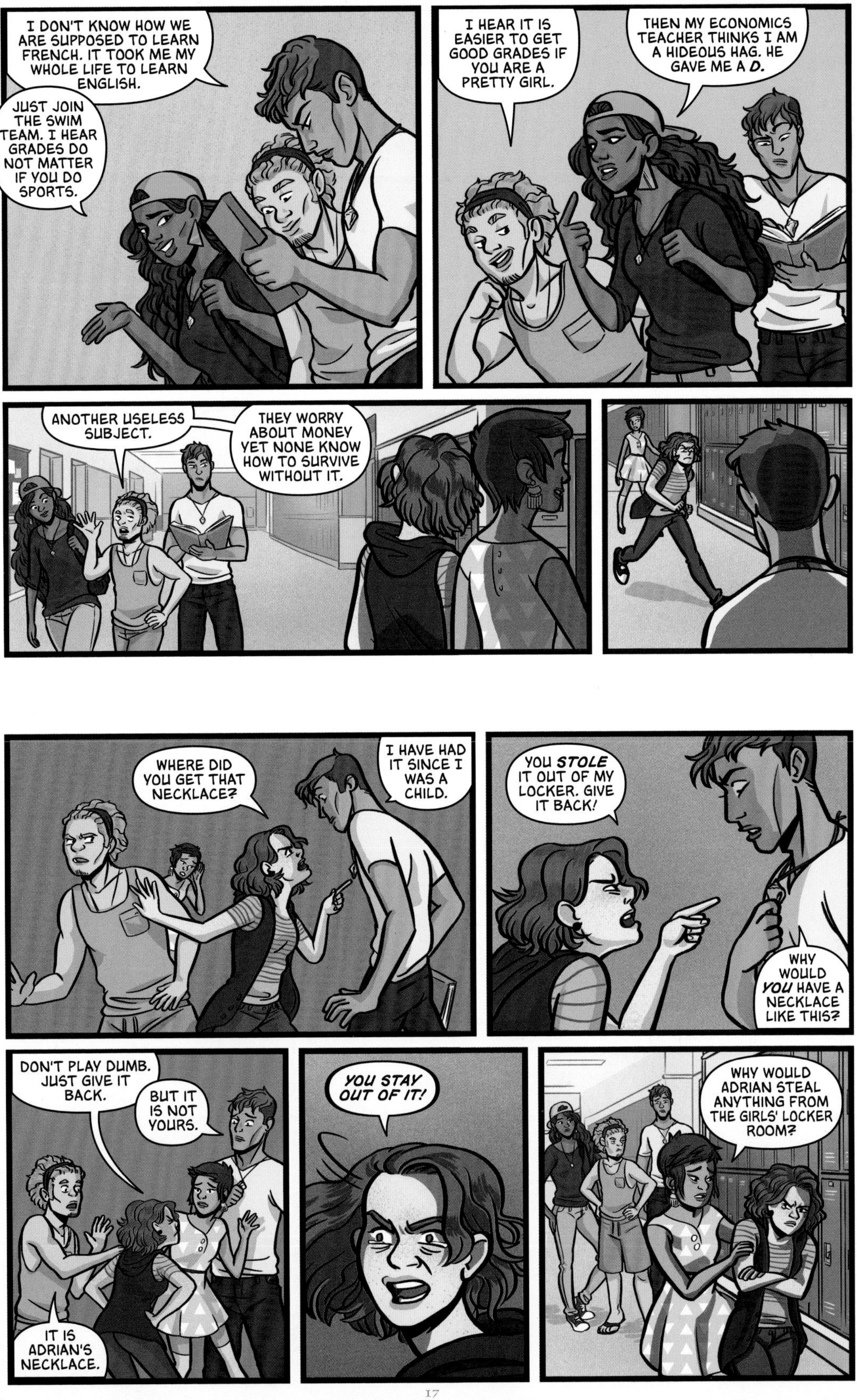
I DON'T KNOW HOW WE ARE SUPPOSED TO LEARN FRENCH. IT TOOK ME MY WHOLE LIFE TO LEARN ENGLISH.
JUST JOIN THE SWIM TEAM. I HEAR GRADES DO NOT MATTER IF YOU DO SPORTS.
I HEAR IT IS EASIER TO GET GOOD GRADES IF YOU ARE A PRETTY GIRL.
THEN MY ECONOMICS TEACHER THINKS I AM A HIDEOUS HAG. HE GAVE ME A D.
ANOTHER USELESS SUBJECT.
THEY WORRY ABOUT MONEY YET NONE KNOW HOW TO SURVIVE WITHOUT IT.
WHERE DID YOU GET THAT NECKLACE?
I HAVE HAD IT SINCE I WAS A CHILD.
YOU STOLE IT OUT OF MY LOCKER. GIVE IT BACK!
WHY WOULD YOU HAVE A NECKLACE LIKE THIS?
DON'T PLAY DUMB. JUST GIVE IT BACK.
BUT IT IS NOT YOURS.
IT IS ADRIAN'S NECKLACE.
YOU STAY OUT OF IT!
WHY WOULD ADRIAN STEAL ANYTHING FROM THE GIRLS' LOCKER ROOM?

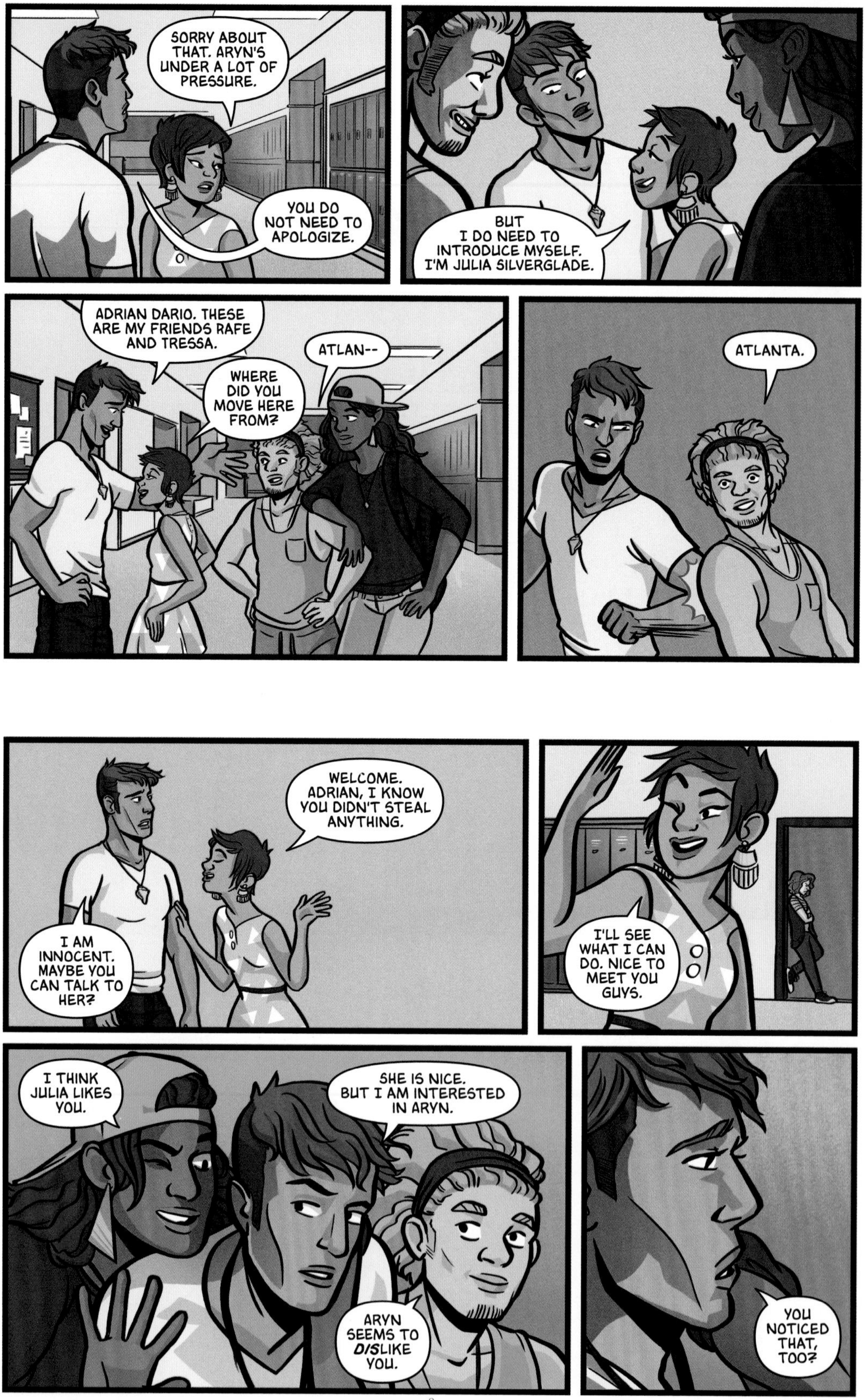
SORRY ABOUT THAT. ARYN'S UNDER A LOT OF PRESSURE.
YOU DO NOT NEED TO APOLOGIZE.
BUT I DO NEED TO INTRODUCE MYSELF. I'M JULIA SILVERGLADE.
ADRIAN DARIO. THESE ARE MY FRIENDS RAFE AND TRESSA.
WHERE DID YOU MOVE HERE FROM?
ATLAN--
ATLANTA.
WELCOME. ADRIAN, I KNOW YOU DIDN'T STEAL ANYTHING.
I AM INNOCENT. MAYBE YOU CAN TALK TO HER?
I'LL SEE WHAT I CAN DO. NICE TO MEET YOU GUYS.
I THINK JULIA LIKES YOU.
SHE IS NICE. BUT I AM INTERESTED IN ARYN.
ARYN SEEMS TO *DIS*LIKE YOU.
YOU NOTICED THAT, TOO?

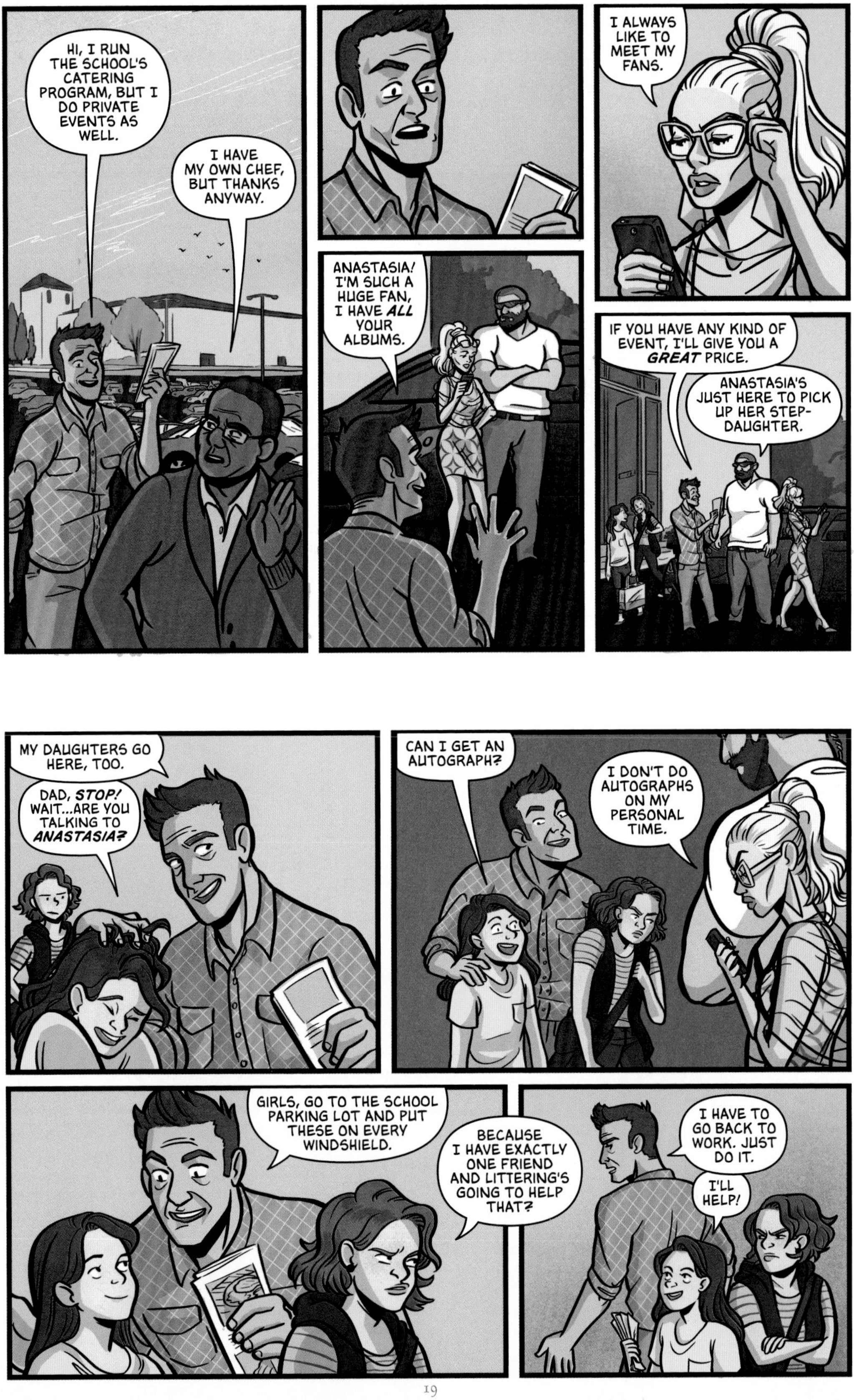
HI, I RUN THE SCHOOL'S CATERING PROGRAM, BUT I DO PRIVATE EVENTS AS WELL.
I HAVE MY OWN CHEF, BUT THANKS ANYWAY.
ANASTASIA! I'M SUCH A HUGE FAN, I HAVE ALL YOUR ALBUMS.
I ALWAYS LIKE TO MEET MY FANS.
IF YOU HAVE ANY KIND OF EVENT, I'LL GIVE YOU A GREAT PRICE.
ANASTASIA'S JUST HERE TO PICK UP HER STEP-DAUGHTER.
MY DAUGHTERS GO HERE, TOO.
DAD, STOP! WAIT...ARE YOU TALKING TO ANASTASIA?
CAN I GET AN AUTOGRAPH?
I DON'T DO AUTOGRAPHS ON MY PERSONAL TIME.
GIRLS, GO TO THE SCHOOL PARKING LOT AND PUT THESE ON EVERY WINDSHIELD.
BECAUSE I HAVE EXACTLY ONE FRIEND AND LITTERING'S GOING TO HELP THAT?
I HAVE TO GO BACK TO WORK. JUST DO IT.
I'LL HELP!

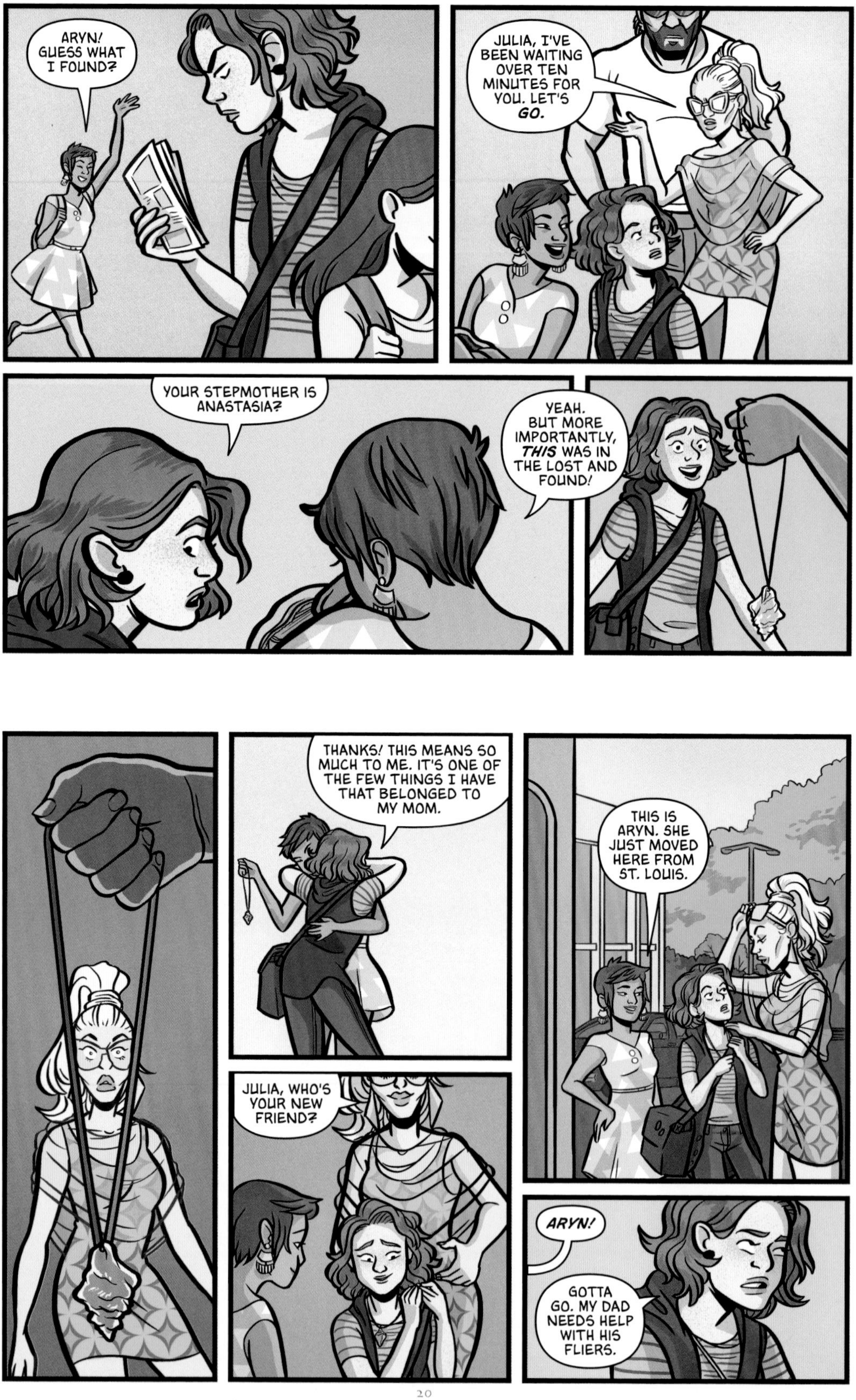
ARYN! GUESS WHAT I FOUND?
JULIA, I'VE BEEN WAITING OVER TEN MINUTES FOR YOU. LET'S GO.
YOUR STEPMOTHER IS ANASTASIA?
YEAH. BUT MORE IMPORTANTLY, THIS WAS IN THE LOST AND FOUND!
THANKS! THIS MEANS SO MUCH TO ME. IT'S ONE OF THE FEW THINGS I HAVE THAT BELONGED TO MY MOM.
JULIA, WHO'S YOUR NEW FRIEND?
THIS IS ARYN. SHE JUST MOVED HERE FROM ST. LOUIS.
ARYN!
GOTTA GO. MY DAD NEEDS HELP WITH HIS FLIERS.

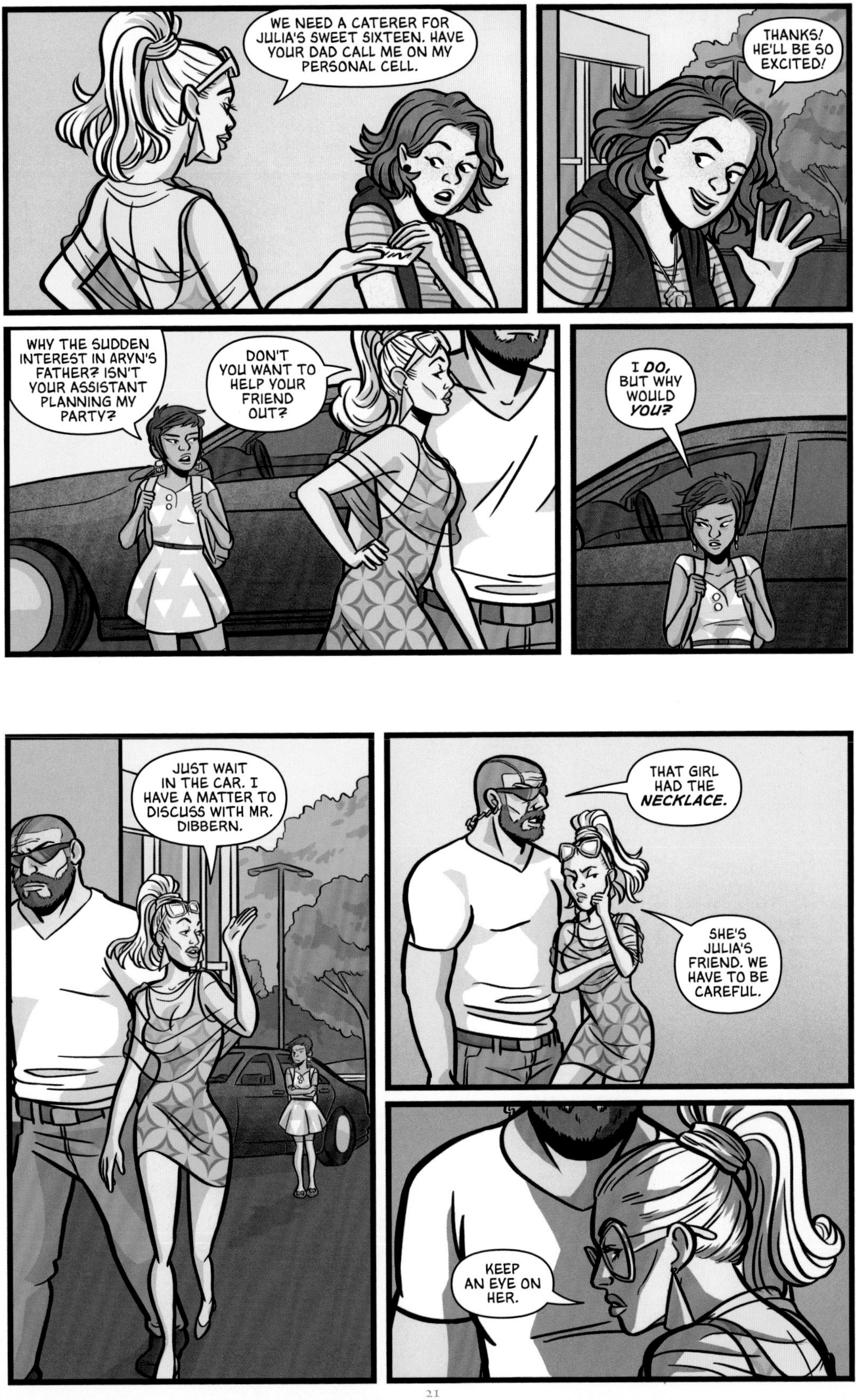
WE NEED A CATERER FOR JULIA'S SWEET SIXTEEN. HAVE YOUR DAD CALL ME ON MY PERSONAL CELL.
THANKS! HE'LL BE SO EXCITED!
WHY THE SUDDEN INTEREST IN ARYN'S FATHER? ISN'T YOUR ASSISTANT PLANNING MY PARTY?
DON'T YOU WANT TO HELP YOUR FRIEND OUT?
I DO, BUT WHY WOULD YOU?
JUST WAIT IN THE CAR. I HAVE A MATTER TO DISCUSS WITH MR. DIBBERN.
THAT GIRL HAD THE NECKLACE.
SHE'S JULIA'S FRIEND. WE HAVE TO BE CAREFUL.
KEEP AN EYE ON HER.

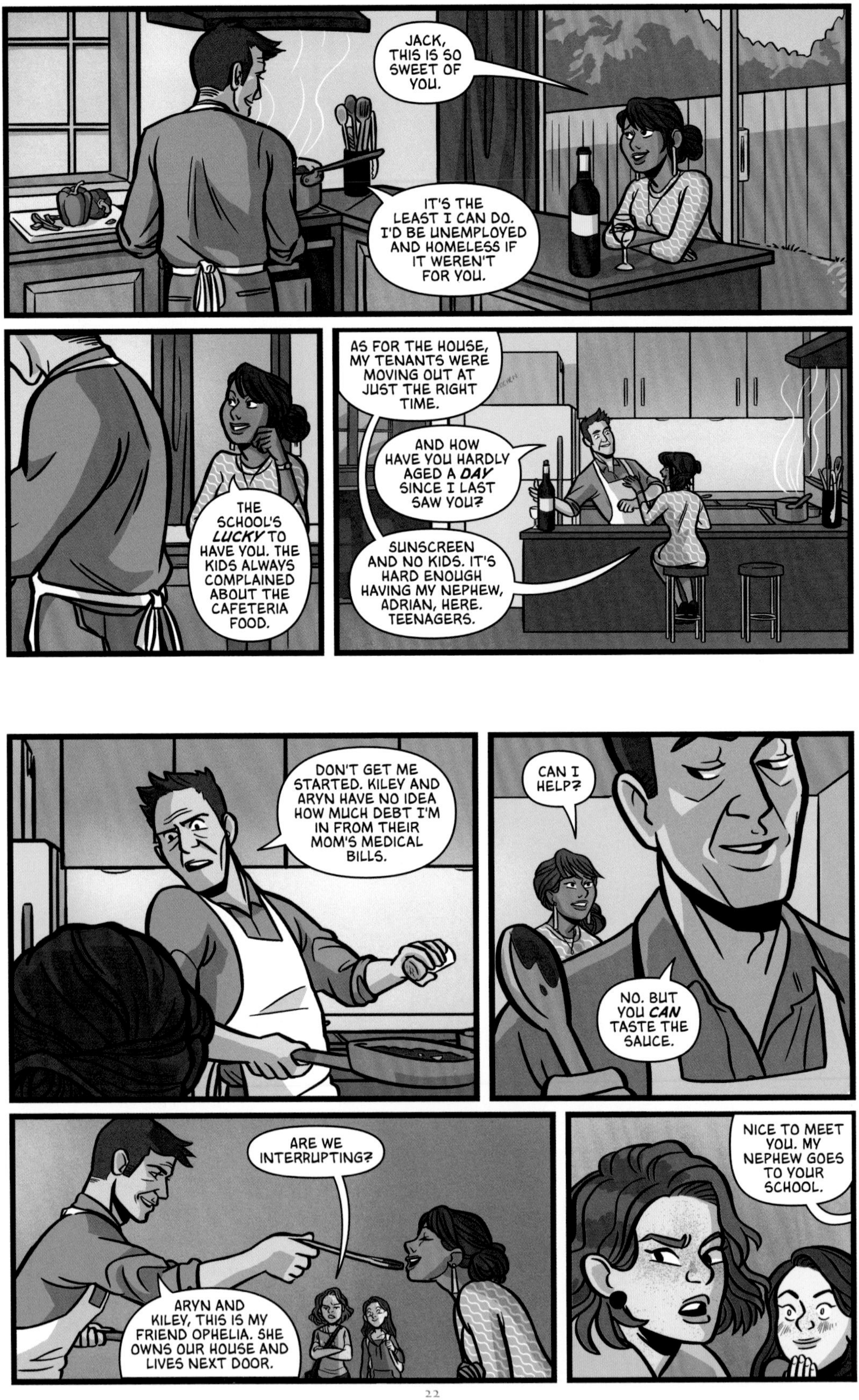
JACK, THIS IS SO SWEET OF YOU.
IT'S THE LEAST I CAN DO. I'D BE UNEMPLOYED AND HOMELESS IF IT WEREN'T FOR YOU.
THE SCHOOL'S *LUCKY* TO HAVE YOU. THE KIDS ALWAYS COMPLAINED ABOUT THE CAFETERIA FOOD.
AS FOR THE HOUSE, MY TENANTS WERE MOVING OUT AT JUST THE RIGHT TIME.
AND HOW HAVE YOU HARDLY AGED A *DAY* SINCE I LAST SAW YOU?
SUNSCREEN AND NO KIDS. IT'S HARD ENOUGH HAVING MY NEPHEW, ADRIAN, HERE. TEENAGERS.
DON'T GET ME STARTED. KILEY AND ARYN HAVE NO IDEA HOW MUCH DEBT I'M IN FROM THEIR MOM'S MEDICAL BILLS.
CAN I HELP?
NO. BUT YOU *CAN* TASTE THE SAUCE.
ARE WE INTERRUPTING?
ARYN AND KILEY, THIS IS MY FRIEND OPHELIA. SHE OWNS OUR HOUSE AND LIVES NEXT DOOR.
NICE TO MEET YOU. MY NEPHEW GOES TO YOUR SCHOOL.

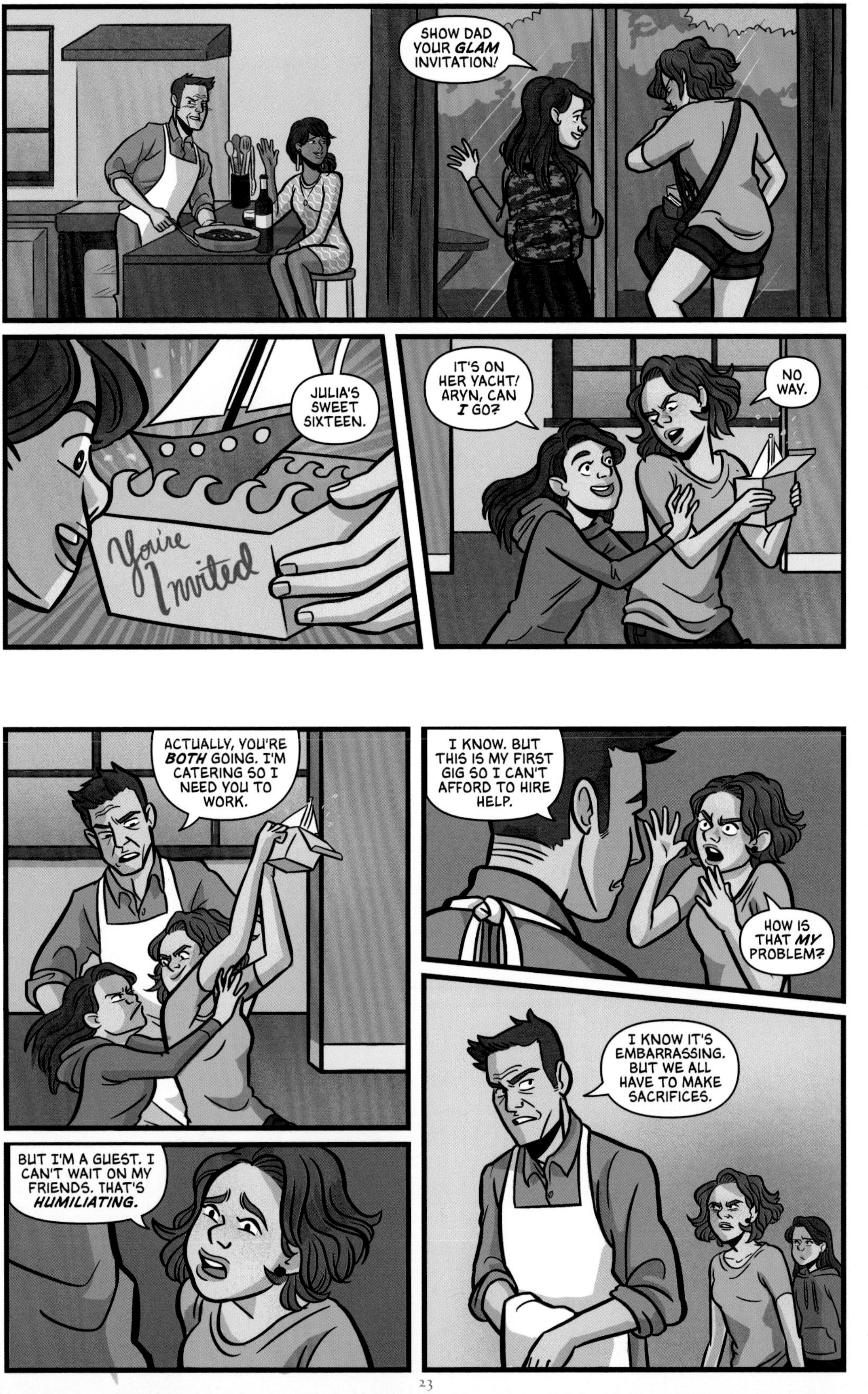
SHOW DAD YOUR GLAM INVITATION!
JULIA'S SWEET SIXTEEN.
You're Invited
IT'S ON HER YACHT! ARYN, CAN I GO?
NO WAY.
ACTUALLY, YOU'RE BOTH GOING. I'M CATERING SO I NEED YOU TO WORK.
I KNOW. BUT THIS IS MY FIRST GIG SO I CAN'T AFFORD TO HIRE HELP.
HOW IS THAT MY PROBLEM?
BUT I'M A GUEST. I CAN'T WAIT ON MY FRIENDS. THAT'S HUMILIATING.
I KNOW IT'S EMBARRASSING. BUT WE ALL HAVE TO MAKE SACRIFICES.

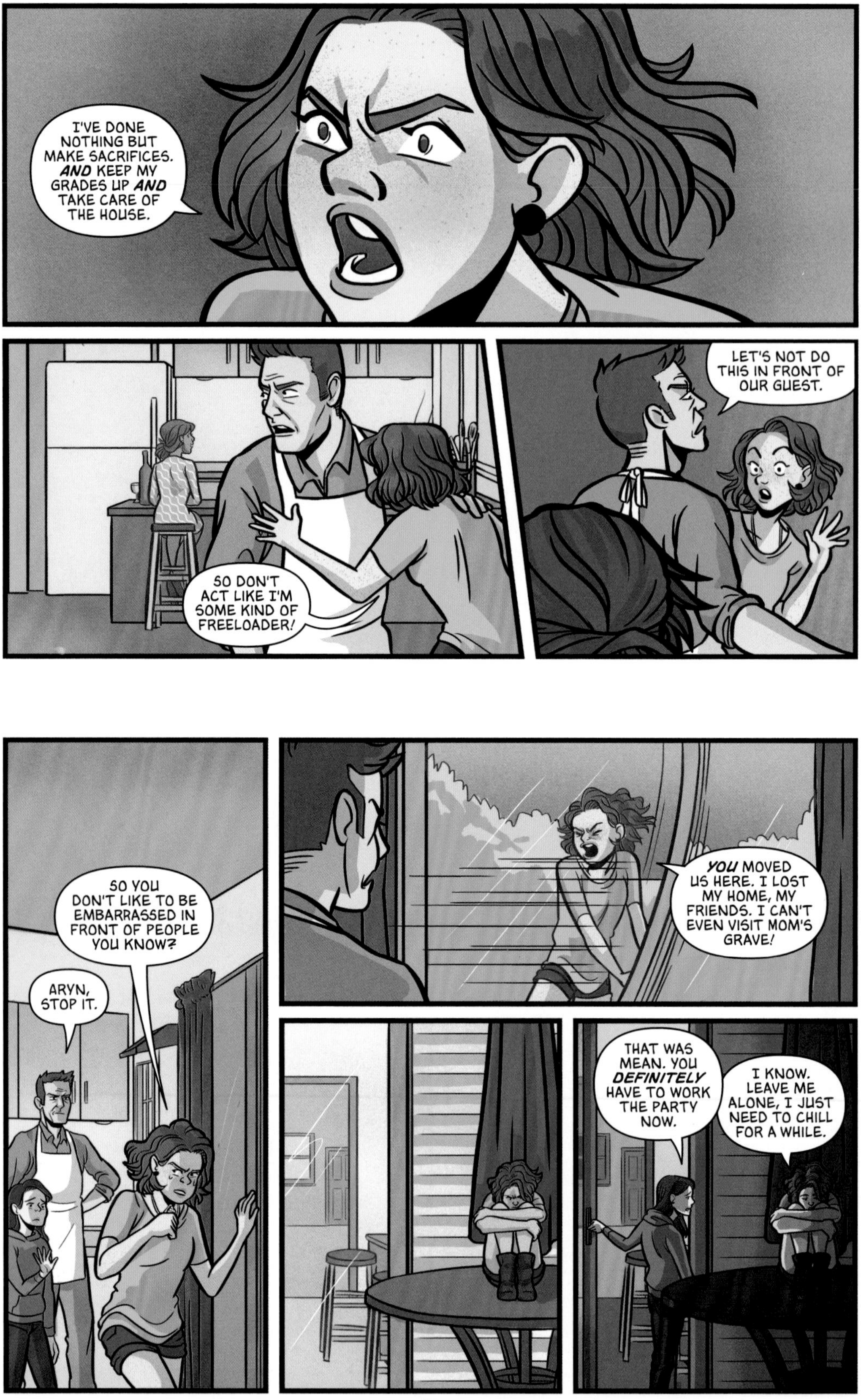

I'VE DONE NOTHING BUT MAKE SACRIFICES. ***AND*** KEEP MY GRADES UP ***AND*** TAKE CARE OF THE HOUSE.
SO DON'T ACT LIKE I'M SOME KIND OF FREELOADER!
LET'S NOT DO THIS IN FRONT OF OUR GUEST.
SO YOU DON'T LIKE TO BE EMBARRASSED IN FRONT OF PEOPLE YOU KNOW?
ARYN, STOP IT.
YOU MOVED US HERE. I LOST MY HOME, MY FRIENDS. I CAN'T EVEN VISIT MOM'S GRAVE!
THAT WAS MEAN. YOU ***DEFINITELY*** HAVE TO WORK THE PARTY NOW.
I KNOW. LEAVE ME ALONE, I JUST NEED TO CHILL FOR A WHILE.

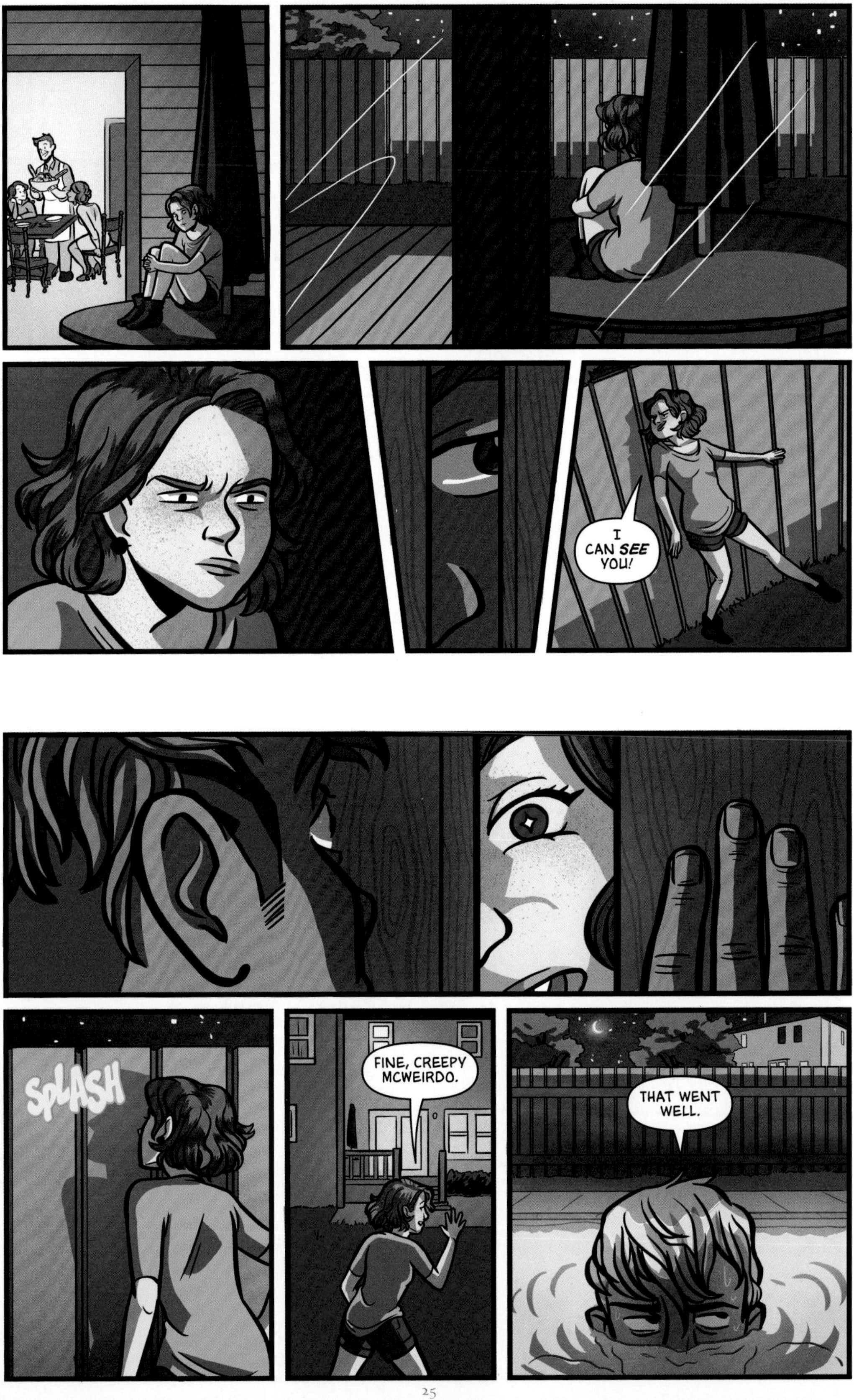
I CAN SEE YOU!
SPLASH
FINE, CREEPY MCWEIRDO.
THAT WENT WELL.

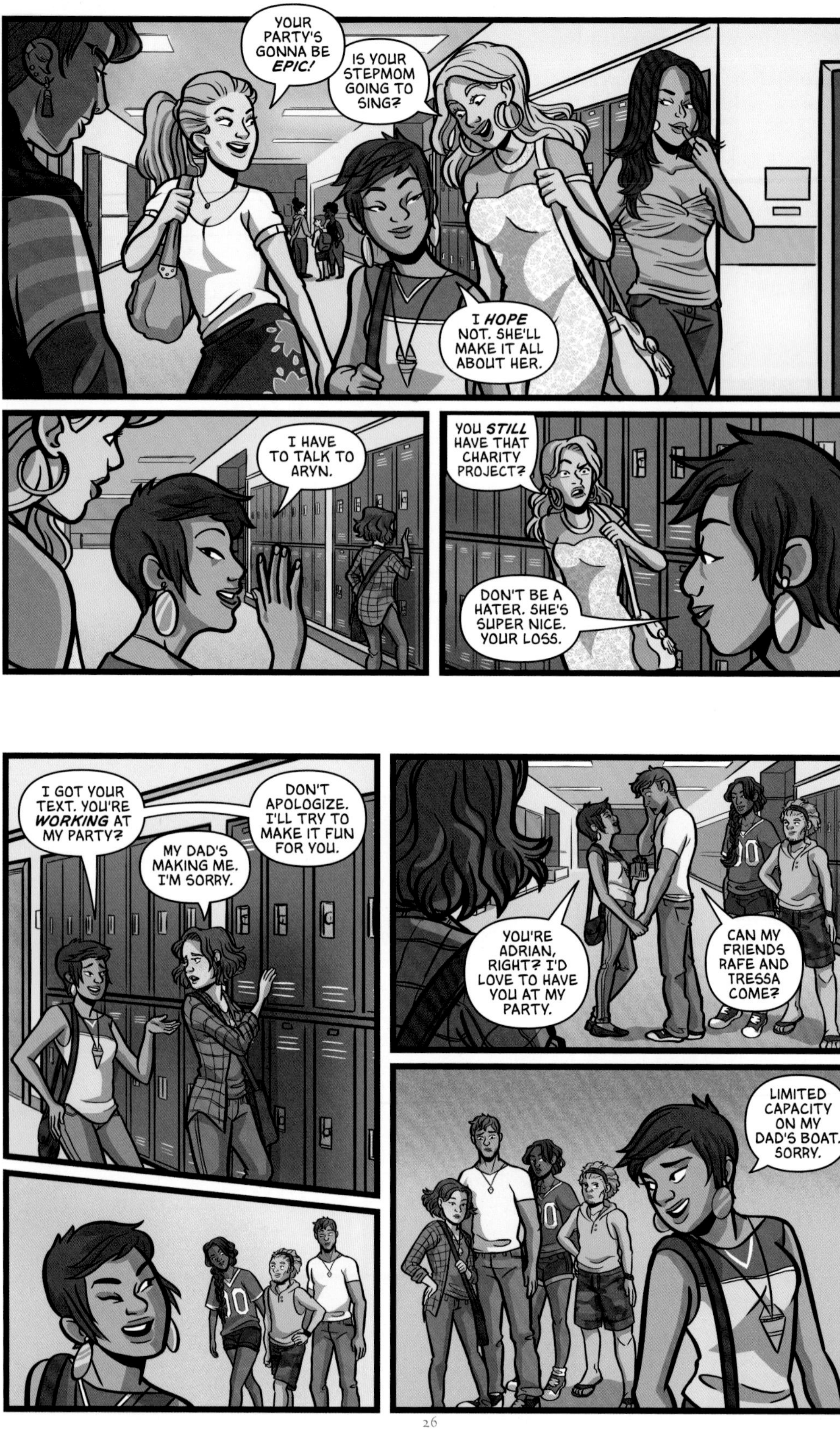
YOUR PARTY'S GONNA BE *EPIC!*
IS YOUR STEPMOM GOING TO SING?
I *HOPE* NOT. SHE'LL MAKE IT ALL ABOUT HER.
I HAVE TO TALK TO ARYN.
YOU *STILL* HAVE THAT CHARITY PROJECT?
DON'T BE A HATER. SHE'S SUPER NICE. YOUR LOSS.
I GOT YOUR TEXT. YOU'RE *WORKING* AT MY PARTY?
MY DAD'S MAKING ME. I'M SORRY.
DON'T APOLOGIZE. I'LL TRY TO MAKE IT FUN FOR YOU.
YOU'RE ADRIAN, RIGHT? I'D LOVE TO HAVE YOU AT MY PARTY.
CAN MY FRIENDS RAFE AND TRESSA COME?
LIMITED CAPACITY ON MY DAD'S BOAT. SORRY.

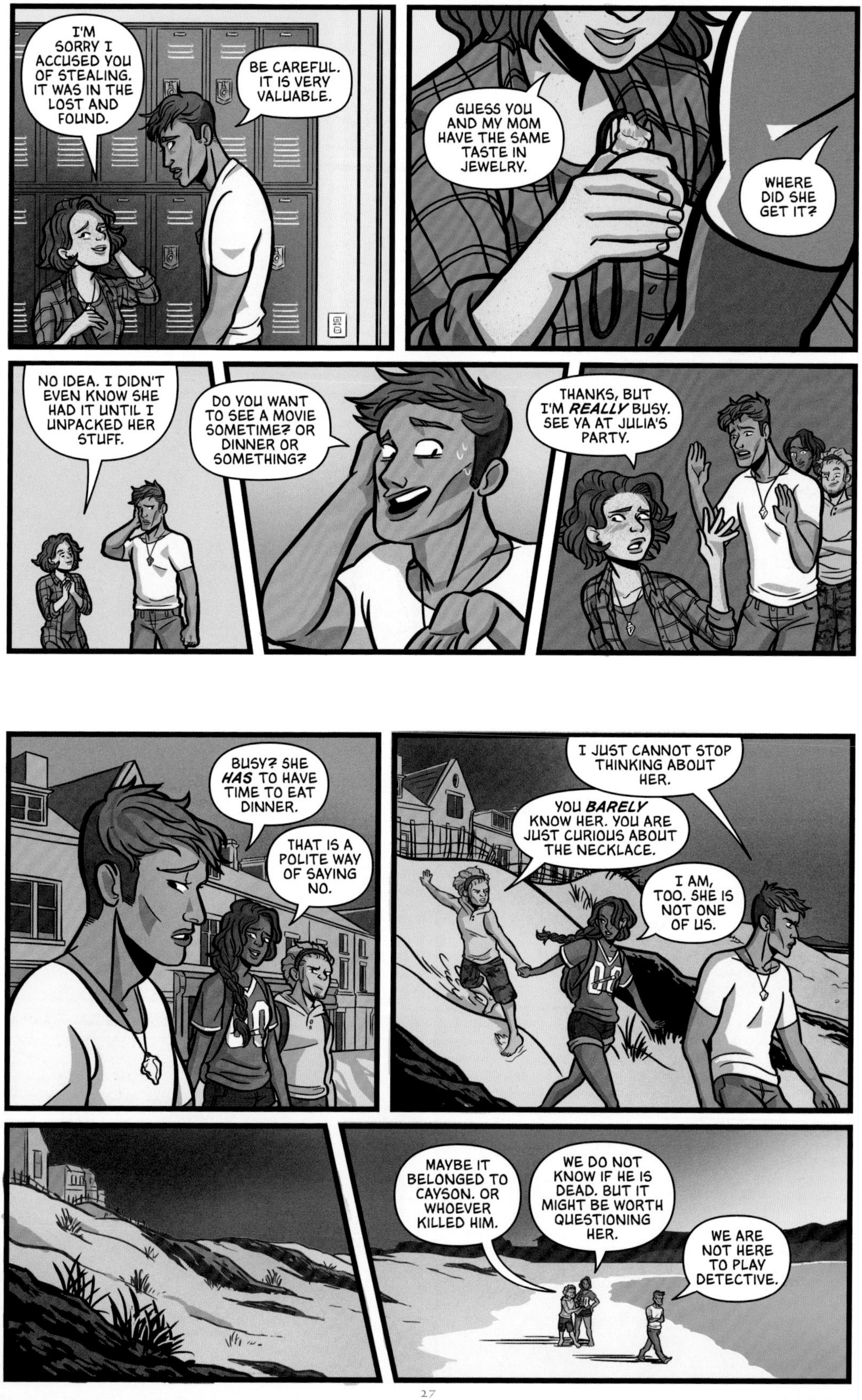
I'M SORRY I ACCUSED YOU OF STEALING. IT WAS IN THE LOST AND FOUND.
BE CAREFUL. IT IS VERY VALUABLE.
GUESS YOU AND MY MOM HAVE THE SAME TASTE IN JEWELRY.
WHERE DID SHE GET IT?
NO IDEA. I DIDN'T EVEN KNOW SHE HAD IT UNTIL I UNPACKED HER STUFF.
DO YOU WANT TO SEE A MOVIE SOMETIME? OR DINNER OR SOMETHING?
THANKS, BUT I'M *REALLY* BUSY. SEE YA AT JULIA'S PARTY.
BUSY? SHE *HAS* TO HAVE TIME TO EAT DINNER.
THAT IS A POLITE WAY OF SAYING NO.
I JUST CANNOT STOP THINKING ABOUT HER.
YOU *BARELY* KNOW HER. YOU ARE JUST CURIOUS ABOUT THE NECKLACE.
I AM, TOO. SHE IS NOT ONE OF US.
MAYBE IT BELONGED TO CAYSON. OR WHOEVER KILLED HIM.
WE DO NOT KNOW IF HE IS DEAD. BUT IT MIGHT BE WORTH QUESTIONING HER.
WE ARE NOT HERE TO PLAY DETECTIVE.

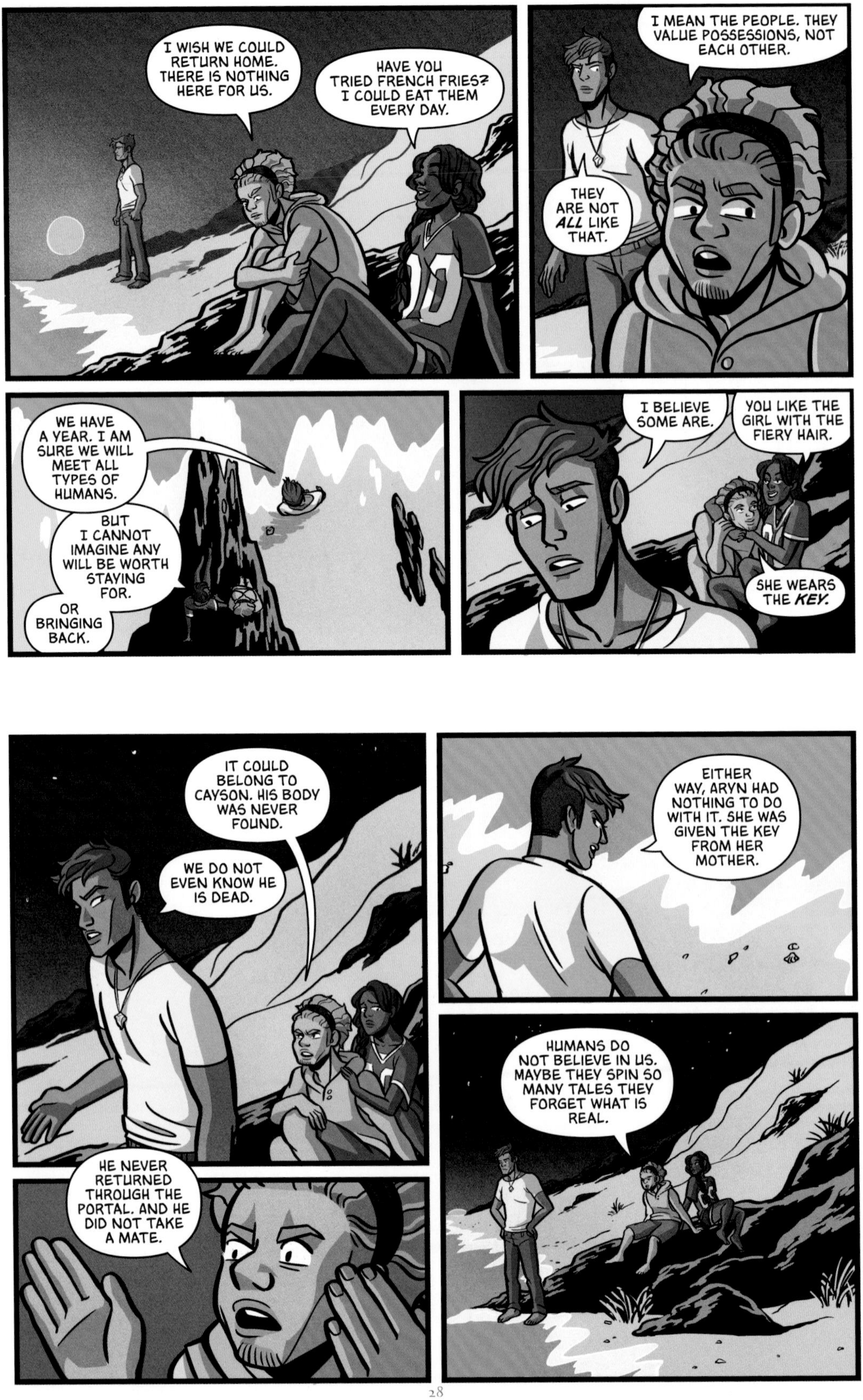
I WISH WE COULD RETURN HOME. THERE IS NOTHING HERE FOR US.
HAVE YOU TRIED FRENCH FRIES? I COULD EAT THEM EVERY DAY.
I MEAN THE PEOPLE. THEY VALUE POSSESSIONS, NOT EACH OTHER.
THEY ARE NOT ALL LIKE THAT.
WE HAVE A YEAR. I AM SURE WE WILL MEET ALL TYPES OF HUMANS.
BUT I CANNOT IMAGINE ANY WILL BE WORTH STAYING FOR.
OR BRINGING BACK.
I BELIEVE SOME ARE.
YOU LIKE THE GIRL WITH THE FIERY HAIR.
SHE WEARS THE KEY.
IT COULD BELONG TO CAYSON. HIS BODY WAS NEVER FOUND.
WE DO NOT EVEN KNOW HE IS DEAD.
HE NEVER RETURNED THROUGH THE PORTAL. AND HE DID NOT TAKE A MATE.
EITHER WAY, ARYN HAD NOTHING TO DO WITH IT. SHE WAS GIVEN THE KEY FROM HER MOTHER.
HUMANS DO NOT BELIEVE IN US. MAYBE THEY SPIN SO MANY TALES THEY FORGET WHAT IS REAL.

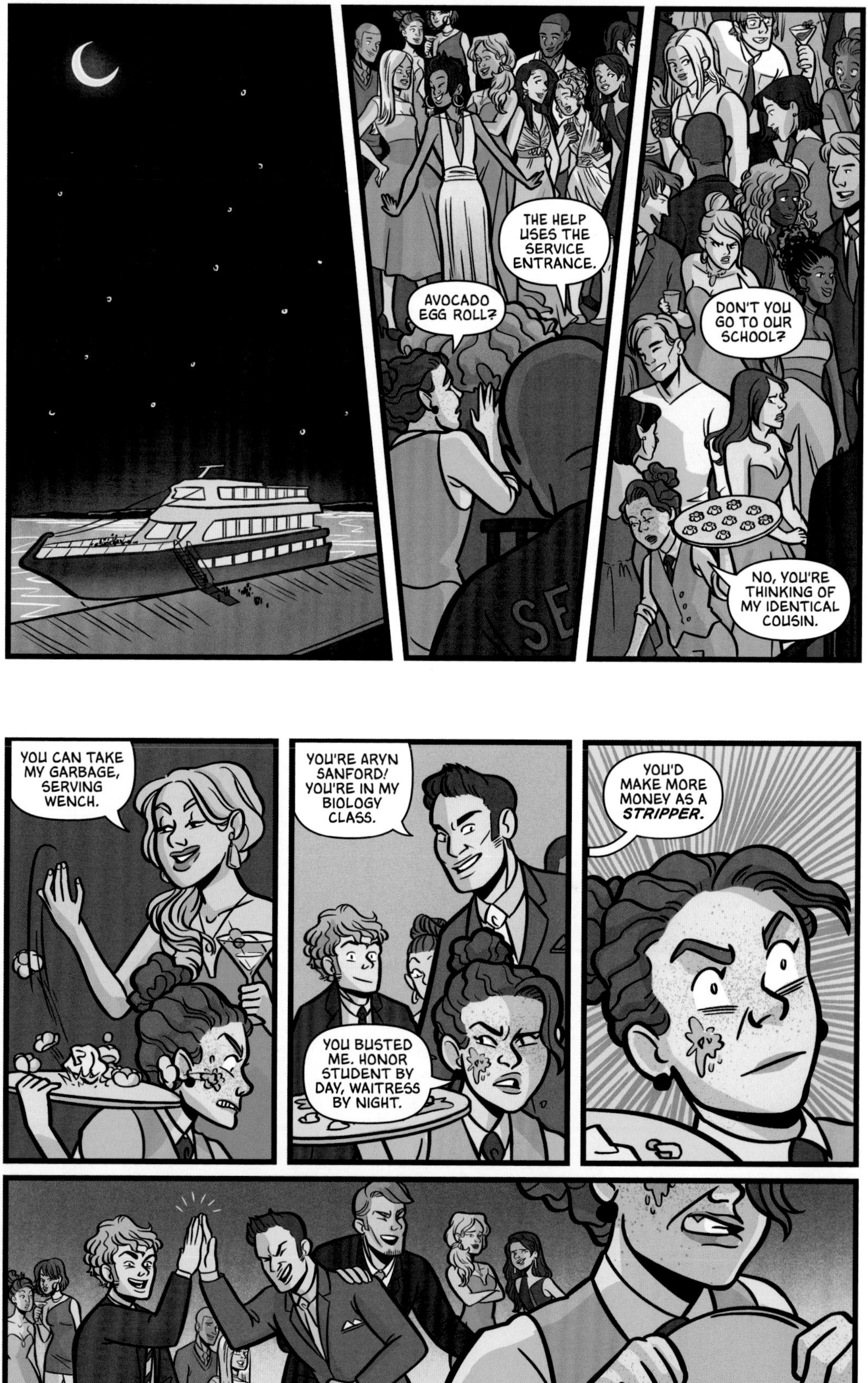
THE HELP USES THE SERVICE ENTRANCE.
AVOCADO EGG ROLL?
DON'T YOU GO TO OUR SCHOOL?
NO, YOU'RE THINKING OF MY IDENTICAL COUSIN.
YOU CAN TAKE MY GARBAGE, SERVING WENCH.
YOU'RE ARYN SANFORD! YOU'RE IN MY BIOLOGY CLASS.
YOU BUSTED ME. HONOR STUDENT BY DAY, WAITRESS BY NIGHT.
YOU'D MAKE MORE MONEY AS A *STRIPPER.*

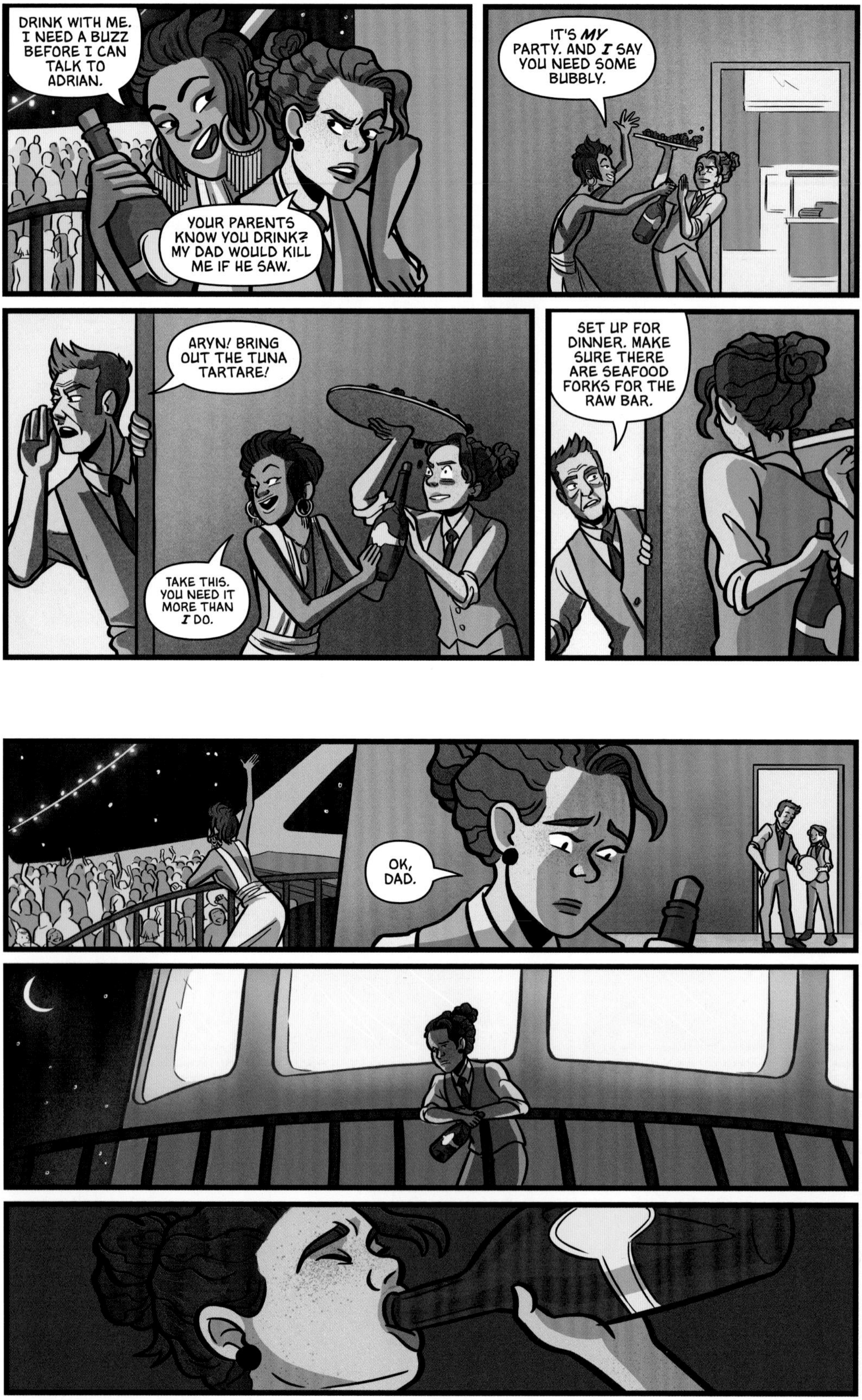
DRINK WITH ME. I NEED A BUZZ BEFORE I CAN TALK TO ADRIAN.
YOUR PARENTS KNOW YOU DRINK? MY DAD WOULD KILL ME IF HE SAW.
IT'S MY PARTY. AND I SAY YOU NEED SOME BUBBLY.
ARYN! BRING OUT THE TUNA TARTARE!
TAKE THIS. YOU NEED IT MORE THAN I DO.
SET UP FOR DINNER. MAKE SURE THERE ARE SEAFOOD FORKS FOR THE RAW BAR.
OK, DAD.

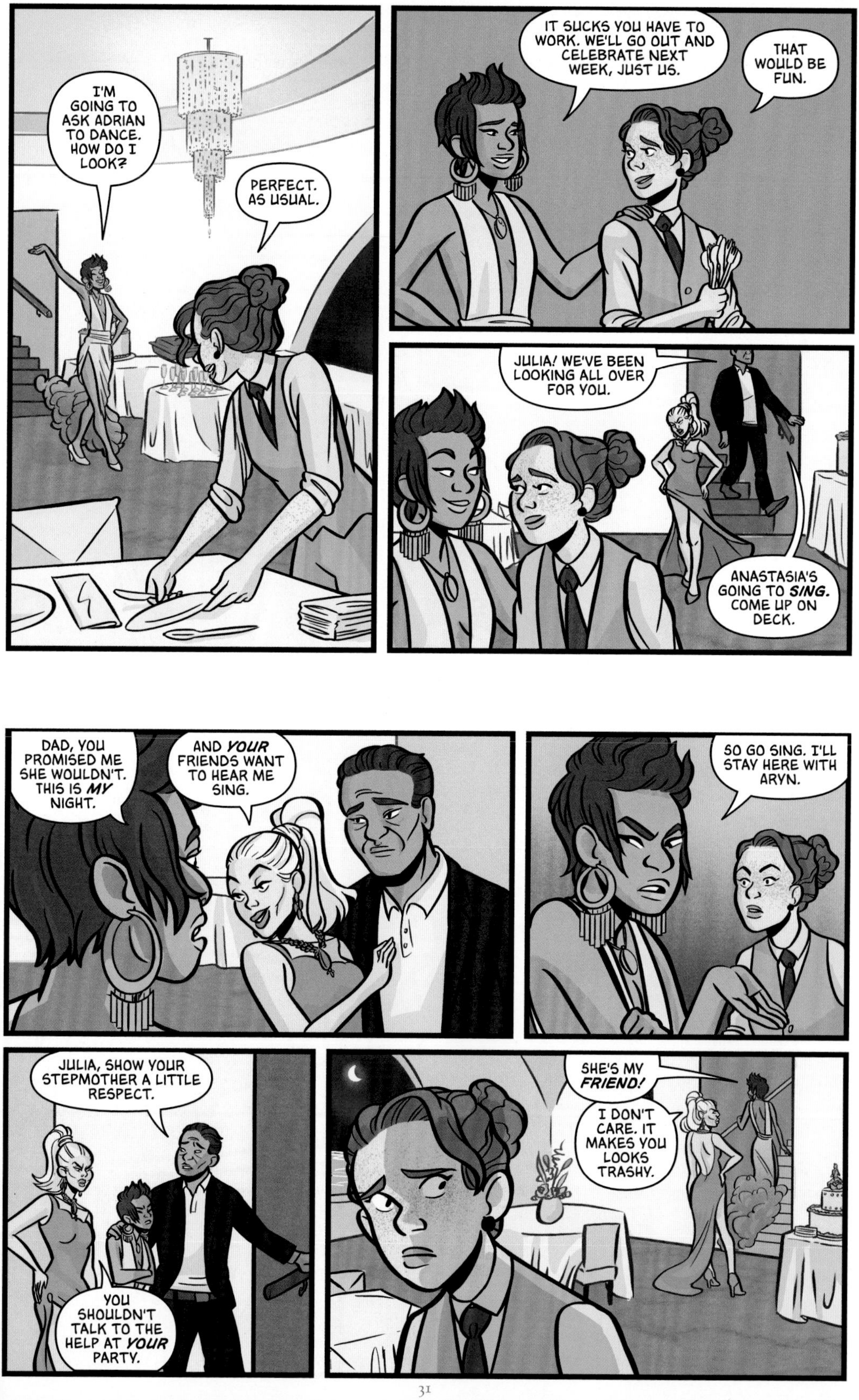
I'M GOING TO ASK ADRIAN TO DANCE. HOW DO I LOOK?
PERFECT. AS USUAL.
IT SUCKS YOU HAVE TO WORK. WE'LL GO OUT AND CELEBRATE NEXT WEEK, JUST US.
THAT WOULD BE FUN.
JULIA! WE'VE BEEN LOOKING ALL OVER FOR YOU.
ANASTASIA'S GOING TO SING. COME UP ON DECK.
DAD, YOU PROMISED ME SHE WOULDN'T. THIS IS MY NIGHT.
AND YOUR FRIENDS WANT TO HEAR ME SING.
SO GO SING. I'LL STAY HERE WITH ARYN.
JULIA, SHOW YOUR STEPMOTHER A LITTLE RESPECT.
YOU SHOULDN'T TALK TO THE HELP AT YOUR PARTY.
SHE'S MY FRIEND!
I DON'T CARE. IT MAKES YOU LOOKS TRASHY.

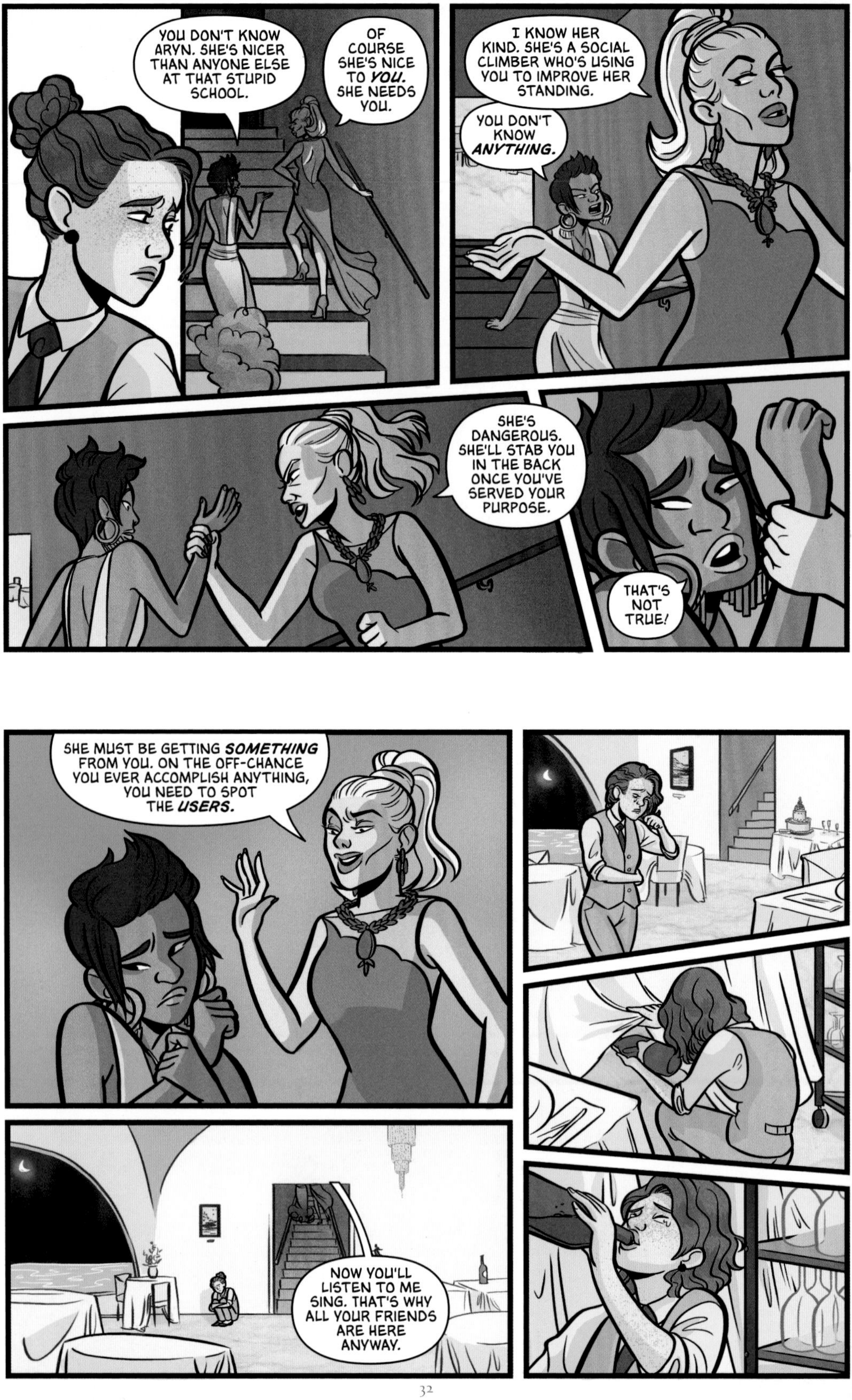
YOU DON'T KNOW ARYN. SHE'S NICER THAN ANYONE ELSE AT THAT STUPID SCHOOL.
OF COURSE SHE'S NICE TO *YOU.* SHE NEEDS YOU.
I KNOW HER KIND. SHE'S A SOCIAL CLIMBER WHO'S USING YOU TO IMPROVE HER STANDING.
YOU DON'T KNOW ***ANYTHING.***
SHE'S DANGEROUS. SHE'LL STAB YOU IN THE BACK ONCE YOU'VE SERVED YOUR PURPOSE.
THAT'S NOT TRUE!
SHE MUST BE GETTING ***SOMETHING*** FROM YOU. ON THE OFF-CHANCE YOU EVER ACCOMPLISH ANYTHING, YOU NEED TO SPOT THE ***USERS.***
NOW YOU'LL LISTEN TO ME SING. THAT'S WHY ALL YOUR FRIENDS ARE HERE ANYWAY.

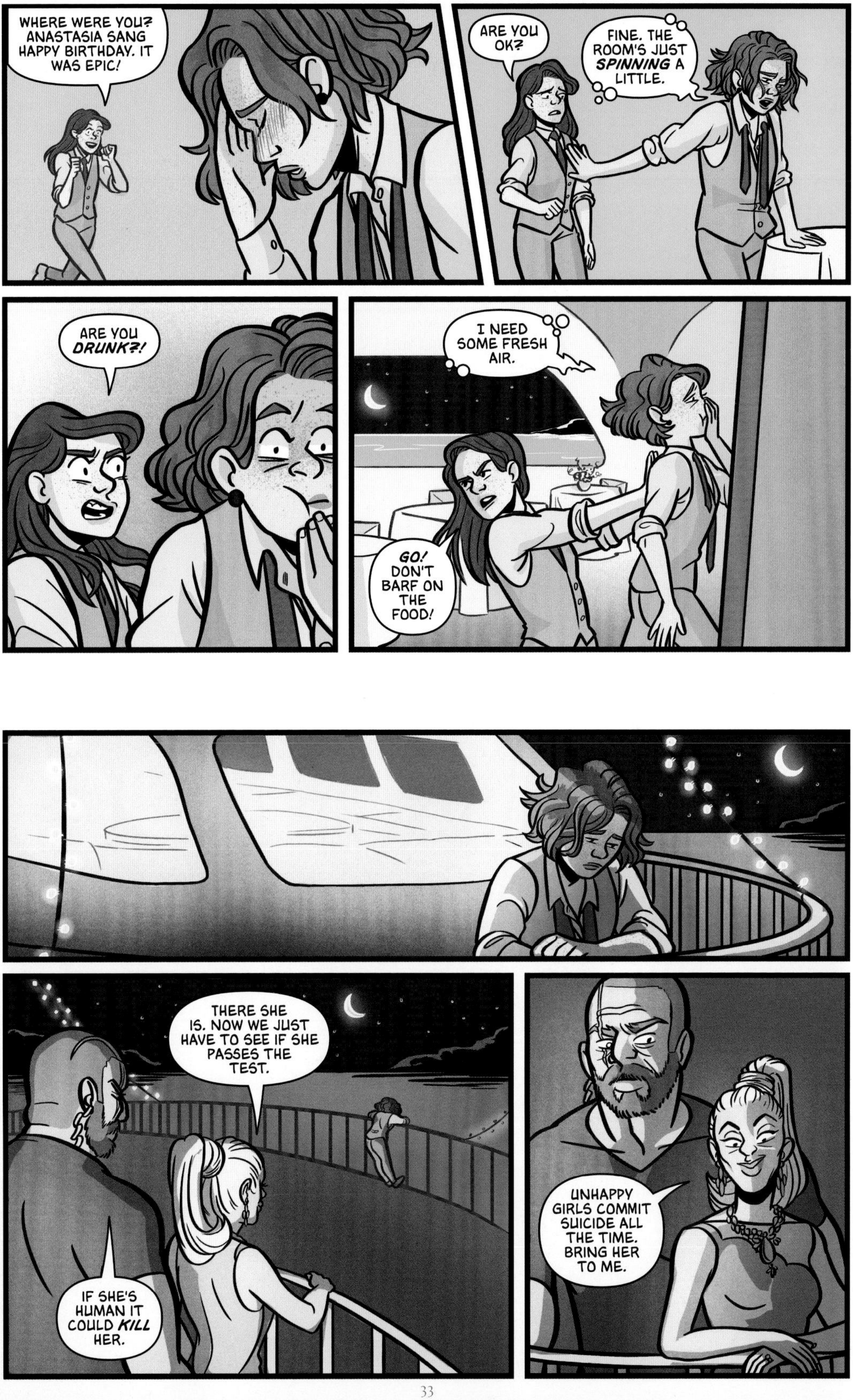
WHERE WERE YOU? ANASTASIA SANG HAPPY BIRTHDAY. IT WAS EPIC!
ARE YOU OK?
FINE. THE ROOM'S JUST SPINNING A LITTLE.
ARE YOU DRUNK?!
I NEED SOME FRESH AIR.
GO! DON'T BARF ON THE FOOD!
THERE SHE IS. NOW WE JUST HAVE TO SEE IF SHE PASSES THE TEST.
IF SHE'S HUMAN IT COULD KILL HER.
UNHAPPY GIRLS COMMIT SUICIDE ALL THE TIME. BRING HER TO ME.

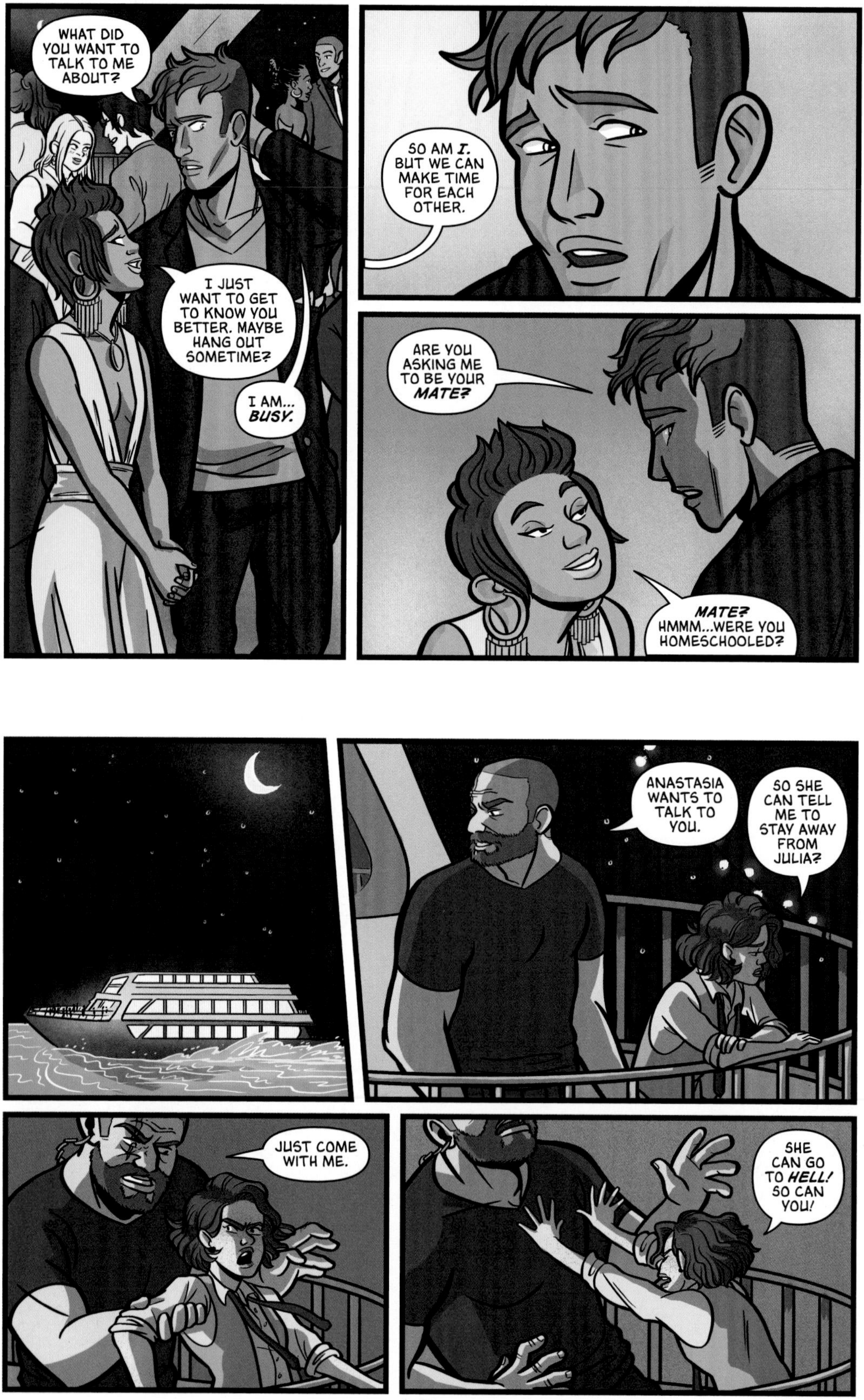
WHAT DID YOU WANT TO TALK TO ME ABOUT?
I JUST WANT TO GET TO KNOW YOU BETTER. MAYBE HANG OUT SOMETIME?
I AM... *BUSY.*
SO AM *I.* BUT WE CAN MAKE TIME FOR EACH OTHER.
ARE YOU ASKING ME TO BE YOUR *MATE?*
MATE? HMMM...WERE YOU HOMESCHOOLED?
ANASTASIA WANTS TO TALK TO YOU.
SO SHE CAN TELL ME TO STAY AWAY FROM JULIA?
JUST COME WITH ME.
SHE CAN GO TO *HELL!* SO CAN YOU!

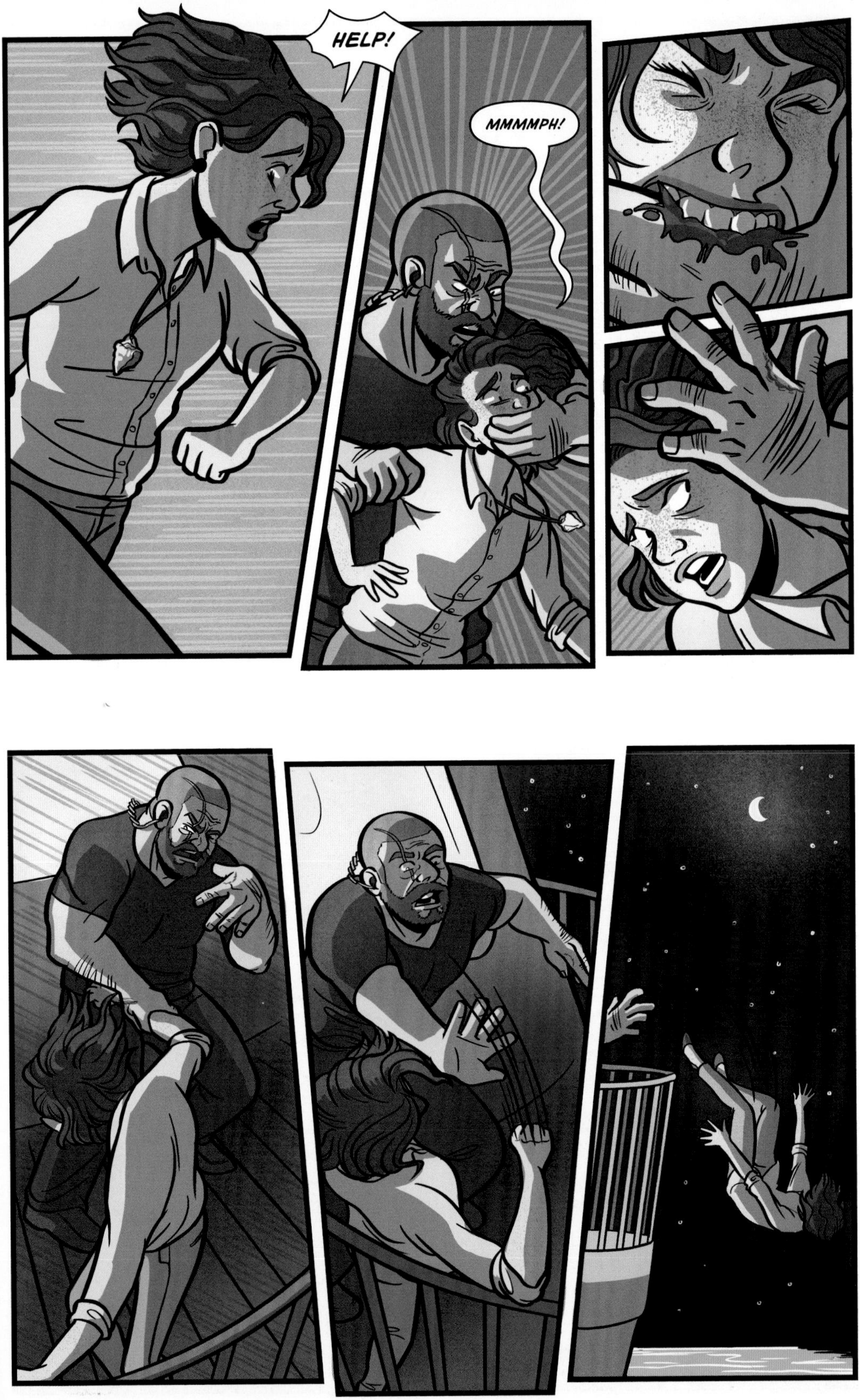
HELP!
MMMMPH!

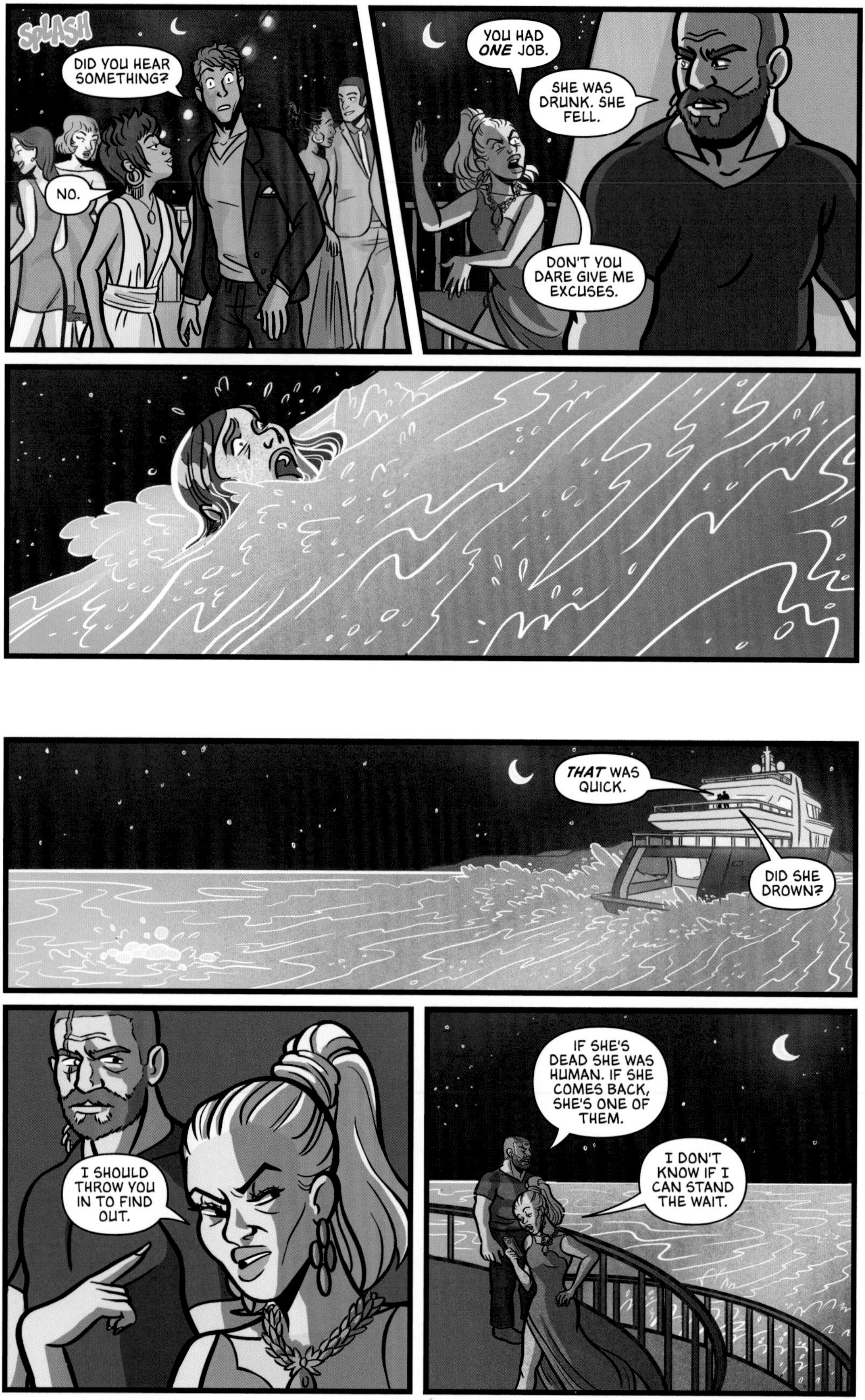
SPLASH
DID YOU HEAR SOMETHING?
NO.
YOU HAD ONE JOB.
SHE WAS DRUNK. SHE FELL.
DON'T YOU DARE GIVE ME EXCUSES.
THAT WAS QUICK.
DID SHE DROWN?
I SHOULD THROW YOU IN TO FIND OUT.
IF SHE'S DEAD SHE WAS HUMAN. IF SHE COMES BACK, SHE'S ONE OF THEM.
I DON'T KNOW IF I CAN STAND THE WAIT.

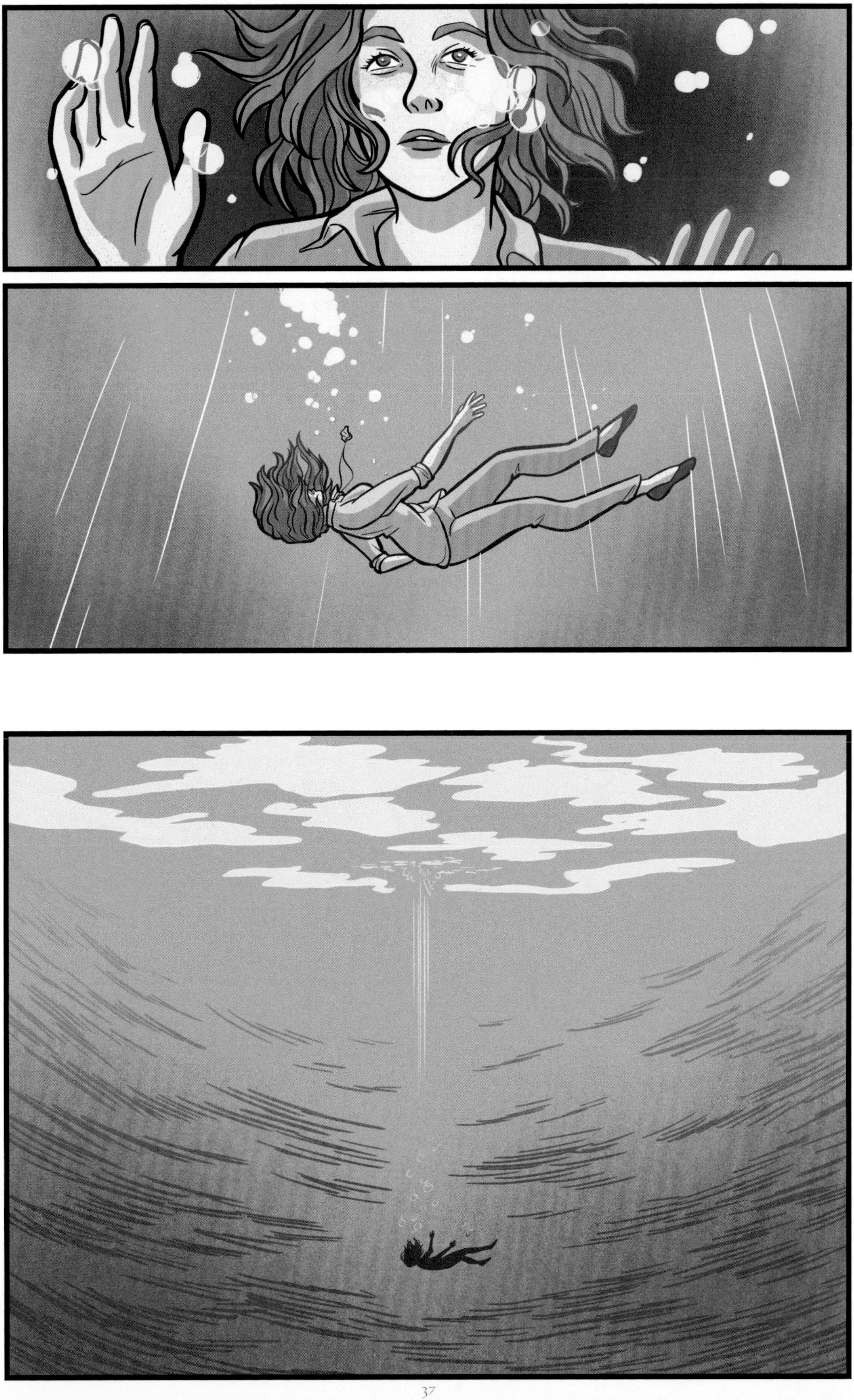

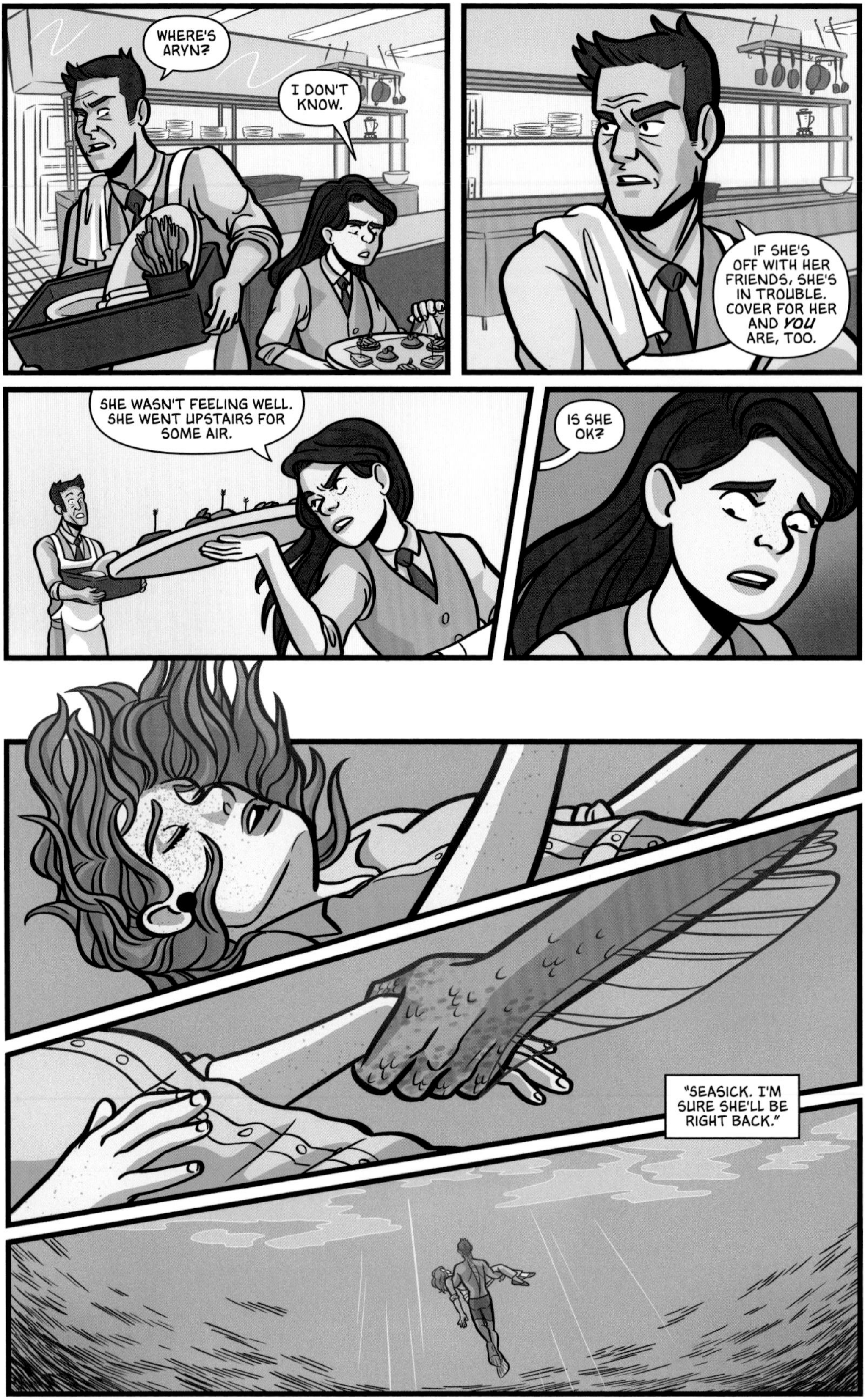
WHERE'S ARYN?
I DON'T KNOW.
IF SHE'S OFF WITH HER FRIENDS, SHE'S IN TROUBLE. COVER FOR HER AND *YOU* ARE, TOO.
SHE WASN'T FEELING WELL. SHE WENT UPSTAIRS FOR SOME AIR.
IS SHE OK?
"SEASICK. I'M SURE SHE'LL BE RIGHT BACK."

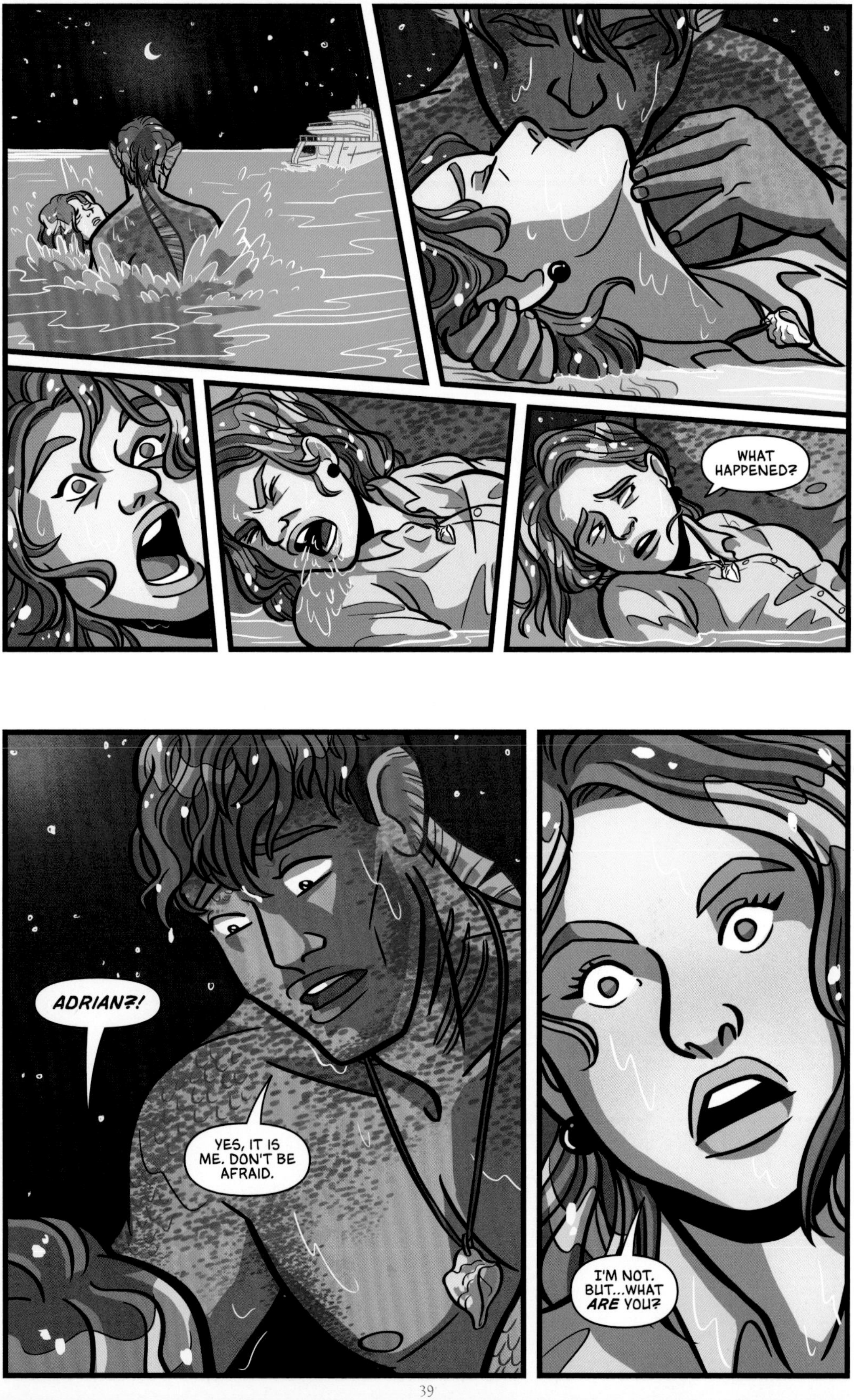
WHAT HAPPENED?
ADRIAN?!
YES, IT IS ME. DON'T BE AFRAID.
I'M NOT. BUT...WHAT ARE YOU?

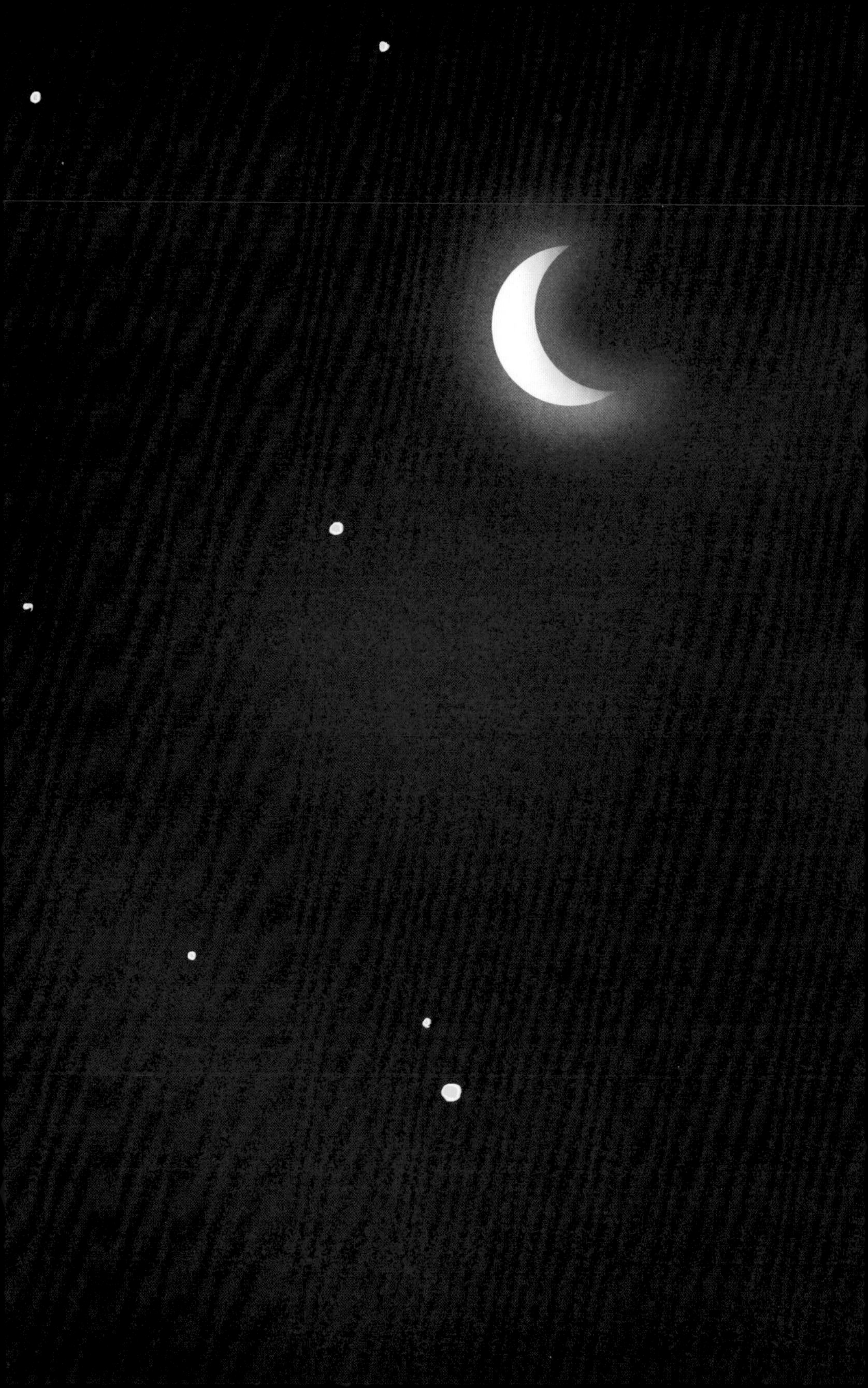

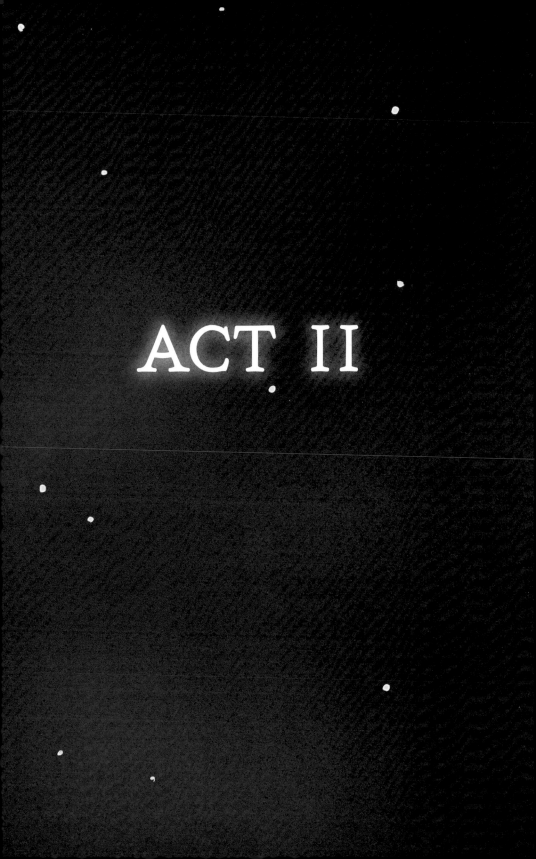

ACT II

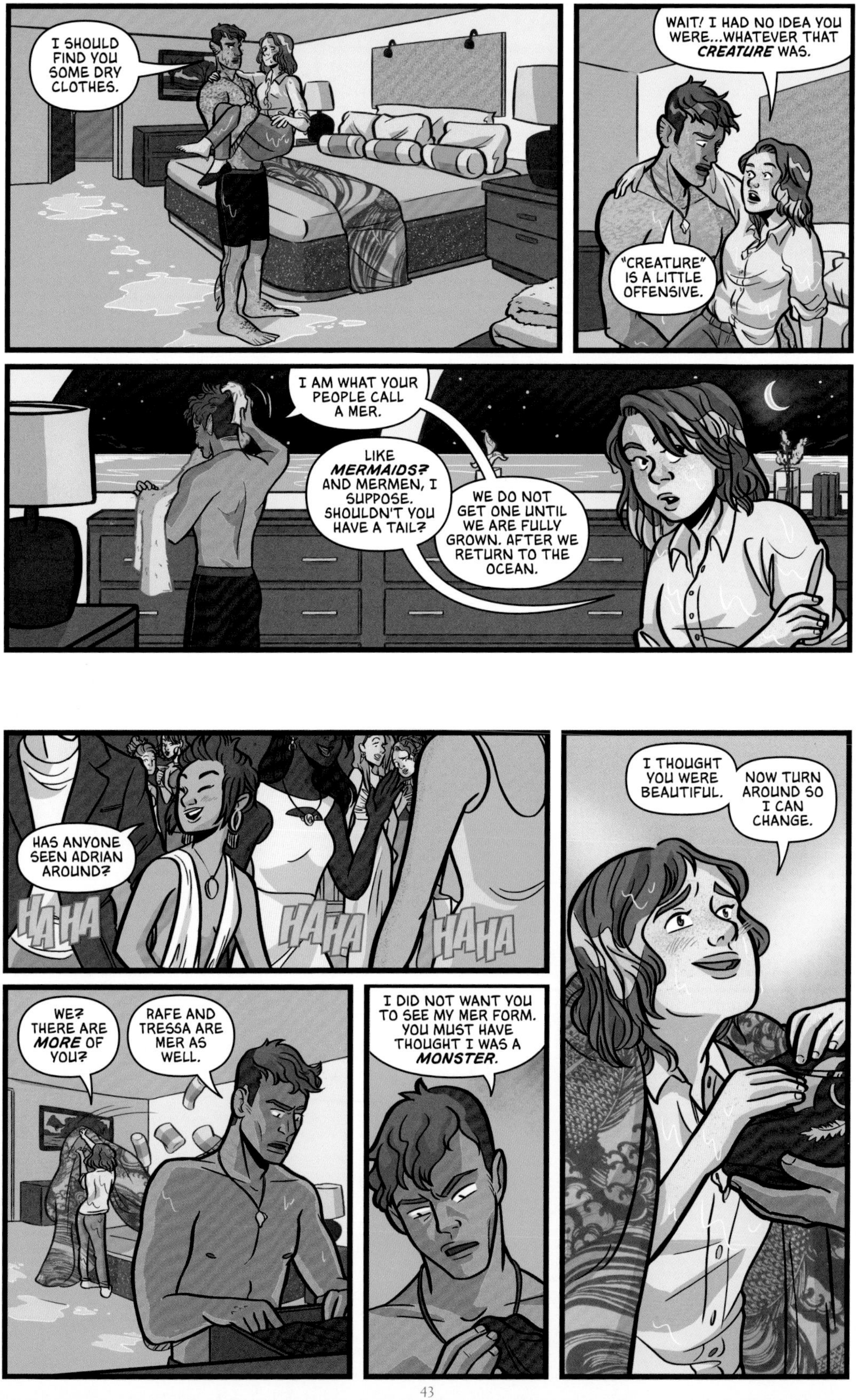

I SHOULD FIND YOU SOME DRY CLOTHES.
WAIT! I HAD NO IDEA YOU WERE...WHATEVER THAT *CREATURE* WAS.
"CREATURE" IS A LITTLE OFFENSIVE.
I AM WHAT YOUR PEOPLE CALL A MER.
LIKE *MERMAIDS?* AND MERMEN, I SUPPOSE. SHOULDN'T YOU HAVE A TAIL?
WE DO NOT GET ONE UNTIL WE ARE FULLY GROWN. AFTER WE RETURN TO THE OCEAN.
HAS ANYONE SEEN ADRIAN AROUND?
HAHA
HAHA
HAHA
WE? THERE ARE *MORE* OF YOU?
RAFE AND TRESSA ARE MER AS WELL.
I DID NOT WANT YOU TO SEE MY MER FORM. YOU MUST HAVE THOUGHT I WAS A *MONSTER.*
I THOUGHT YOU WERE BEAUTIFUL.
NOW TURN AROUND SO I CAN CHANGE.

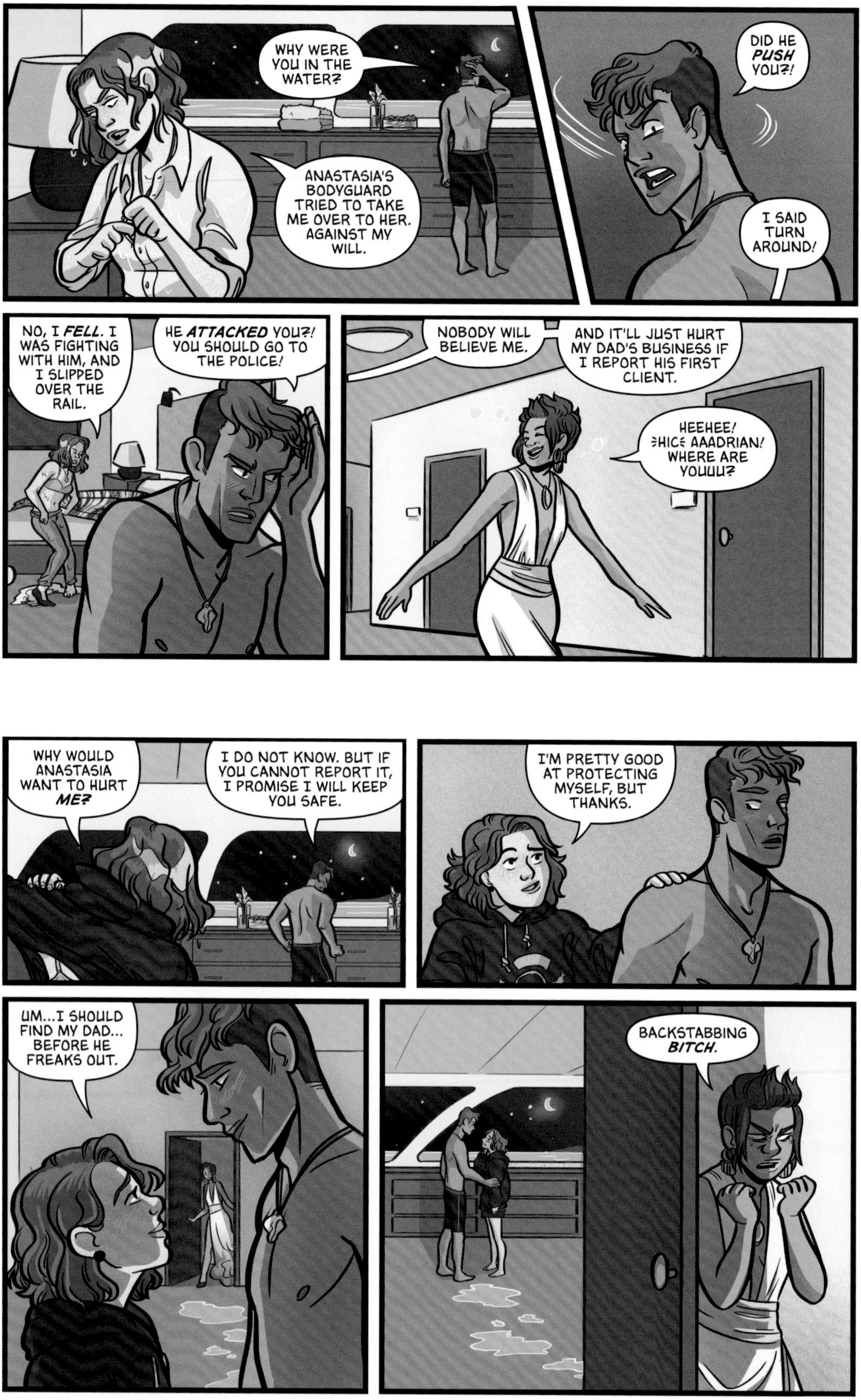
WHY WERE YOU IN THE WATER?
ANASTASIA'S BODYGUARD TRIED TO TAKE ME OVER TO HER. AGAINST MY WILL.
DID HE PUSH YOU?!
I SAID TURN AROUND!
NO, I FELL. I WAS FIGHTING WITH HIM, AND I SLIPPED OVER THE RAIL.
HE ATTACKED YOU?! YOU SHOULD GO TO THE POLICE!
NOBODY WILL BELIEVE ME.
AND IT'LL JUST HURT MY DAD'S BUSINESS IF I REPORT HIS FIRST CLIENT.
HEEHEE! *HIC* AAADRIAN! WHERE ARE YOUUU?
WHY WOULD ANASTASIA WANT TO HURT ME?
I DO NOT KNOW. BUT IF YOU CANNOT REPORT IT, I PROMISE I WILL KEEP YOU SAFE.
I'M PRETTY GOOD AT PROTECTING MYSELF, BUT THANKS.
UM...I SHOULD FIND MY DAD... BEFORE HE FREAKS OUT.
BACKSTABBING BITCH.

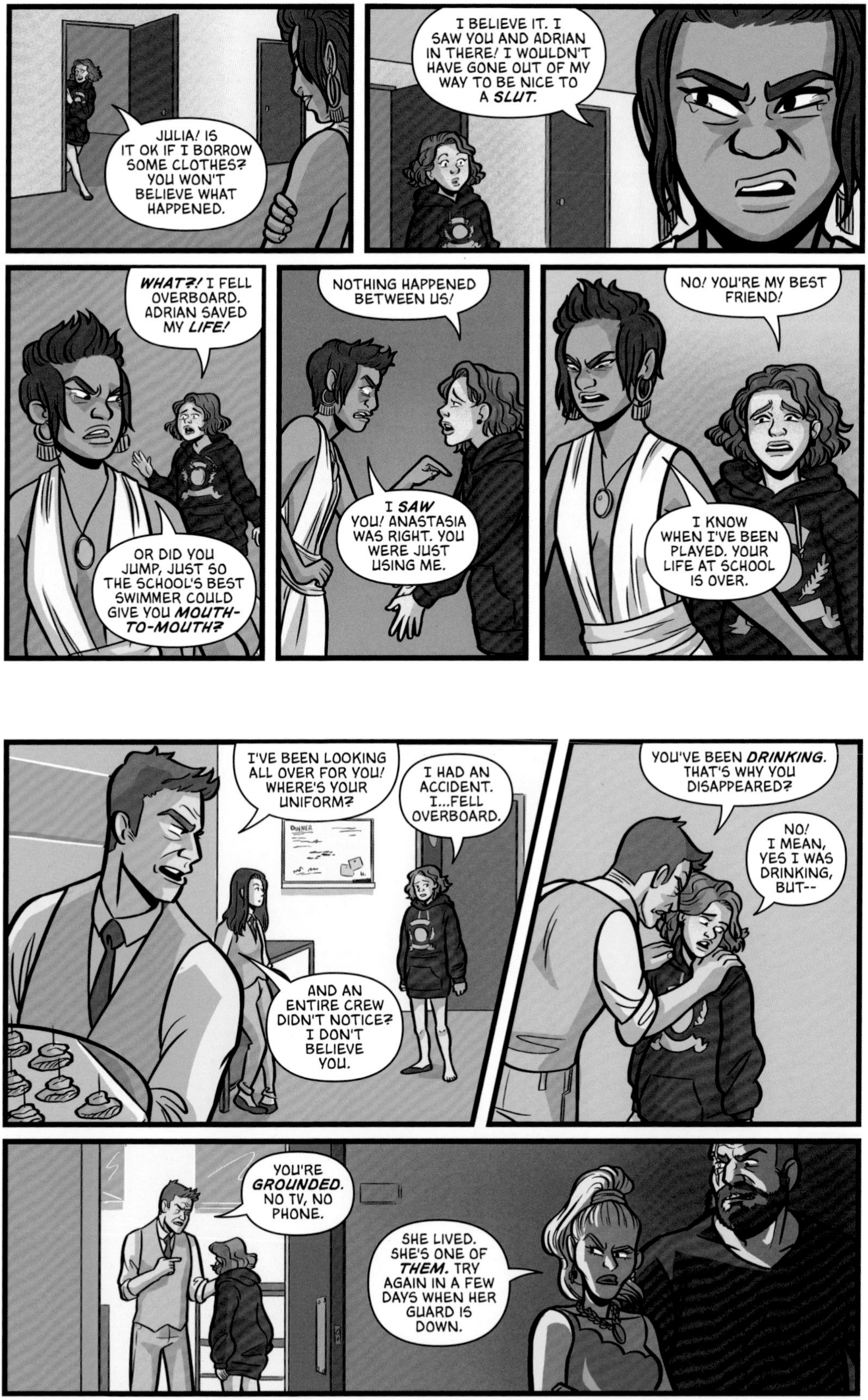
JULIA! IS IT OK IF I BORROW SOME CLOTHES? YOU WON'T BELIEVE WHAT HAPPENED.
I BELIEVE IT. I SAW YOU AND ADRIAN IN THERE! I WOULDN'T HAVE GONE OUT OF MY WAY TO BE NICE TO A SLUT.
WHAT?! I FELL OVERBOARD. ADRIAN SAVED MY LIFE!
OR DID YOU JUMP, JUST SO THE SCHOOL'S BEST SWIMMER COULD GIVE YOU MOUTH-TO-MOUTH?
NOTHING HAPPENED BETWEEN US!
I SAW YOU! ANASTASIA WAS RIGHT. YOU WERE JUST USING ME.
NO! YOU'RE MY BEST FRIEND!
I KNOW WHEN I'VE BEEN PLAYED. YOUR LIFE AT SCHOOL IS OVER.
I'VE BEEN LOOKING ALL OVER FOR YOU! WHERE'S YOUR UNIFORM?
I HAD AN ACCIDENT. I...FELL OVERBOARD.
AND AN ENTIRE CREW DIDN'T NOTICE? I DON'T BELIEVE YOU.
YOU'VE BEEN DRINKING. THAT'S WHY YOU DISAPPEARED?
NO! I MEAN, YES I WAS DRINKING, BUT--
YOU'RE GROUNDED. NO TV, NO PHONE.
SHE LIVED. SHE'S ONE OF THEM. TRY AGAIN IN A FEW DAYS WHEN HER GUARD IS DOWN.

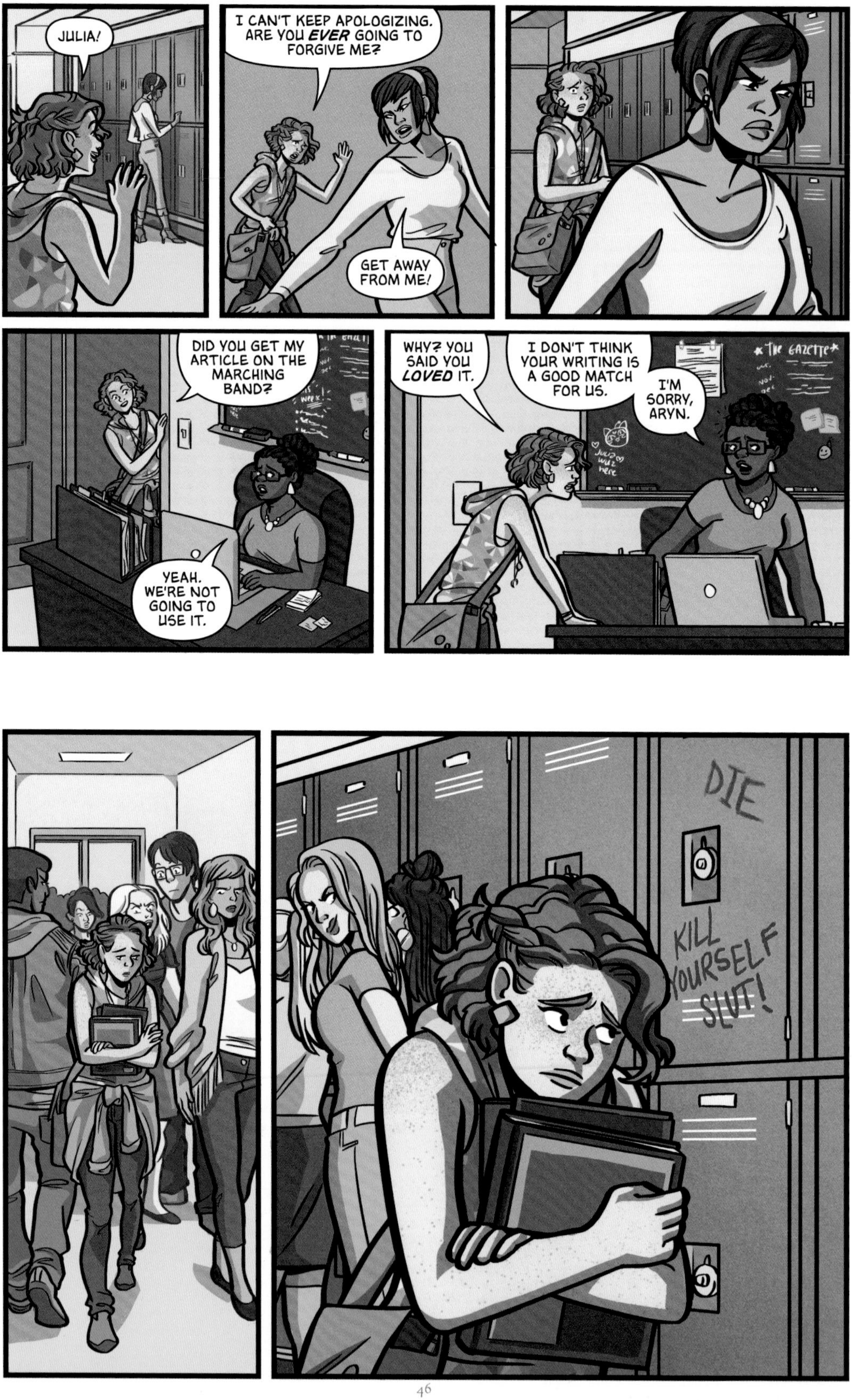
JULIA!
I CAN'T KEEP APOLOGIZING. ARE YOU EVER GOING TO FORGIVE ME?
GET AWAY FROM ME!
DID YOU GET MY ARTICLE ON THE MARCHING BAND?
YEAH. WE'RE NOT GOING TO USE IT.
WHY? YOU SAID YOU LOVED IT.
I DON'T THINK YOUR WRITING IS A GOOD MATCH FOR US.
I'M SORRY, ARYN.
THE GAZETTE
DIE
KILL YOURSELF SLUT!

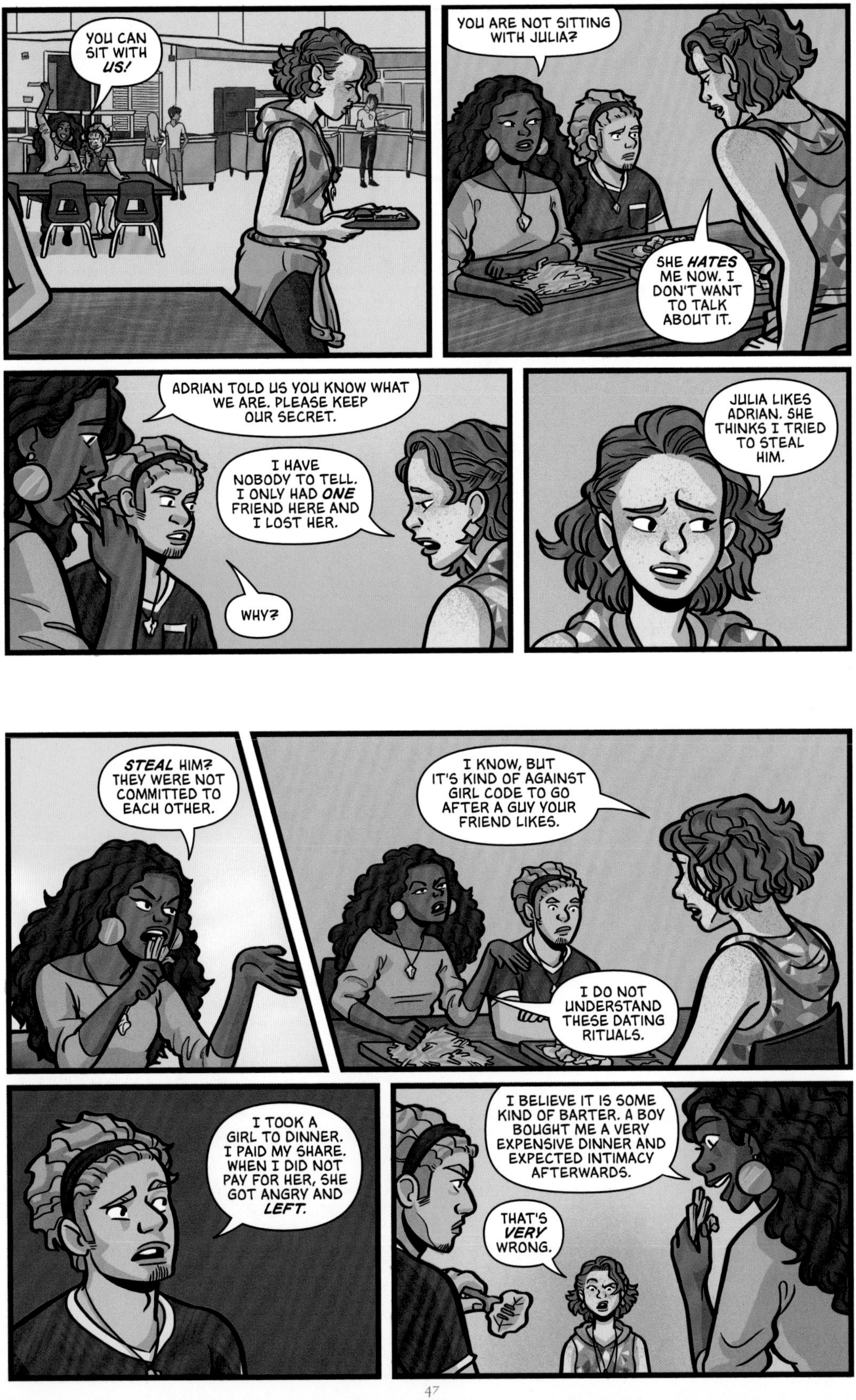

YOU CAN SIT WITH US!
YOU ARE NOT SITTING WITH JULIA?
SHE HATES ME NOW. I DON'T WANT TO TALK ABOUT IT.
ADRIAN TOLD US YOU KNOW WHAT WE ARE. PLEASE KEEP OUR SECRET.
I HAVE NOBODY TO TELL. I ONLY HAD ONE FRIEND HERE AND I LOST HER.
WHY?
JULIA LIKES ADRIAN. SHE THINKS I TRIED TO STEAL HIM.
STEAL HIM? THEY WERE NOT COMMITTED TO EACH OTHER.
I KNOW, BUT IT'S KIND OF AGAINST GIRL CODE TO GO AFTER A GUY YOUR FRIEND LIKES.
I DO NOT UNDERSTAND THESE DATING RITUALS.
I TOOK A GIRL TO DINNER. I PAID MY SHARE. WHEN I DID NOT PAY FOR HER, SHE GOT ANGRY AND LEFT.
I BELIEVE IT IS SOME KIND OF BARTER. A BOY BOUGHT ME A VERY EXPENSIVE DINNER AND EXPECTED INTIMACY AFTERWARDS.
THAT'S VERY WRONG.

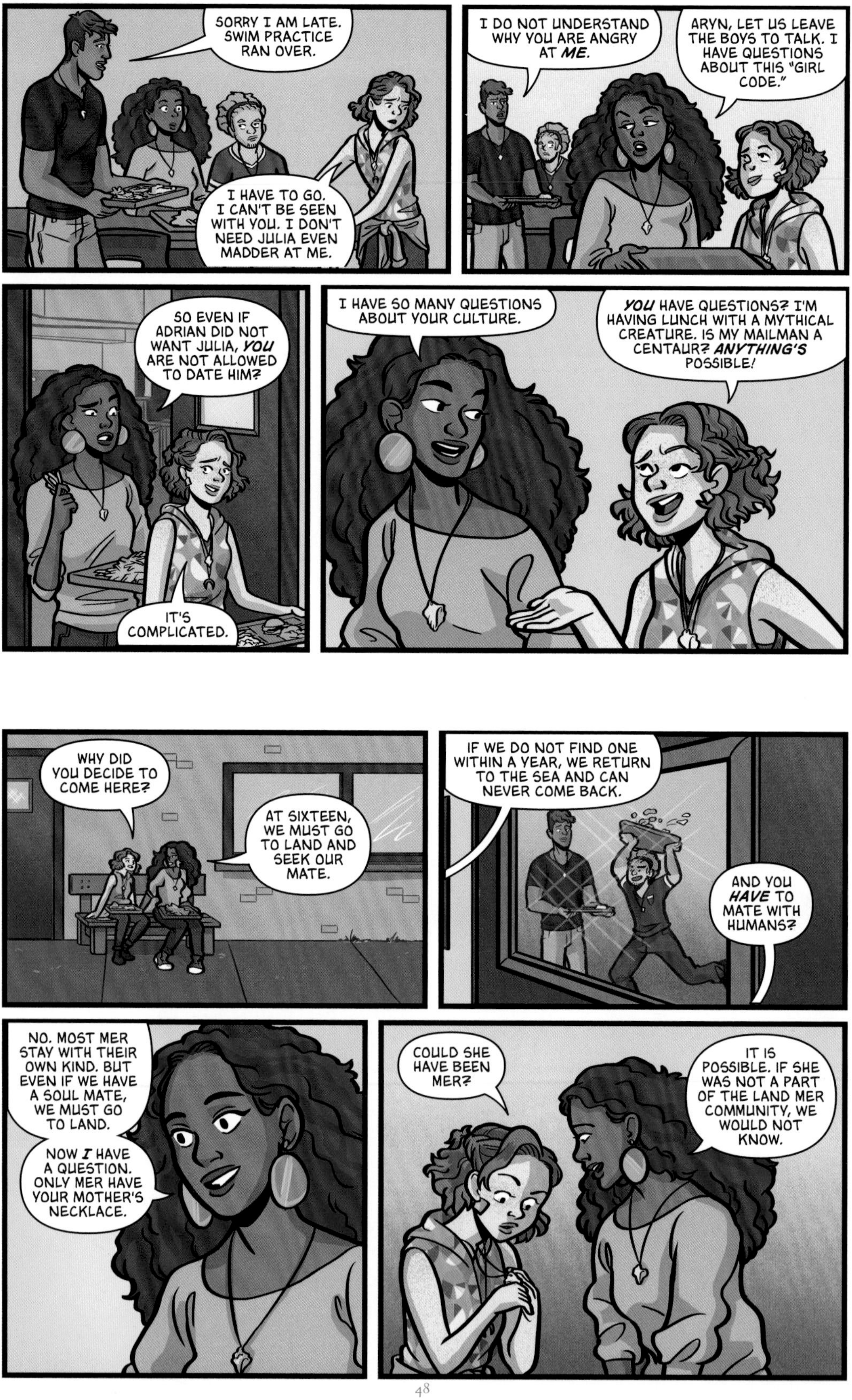
SORRY I AM LATE. SWIM PRACTICE RAN OVER.
I HAVE TO GO. I CAN'T BE SEEN WITH YOU. I DON'T NEED JULIA EVEN MADDER AT ME.
I DO NOT UNDERSTAND WHY YOU ARE ANGRY AT ME.
ARYN, LET US LEAVE THE BOYS TO TALK. I HAVE QUESTIONS ABOUT THIS "GIRL CODE."
SO EVEN IF ADRIAN DID NOT WANT JULIA, YOU ARE NOT ALLOWED TO DATE HIM?
IT'S COMPLICATED.
I HAVE SO MANY QUESTIONS ABOUT YOUR CULTURE.
YOU HAVE QUESTIONS? I'M HAVING LUNCH WITH A MYTHICAL CREATURE. IS MY MAILMAN A CENTAUR? ANYTHING'S POSSIBLE!
WHY DID YOU DECIDE TO COME HERE?
AT SIXTEEN, WE MUST GO TO LAND AND SEEK OUR MATE.
IF WE DO NOT FIND ONE WITHIN A YEAR, WE RETURN TO THE SEA AND CAN NEVER COME BACK.
AND YOU HAVE TO MATE WITH HUMANS?
NO. MOST MER STAY WITH THEIR OWN KIND. BUT EVEN IF WE HAVE A SOUL MATE, WE MUST GO TO LAND.
NOW I HAVE A QUESTION. ONLY MER HAVE YOUR MOTHER'S NECKLACE.
COULD SHE HAVE BEEN MER?
IT IS POSSIBLE. IF SHE WAS NOT A PART OF THE LAND MER COMMUNITY, WE WOULD NOT KNOW.

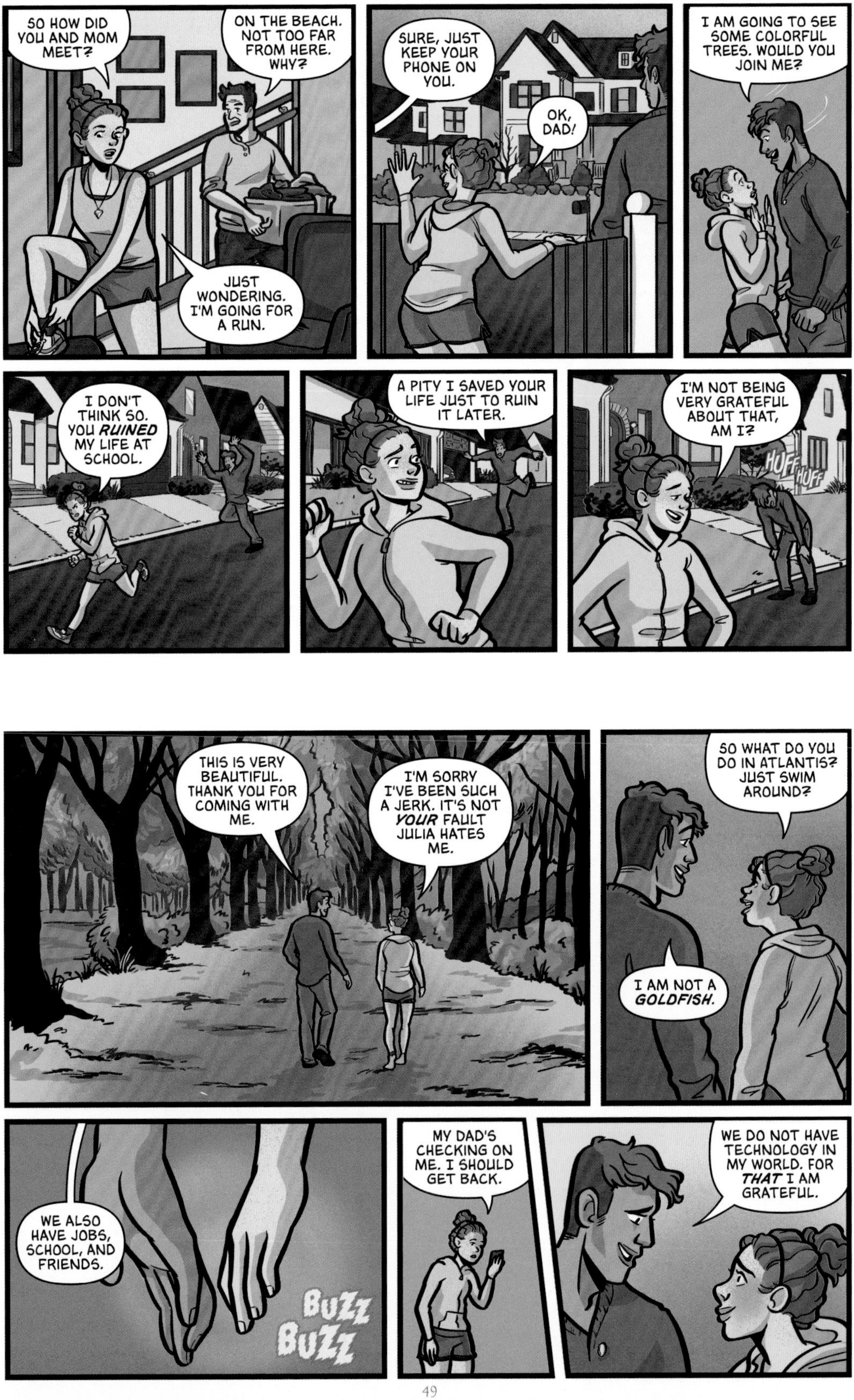
SO HOW DID YOU AND MOM MEET?
ON THE BEACH. NOT TOO FAR FROM HERE. WHY?
JUST WONDERING. I'M GOING FOR A RUN.
SURE, JUST KEEP YOUR PHONE ON YOU.
OK, DAD!
I AM GOING TO SEE SOME COLORFUL TREES. WOULD YOU JOIN ME?
I DON'T THINK SO. YOU *RUINED* MY LIFE AT SCHOOL.
A PITY I SAVED YOUR LIFE JUST TO RUIN IT LATER.
I'M NOT BEING VERY GRATEFUL ABOUT THAT, AM I?
HUFF HUFF
THIS IS VERY BEAUTIFUL. THANK YOU FOR COMING WITH ME.
I'M SORRY I'VE BEEN SUCH A JERK. IT'S NOT *YOUR* FAULT JULIA HATES ME.
SO WHAT DO YOU DO IN ATLANTIS? JUST SWIM AROUND?
I AM NOT A *GOLDFISH.*
WE ALSO HAVE JOBS, SCHOOL, AND FRIENDS.
BUZZ BUZZ
MY DAD'S CHECKING ON ME. I SHOULD GET BACK.
WE DO NOT HAVE TECHNOLOGY IN MY WORLD. FOR *THAT* I AM GRATEFUL.

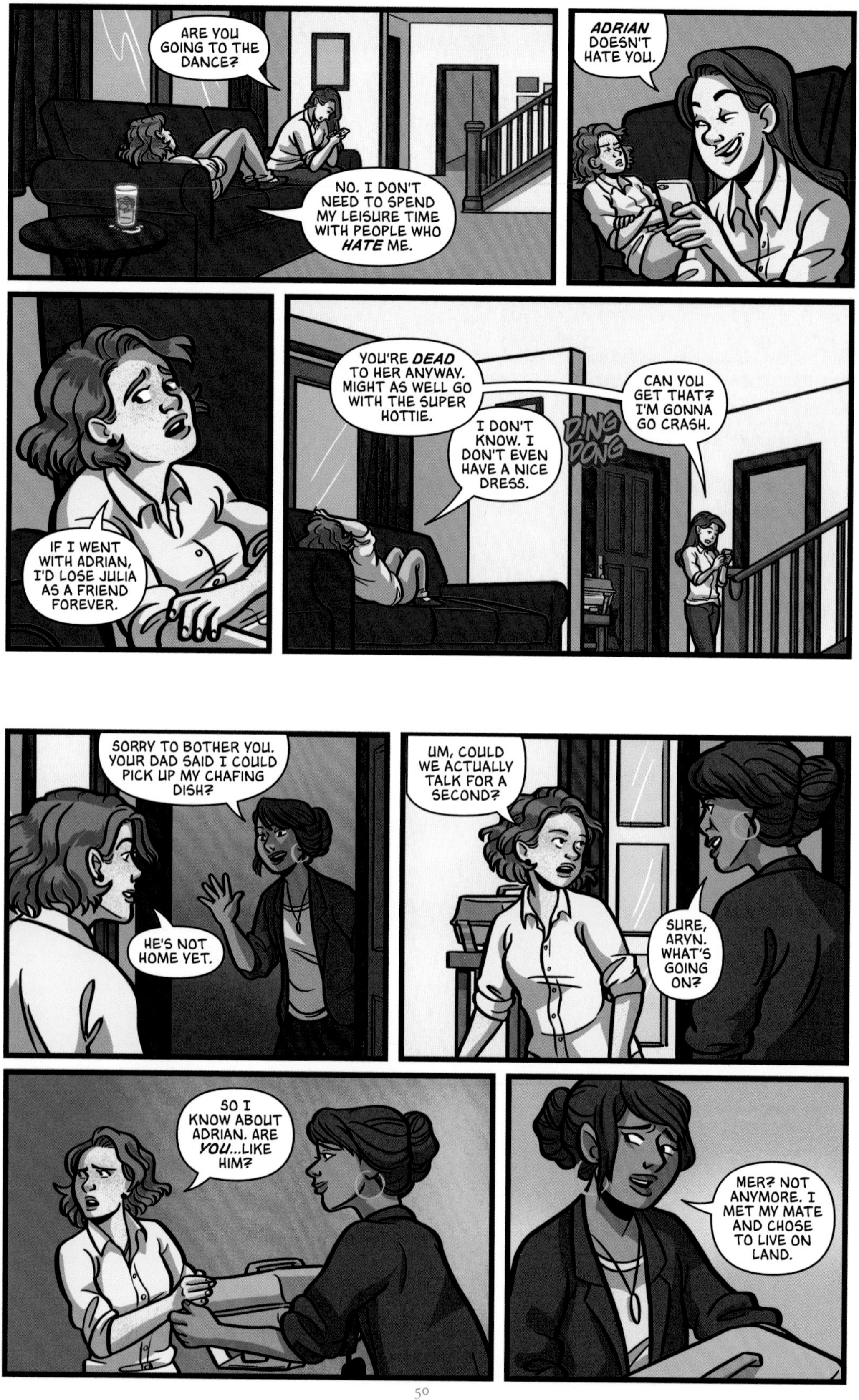
ARE YOU GOING TO THE DANCE?
NO. I DON'T NEED TO SPEND MY LEISURE TIME WITH PEOPLE WHO HATE ME.
ADRIAN DOESN'T HATE YOU.
IF I WENT WITH ADRIAN, I'D LOSE JULIA AS A FRIEND FOREVER.
YOU'RE DEAD TO HER ANYWAY. MIGHT AS WELL GO WITH THE SUPER HOTTIE.
I DON'T KNOW. I DON'T EVEN HAVE A NICE DRESS.
DING DONG
CAN YOU GET THAT? I'M GONNA GO CRASH.
SORRY TO BOTHER YOU. YOUR DAD SAID I COULD PICK UP MY CHAFING DISH?
HE'S NOT HOME YET.
UM, COULD WE ACTUALLY TALK FOR A SECOND?
SURE, ARYN. WHAT'S GOING ON?
SO I KNOW ABOUT ADRIAN. ARE YOU...LIKE HIM?
MER? NOT ANYMORE. I MET MY MATE AND CHOSE TO LIVE ON LAND.

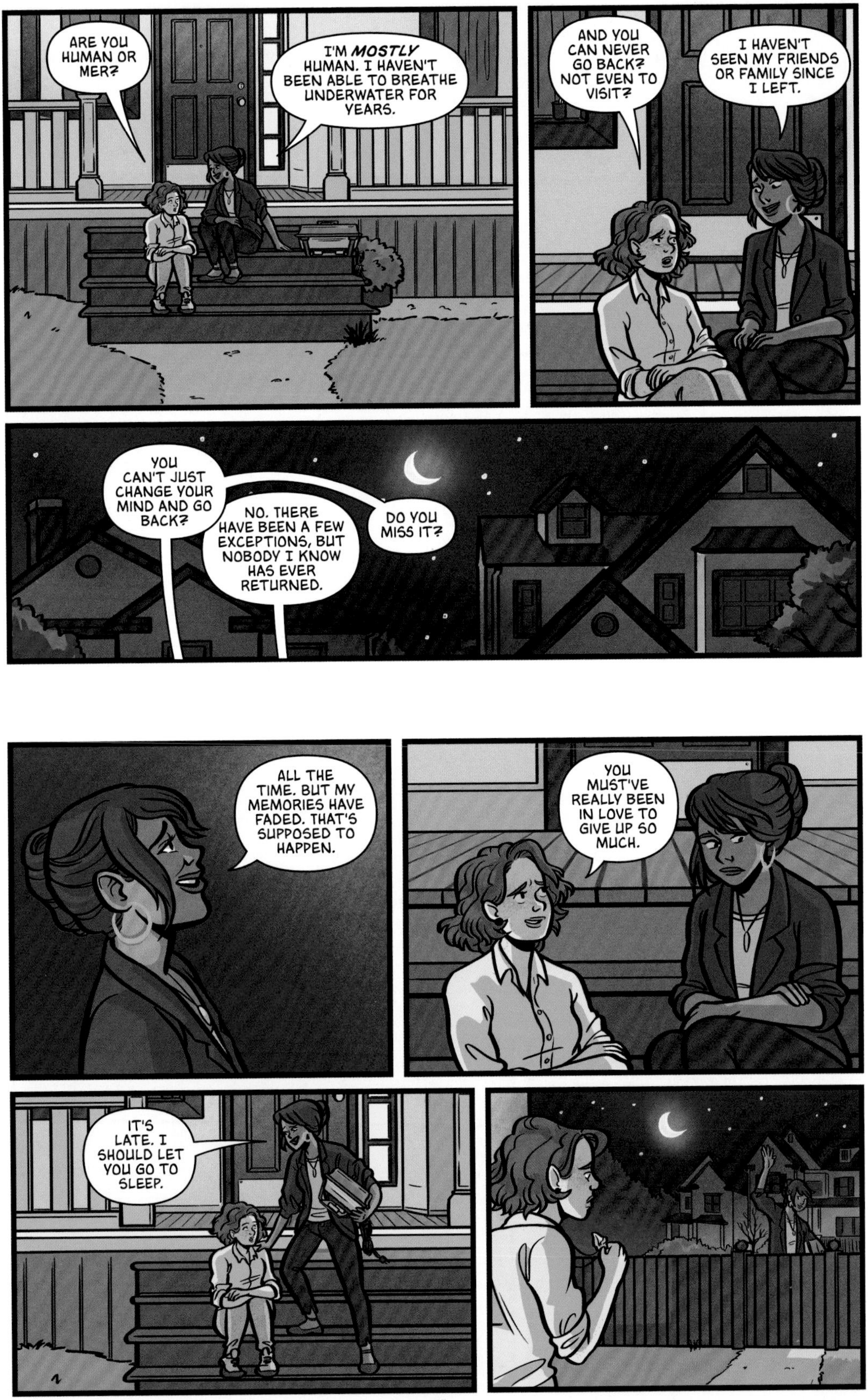
ARE YOU HUMAN OR MER?
I'M **MOSTLY** HUMAN. I HAVEN'T BEEN ABLE TO BREATHE UNDERWATER FOR YEARS.
AND YOU CAN NEVER GO BACK? NOT EVEN TO VISIT?
I HAVEN'T SEEN MY FRIENDS OR FAMILY SINCE I LEFT.
YOU CAN'T JUST CHANGE YOUR MIND AND GO BACK?
NO. THERE HAVE BEEN A FEW EXCEPTIONS, BUT NOBODY I KNOW HAS EVER RETURNED.
DO YOU MISS IT?
ALL THE TIME. BUT MY MEMORIES HAVE FADED. THAT'S SUPPOSED TO HAPPEN.
YOU MUST'VE REALLY BEEN IN LOVE TO GIVE UP SO MUCH.
IT'S LATE. I SHOULD LET YOU GO TO SLEEP.

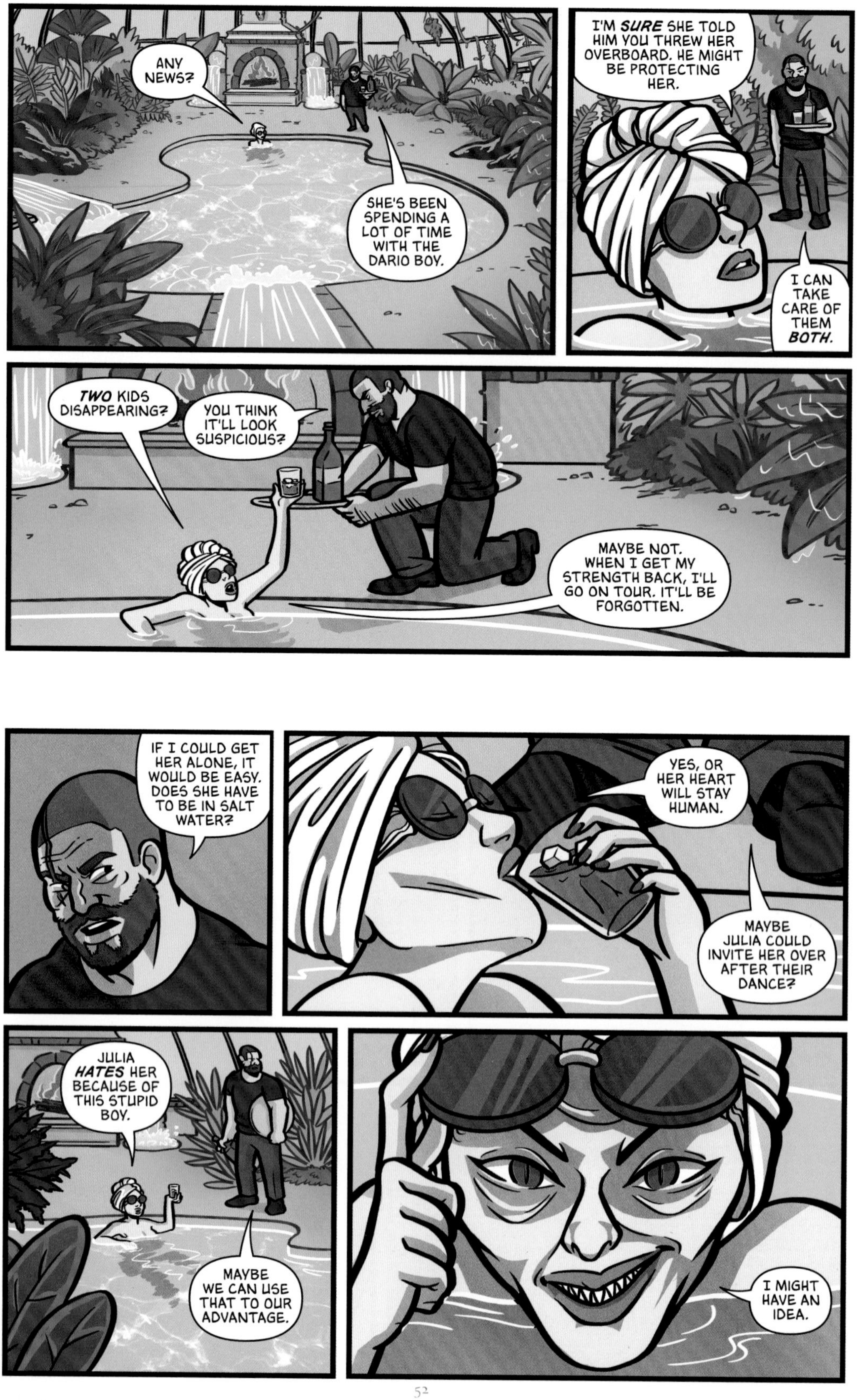
ANY NEWS?
SHE'S BEEN SPENDING A LOT OF TIME WITH THE DARIO BOY.
I'M SURE SHE TOLD HIM YOU THREW HER OVERBOARD. HE MIGHT BE PROTECTING HER.
I CAN TAKE CARE OF THEM BOTH.
TWO KIDS DISAPPEARING?
YOU THINK IT'LL LOOK SUSPICIOUS?
MAYBE NOT. WHEN I GET MY STRENGTH BACK, I'LL GO ON TOUR. IT'LL BE FORGOTTEN.
IF I COULD GET HER ALONE, IT WOULD BE EASY. DOES SHE HAVE TO BE IN SALT WATER?
YES, OR HER HEART WILL STAY HUMAN.
MAYBE JULIA COULD INVITE HER OVER AFTER THEIR DANCE?
JULIA HATES HER BECAUSE OF THIS STUPID BOY.
MAYBE WE CAN USE THAT TO OUR ADVANTAGE.
I MIGHT HAVE AN IDEA.

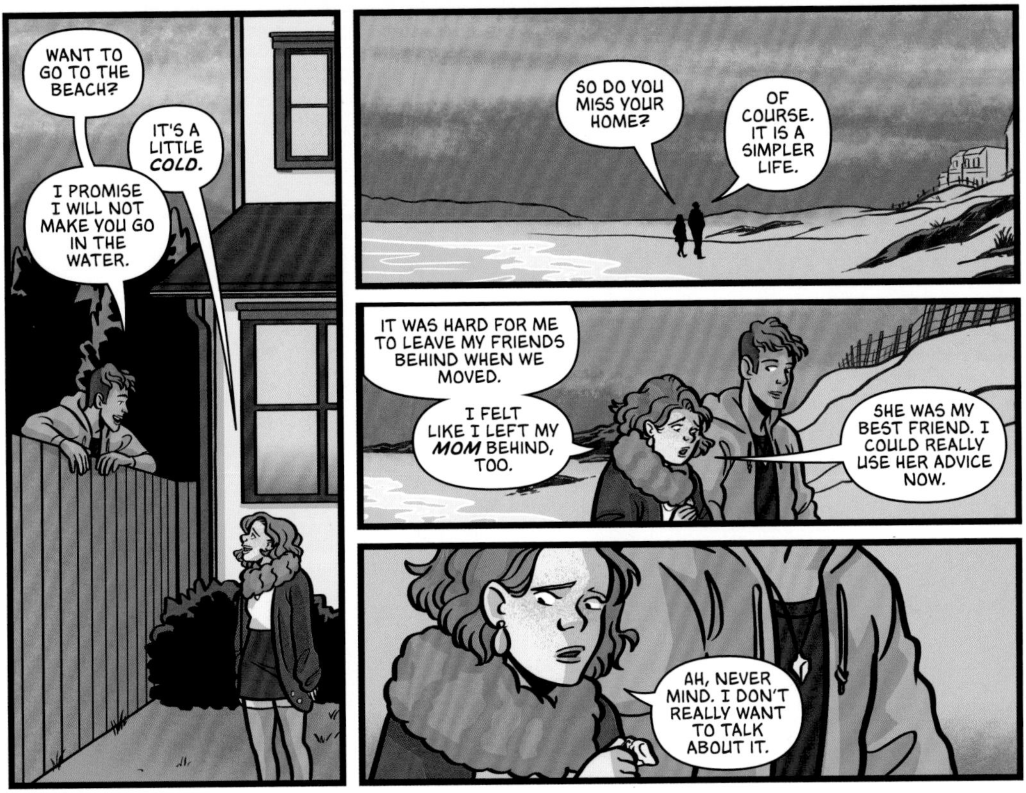
WANT TO GO TO THE BEACH?
IT'S A LITTLE *COLD.*
I PROMISE I WILL NOT MAKE YOU GO IN THE WATER.
SO DO YOU MISS YOUR HOME?
OF COURSE. IT IS A SIMPLER LIFE.
IT WAS HARD FOR ME TO LEAVE MY FRIENDS BEHIND WHEN WE MOVED.
I FELT LIKE I LEFT MY *MOM* BEHIND, TOO.
SHE WAS MY BEST FRIEND. I COULD REALLY USE HER ADVICE NOW.
AH, NEVER MIND. I DON'T REALLY WANT TO TALK ABOUT IT.

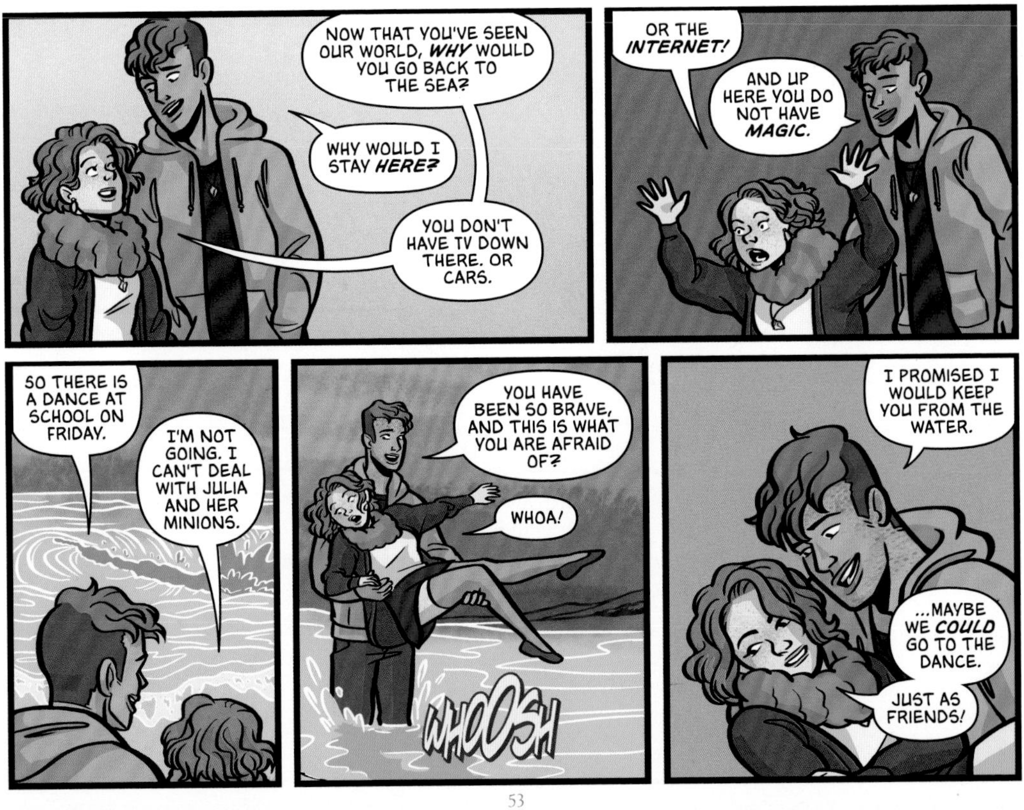
NOW THAT YOU'VE SEEN OUR WORLD, *WHY* WOULD YOU GO BACK TO THE SEA?
WHY WOULD I STAY *HERE?*
YOU DON'T HAVE TV DOWN THERE. OR CARS.
OR THE *INTERNET!*
AND UP HERE YOU DO NOT HAVE *MAGIC.*
SO THERE IS A DANCE AT SCHOOL ON FRIDAY.
I'M NOT GOING. I CAN'T DEAL WITH JULIA AND HER MINIONS.
YOU HAVE BEEN SO BRAVE, AND THIS IS WHAT YOU ARE AFRAID OF?
WHOA!
WHOOSH
I PROMISED I WOULD KEEP YOU FROM THE WATER.
...MAYBE WE *COULD* GO TO THE DANCE.
JUST AS FRIENDS!

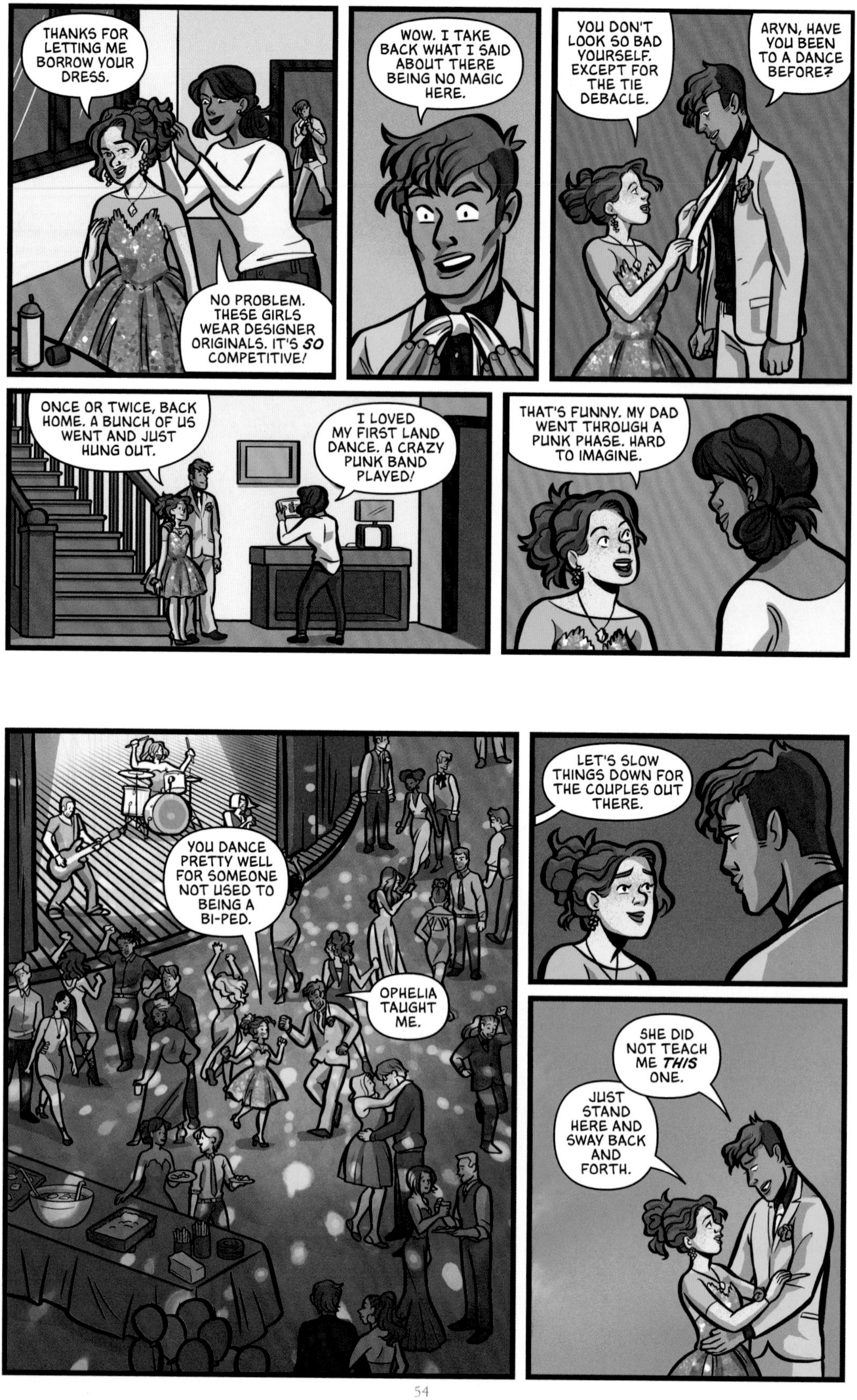
THANKS FOR LETTING ME BORROW YOUR DRESS.
NO PROBLEM. THESE GIRLS WEAR DESIGNER ORIGINALS. IT'S *SO* COMPETITIVE!
WOW. I TAKE BACK WHAT I SAID ABOUT THERE BEING NO MAGIC HERE.
YOU DON'T LOOK SO BAD YOURSELF. EXCEPT FOR THE TIE DEBACLE.
ARYN, HAVE YOU BEEN TO A DANCE BEFORE?
ONCE OR TWICE, BACK HOME. A BUNCH OF US WENT AND JUST HUNG OUT.
I LOVED MY FIRST LAND DANCE. A CRAZY PUNK BAND PLAYED!
THAT'S FUNNY. MY DAD WENT THROUGH A PUNK PHASE. HARD TO IMAGINE.
YOU DANCE PRETTY WELL FOR SOMEONE NOT USED TO BEING A BI-PED.
OPHELIA TAUGHT ME.
LET'S SLOW THINGS DOWN FOR THE COUPLES OUT THERE.
SHE DID NOT TEACH ME *THIS* ONE.
JUST STAND HERE AND SWAY BACK AND FORTH.

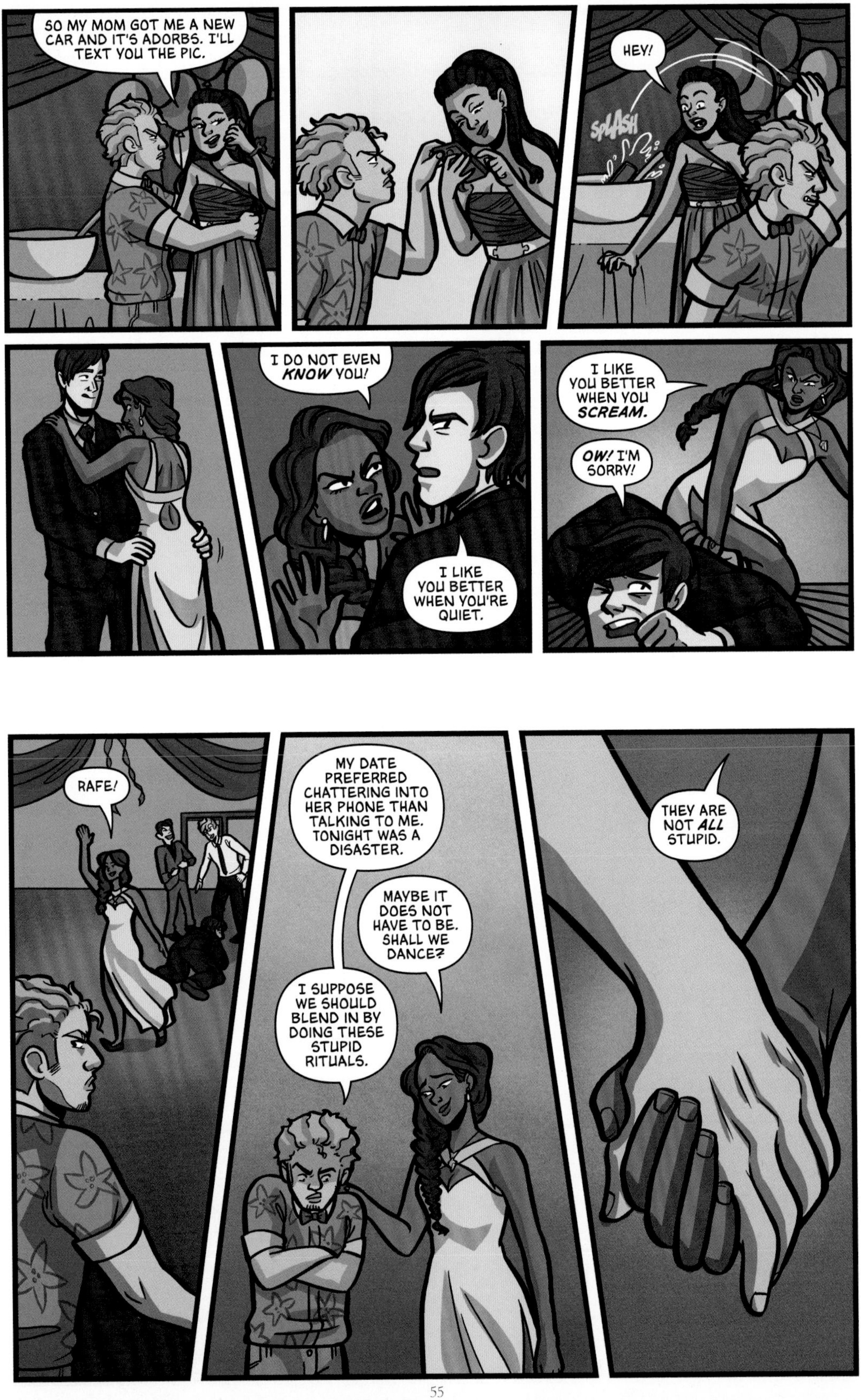
SO MY MOM GOT ME A NEW CAR AND IT'S ADORBS. I'LL TEXT YOU THE PIC.
HEY!
SPLASH
I DO NOT EVEN *KNOW* YOU!
I LIKE YOU BETTER WHEN YOU'RE QUIET.
I LIKE YOU BETTER WHEN YOU *SCREAM.*
OW! I'M SORRY!
RAFE!
MY DATE PREFERRED CHATTERING INTO HER PHONE THAN TALKING TO ME. TONIGHT WAS A DISASTER.
MAYBE IT DOES NOT HAVE TO BE. SHALL WE DANCE?
I SUPPOSE WE SHOULD BLEND IN BY DOING THESE STUPID RITUALS.
THEY ARE NOT *ALL* STUPID.

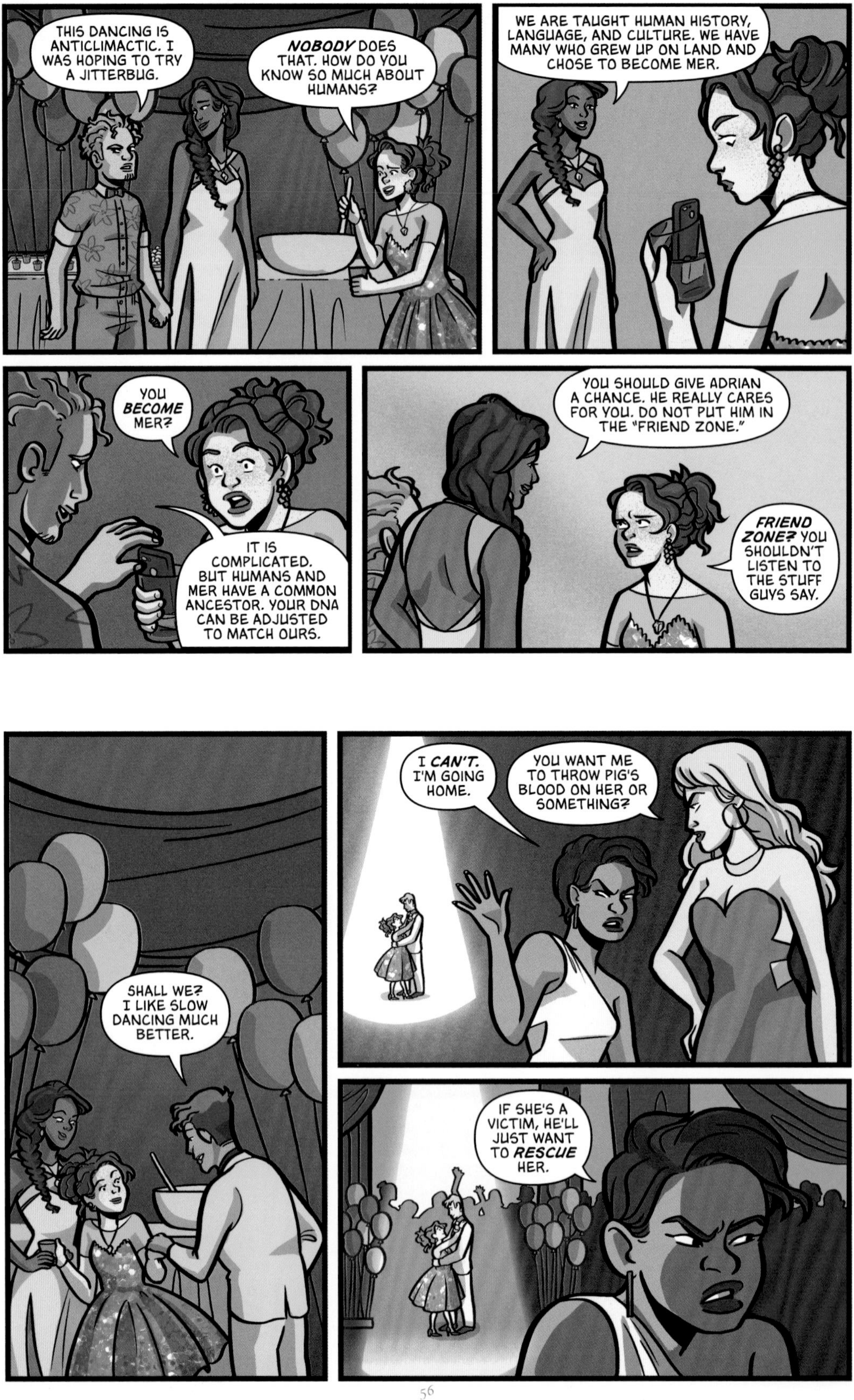
THIS DANCING IS ANTICLIMACTIC. I WAS HOPING TO TRY A JITTERBUG.
NOBODY DOES THAT. HOW DO YOU KNOW SO MUCH ABOUT HUMANS?
WE ARE TAUGHT HUMAN HISTORY, LANGUAGE, AND CULTURE. WE HAVE MANY WHO GREW UP ON LAND AND CHOSE TO BECOME MER.
YOU BECOME MER?
IT IS COMPLICATED. BUT HUMANS AND MER HAVE A COMMON ANCESTOR. YOUR DNA CAN BE ADJUSTED TO MATCH OURS.
YOU SHOULD GIVE ADRIAN A CHANCE. HE REALLY CARES FOR YOU. DO NOT PUT HIM IN THE "FRIEND ZONE."
FRIEND ZONE? YOU SHOULDN'T LISTEN TO THE STUFF GUYS SAY.
SHALL WE? I LIKE SLOW DANCING MUCH BETTER.
I CAN'T. I'M GOING HOME.
YOU WANT ME TO THROW PIG'S BLOOD ON HER OR SOMETHING?
IF SHE'S A VICTIM, HE'LL JUST WANT TO RESCUE HER.

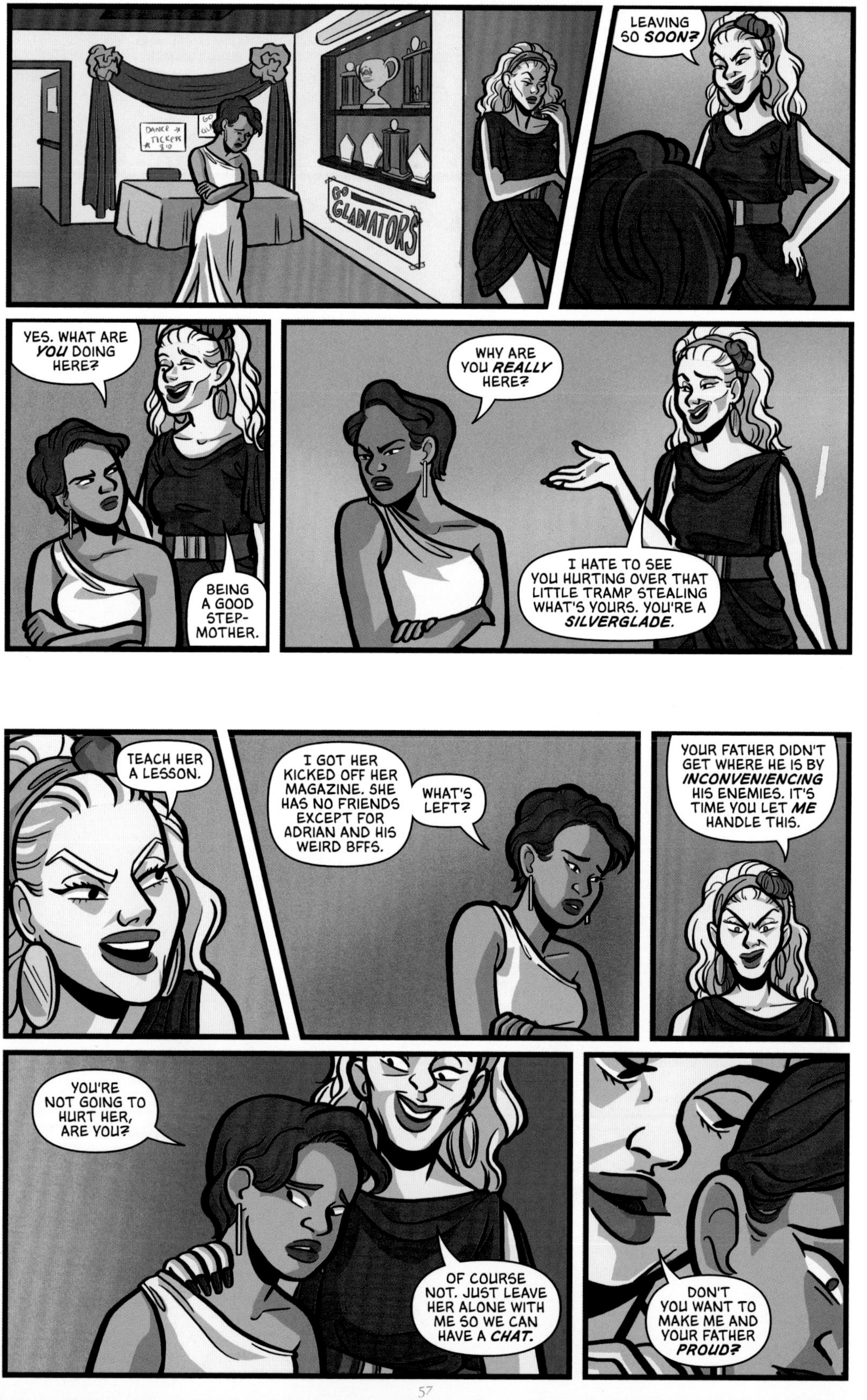
DANCE TICKETS $10
GO GLADIATORS
LEAVING SO SOON?
YES. WHAT ARE YOU DOING HERE?
BEING A GOOD STEP-MOTHER.
WHY ARE YOU REALLY HERE?
I HATE TO SEE YOU HURTING OVER THAT LITTLE TRAMP STEALING WHAT'S YOURS. YOU'RE A SILVERGLADE.
TEACH HER A LESSON.
I GOT HER KICKED OFF HER MAGAZINE. SHE HAS NO FRIENDS EXCEPT FOR ADRIAN AND HIS WEIRD BFFS.
WHAT'S LEFT?
YOUR FATHER DIDN'T GET WHERE HE IS BY INCONVENIENCING HIS ENEMIES. IT'S TIME YOU LET ME HANDLE THIS.
YOU'RE NOT GOING TO HURT HER, ARE YOU?
OF COURSE NOT. JUST LEAVE HER ALONE WITH ME SO WE CAN HAVE A CHAT.
DON'T YOU WANT TO MAKE ME AND YOUR FATHER PROUD?

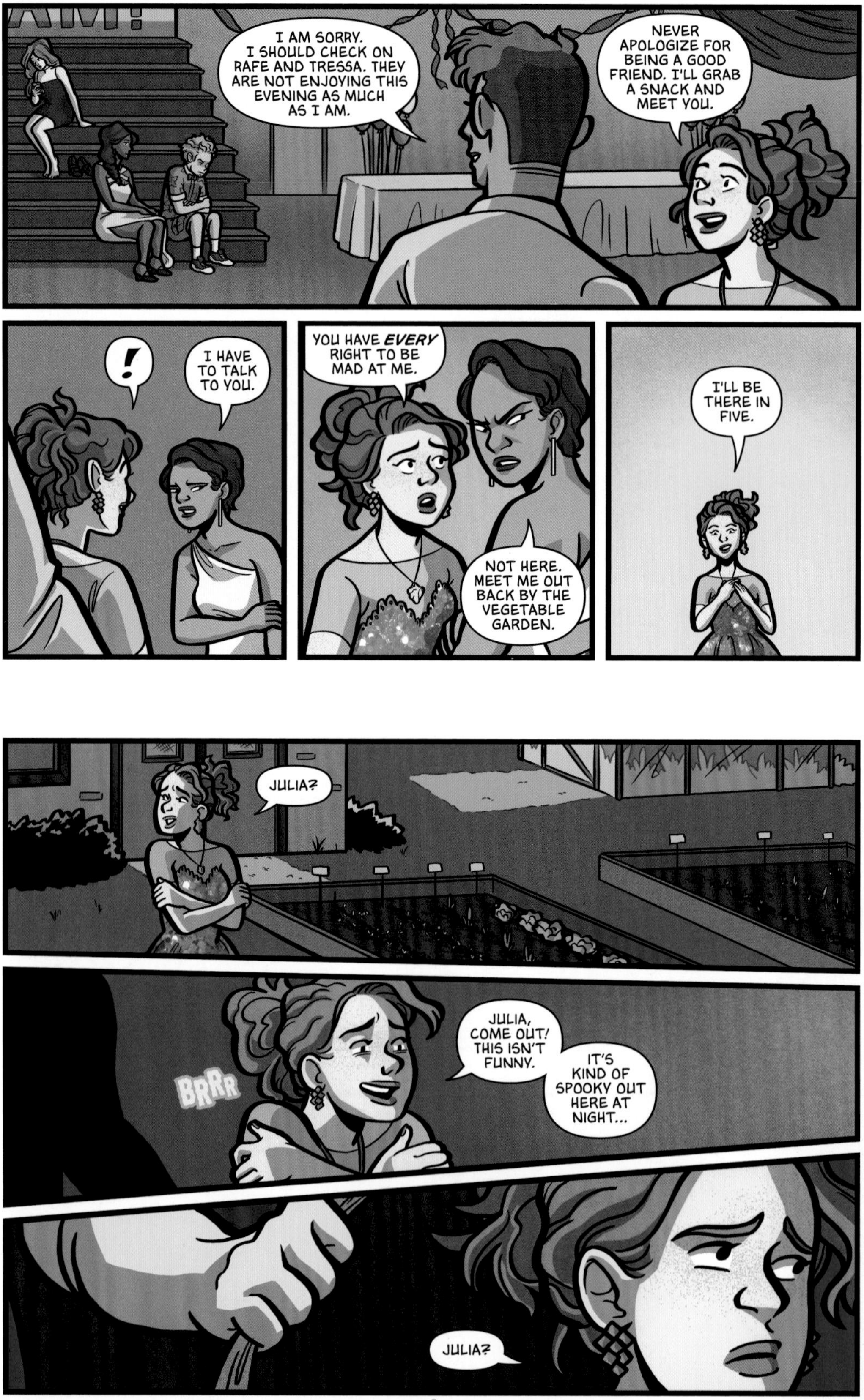
I AM SORRY. I SHOULD CHECK ON RAFE AND TRESSA. THEY ARE NOT ENJOYING THIS EVENING AS MUCH AS I AM.
NEVER APOLOGIZE FOR BEING A GOOD FRIEND. I'LL GRAB A SNACK AND MEET YOU.
!
I HAVE TO TALK TO YOU.
YOU HAVE EVERY RIGHT TO BE MAD AT ME.
NOT HERE. MEET ME OUT BACK BY THE VEGETABLE GARDEN.
I'LL BE THERE IN FIVE.
JULIA?
BRRR
JULIA, COME OUT! THIS ISN'T FUNNY.
IT'S KIND OF SPOOKY OUT HERE AT NIGHT...
JULIA?

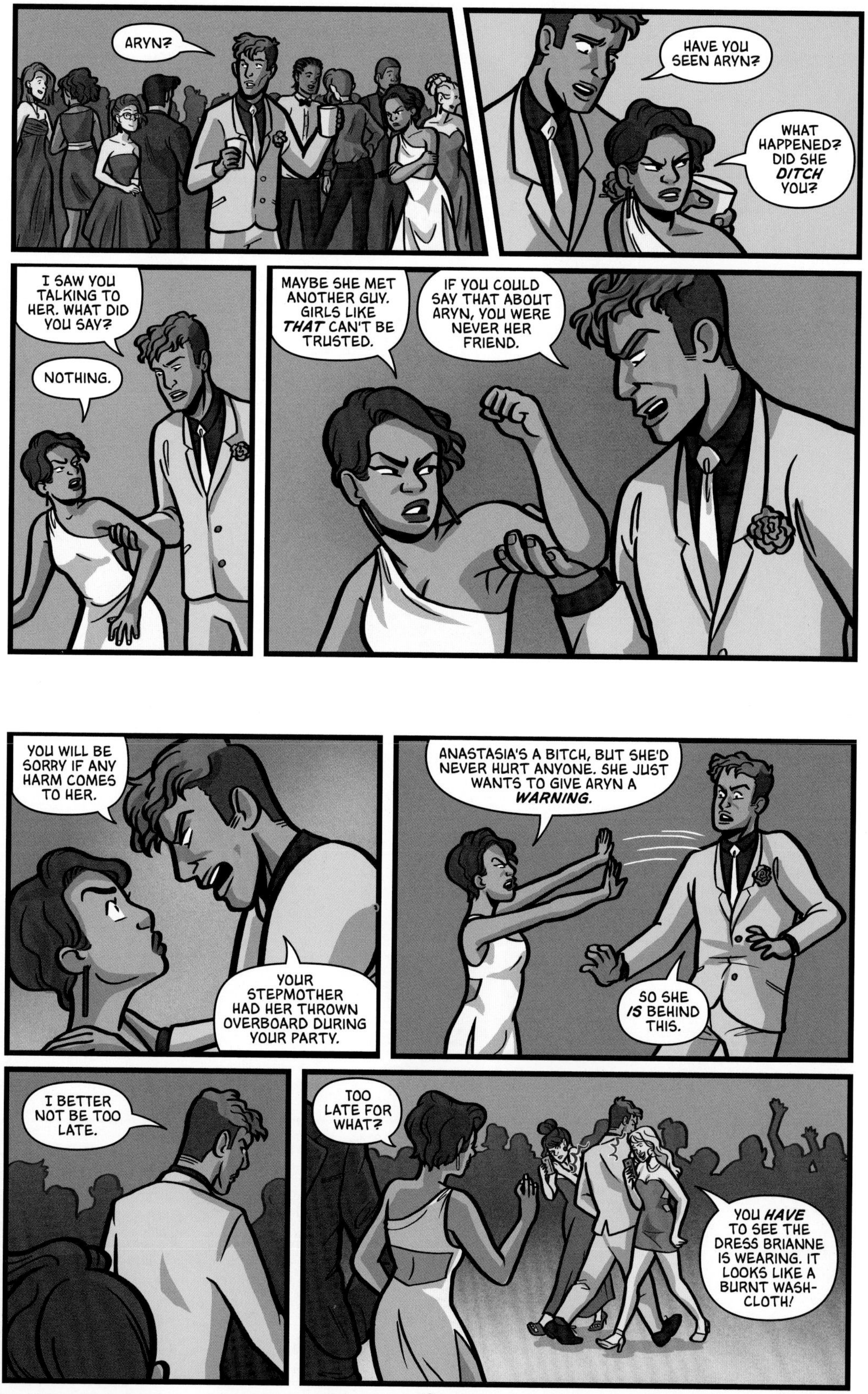
ARYN?
HAVE YOU SEEN ARYN?
WHAT HAPPENED? DID SHE *DITCH* YOU?
I SAW YOU TALKING TO HER. WHAT DID YOU SAY?
NOTHING.
MAYBE SHE MET ANOTHER GUY. GIRLS LIKE *THAT* CAN'T BE TRUSTED.
IF YOU COULD SAY THAT ABOUT ARYN, YOU WERE NEVER HER FRIEND.
YOU WILL BE SORRY IF ANY HARM COMES TO HER.
YOUR STEPMOTHER HAD HER THROWN OVERBOARD DURING YOUR PARTY.
ANASTASIA'S A BITCH, BUT SHE'D NEVER HURT ANYONE. SHE JUST WANTS TO GIVE ARYN A *WARNING*.
SO SHE *IS* BEHIND THIS.
I BETTER NOT BE TOO LATE.
TOO LATE FOR WHAT?
YOU *HAVE* TO SEE THE DRESS BRIANNE IS WEARING. IT LOOKS LIKE A BURNT WASH-CLOTH!

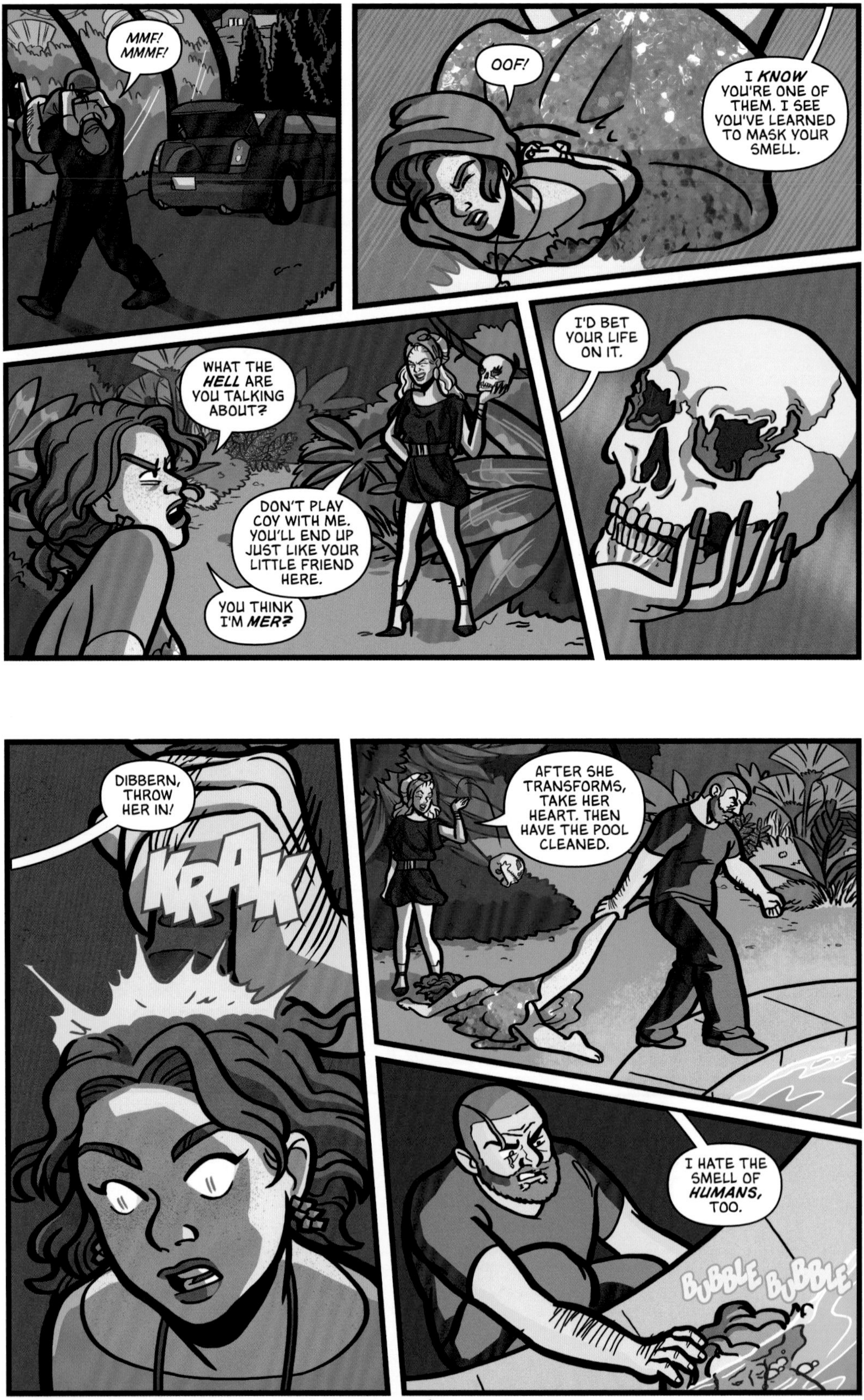
MMF! MMMF!
OOF!
I KNOW YOU'RE ONE OF THEM. I SEE YOU'VE LEARNED TO MASK YOUR SMELL.
WHAT THE HELL ARE YOU TALKING ABOUT?
DON'T PLAY COY WITH ME. YOU'LL END UP JUST LIKE YOUR LITTLE FRIEND HERE.
YOU THINK I'M MER?
I'D BET YOUR LIFE ON IT.
DIBBERN, THROW HER IN!
KRAK
AFTER SHE TRANSFORMS, TAKE HER HEART. THEN HAVE THE POOL CLEANED.
I HATE THE SMELL OF HUMANS, TOO.
BUBBLE BUBBLE

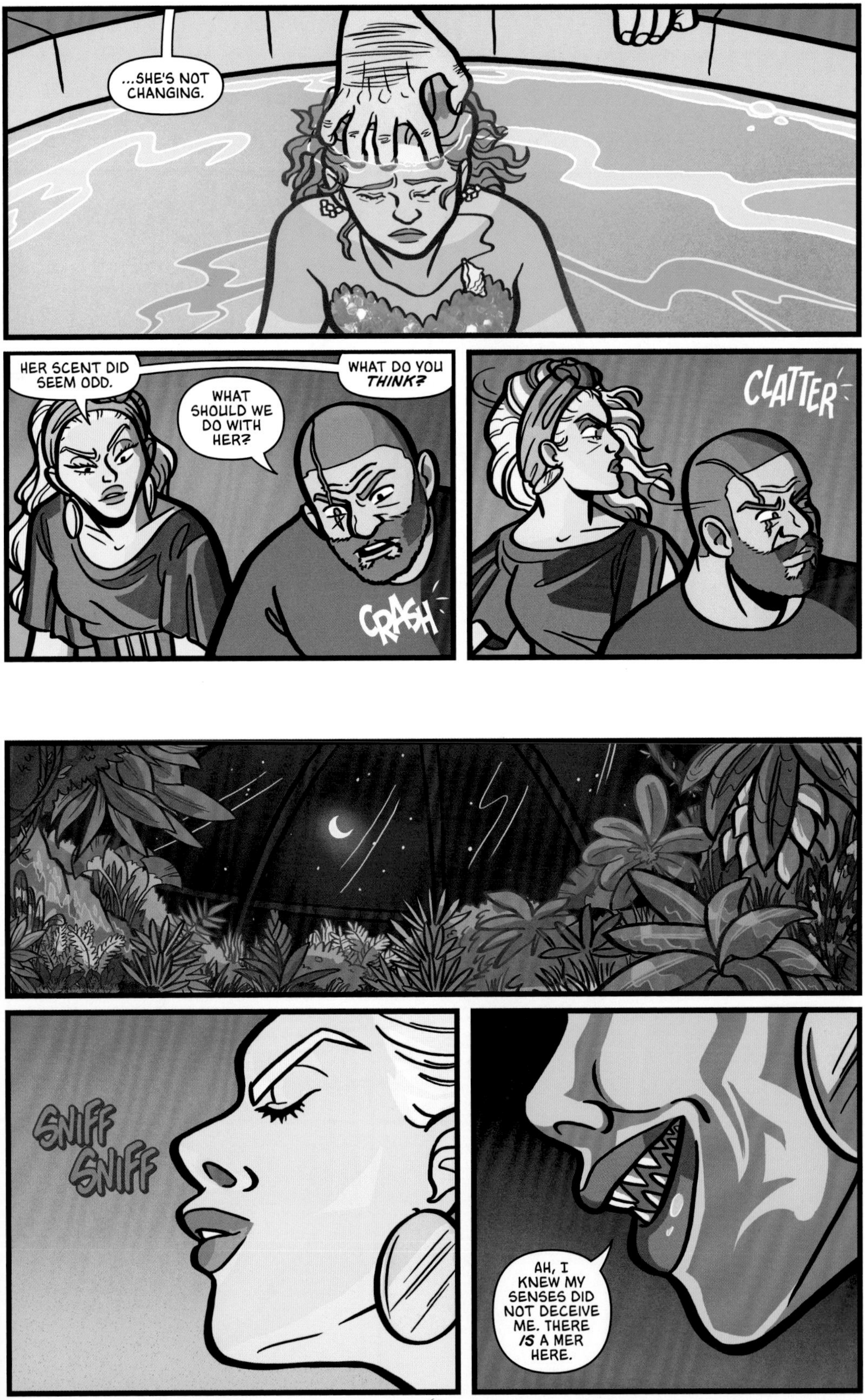
...SHE'S NOT CHANGING.
HER SCENT DID SEEM ODD.
WHAT SHOULD WE DO WITH HER?
WHAT DO YOU *THINK?*
CRASH
CLATTER
SNIFF SNIFF
AH, I KNEW MY SENSES DID NOT DECEIVE ME. THERE *IS* A MER HERE.

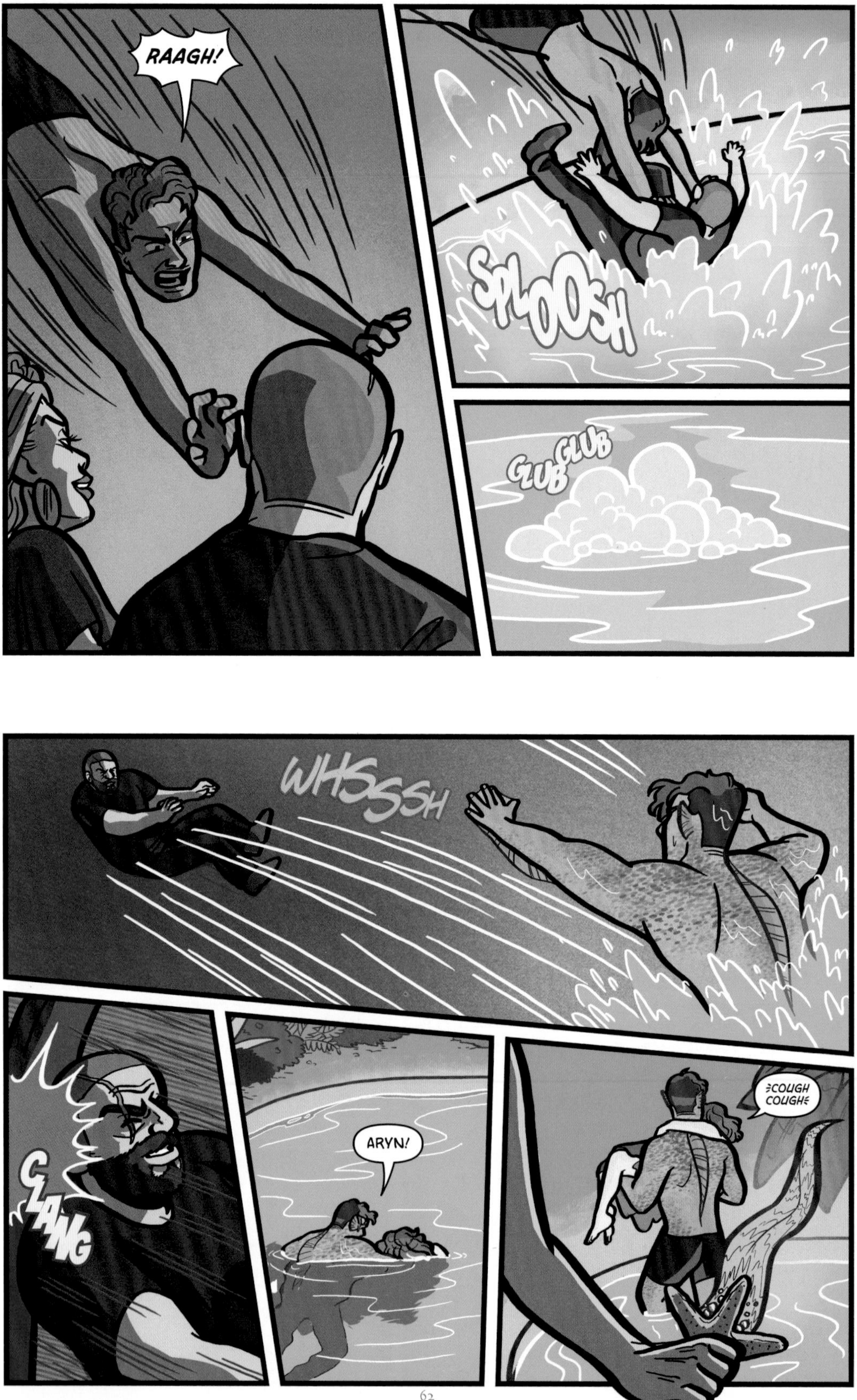
RAAGH!
SPLOOSH
GLUB GLUB
WHSSSH
CLANG
ARYN!
COUGH COUGH

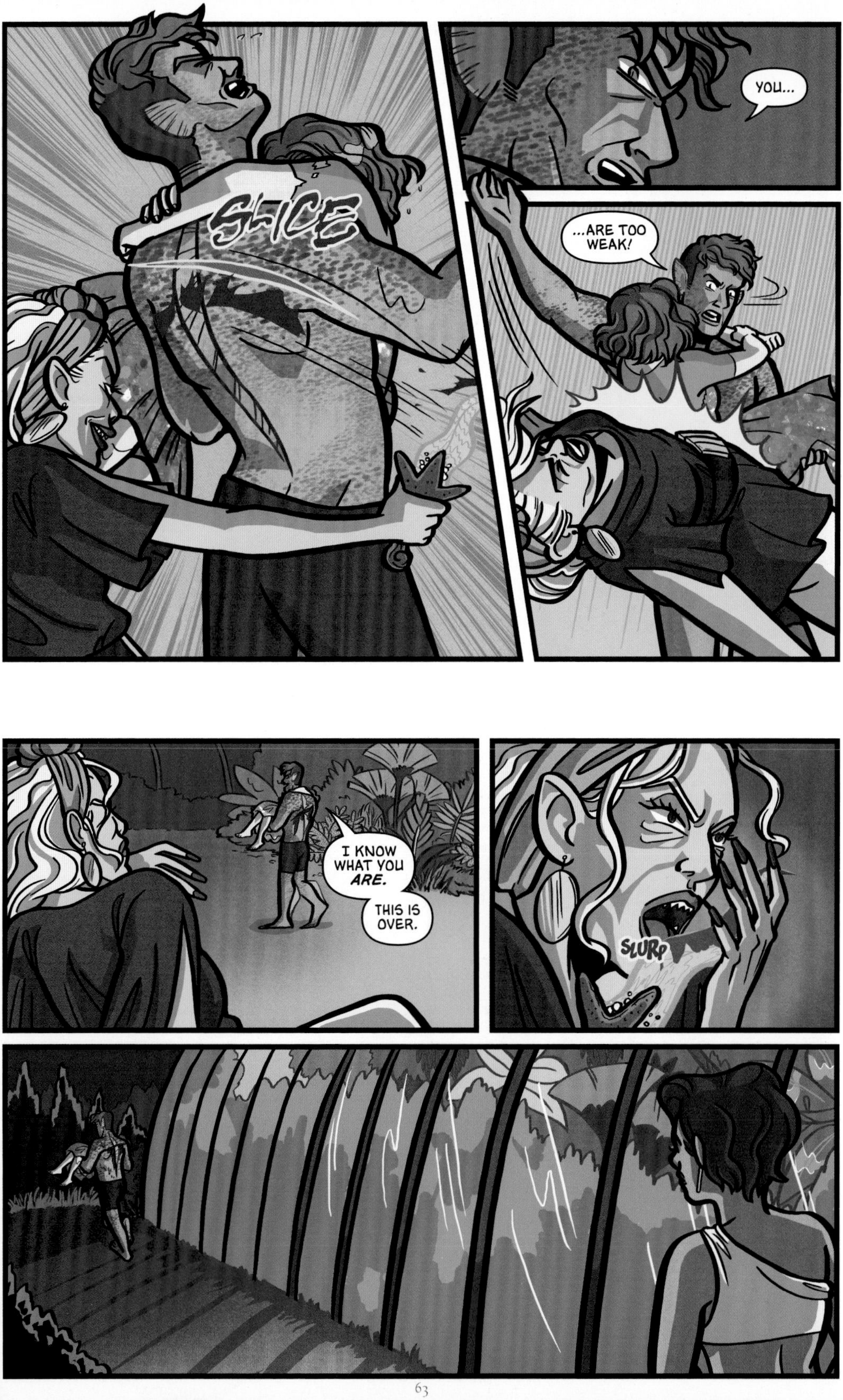
SLICE
YOU...
...ARE TOO WEAK!
I KNOW WHAT YOU ARE.
THIS IS OVER.
SLURP

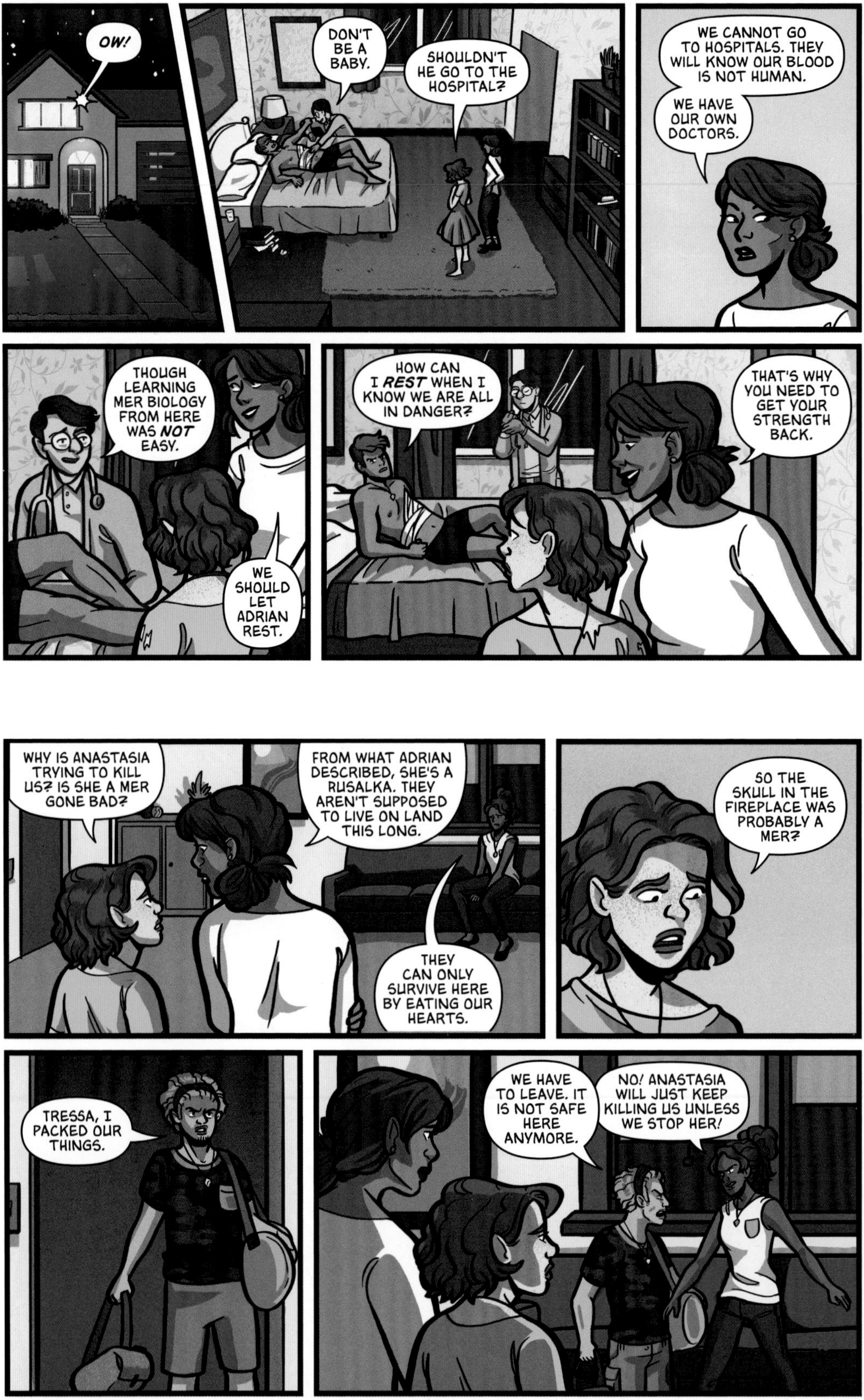
OW!
DON'T BE A BABY.
SHOULDN'T HE GO TO THE HOSPITAL?
WE CANNOT GO TO HOSPITALS. THEY WILL KNOW OUR BLOOD IS NOT HUMAN.
WE HAVE OUR OWN DOCTORS.
THOUGH LEARNING MER BIOLOGY FROM HERE WAS NOT EASY.
WE SHOULD LET ADRIAN REST.
HOW CAN I REST WHEN I KNOW WE ARE ALL IN DANGER?
THAT'S WHY YOU NEED TO GET YOUR STRENGTH BACK.
WHY IS ANASTASIA TRYING TO KILL US? IS SHE A MER GONE BAD?
FROM WHAT ADRIAN DESCRIBED, SHE'S A RUSALKA. THEY AREN'T SUPPOSED TO LIVE ON LAND THIS LONG.
THEY CAN ONLY SURVIVE HERE BY EATING OUR HEARTS.
SO THE SKULL IN THE FIREPLACE WAS PROBABLY A MER?
TRESSA, I PACKED OUR THINGS.
WE HAVE TO LEAVE. IT IS NOT SAFE HERE ANYMORE.
NO! ANASTASIA WILL JUST KEEP KILLING US UNLESS WE STOP HER!

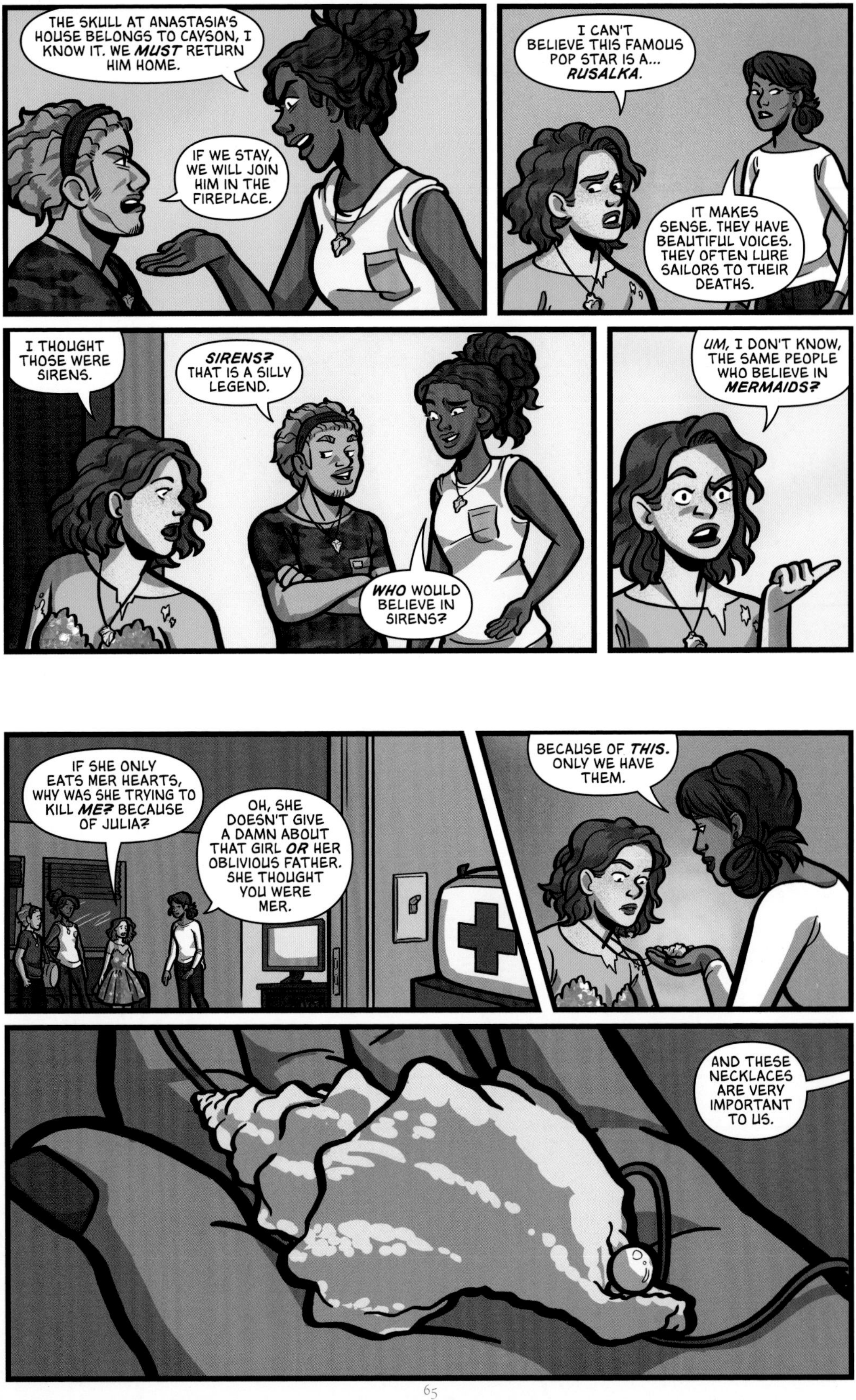
THE SKULL AT ANASTASIA'S HOUSE BELONGS TO CAYSON, I KNOW IT. WE *MUST* RETURN HIM HOME.
IF WE STAY, WE WILL JOIN HIM IN THE FIREPLACE.
I CAN'T BELIEVE THIS FAMOUS POP STAR IS A... *RUSALKA*.
IT MAKES SENSE. THEY HAVE BEAUTIFUL VOICES. THEY OFTEN LURE SAILORS TO THEIR DEATHS.
I THOUGHT THOSE WERE SIRENS.
SIRENS? THAT IS A SILLY LEGEND.
WHO WOULD BELIEVE IN SIRENS?
UM, I DON'T KNOW, THE SAME PEOPLE WHO BELIEVE IN *MERMAIDS?*
IF SHE ONLY EATS MER HEARTS, WHY WAS SHE TRYING TO KILL *ME?* BECAUSE OF JULIA?
OH, SHE DOESN'T GIVE A DAMN ABOUT THAT GIRL *OR* HER OBLIVIOUS FATHER. SHE THOUGHT YOU WERE MER.
BECAUSE OF *THIS*. ONLY WE HAVE THEM.
AND THESE NECKLACES ARE VERY IMPORTANT TO US.

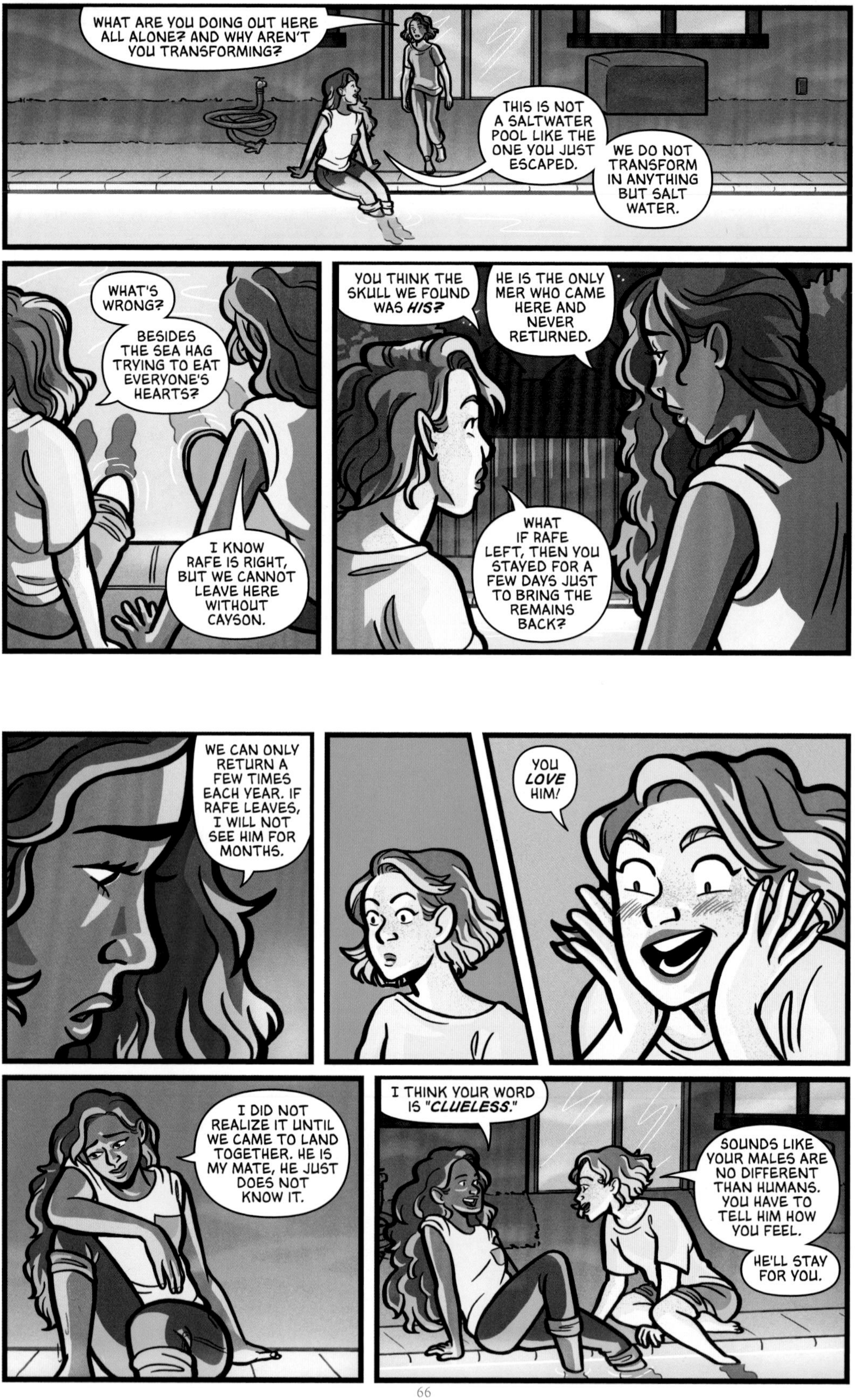
WHAT ARE YOU DOING OUT HERE ALL ALONE? AND WHY AREN'T YOU TRANSFORMING?
THIS IS NOT A SALTWATER POOL LIKE THE ONE YOU JUST ESCAPED.
WE DO NOT TRANSFORM IN ANYTHING BUT SALT WATER.
WHAT'S WRONG?
BESIDES THE SEA HAG TRYING TO EAT EVERYONE'S HEARTS?
I KNOW RAFE IS RIGHT, BUT WE CANNOT LEAVE HERE WITHOUT CAYSON.
YOU THINK THE SKULL WE FOUND WAS *HIS?*
HE IS THE ONLY MER WHO CAME HERE AND NEVER RETURNED.
WHAT IF RAFE LEFT, THEN YOU STAYED FOR A FEW DAYS JUST TO BRING THE REMAINS BACK?
WE CAN ONLY RETURN A FEW TIMES EACH YEAR. IF RAFE LEAVES, I WILL NOT SEE HIM FOR MONTHS.
YOU *LOVE* HIM!
I DID NOT REALIZE IT UNTIL WE CAME TO LAND TOGETHER. HE IS MY MATE, HE JUST DOES NOT KNOW IT.
I THINK YOUR WORD IS "*CLUELESS.*"
SOUNDS LIKE YOUR MALES ARE NO DIFFERENT THAN HUMANS. YOU HAVE TO TELL HIM HOW YOU FEEL.
HE'LL STAY FOR YOU.

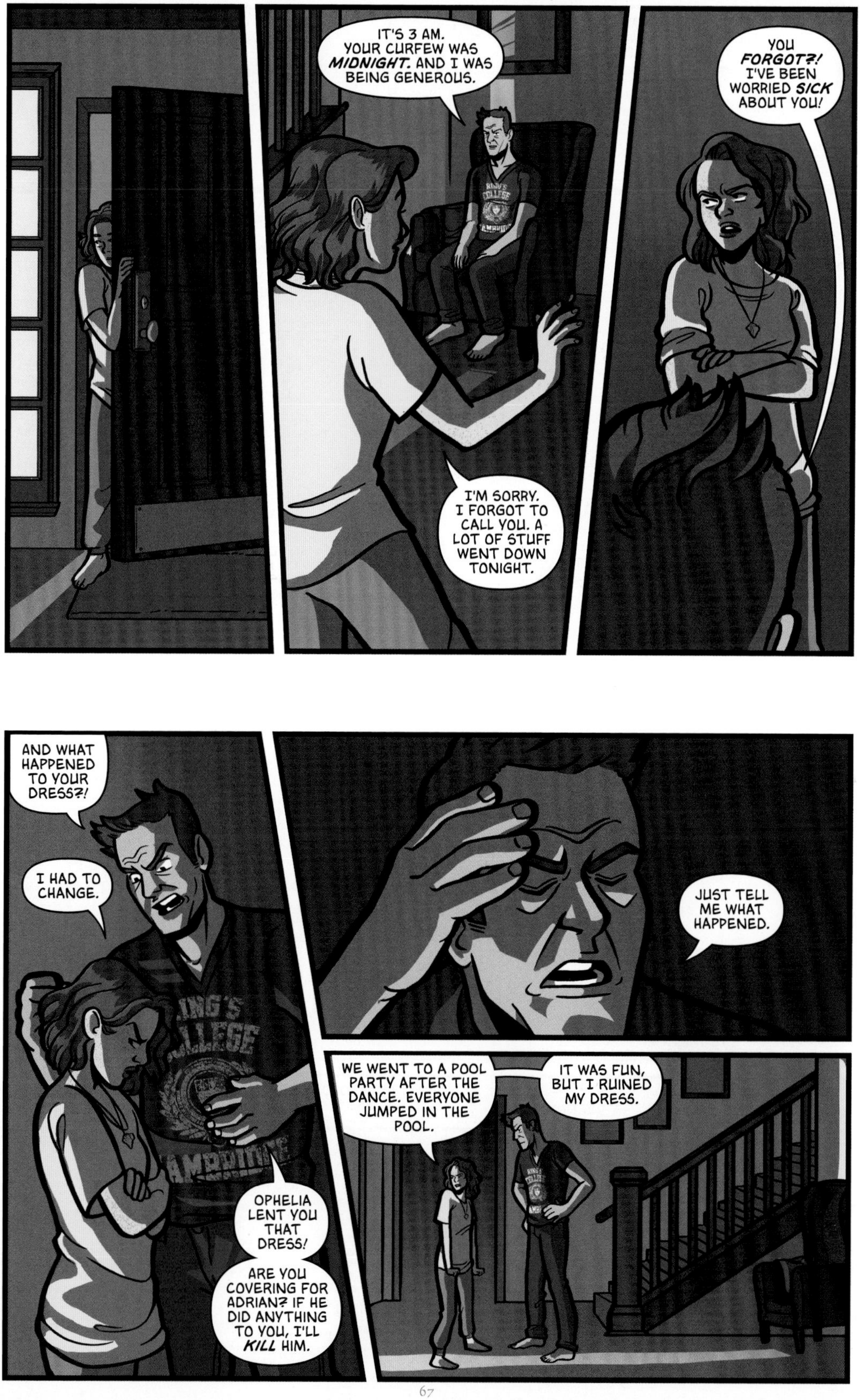
IT'S 3 AM. YOUR CURFEW WAS MIDNIGHT. AND I WAS BEING GENEROUS.
I'M SORRY. I FORGOT TO CALL YOU. A LOT OF STUFF WENT DOWN TONIGHT.
YOU FORGOT?! I'VE BEEN WORRIED SICK ABOUT YOU!
AND WHAT HAPPENED TO YOUR DRESS?!
I HAD TO CHANGE.
OPHELIA LENT YOU THAT DRESS!
ARE YOU COVERING FOR ADRIAN? IF HE DID ANYTHING TO YOU, I'LL KILL HIM.
JUST TELL ME WHAT HAPPENED.
WE WENT TO A POOL PARTY AFTER THE DANCE. EVERYONE JUMPED IN THE POOL.
IT WAS FUN, BUT I RUINED MY DRESS.

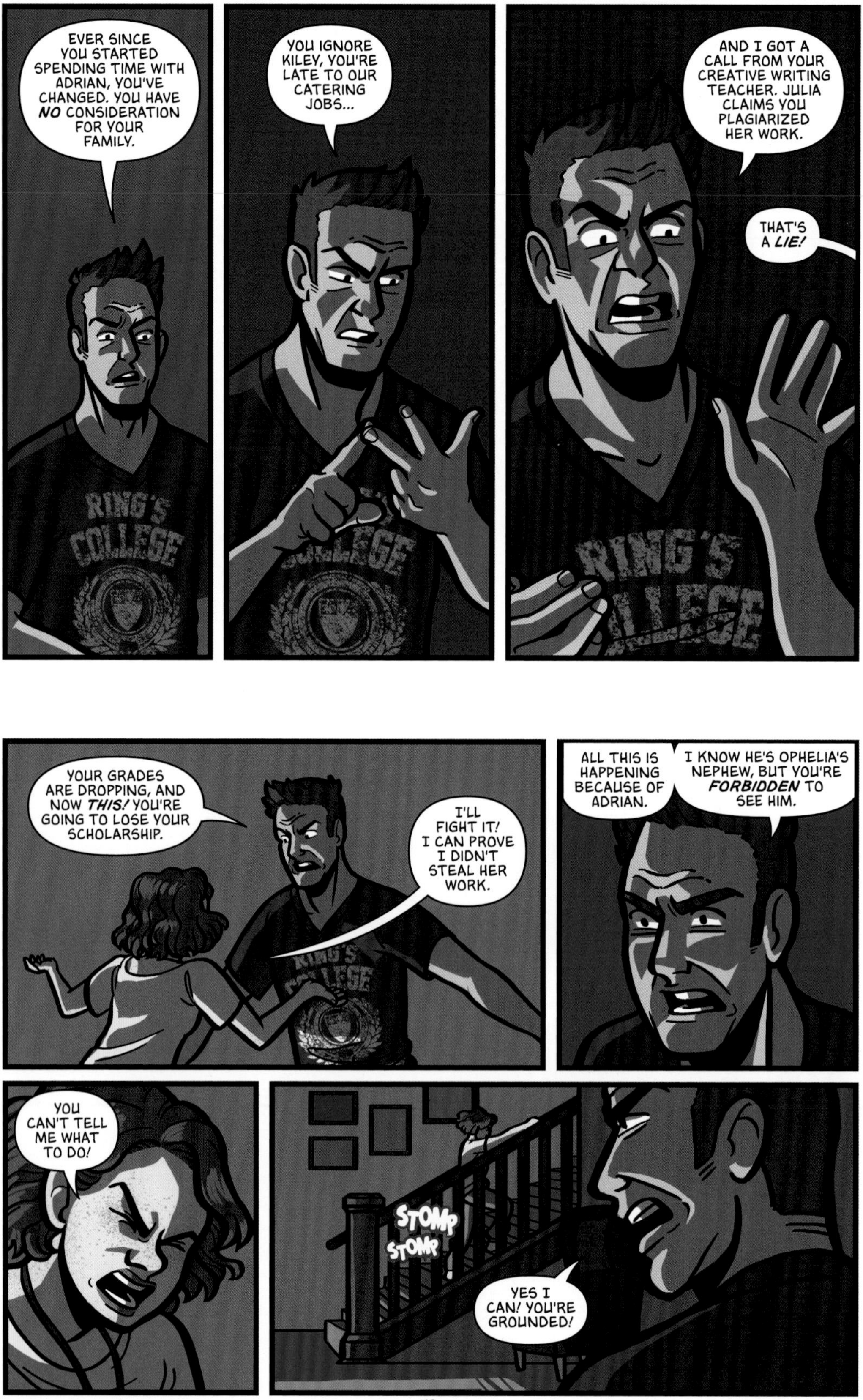
EVER SINCE YOU STARTED SPENDING TIME WITH ADRIAN, YOU'VE CHANGED. YOU HAVE *NO* CONSIDERATION FOR YOUR FAMILY.
YOU IGNORE KILEY, YOU'RE LATE TO OUR CATERING JOBS...
AND I GOT A CALL FROM YOUR CREATIVE WRITING TEACHER. JULIA CLAIMS YOU PLAGIARIZED HER WORK.
THAT'S A *LIE!*
RING'S COLLEGE
YOUR GRADES ARE DROPPING, AND NOW *THIS!* YOU'RE GOING TO LOSE YOUR SCHOLARSHIP.
I'LL FIGHT IT! I CAN PROVE I DIDN'T STEAL HER WORK.
ALL THIS IS HAPPENING BECAUSE OF ADRIAN.
I KNOW HE'S OPHELIA'S NEPHEW, BUT YOU'RE *FORBIDDEN* TO SEE HIM.
YOU CAN'T TELL ME WHAT TO DO!
STOMP
STOMP
YES I CAN! YOU'RE GROUNDED!

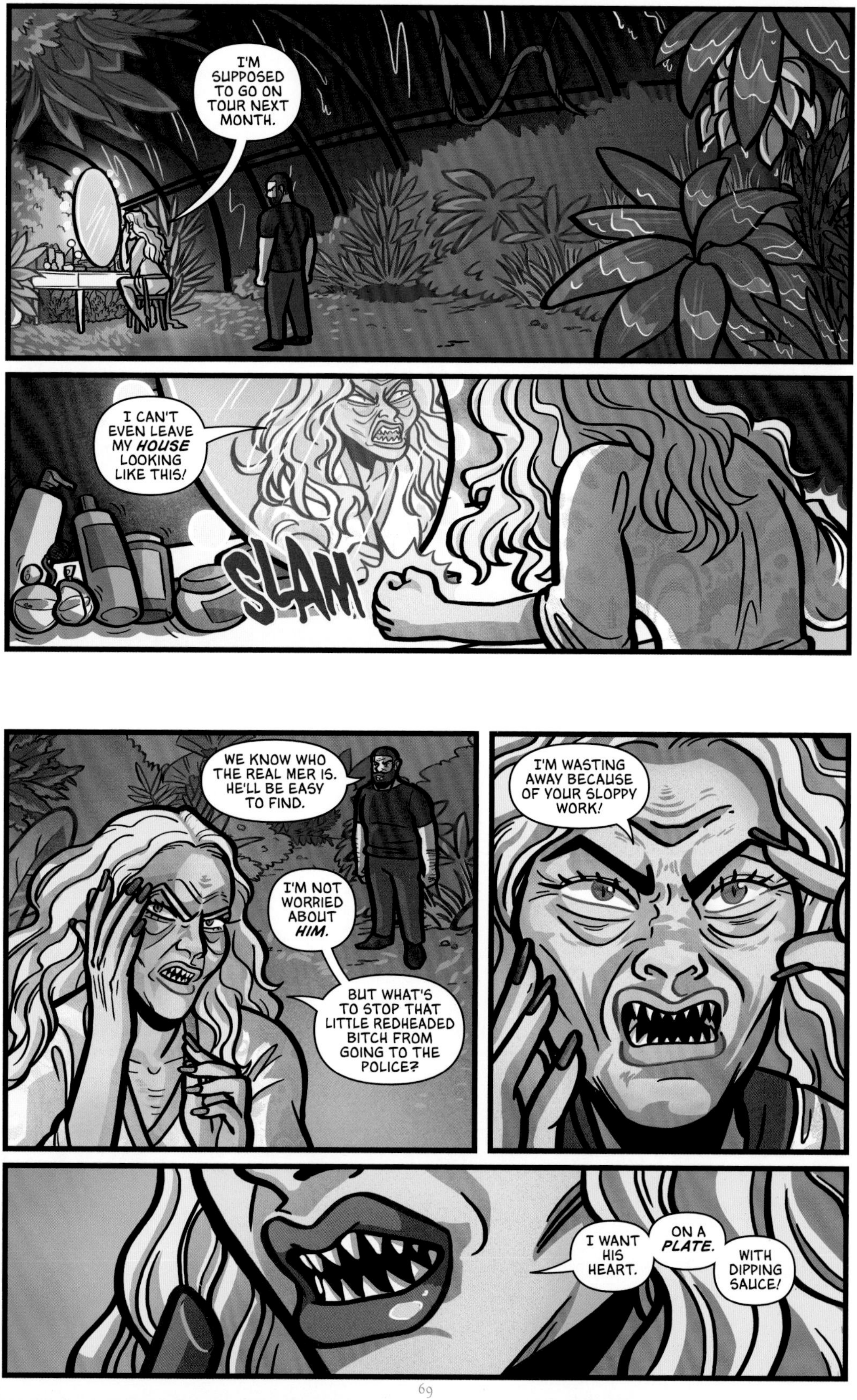
I'M SUPPOSED TO GO ON TOUR NEXT MONTH.
I CAN'T EVEN LEAVE MY *HOUSE* LOOKING LIKE THIS!
SLAM
WE KNOW WHO THE REAL MER IS. HE'LL BE EASY TO FIND.
I'M NOT WORRIED ABOUT *HIM*.
BUT WHAT'S TO STOP THAT LITTLE REDHEADED BITCH FROM GOING TO THE POLICE?
I'M WASTING AWAY BECAUSE OF YOUR SLOPPY WORK!
I WANT HIS HEART.
ON A *PLATE*.
WITH DIPPING SAUCE!

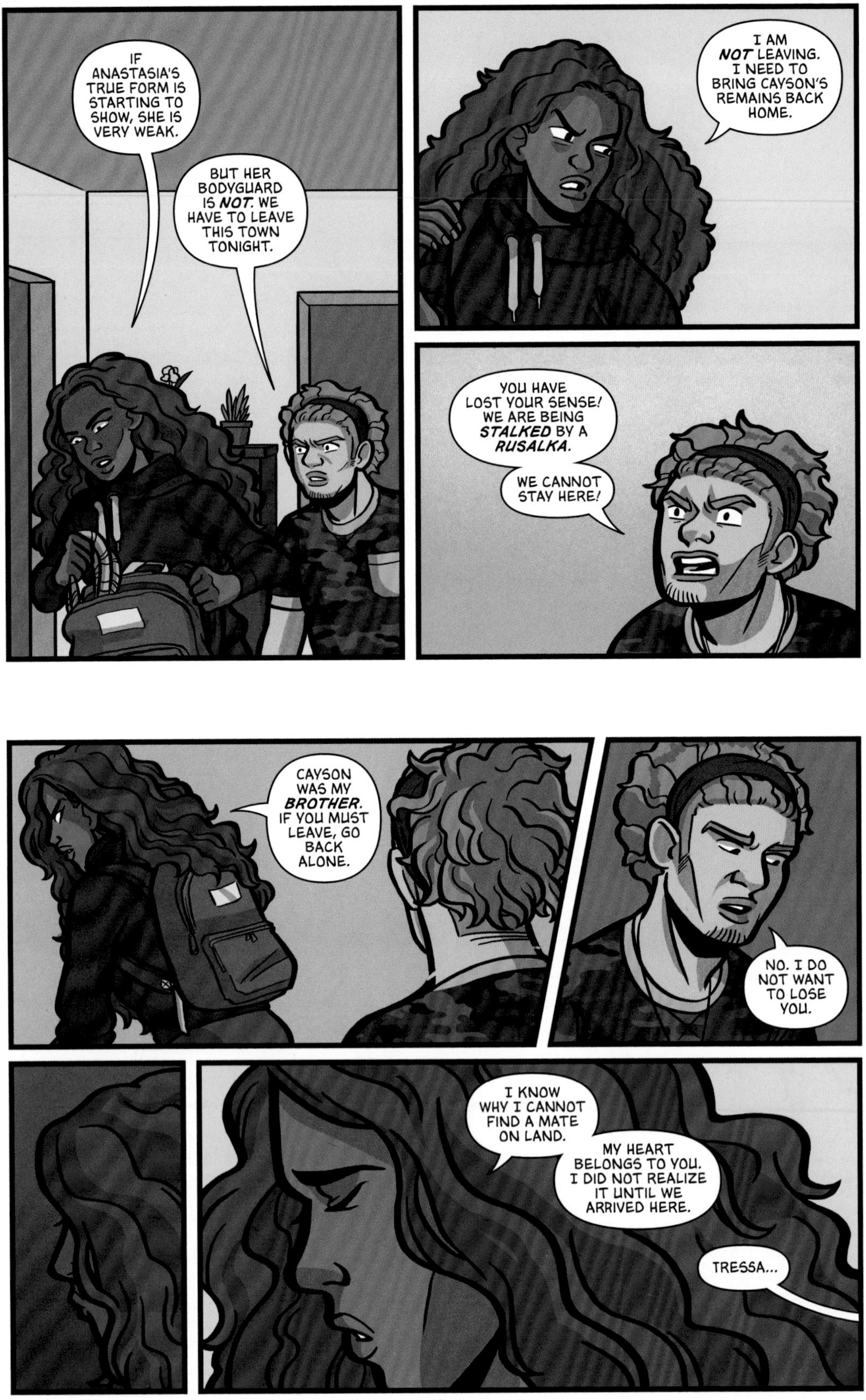
IF ANASTASIA'S TRUE FORM IS STARTING TO SHOW, SHE IS VERY WEAK.
BUT HER BODYGUARD IS ***NOT***. WE HAVE TO LEAVE THIS TOWN TONIGHT.
I AM ***NOT*** LEAVING. I NEED TO BRING CAYSON'S REMAINS BACK HOME.
YOU HAVE LOST YOUR SENSE! WE ARE BEING ***STALKED*** BY A ***RUSALKA***.
WE CANNOT STAY HERE!
CAYSON WAS MY ***BROTHER***. IF YOU MUST LEAVE, GO BACK ALONE.
NO. I DO NOT WANT TO LOSE YOU.
I KNOW WHY I CANNOT FIND A MATE ON LAND.
MY HEART BELONGS TO YOU. I DID NOT REALIZE IT UNTIL WE ARRIVED HERE.
TRESSA...

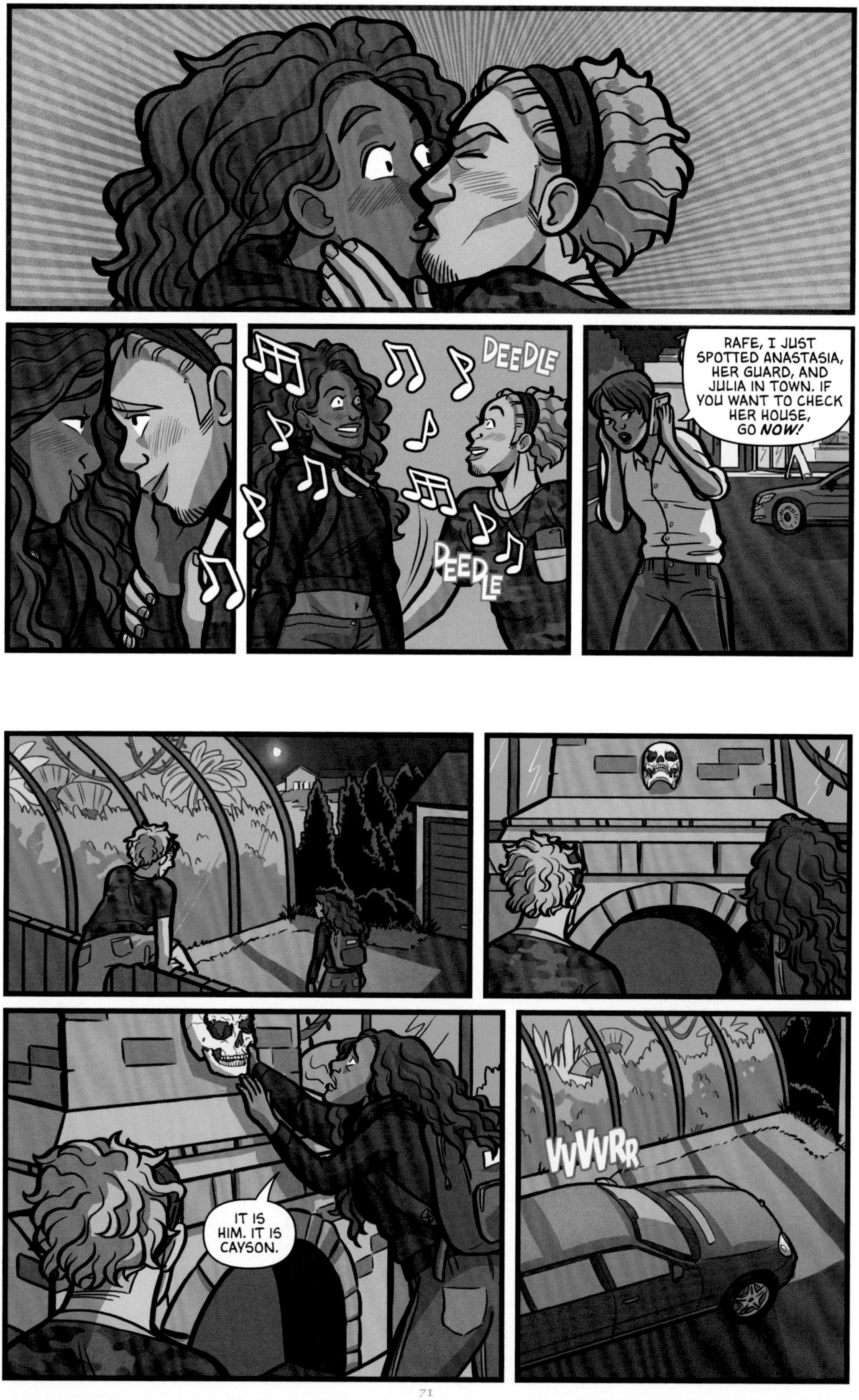
DEEDLE
DEEDLE
RAFE, I JUST SPOTTED ANASTASIA, HER GUARD, AND JULIA IN TOWN. IF YOU WANT TO CHECK HER HOUSE, GO NOW!
IT IS HIM. IT IS CAYSON.
VVVVRR

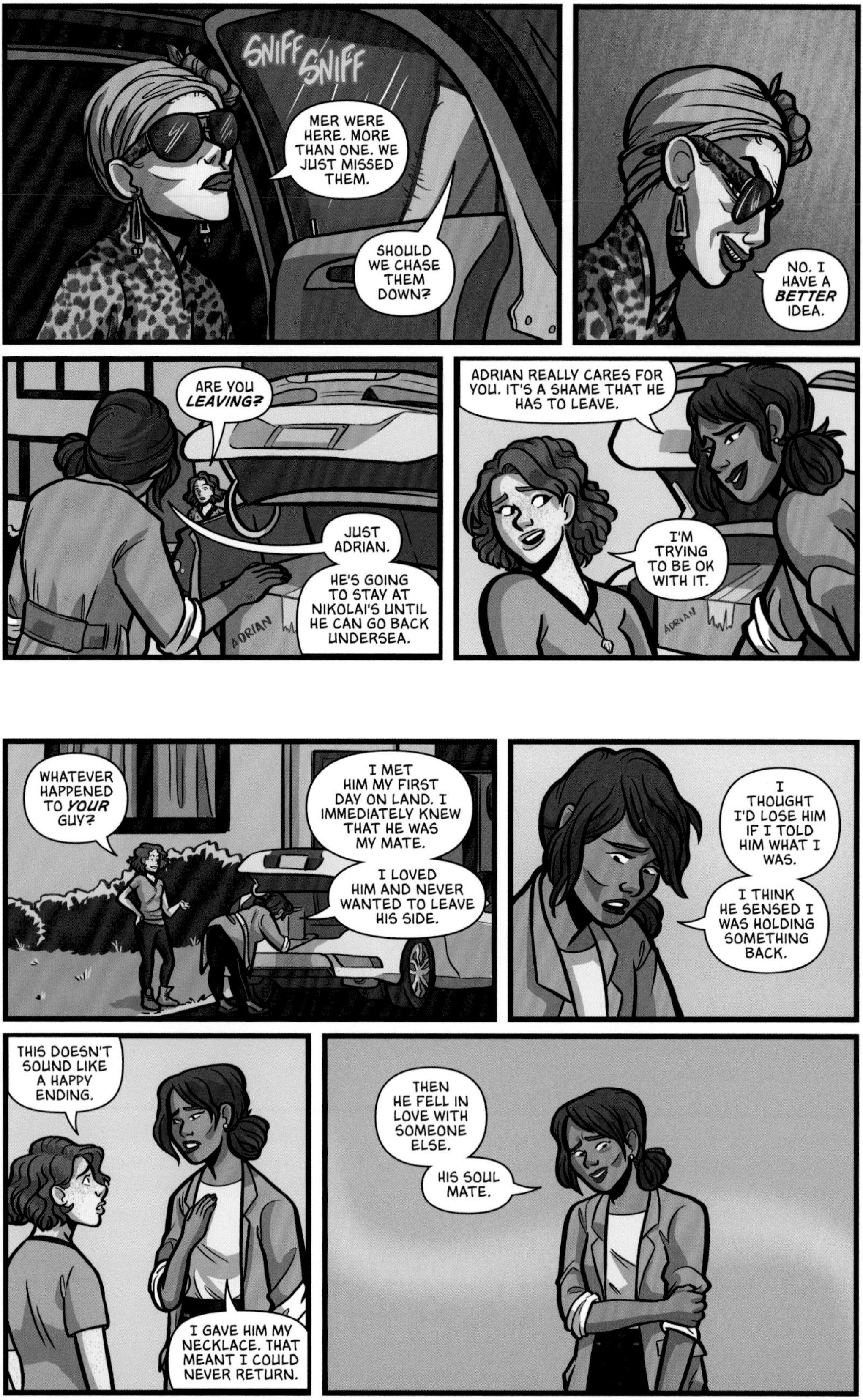
SNIFF SNIFF
MER WERE HERE. MORE THAN ONE. WE JUST MISSED THEM.
SHOULD WE CHASE THEM DOWN?
NO. I HAVE A *BETTER* IDEA.
ARE YOU *LEAVING?*
JUST ADRIAN.
HE'S GOING TO STAY AT NIKOLAI'S UNTIL HE CAN GO BACK UNDERSEA.
ADRIAN
ADRIAN REALLY CARES FOR YOU. IT'S A SHAME THAT HE HAS TO LEAVE.
I'M TRYING TO BE OK WITH IT.
ADRIAN
WHATEVER HAPPENED TO *YOUR* GUY?
I MET HIM MY FIRST DAY ON LAND. I IMMEDIATELY KNEW THAT HE WAS MY MATE.
I LOVED HIM AND NEVER WANTED TO LEAVE HIS SIDE.
I THOUGHT I'D LOSE HIM IF I TOLD HIM WHAT I WAS.
I THINK HE SENSED I WAS HOLDING SOMETHING BACK.
THIS DOESN'T SOUND LIKE A HAPPY ENDING.
I GAVE HIM MY NECKLACE. THAT MEANT I COULD NEVER RETURN.
THEN HE FELL IN LOVE WITH SOMEONE ELSE.
HIS SOUL MATE.

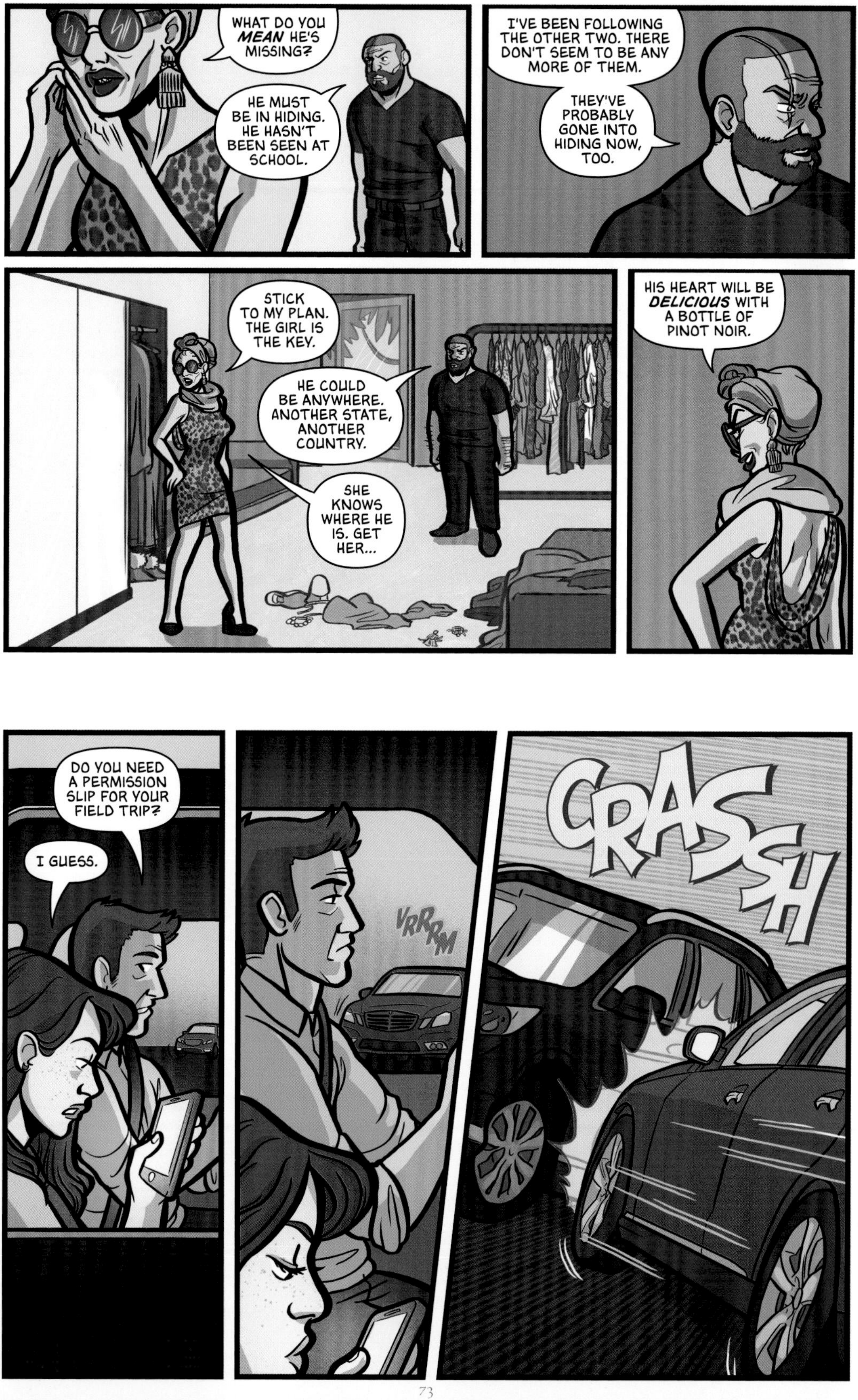
WHAT DO YOU *MEAN* HE'S MISSING?
HE MUST BE IN HIDING. HE HASN'T BEEN SEEN AT SCHOOL.
I'VE BEEN FOLLOWING THE OTHER TWO. THERE DON'T SEEM TO BE ANY MORE OF THEM.
THEY'VE PROBABLY GONE INTO HIDING NOW, TOO.
STICK TO MY PLAN. THE GIRL IS THE KEY.
HE COULD BE ANYWHERE. ANOTHER STATE, ANOTHER COUNTRY.
SHE KNOWS WHERE HE IS. GET HER...
HIS HEART WILL BE *DELICIOUS* WITH A BOTTLE OF PINOT NOIR.
DO YOU NEED A PERMISSION SLIP FOR YOUR FIELD TRIP?
I GUESS.
VRRRM
CRASSH

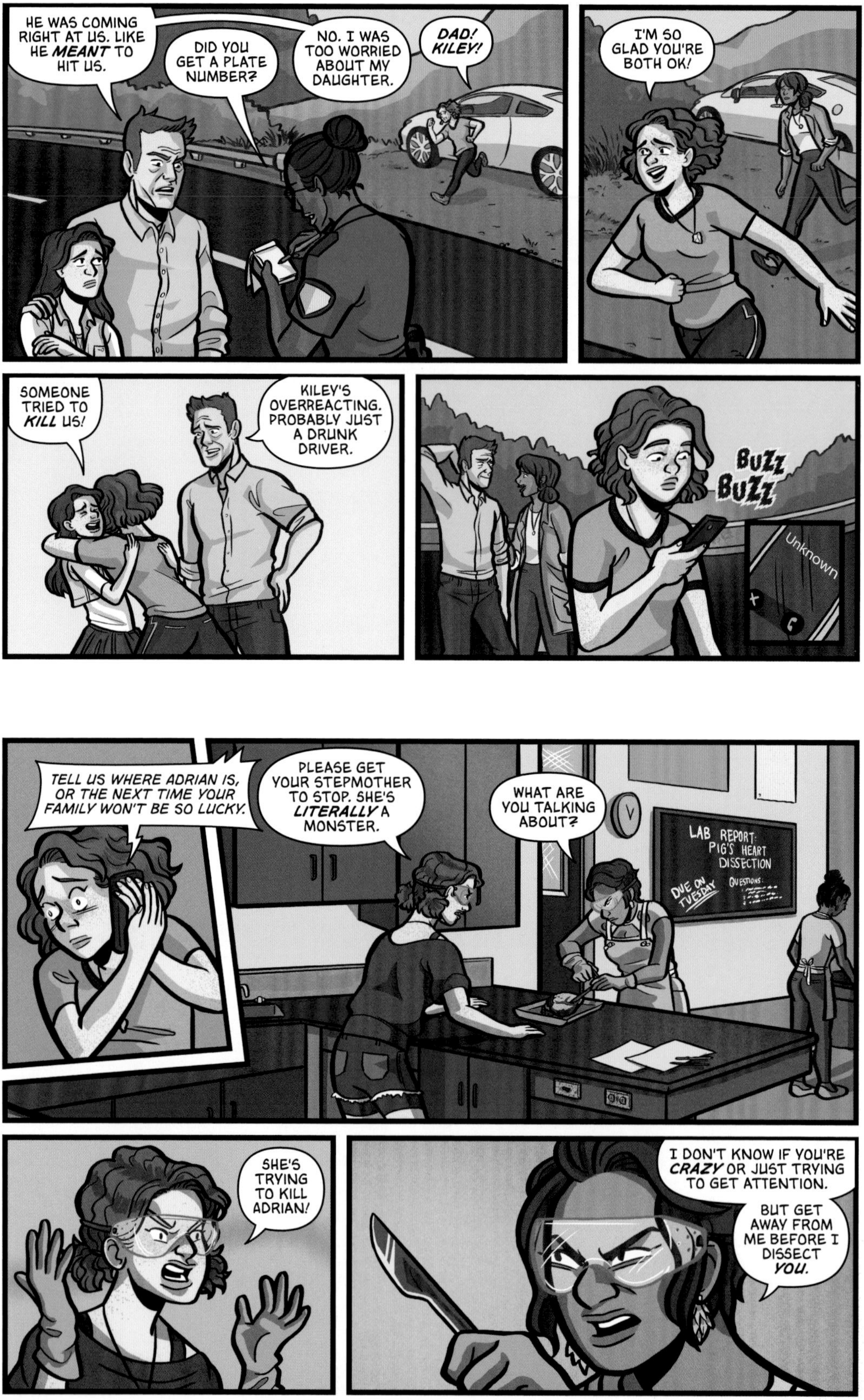
HE WAS COMING RIGHT AT US. LIKE HE MEANT TO HIT US.
DID YOU GET A PLATE NUMBER?
NO. I WAS TOO WORRIED ABOUT MY DAUGHTER.
DAD! KILEY!
I'M SO GLAD YOU'RE BOTH OK!
SOMEONE TRIED TO KILL US!
KILEY'S OVERREACTING. PROBABLY JUST A DRUNK DRIVER.
BUZZ BUZZ
Unknown
TELL US WHERE ADRIAN IS, OR THE NEXT TIME YOUR FAMILY WON'T BE SO LUCKY.
PLEASE GET YOUR STEPMOTHER TO STOP. SHE'S LITERALLY A MONSTER.
WHAT ARE YOU TALKING ABOUT?
LAB REPORT: PIG'S HEART DISSECTION
DUE ON TUESDAY
QUESTIONS:
SHE'S TRYING TO KILL ADRIAN!
I DON'T KNOW IF YOU'RE CRAZY OR JUST TRYING TO GET ATTENTION.
BUT GET AWAY FROM ME BEFORE I DISSECT YOU.

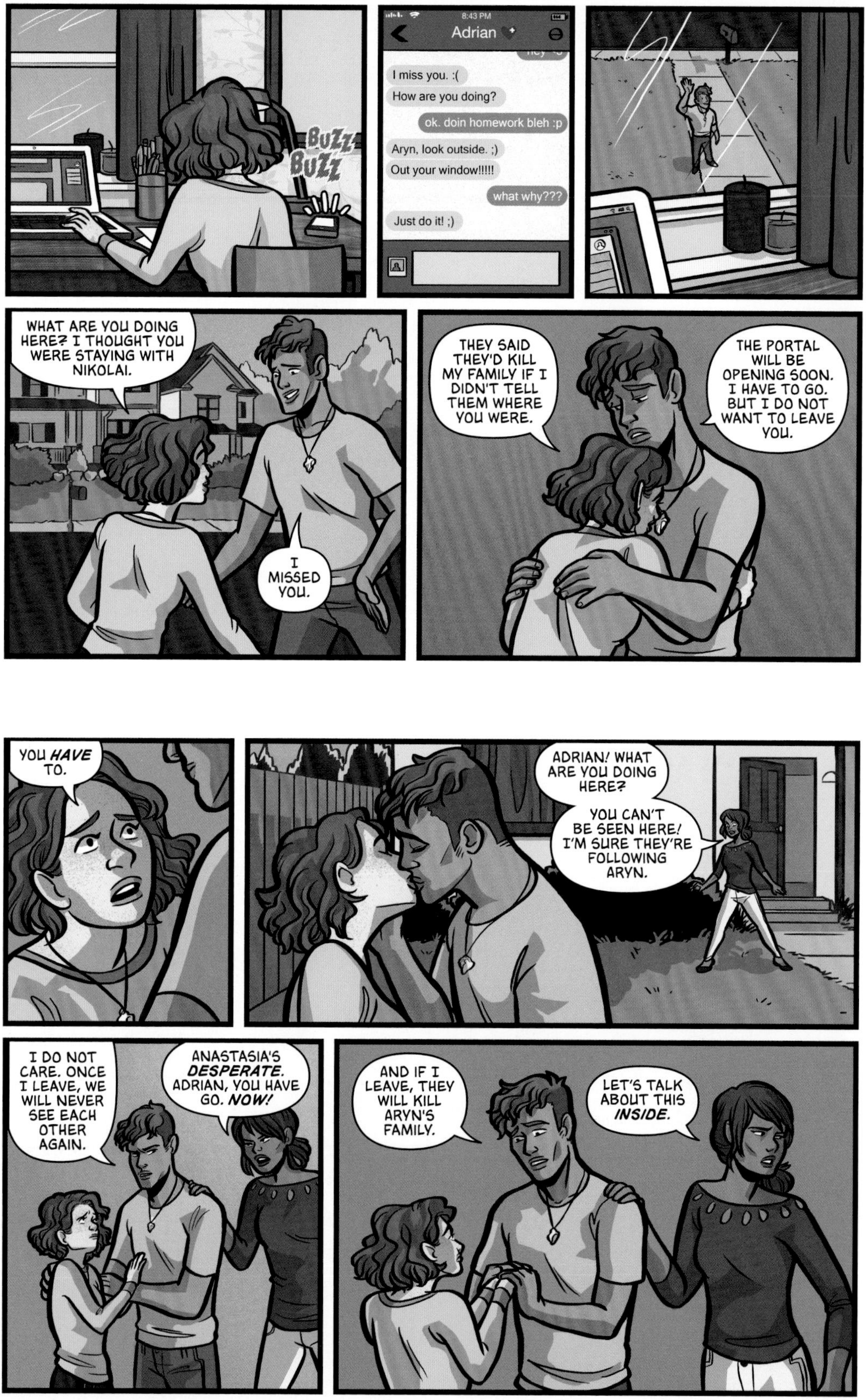
BUZZ
BUZZ
8:43 PM
Adrian
I miss you. :(
How are you doing?
ok. doin homework bleh :p
Aryn, look outside. ;)
Out your window!!!!!
what why???
Just do it! ;)
WHAT ARE YOU DOING HERE? I THOUGHT YOU WERE STAYING WITH NIKOLAI.
I MISSED YOU.
THEY SAID THEY'D KILL MY FAMILY IF I DIDN'T TELL THEM WHERE YOU WERE.
THE PORTAL WILL BE OPENING SOON. I HAVE TO GO. BUT I DO NOT WANT TO LEAVE YOU.
YOU *HAVE* TO.
ADRIAN! WHAT ARE YOU DOING HERE?
YOU CAN'T BE SEEN HERE! I'M SURE THEY'RE FOLLOWING ARYN.
I DO NOT CARE. ONCE I LEAVE, WE WILL NEVER SEE EACH OTHER AGAIN.
ANASTASIA'S *DESPERATE*. ADRIAN, YOU HAVE GO. *NOW!*
AND IF I LEAVE, THEY WILL KILL ARYN'S FAMILY.
LET'S TALK ABOUT THIS *INSIDE*.

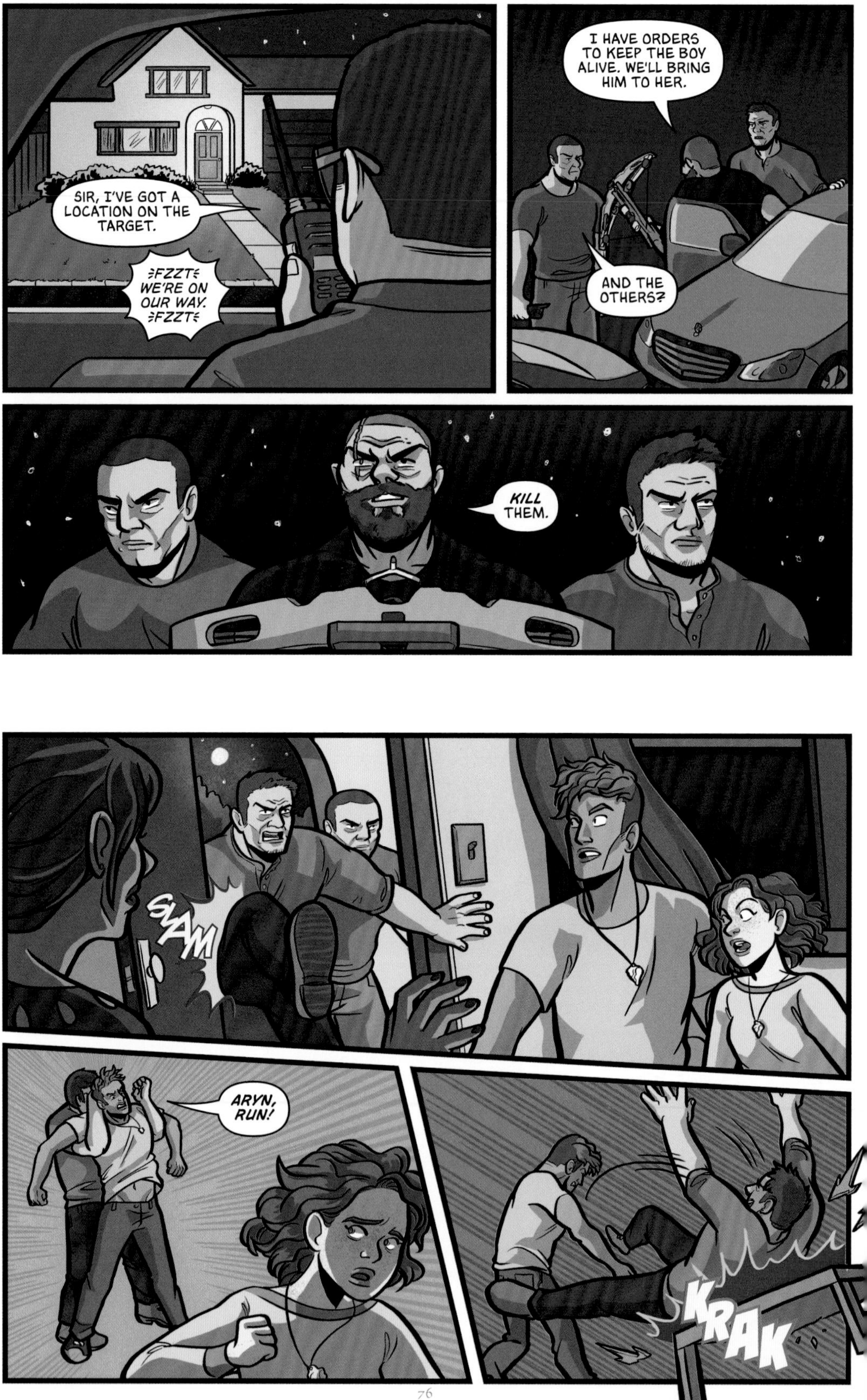
SIR, I'VE GOT A LOCATION ON THE TARGET.
FZZT WE'RE ON OUR WAY. FZZT
I HAVE ORDERS TO KEEP THE BOY ALIVE. WE'LL BRING HIM TO HER.
AND THE OTHERS?
KILL THEM.
SLAM
ARYN, RUN!
KRAK

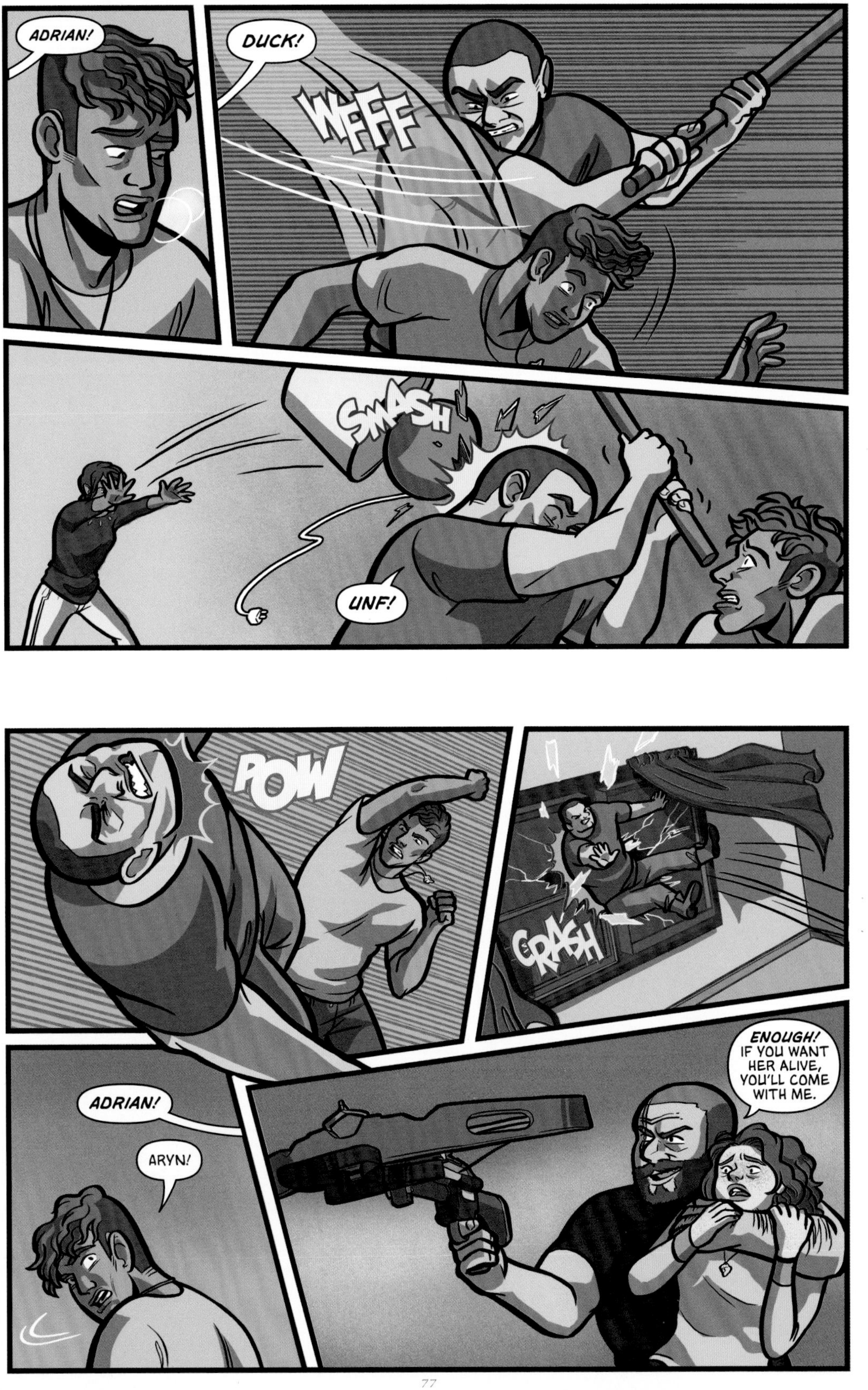
ADRIAN!
DUCK!
WFFF
SMASH
UNF!
POW
CRASH
ENOUGH! IF YOU WANT HER ALIVE, YOU'LL COME WITH ME.
ADRIAN!
ARYN!

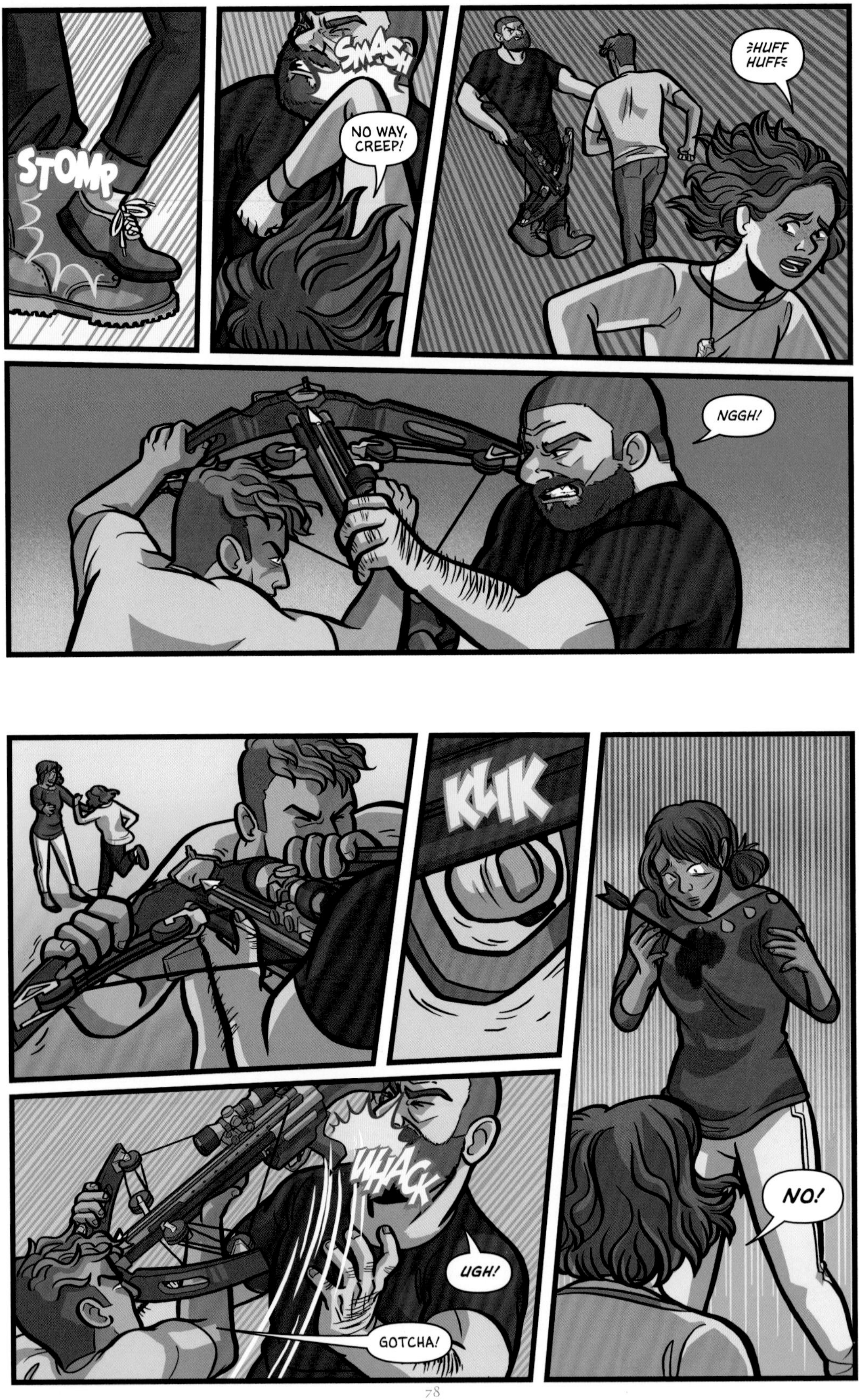
STOMP
SMASH
NO WAY, CREEP!
HUFF HUFF
NGGH!
KLIK
WHACK
UGH!
GOTCHA!
NO!

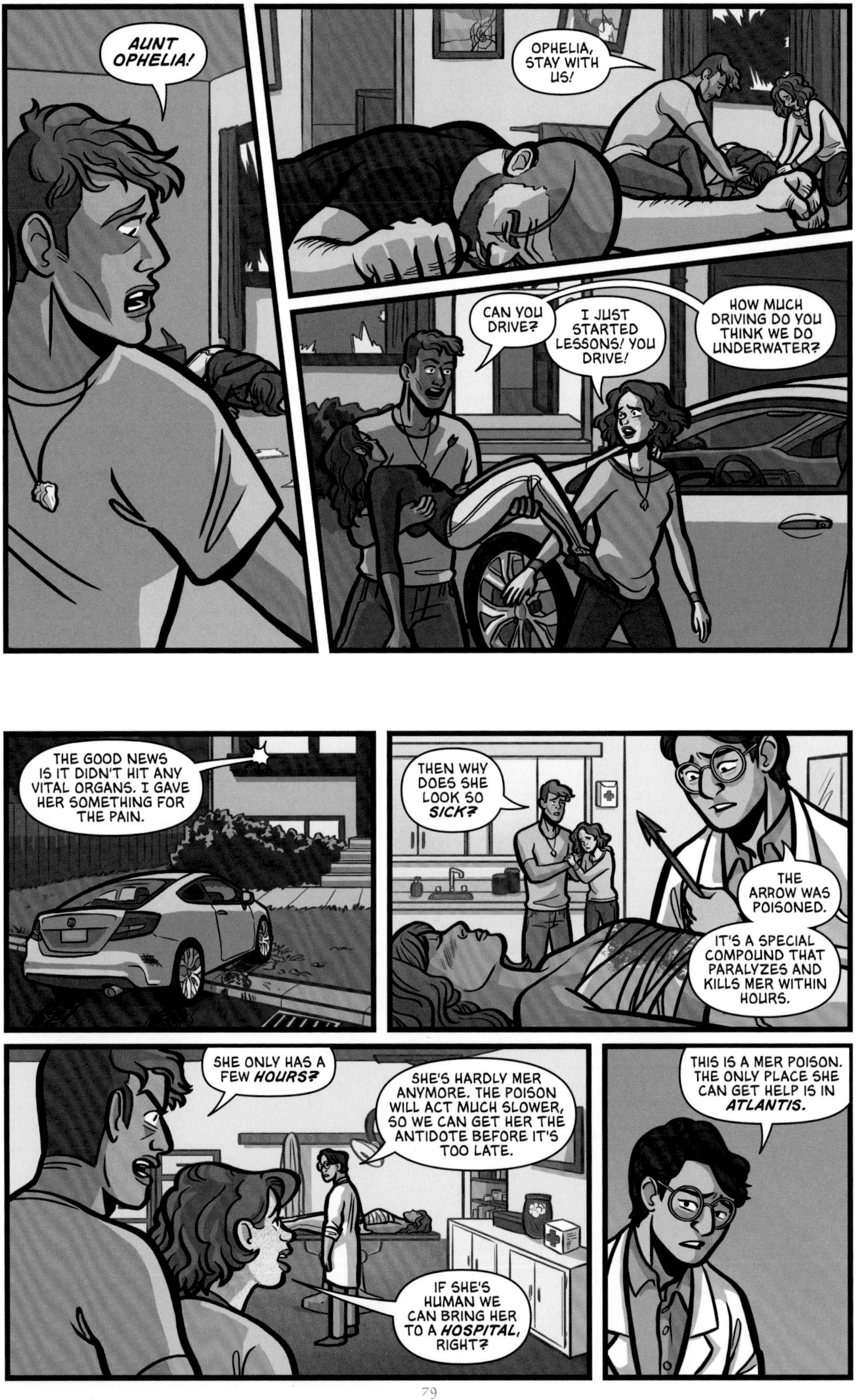
AUNT OPHELIA!
OPHELIA, STAY WITH US!
CAN YOU DRIVE?
I JUST STARTED LESSONS! YOU DRIVE!
HOW MUCH DRIVING DO YOU THINK WE DO UNDERWATER?
THE GOOD NEWS IS IT DIDN'T HIT ANY VITAL ORGANS. I GAVE HER SOMETHING FOR THE PAIN.
THEN WHY DOES SHE LOOK SO SICK?
THE ARROW WAS POISONED.
IT'S A SPECIAL COMPOUND THAT PARALYZES AND KILLS MER WITHIN HOURS.
SHE ONLY HAS A FEW HOURS?
SHE'S HARDLY MER ANYMORE. THE POISON WILL ACT MUCH SLOWER, SO WE CAN GET HER THE ANTIDOTE BEFORE IT'S TOO LATE.
IF SHE'S HUMAN WE CAN BRING HER TO A HOSPITAL, RIGHT?
THIS IS A MER POISON. THE ONLY PLACE SHE CAN GET HELP IS IN ATLANTIS.

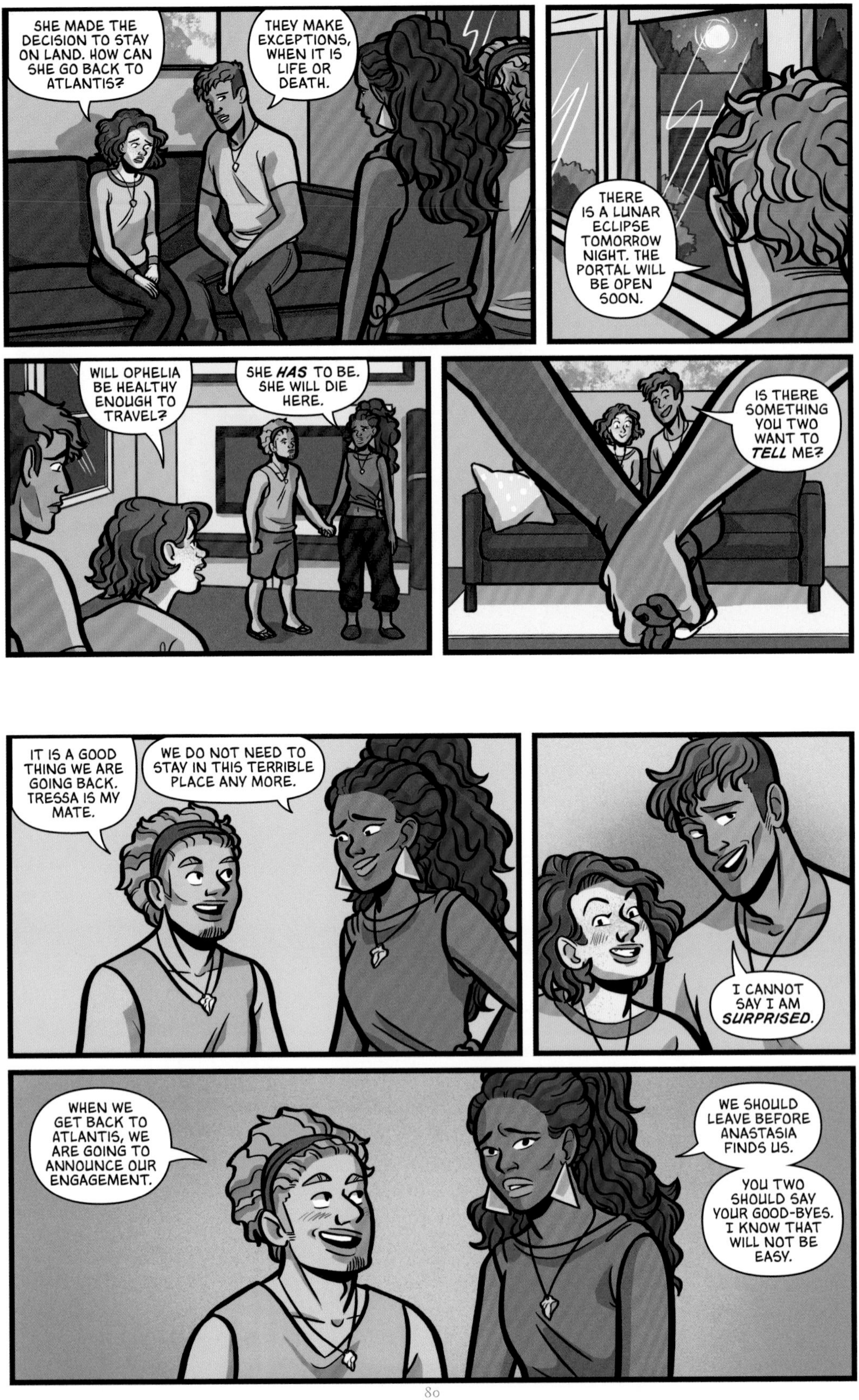

SHE MADE THE DECISION TO STAY ON LAND. HOW CAN SHE GO BACK TO ATLANTIS?
THEY MAKE EXCEPTIONS, WHEN IT IS LIFE OR DEATH.
THERE IS A LUNAR ECLIPSE TOMORROW NIGHT. THE PORTAL WILL BE OPEN SOON.
WILL OPHELIA BE HEALTHY ENOUGH TO TRAVEL?
SHE *HAS* TO BE. SHE WILL DIE HERE.
IS THERE SOMETHING YOU TWO WANT TO *TELL* ME?
IT IS A GOOD THING WE ARE GOING BACK. TRESSA IS MY MATE.
WE DO NOT NEED TO STAY IN THIS TERRIBLE PLACE ANY MORE.
I CANNOT SAY I AM *SURPRISED.*
WHEN WE GET BACK TO ATLANTIS, WE ARE GOING TO ANNOUNCE OUR ENGAGEMENT.
WE SHOULD LEAVE BEFORE ANASTASIA FINDS US.
YOU TWO SHOULD SAY YOUR GOOD-BYES. I KNOW THAT WILL NOT BE EASY.

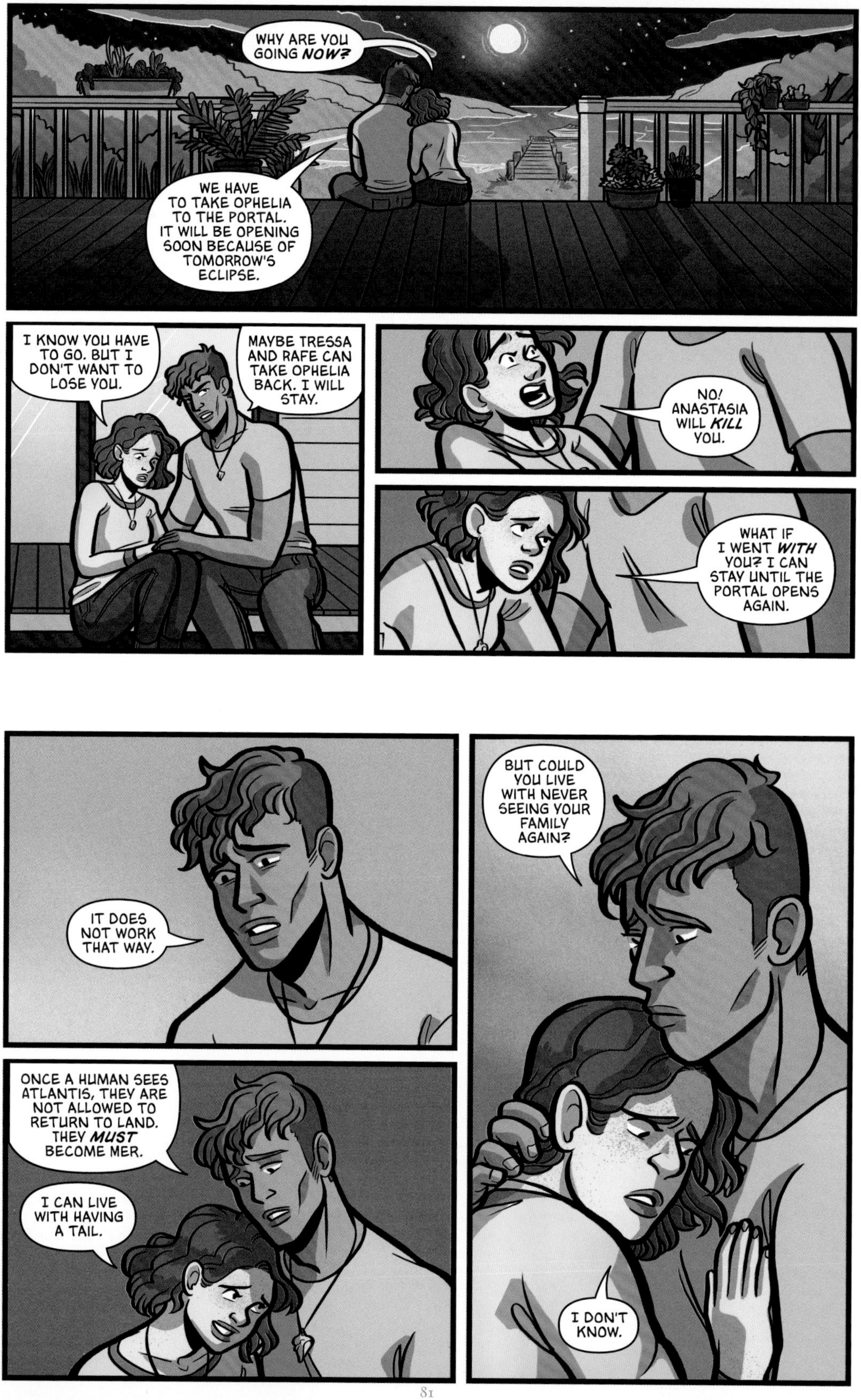
WHY ARE YOU GOING *NOW?*
WE HAVE TO TAKE OPHELIA TO THE PORTAL. IT WILL BE OPENING SOON BECAUSE OF TOMORROW'S ECLIPSE.
I KNOW YOU HAVE TO GO. BUT I DON'T WANT TO LOSE YOU.
MAYBE TRESSA AND RAFE CAN TAKE OPHELIA BACK. I WILL STAY.
NO! ANASTASIA WILL *KILL* YOU.
WHAT IF I WENT *WITH* YOU? I CAN STAY UNTIL THE PORTAL OPENS AGAIN.
IT DOES NOT WORK THAT WAY.
ONCE A HUMAN SEES ATLANTIS, THEY ARE NOT ALLOWED TO RETURN TO LAND. THEY *MUST* BECOME MER.
I CAN LIVE WITH HAVING A TAIL.
BUT COULD YOU LIVE WITH NEVER SEEING YOUR FAMILY AGAIN?
I DON'T KNOW.

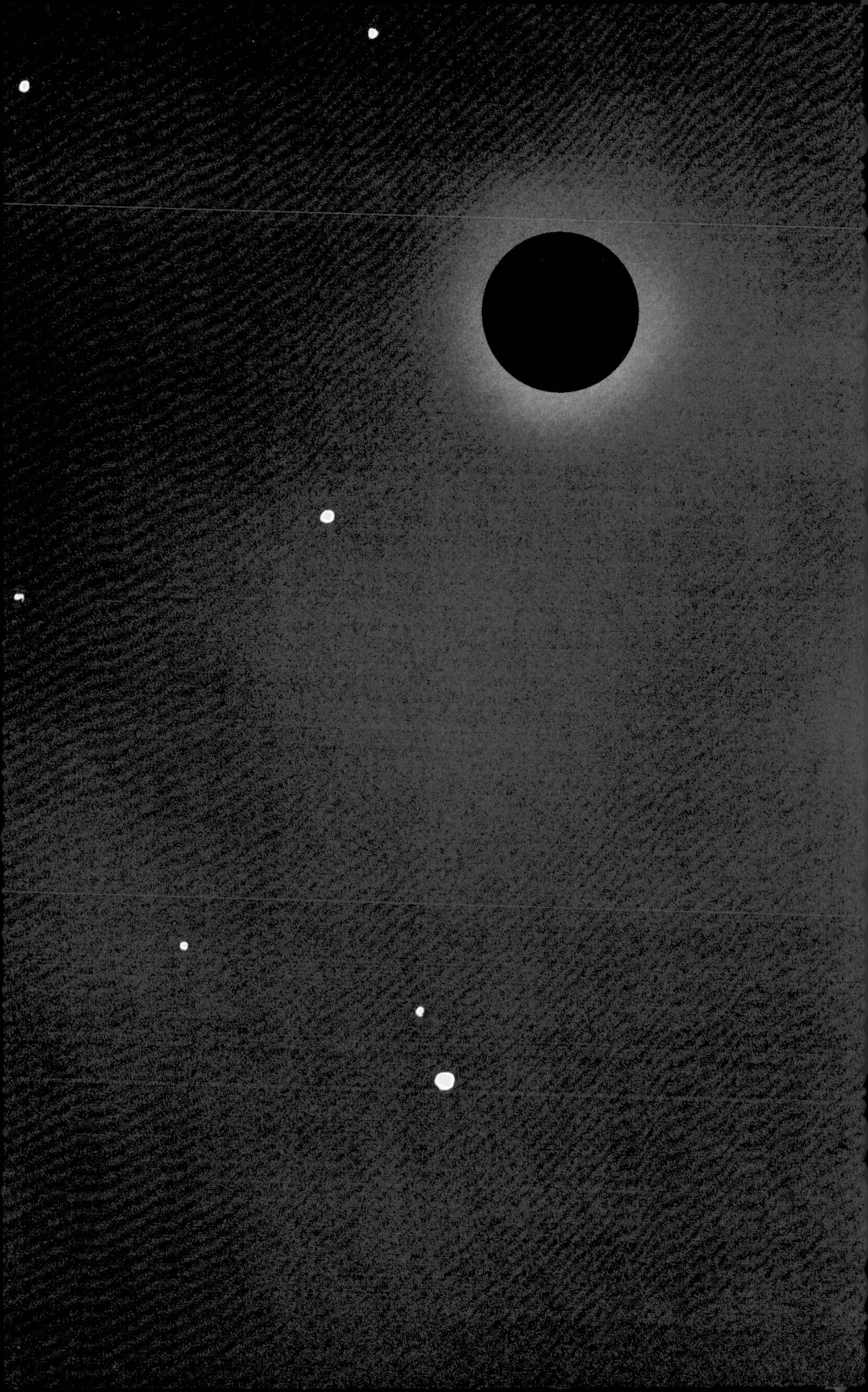

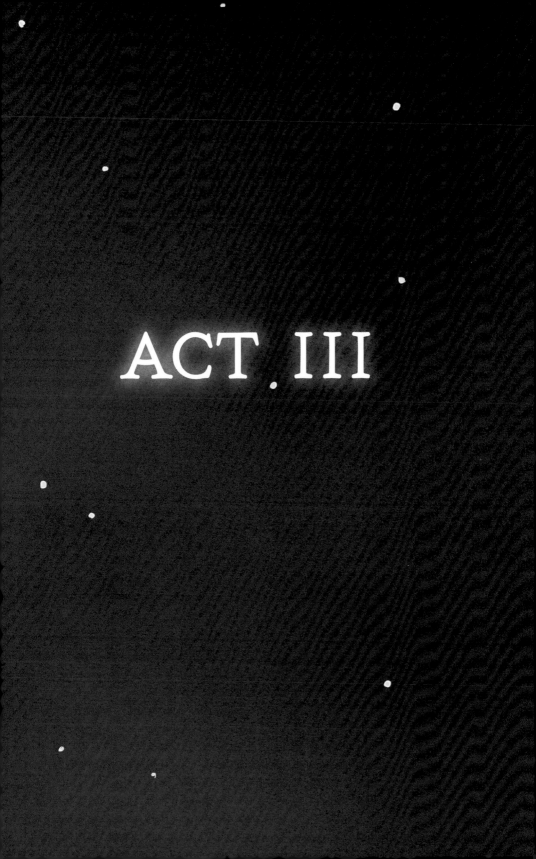

ACT III

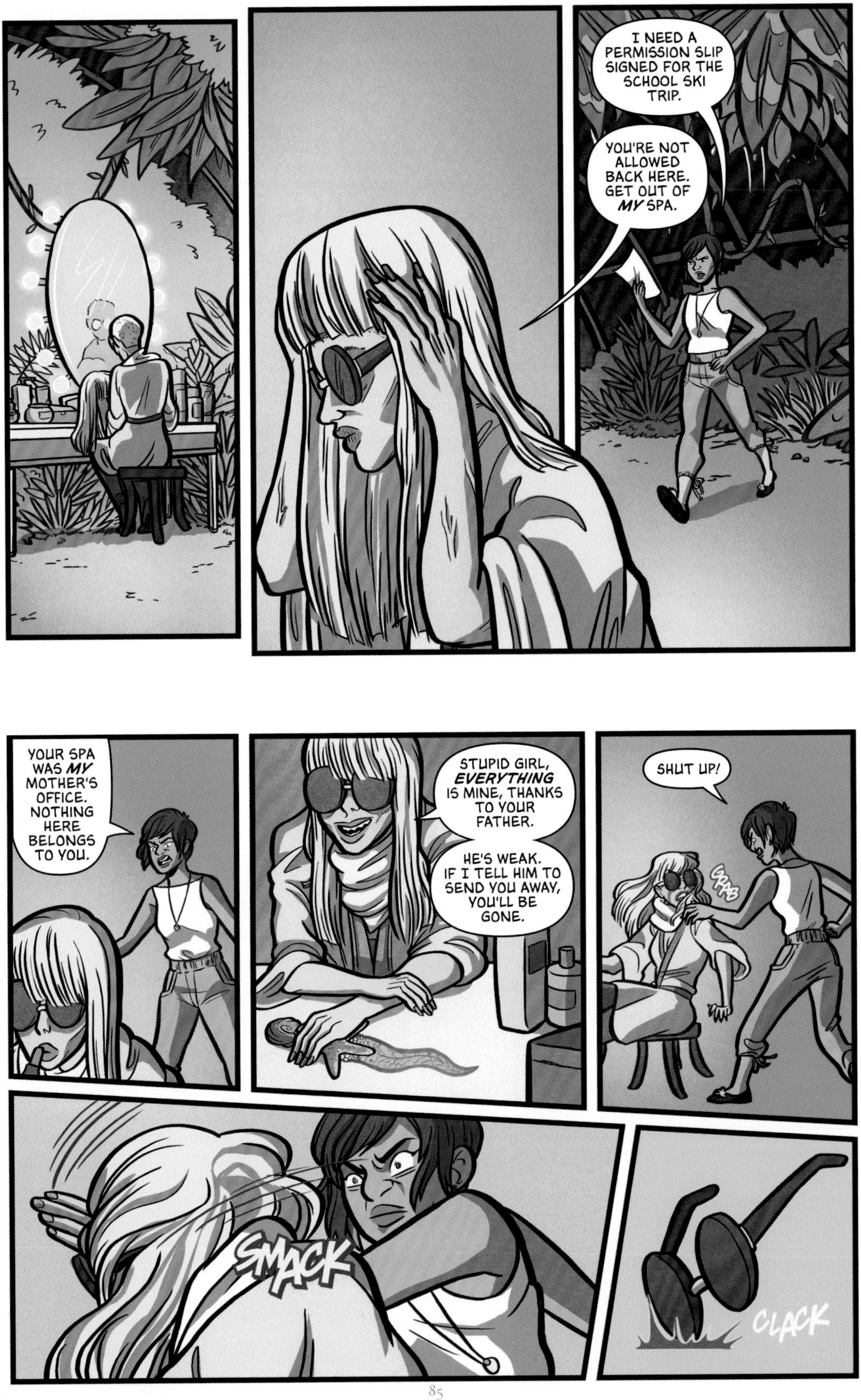
I NEED A PERMISSION SLIP SIGNED FOR THE SCHOOL SKI TRIP.
YOU'RE NOT ALLOWED BACK HERE. GET OUT OF *MY* SPA.
YOUR SPA WAS *MY* MOTHER'S OFFICE. NOTHING HERE BELONGS TO YOU.
STUPID GIRL, *EVERYTHING* IS MINE, THANKS TO YOUR FATHER.
HE'S WEAK. IF I TELL HIM TO SEND YOU AWAY, YOU'LL BE GONE.
SHUT UP!
GRAB
SMACK
CLACK

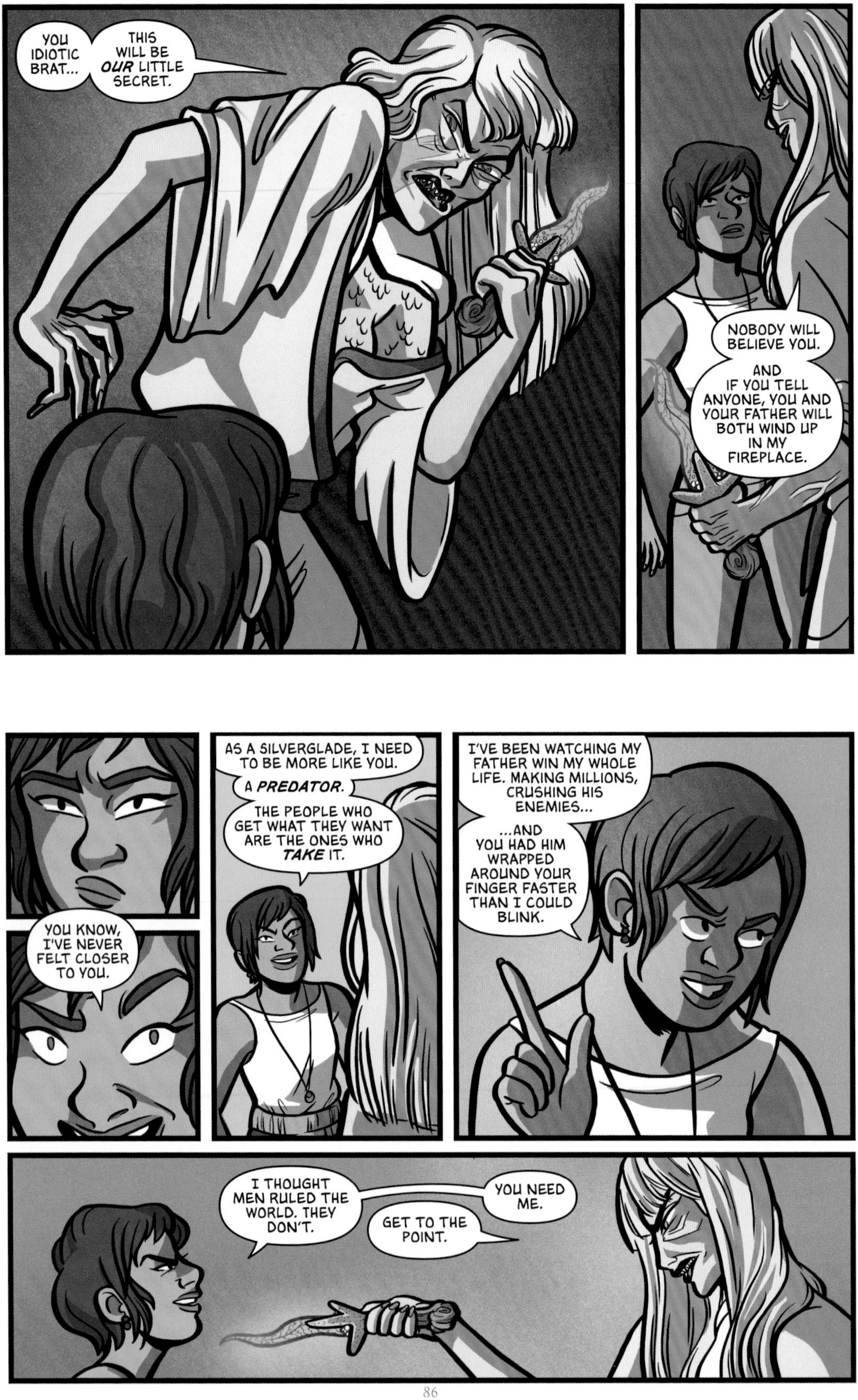
YOU IDIOTIC BRAT...
THIS WILL BE OUR LITTLE SECRET.
NOBODY WILL BELIEVE YOU.
AND IF YOU TELL ANYONE, YOU AND YOUR FATHER WILL BOTH WIND UP IN MY FIREPLACE.
YOU KNOW, I'VE NEVER FELT CLOSER TO YOU.
AS A SILVERGLADE, I NEED TO BE MORE LIKE YOU.
A PREDATOR.
THE PEOPLE WHO GET WHAT THEY WANT ARE THE ONES WHO TAKE IT.
I'VE BEEN WATCHING MY FATHER WIN MY WHOLE LIFE. MAKING MILLIONS, CRUSHING HIS ENEMIES...
...AND YOU HAD HIM WRAPPED AROUND YOUR FINGER FASTER THAN I COULD BLINK.
I THOUGHT MEN RULED THE WORLD. THEY DON'T.
YOU NEED ME.
GET TO THE POINT.

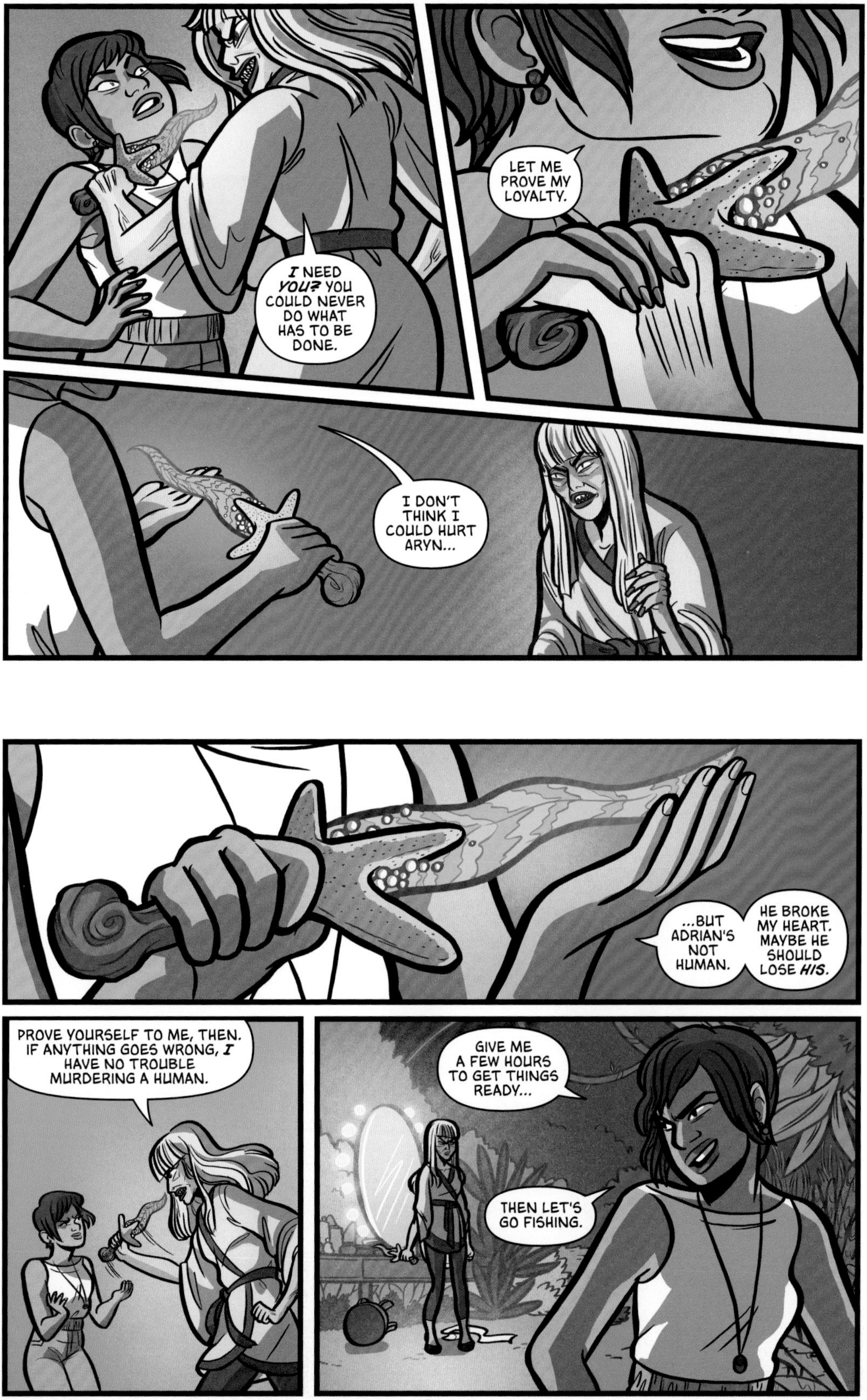
I NEED YOU? YOU COULD NEVER DO WHAT HAS TO BE DONE.
LET ME PROVE MY LOYALTY.
I DON'T THINK I COULD HURT ARYN...
...BUT ADRIAN'S NOT HUMAN.
HE BROKE MY HEART. MAYBE HE SHOULD LOSE HIS.
PROVE YOURSELF TO ME, THEN. IF ANYTHING GOES WRONG, I HAVE NO TROUBLE MURDERING A HUMAN.
GIVE ME A FEW HOURS TO GET THINGS READY...
THEN LET'S GO FISHING.

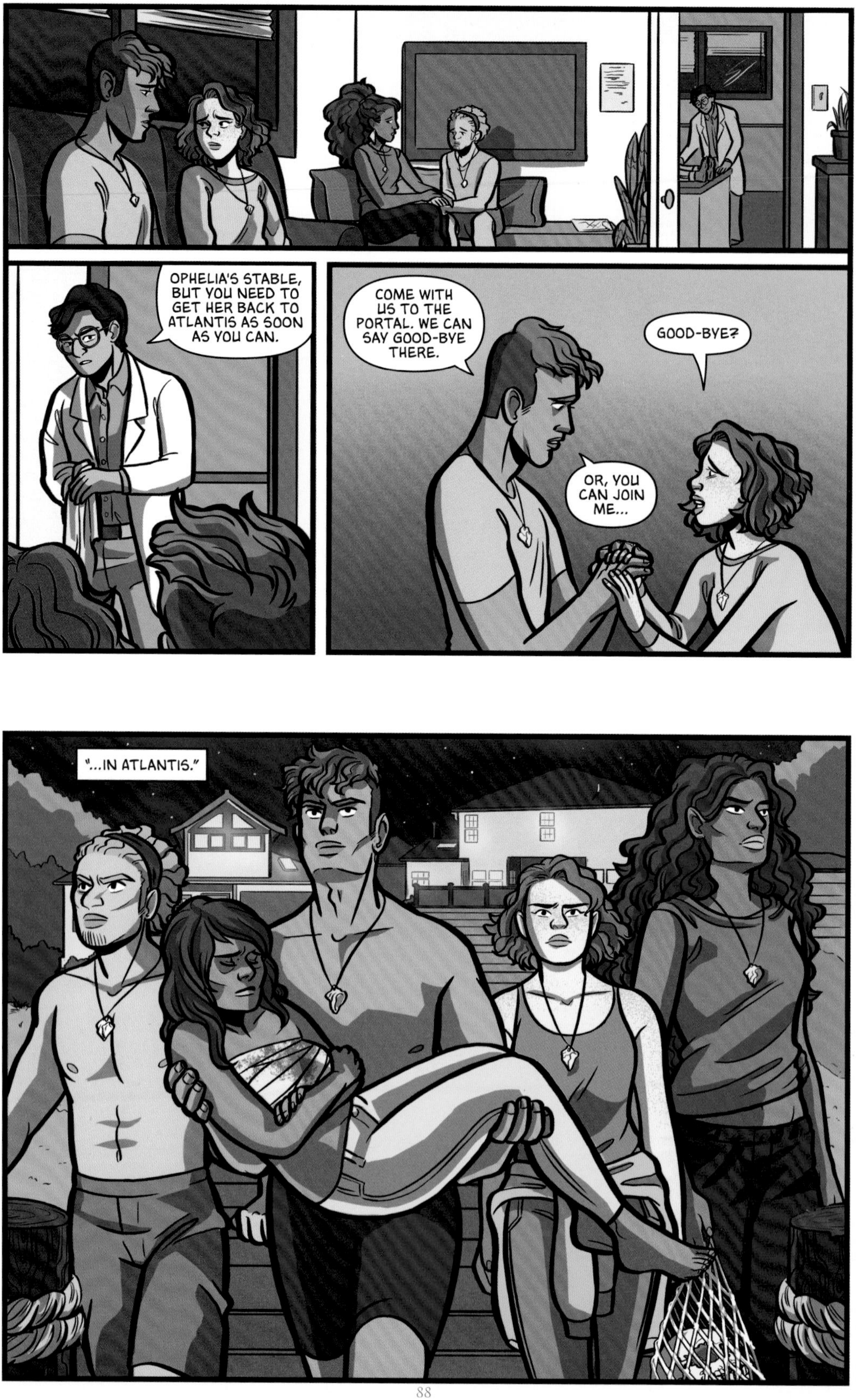
OPHELIA'S STABLE, BUT YOU NEED TO GET HER BACK TO ATLANTIS AS SOON AS YOU CAN.
COME WITH US TO THE PORTAL. WE CAN SAY GOOD-BYE THERE.
GOOD-BYE?
OR, YOU CAN JOIN ME...
"...IN ATLANTIS."

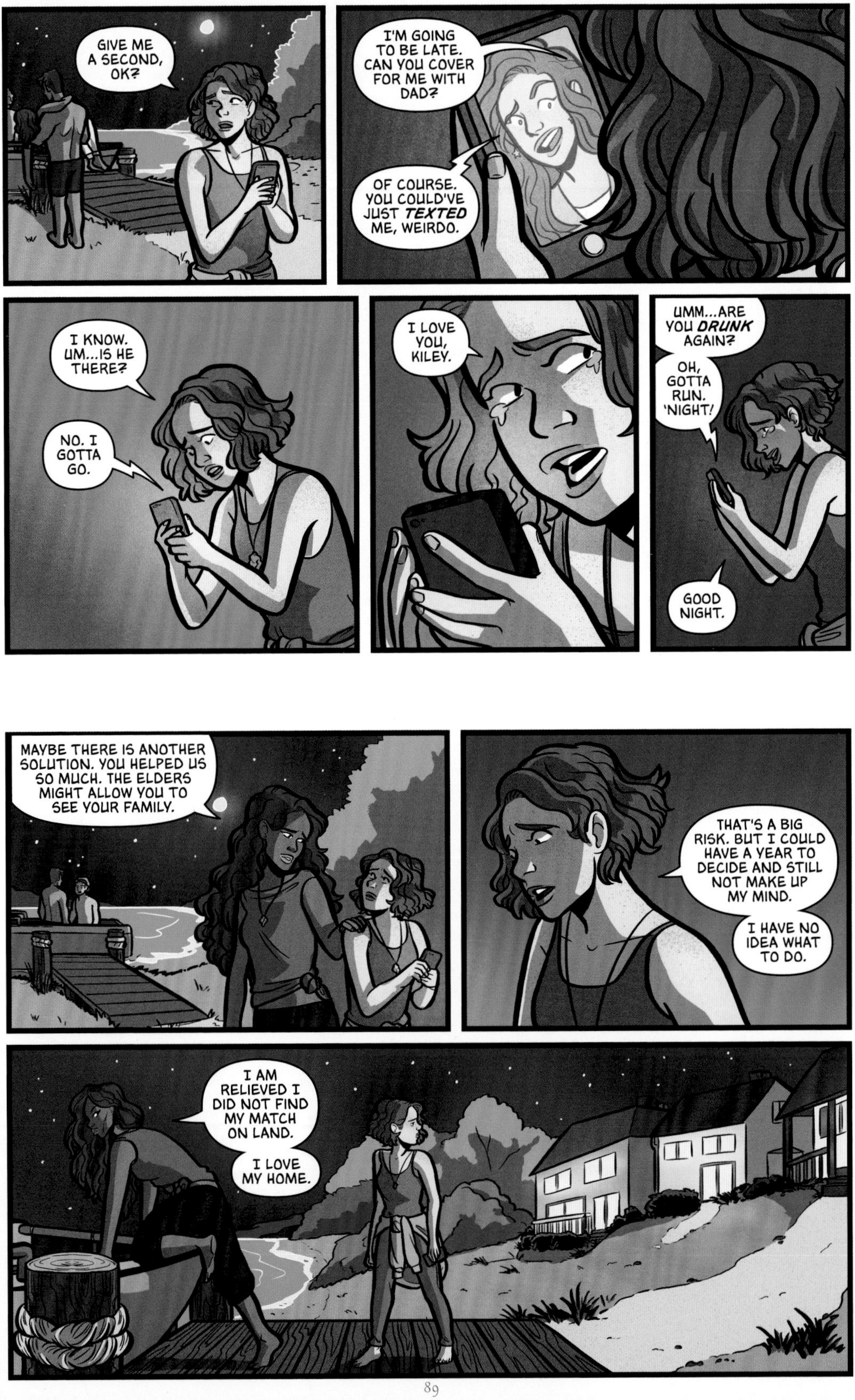
GIVE ME A SECOND, OK?
I'M GOING TO BE LATE. CAN YOU COVER FOR ME WITH DAD?
OF COURSE. YOU COULD'VE JUST TEXTED ME, WEIRDO.
I KNOW. UM...IS HE THERE?
NO. I GOTTA GO.
I LOVE YOU, KILEY.
UMM...ARE YOU DRUNK AGAIN?
OH, GOTTA RUN. 'NIGHT!
GOOD NIGHT.
MAYBE THERE IS ANOTHER SOLUTION. YOU HELPED US SO MUCH. THE ELDERS MIGHT ALLOW YOU TO SEE YOUR FAMILY.
THAT'S A BIG RISK. BUT I COULD HAVE A YEAR TO DECIDE AND STILL NOT MAKE UP MY MIND.
I HAVE NO IDEA WHAT TO DO.
I AM RELIEVED I DID NOT FIND MY MATCH ON LAND.
I LOVE MY HOME.

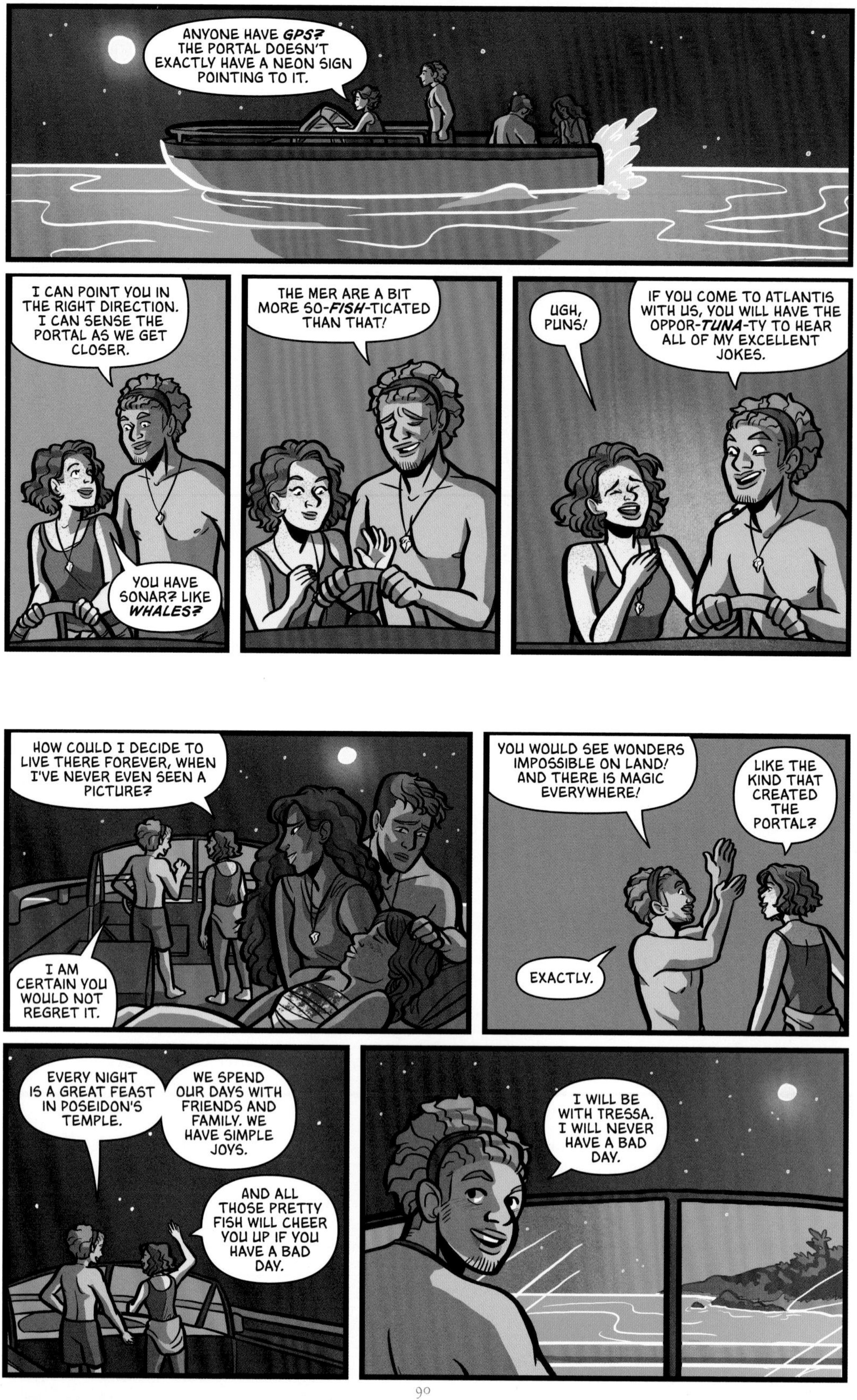
ANYONE HAVE *GPS?* THE PORTAL DOESN'T EXACTLY HAVE A NEON SIGN POINTING TO IT.
I CAN POINT YOU IN THE RIGHT DIRECTION. I CAN SENSE THE PORTAL AS WE GET CLOSER.
YOU HAVE SONAR? LIKE *WHALES?*
THE MER ARE A BIT MORE SO-*FISH*-TICATED THAN THAT!
UGH, PUNS!
IF YOU COME TO ATLANTIS WITH US, YOU WILL HAVE THE OPPOR-*TUNA*-TY TO HEAR ALL OF MY EXCELLENT JOKES.
HOW COULD I DECIDE TO LIVE THERE FOREVER, WHEN I'VE NEVER EVEN SEEN A PICTURE?
I AM CERTAIN YOU WOULD NOT REGRET IT.
YOU WOULD SEE WONDERS IMPOSSIBLE ON LAND! AND THERE IS MAGIC EVERYWHERE!
LIKE THE KIND THAT CREATED THE PORTAL?
EXACTLY.
EVERY NIGHT IS A GREAT FEAST IN POSEIDON'S TEMPLE.
WE SPEND OUR DAYS WITH FRIENDS AND FAMILY. WE HAVE SIMPLE JOYS.
AND ALL THOSE PRETTY FISH WILL CHEER YOU UP IF YOU HAVE A BAD DAY.
I WILL BE WITH TRESSA. I WILL NEVER HAVE A BAD DAY.

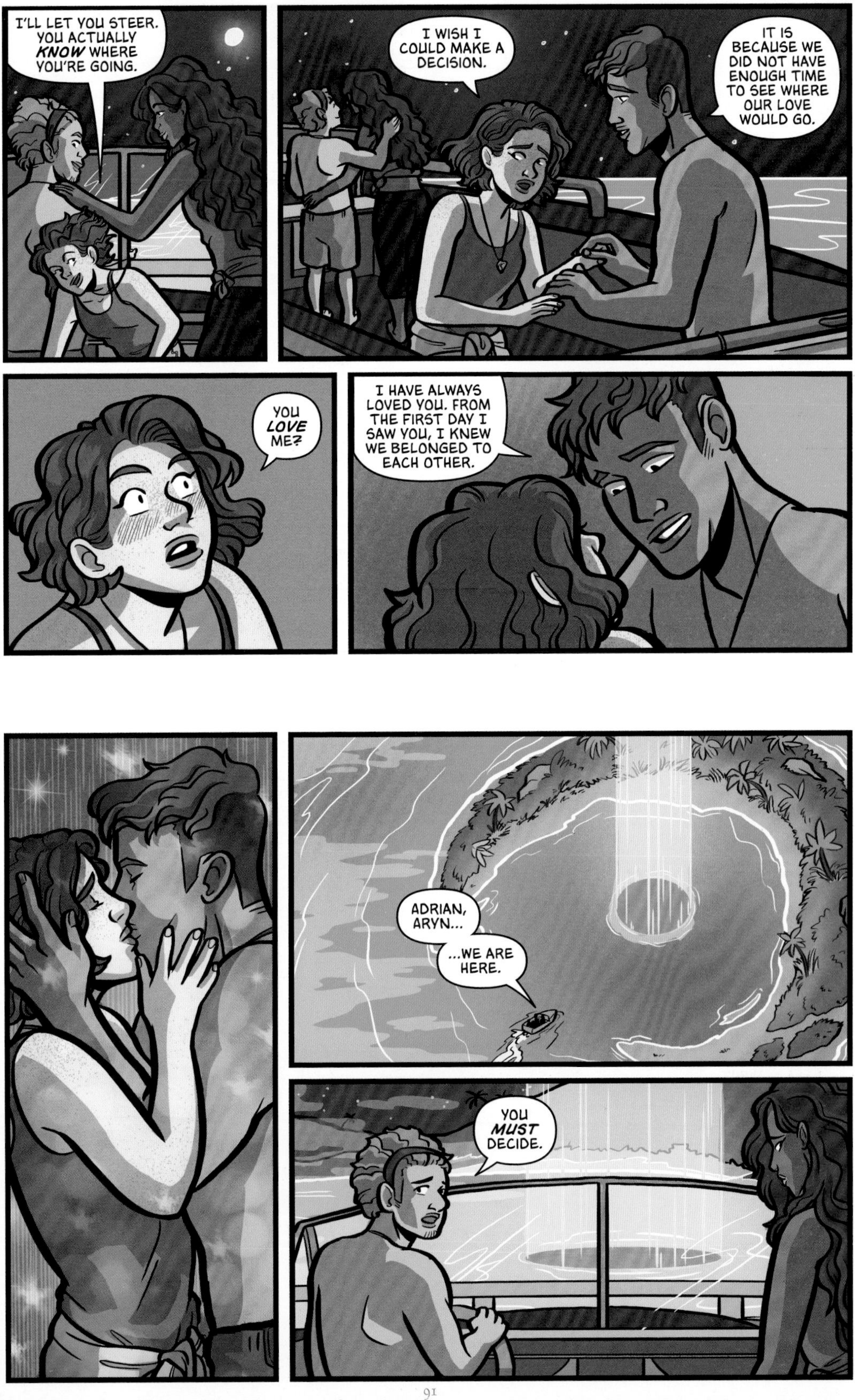
I'LL LET YOU STEER. YOU ACTUALLY KNOW WHERE YOU'RE GOING.
I WISH I COULD MAKE A DECISION.
IT IS BECAUSE WE DID NOT HAVE ENOUGH TIME TO SEE WHERE OUR LOVE WOULD GO.
YOU LOVE ME?
I HAVE ALWAYS LOVED YOU. FROM THE FIRST DAY I SAW YOU, I KNEW WE BELONGED TO EACH OTHER.
ADRIAN, ARYN...
...WE ARE HERE.
YOU MUST DECIDE.

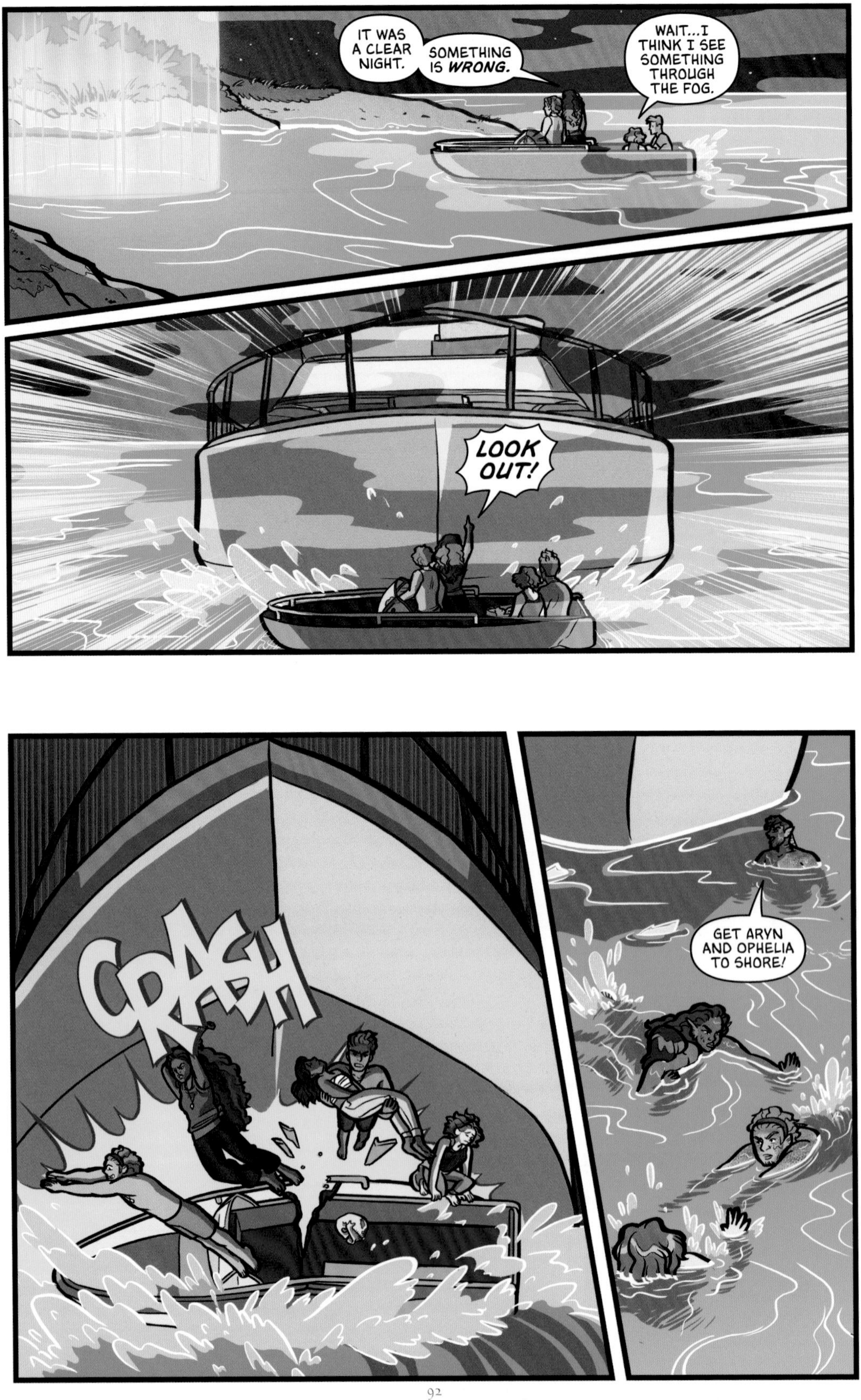
IT WAS A CLEAR NIGHT.
SOMETHING IS WRONG.
WAIT...I THINK I SEE SOMETHING THROUGH THE FOG.
LOOK OUT!
CRASH
GET ARYN AND OPHELIA TO SHORE!

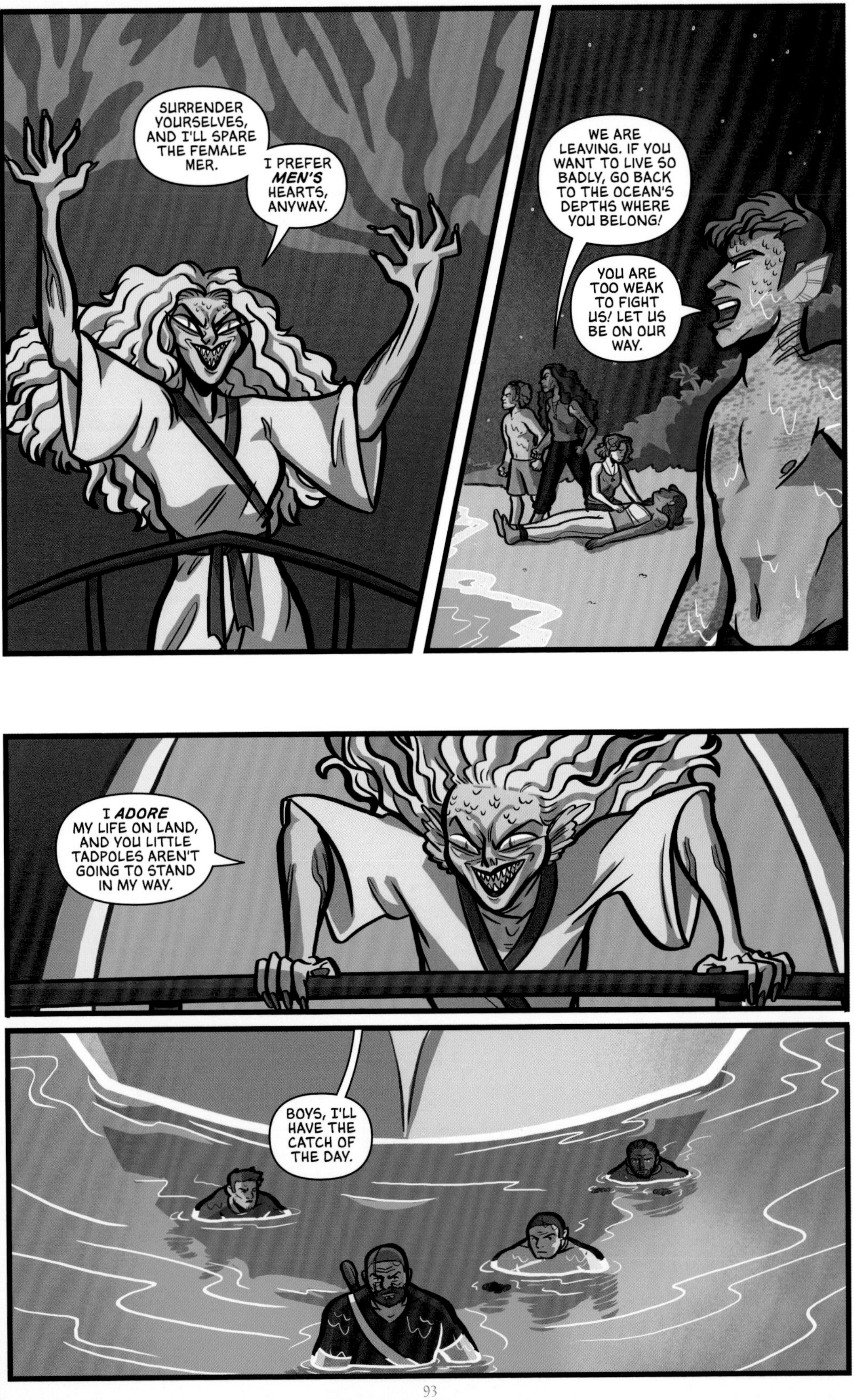
SURRENDER YOURSELVES, AND I'LL SPARE THE FEMALE MER.
I PREFER *MEN'S* HEARTS, ANYWAY.
WE ARE LEAVING. IF YOU WANT TO LIVE SO BADLY, GO BACK TO THE OCEAN'S DEPTHS WHERE YOU BELONG!
YOU ARE TOO WEAK TO FIGHT US! LET US BE ON OUR WAY.
I *ADORE* MY LIFE ON LAND, AND YOU LITTLE TADPOLES AREN'T GOING TO STAND IN MY WAY.
BOYS, I'LL HAVE THE CATCH OF THE DAY.

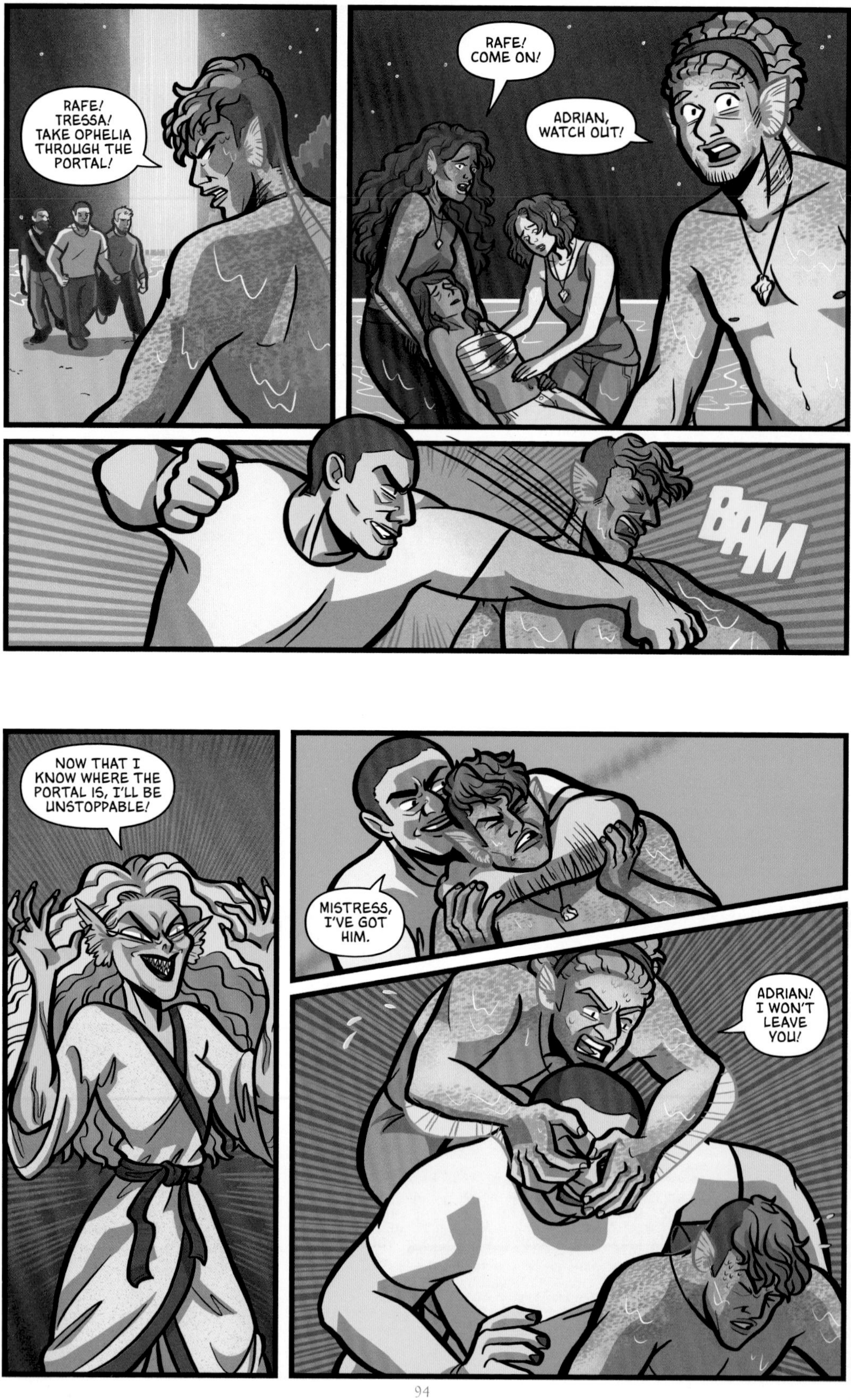
RAFE! TRESSA! TAKE OPHELIA THROUGH THE PORTAL!
RAFE! COME ON!
ADRIAN, WATCH OUT!
BAM
NOW THAT I KNOW WHERE THE PORTAL IS, I'LL BE UNSTOPPABLE!
MISTRESS, I'VE GOT HIM.
ADRIAN! I WON'T LEAVE YOU!

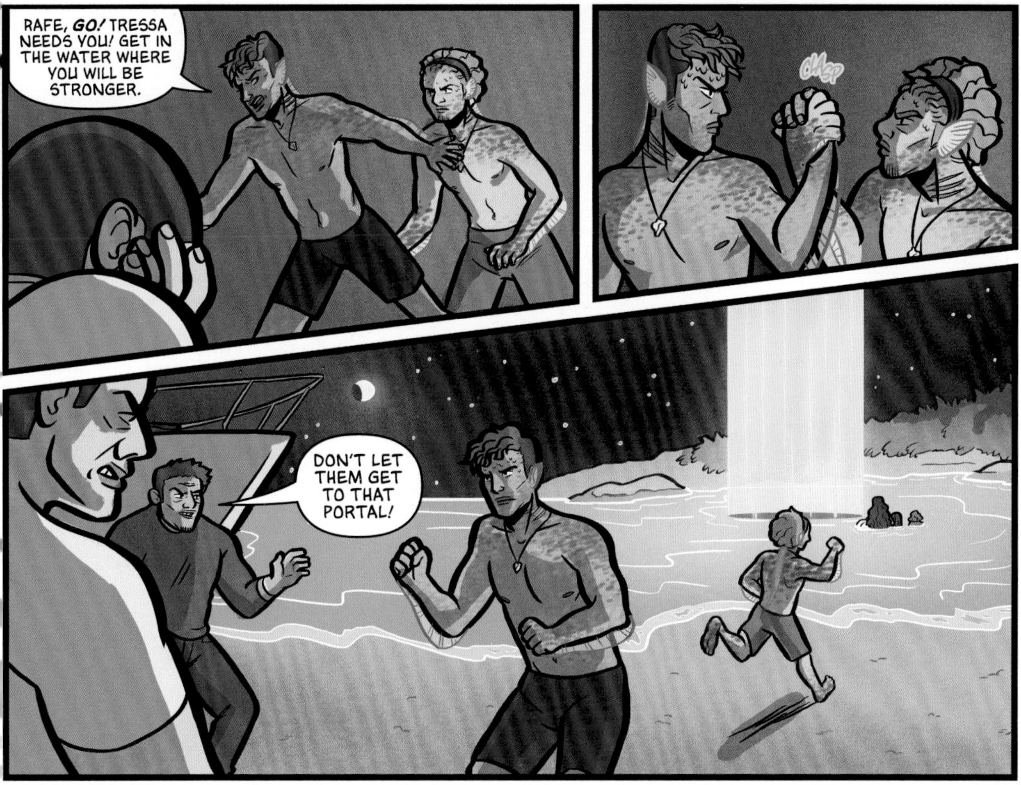
RAFE, GO! TRESSA NEEDS YOU! GET IN THE WATER WHERE YOU WILL BE STRONGER.
CLASP
DON'T LET THEM GET TO THAT PORTAL!

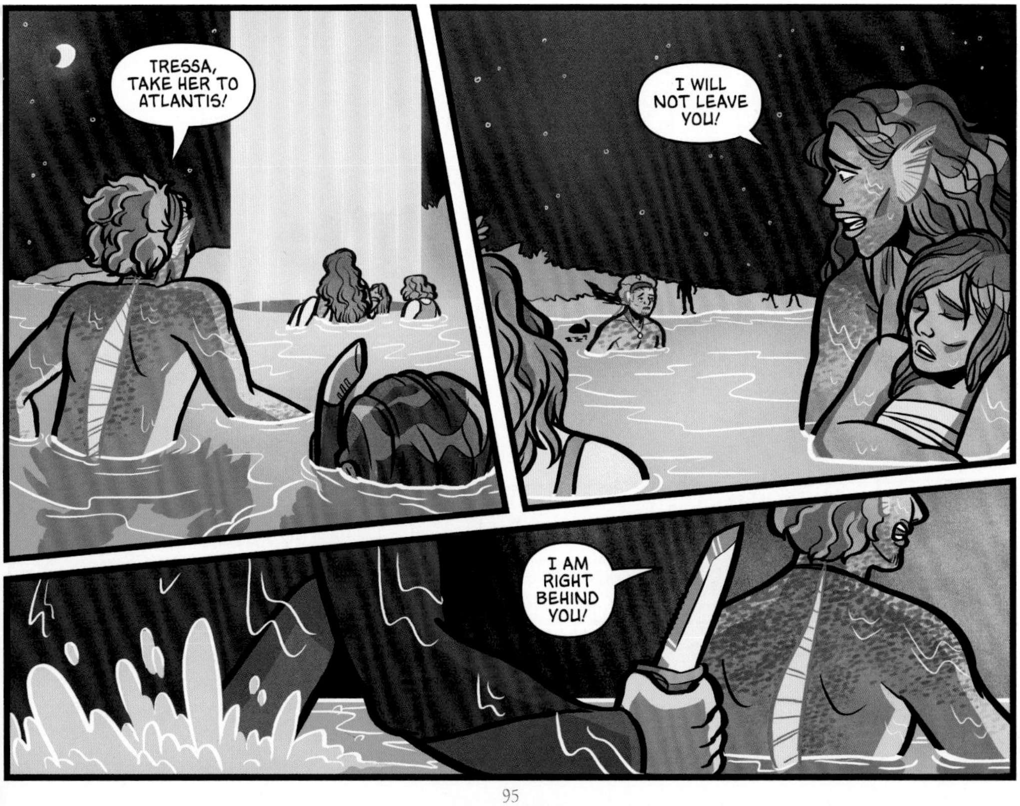
TRESSA, TAKE HER TO ATLANTIS!
I WILL NOT LEAVE YOU!
I AM RIGHT BEHIND YOU!

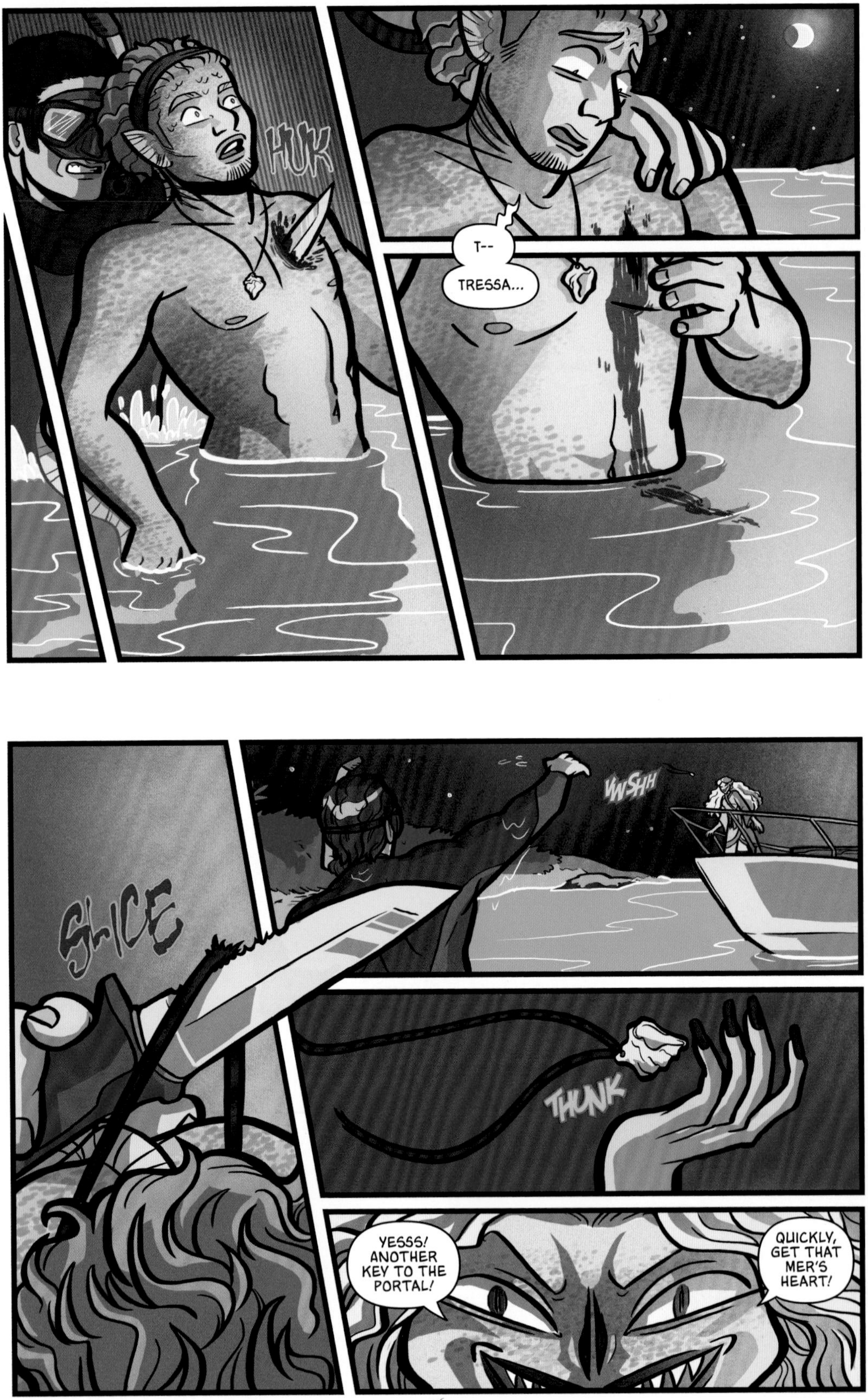
HUK
T--
TRESSA...
SLICE
VWSHH
THUNK
YESSS! ANOTHER KEY TO THE PORTAL!
QUICKLY, GET THAT MER'S HEART!

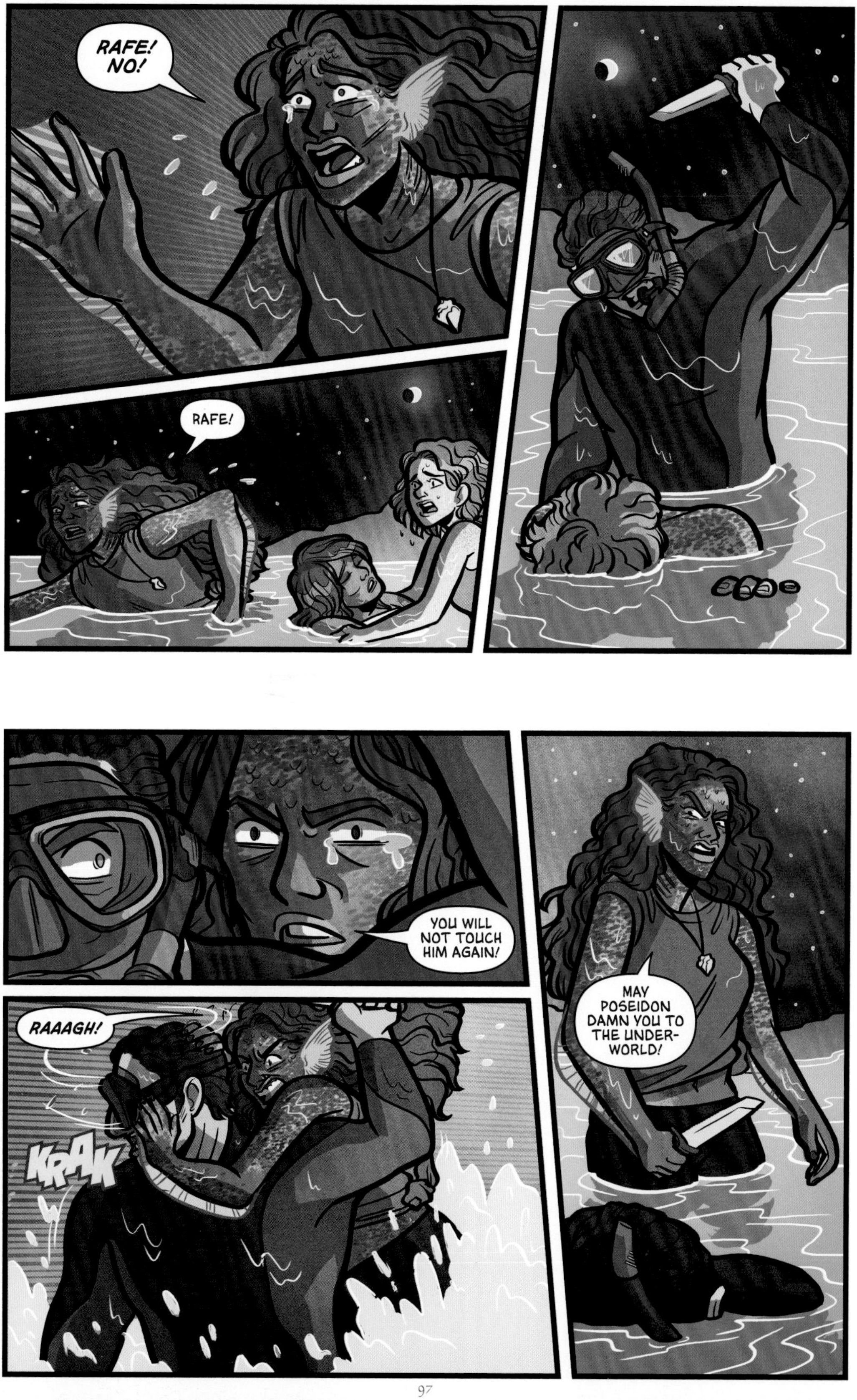
RAFE! NO!
RAFE!
YOU WILL NOT TOUCH HIM AGAIN!
RAAAGH!
KRAK
MAY POSEIDON DAMN YOU TO THE UNDER-WORLD!

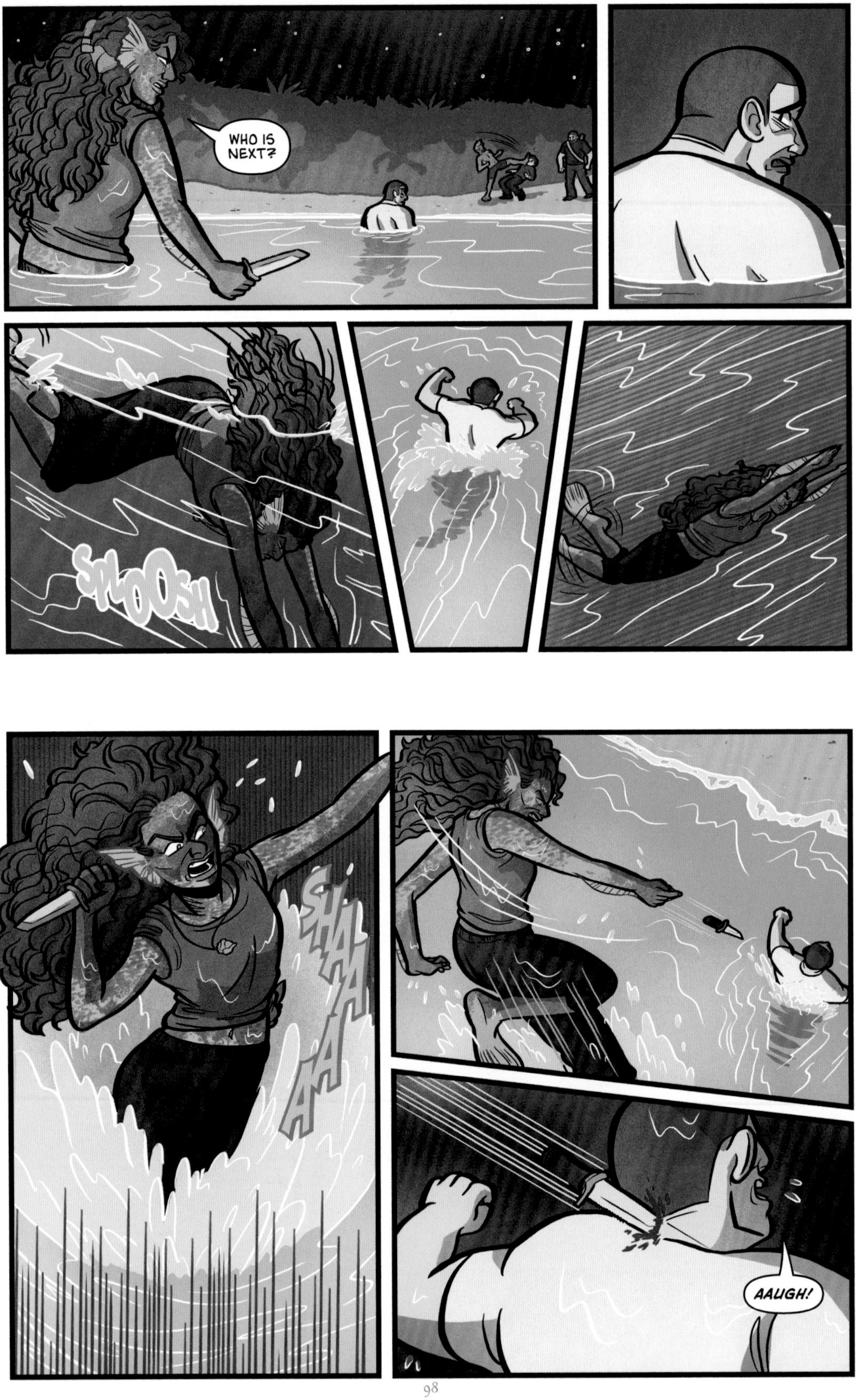
WHO IS NEXT?
SPLOOSH
SHAAAA
AAUGH!

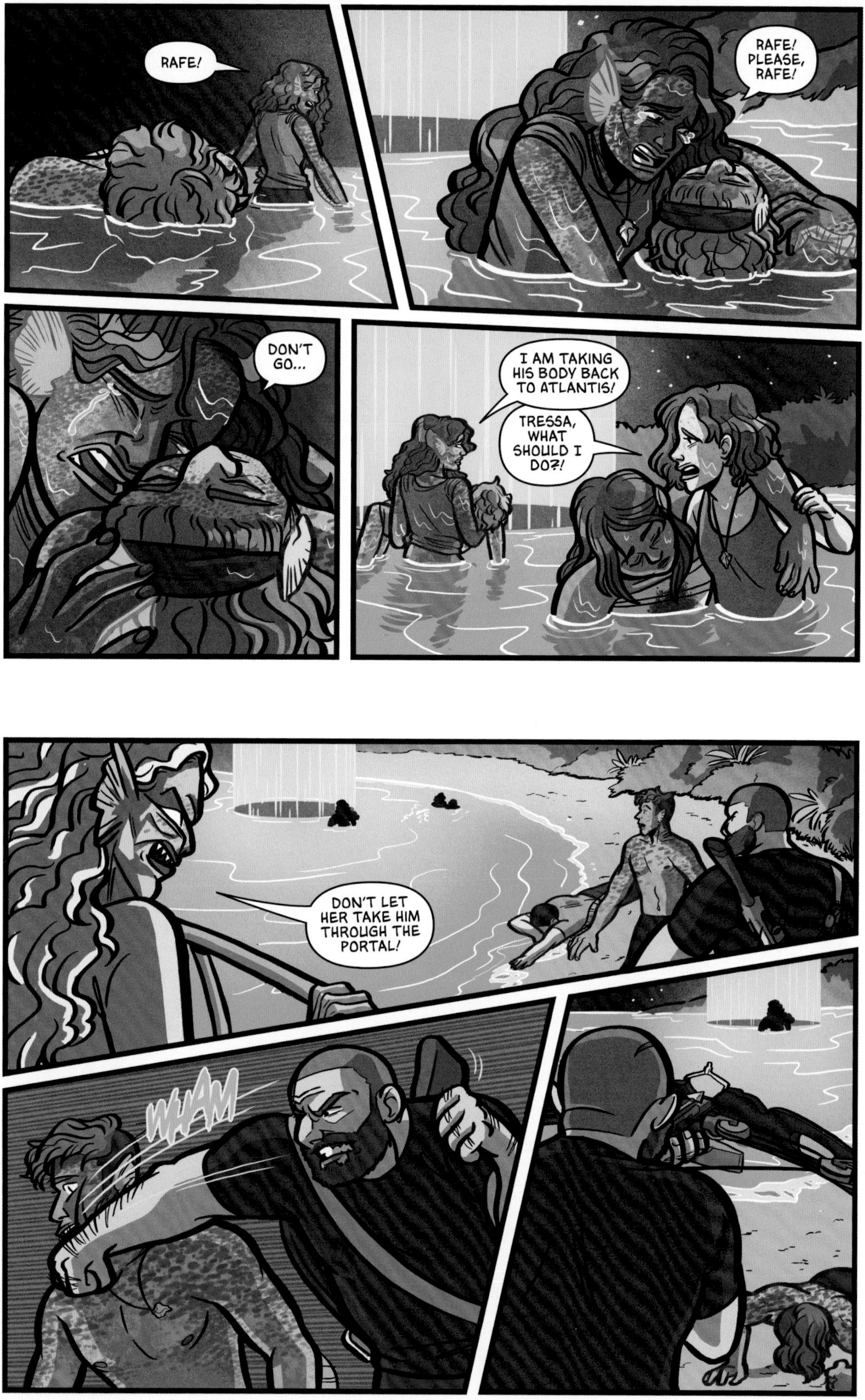
RAFE!
RAFE! PLEASE, RAFE!
DON'T GO...
I AM TAKING HIS BODY BACK TO ATLANTIS!
TRESSA, WHAT SHOULD I DO?!
DON'T LET HER TAKE HIM THROUGH THE PORTAL!
WHAM

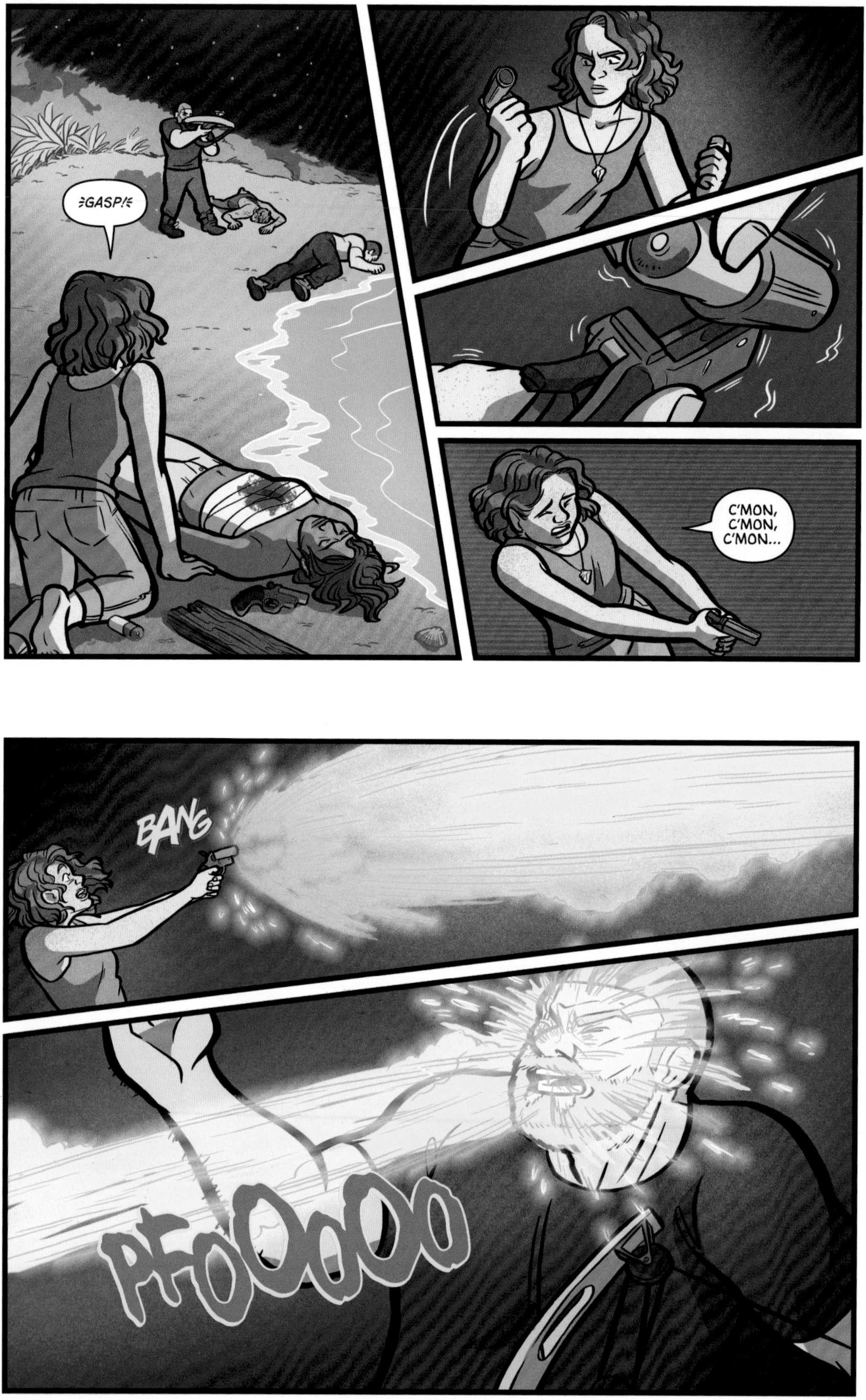

GASP!
C'MON, C'MON, C'MON...
BANG
PFOOOOO

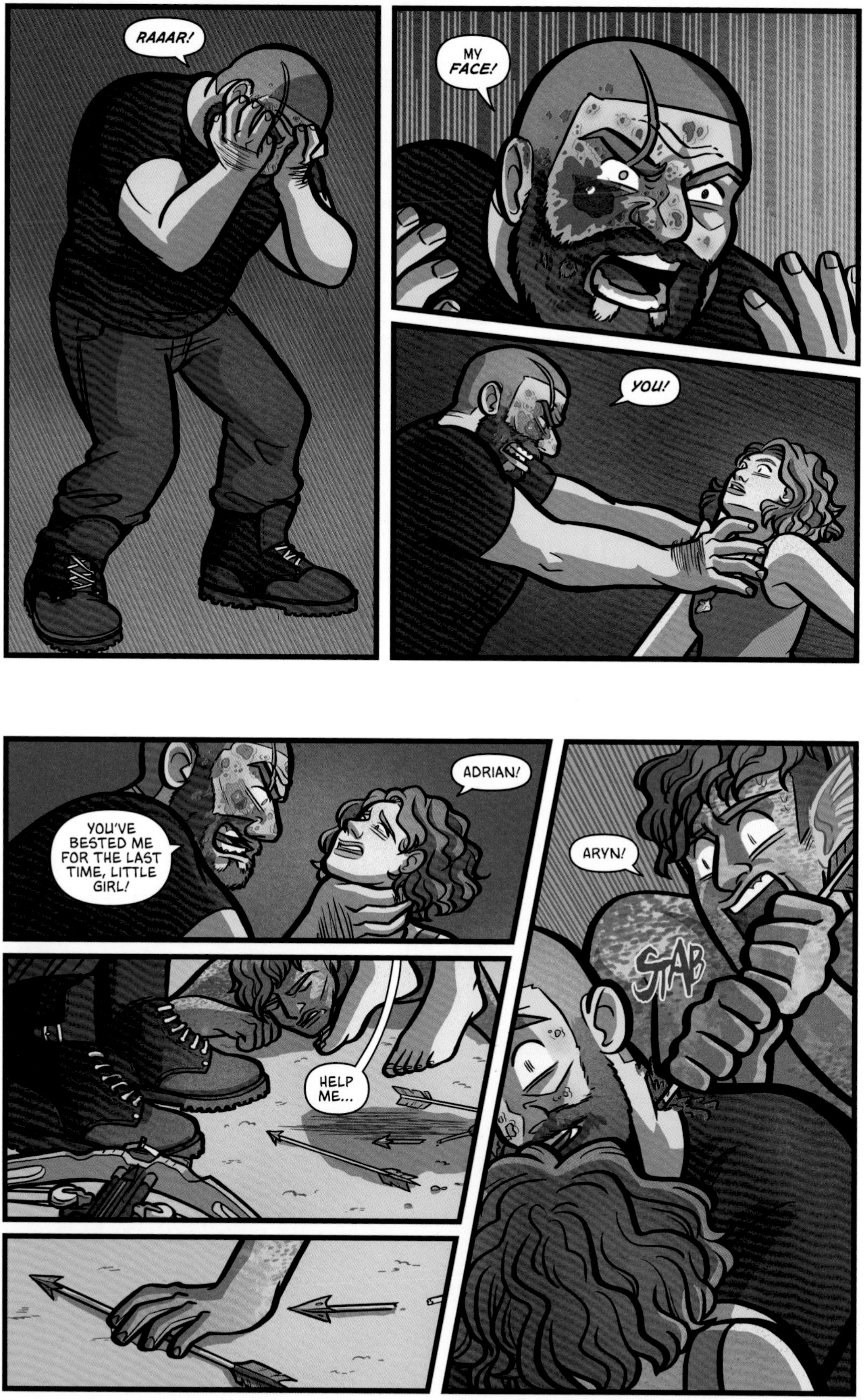
RAAAR!
MY FACE!
YOU!
ADRIAN!
YOU'VE BESTED ME FOR THE LAST TIME, LITTLE GIRL!
HELP ME...
ARYN!
STAB

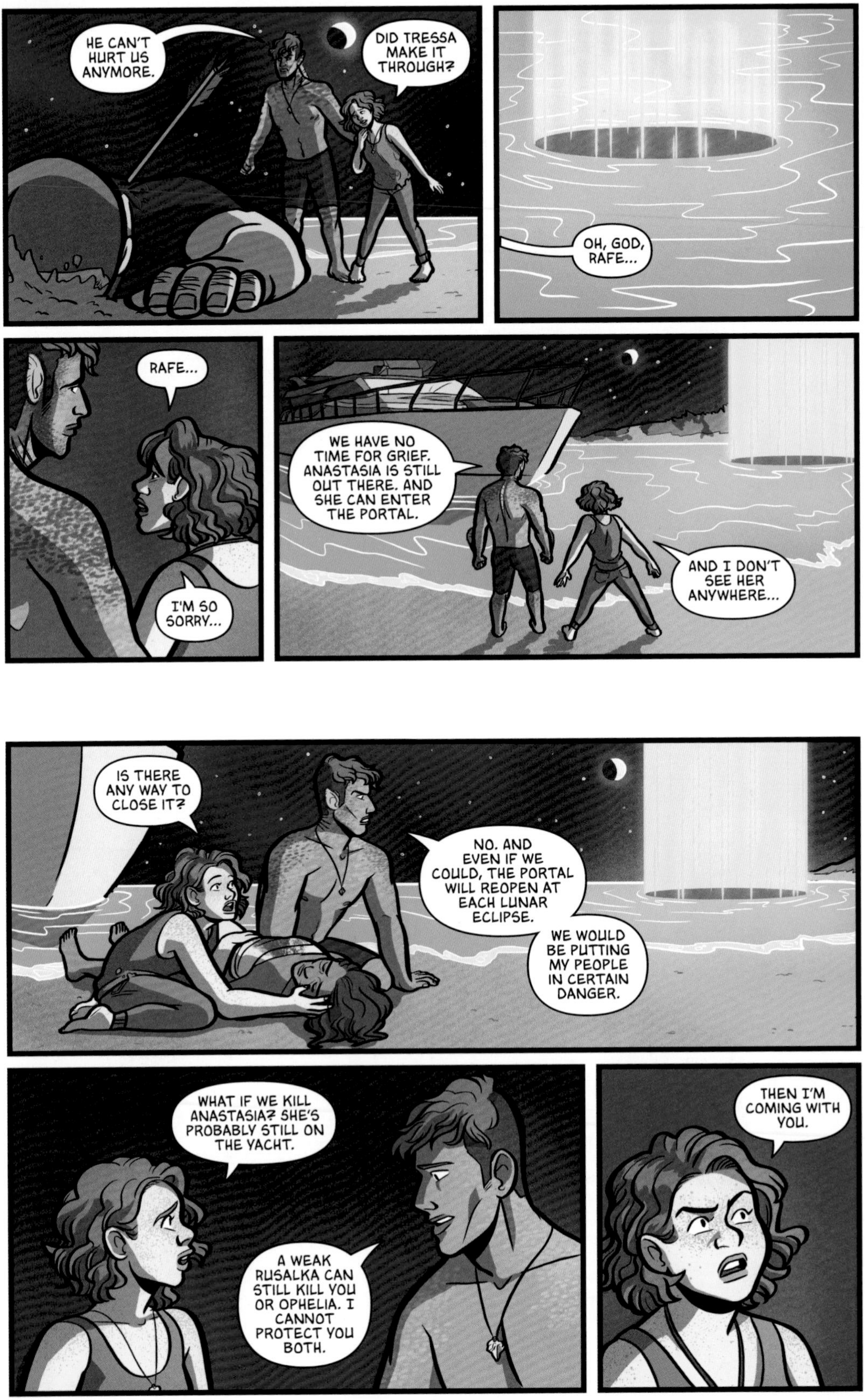
HE CAN'T HURT US ANYMORE.
DID TRESSA MAKE IT THROUGH?
OH, GOD, RAFE...
RAFE...
I'M SO SORRY...
WE HAVE NO TIME FOR GRIEF. ANASTASIA IS STILL OUT THERE. AND SHE CAN ENTER THE PORTAL.
AND I DON'T SEE HER ANYWHERE...
IS THERE ANY WAY TO CLOSE IT?
NO. AND EVEN IF WE COULD, THE PORTAL WILL REOPEN AT EACH LUNAR ECLIPSE.
WE WOULD BE PUTTING MY PEOPLE IN CERTAIN DANGER.
WHAT IF WE KILL ANASTASIA? SHE'S PROBABLY STILL ON THE YACHT.
A WEAK RUSALKA CAN STILL KILL YOU OR OPHELIA. I CANNOT PROTECT YOU BOTH.
THEN I'M COMING WITH YOU.

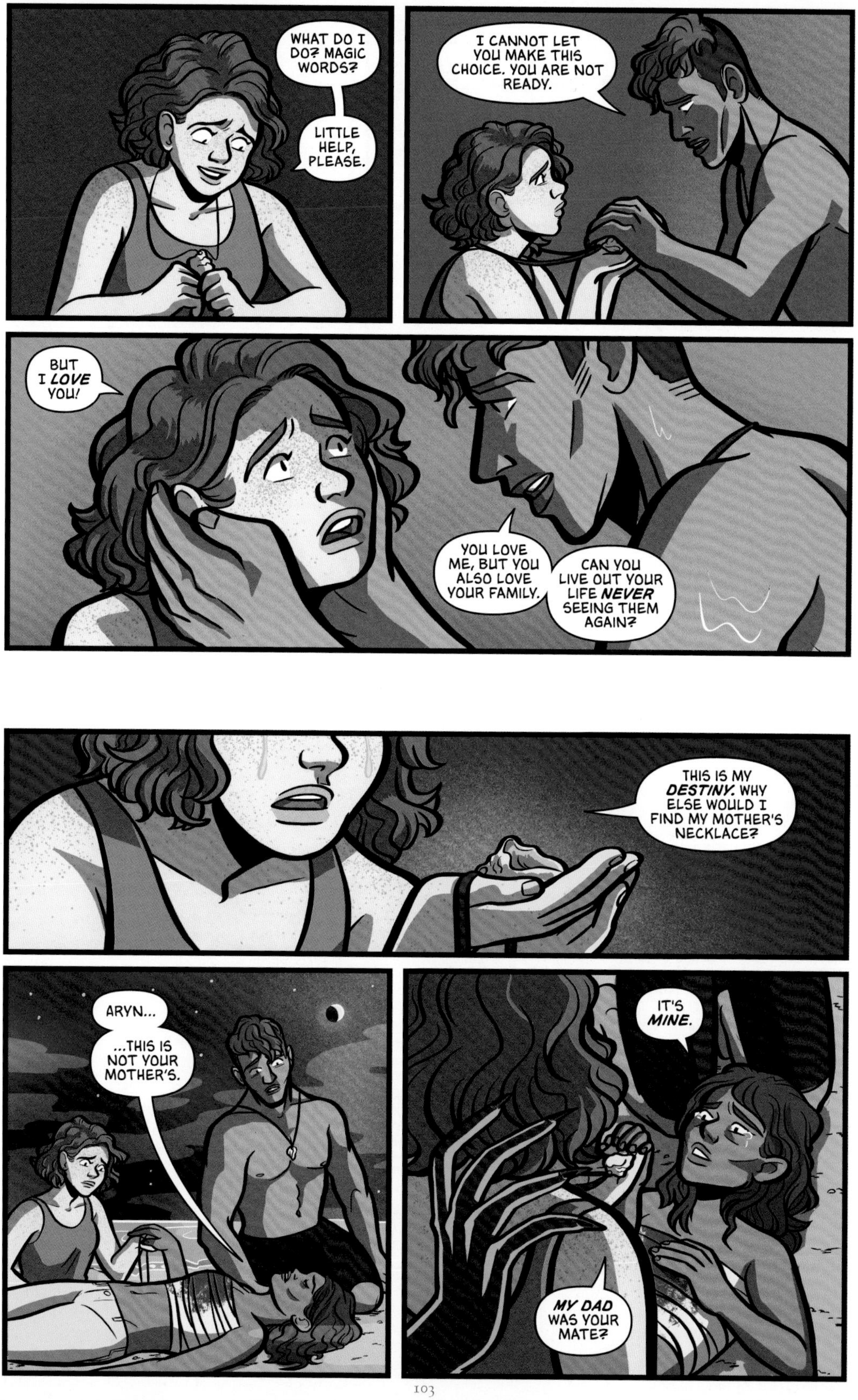
WHAT DO I DO? MAGIC WORDS?
LITTLE HELP, PLEASE.
I CANNOT LET YOU MAKE THIS CHOICE. YOU ARE NOT READY.
BUT I LOVE YOU!
YOU LOVE ME, BUT YOU ALSO LOVE YOUR FAMILY.
CAN YOU LIVE OUT YOUR LIFE NEVER SEEING THEM AGAIN?
THIS IS MY DESTINY. WHY ELSE WOULD I FIND MY MOTHER'S NECKLACE?
ARYN...
...THIS IS NOT YOUR MOTHER'S.
IT'S MINE.
MY DAD WAS YOUR MATE?

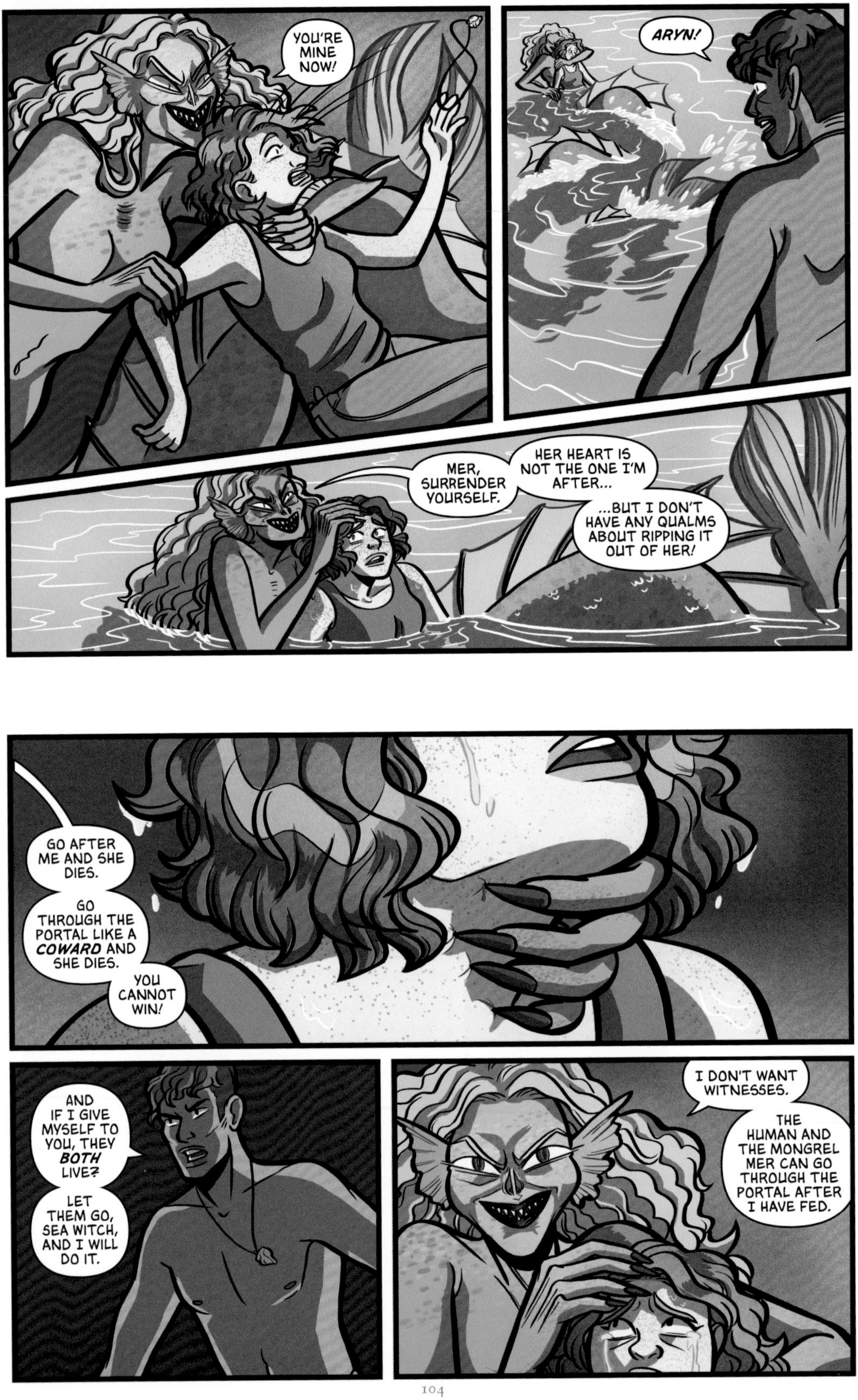

YOU'RE MINE NOW!
ARYN!
MER, SURRENDER YOURSELF.
HER HEART IS NOT THE ONE I'M AFTER...
...BUT I DON'T HAVE ANY QUALMS ABOUT RIPPING IT OUT OF HER!
GO AFTER ME AND SHE DIES.
GO THROUGH THE PORTAL LIKE A *COWARD* AND SHE DIES.
YOU CANNOT WIN!
AND IF I GIVE MYSELF TO YOU, THEY *BOTH* LIVE?
LET THEM GO, SEA WITCH, AND I WILL DO IT.
I DON'T WANT WITNESSES.
THE HUMAN AND THE MONGREL MER CAN GO THROUGH THE PORTAL AFTER I HAVE FED.

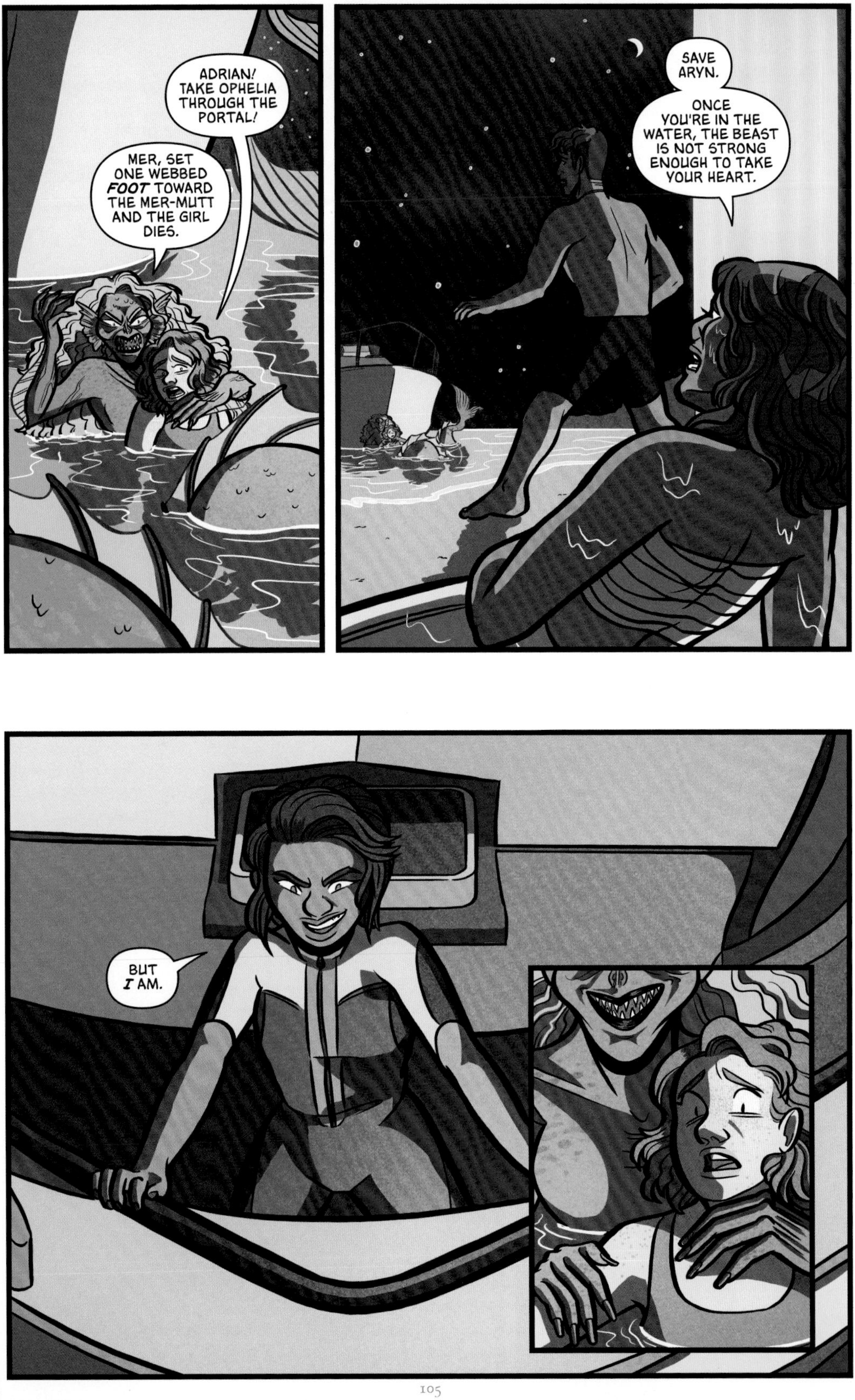
ADRIAN! TAKE OPHELIA THROUGH THE PORTAL!
MER, SET ONE WEBBED FOOT TOWARD THE MER-MUTT AND THE GIRL DIES.
SAVE ARYN.
ONCE YOU'RE IN THE WATER, THE BEAST IS NOT STRONG ENOUGH TO TAKE YOUR HEART.
BUT I AM.

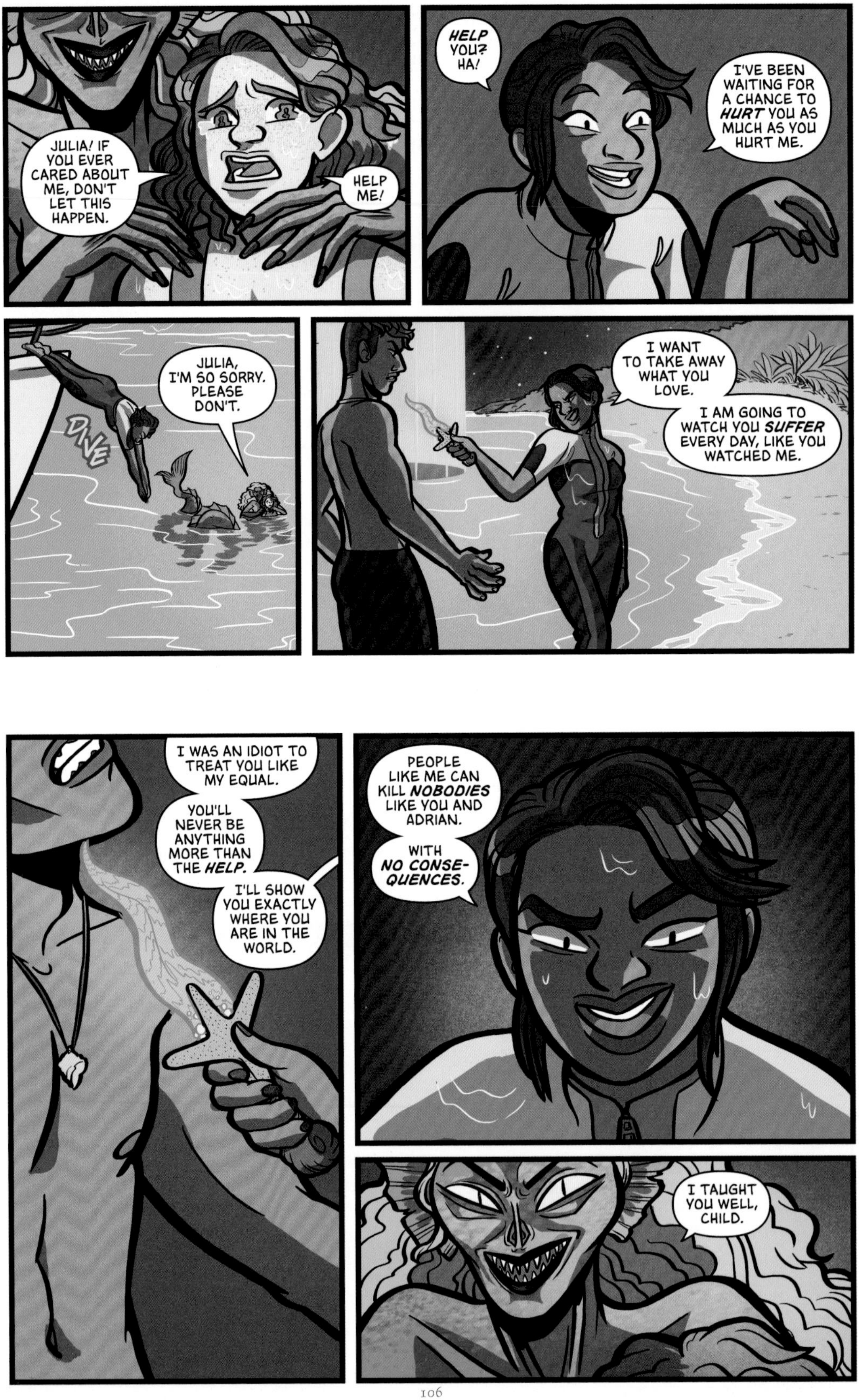
JULIA! IF YOU EVER CARED ABOUT ME, DON'T LET THIS HAPPEN.
HELP ME!
HELP YOU? HA!
I'VE BEEN WAITING FOR A CHANCE TO HURT YOU AS MUCH AS YOU HURT ME.
DIVE
JULIA, I'M SO SORRY. PLEASE DON'T.
I WANT TO TAKE AWAY WHAT YOU LOVE.
I AM GOING TO WATCH YOU SUFFER EVERY DAY, LIKE YOU WATCHED ME.
I WAS AN IDIOT TO TREAT YOU LIKE MY EQUAL.
YOU'LL NEVER BE ANYTHING MORE THAN THE HELP.
I'LL SHOW YOU EXACTLY WHERE YOU ARE IN THE WORLD.
PEOPLE LIKE ME CAN KILL NOBODIES LIKE YOU AND ADRIAN.
WITH NO CONSE-QUENCES.
I TAUGHT YOU WELL, CHILD.

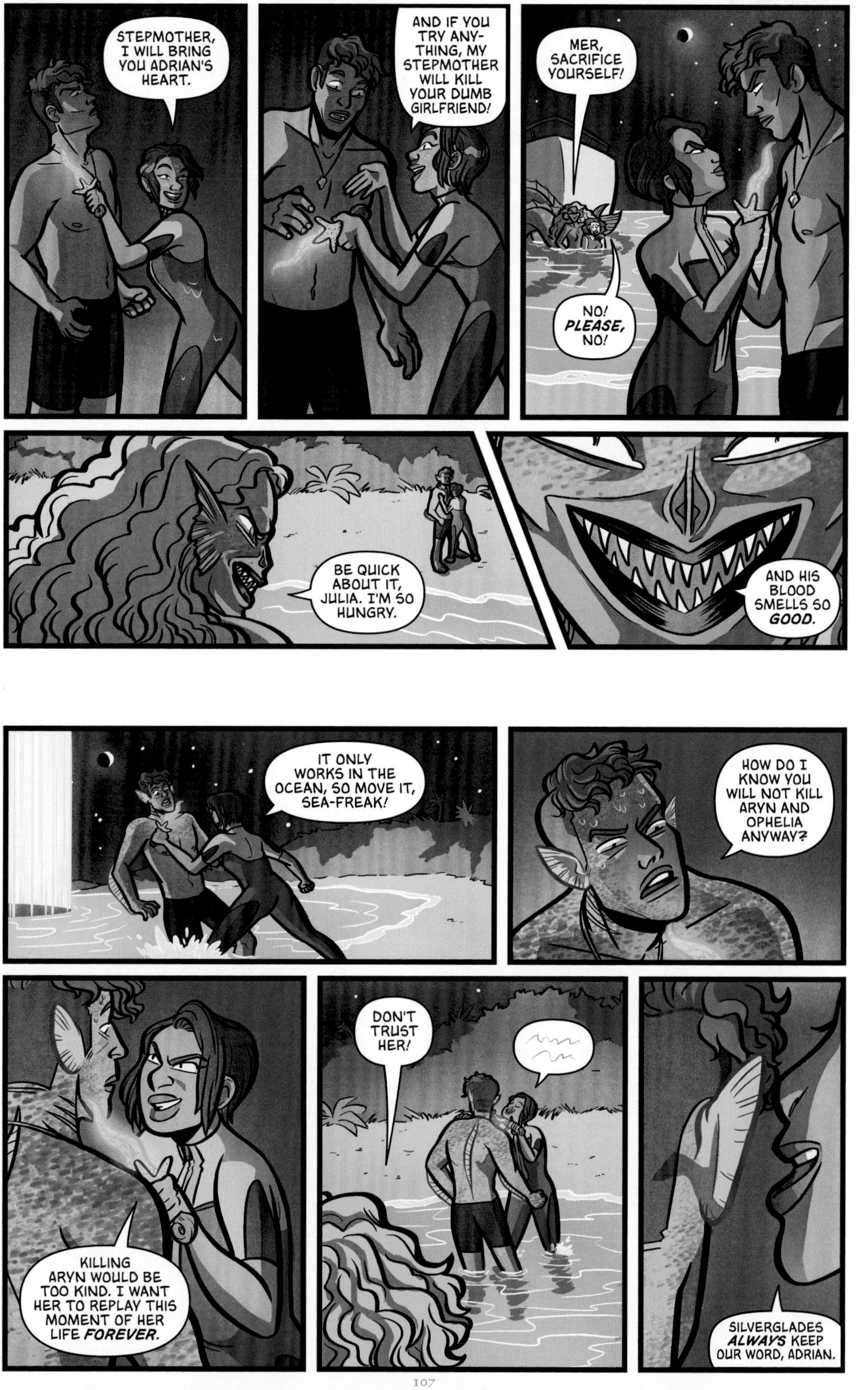
STEPMOTHER, I WILL BRING YOU ADRIAN'S HEART.
AND IF YOU TRY ANY-THING, MY STEPMOTHER WILL KILL YOUR DUMB GIRLFRIEND!
MER, SACRIFICE YOURSELF!
NO! *PLEASE,* NO!
BE QUICK ABOUT IT, JULIA. I'M SO HUNGRY.
AND HIS BLOOD SMELLS SO *GOOD.*
IT ONLY WORKS IN THE OCEAN, SO MOVE IT, SEA-FREAK!
HOW DO I KNOW YOU WILL NOT KILL ARYN AND OPHELIA ANYWAY?
KILLING ARYN WOULD BE TOO KIND. I WANT HER TO REPLAY THIS MOMENT OF HER LIFE *FOREVER.*
DON'T TRUST HER!
SILVERGLADES *ALWAYS* KEEP OUR WORD, ADRIAN.

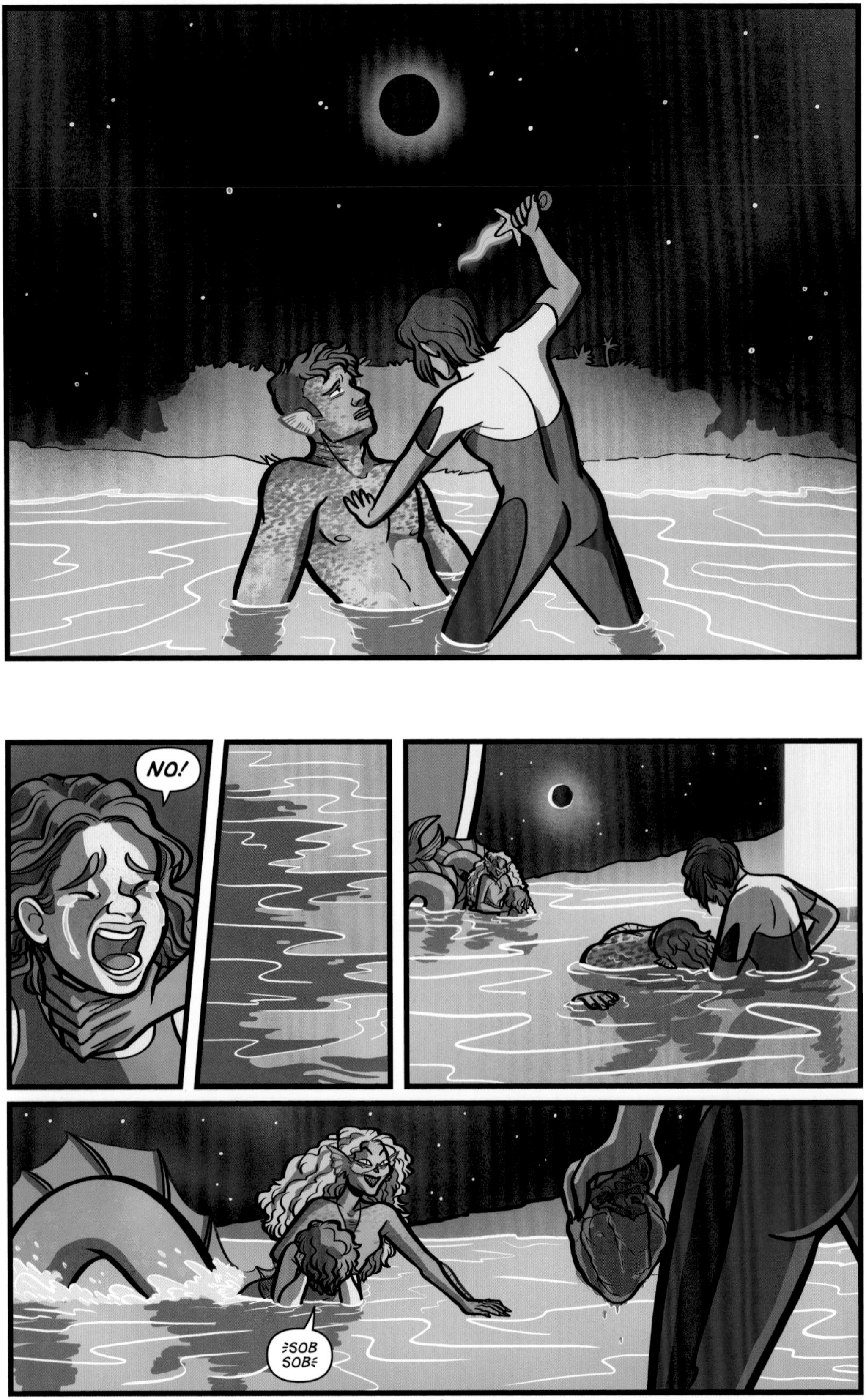
NO!
SOB SOB

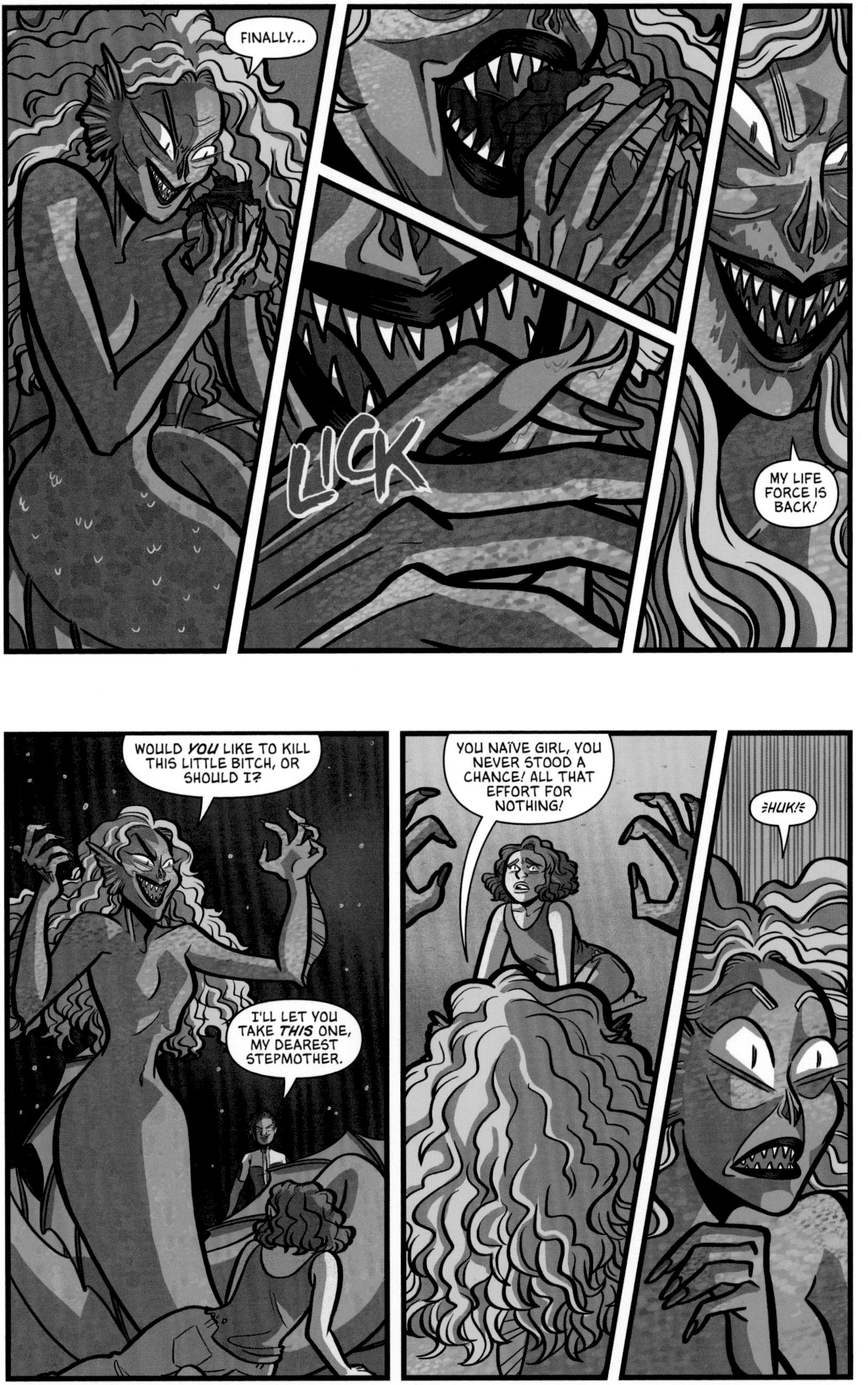
FINALLY...
LICK
MY LIFE FORCE IS BACK!
WOULD YOU LIKE TO KILL THIS LITTLE BITCH, OR SHOULD I?
I'LL LET YOU TAKE THIS ONE, MY DEAREST STEPMOTHER.
YOU NAÏVE GIRL, YOU NEVER STOOD A CHANCE! ALL THAT EFFORT FOR NOTHING!
HUK!

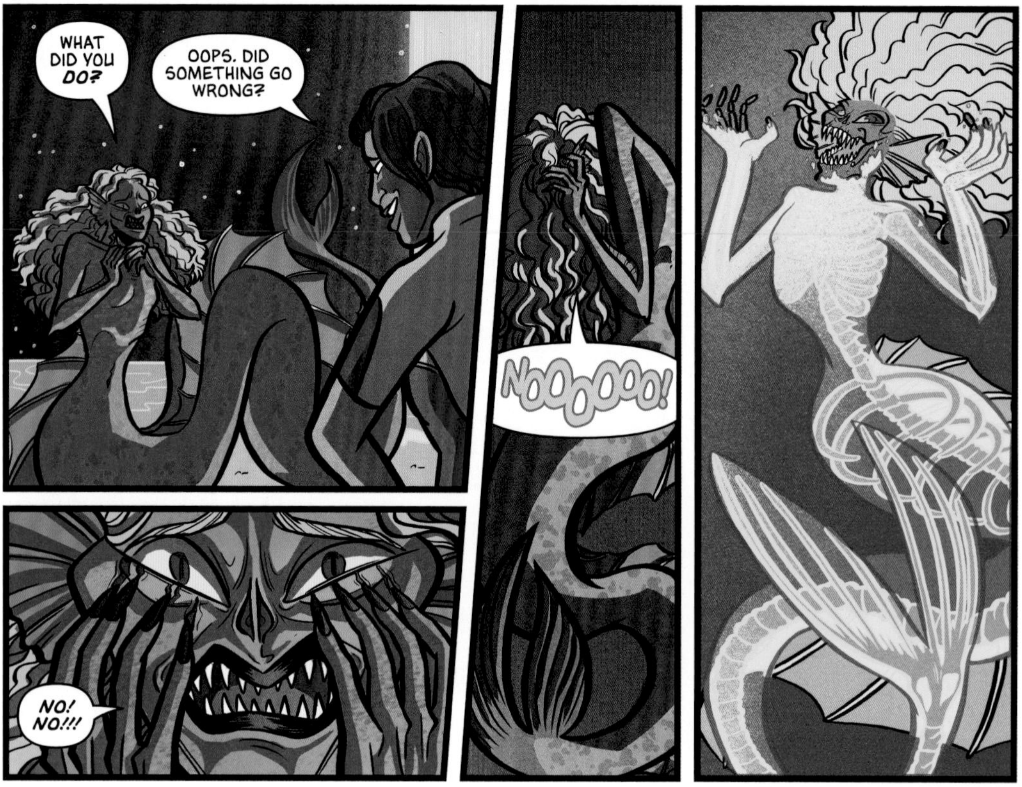
WHAT DID YOU *DO?*
OOPS. DID SOMETHING GO WRONG?
NOOOOOO!
NO! NO!!!

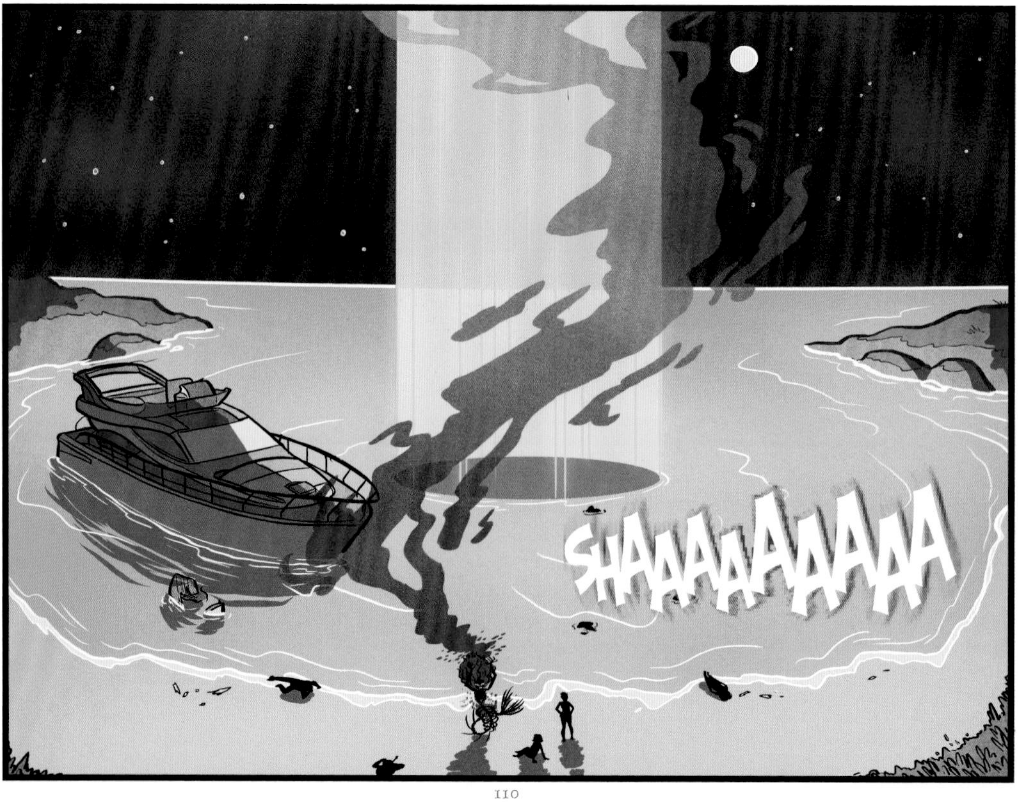
SHAAAAAAAAAA

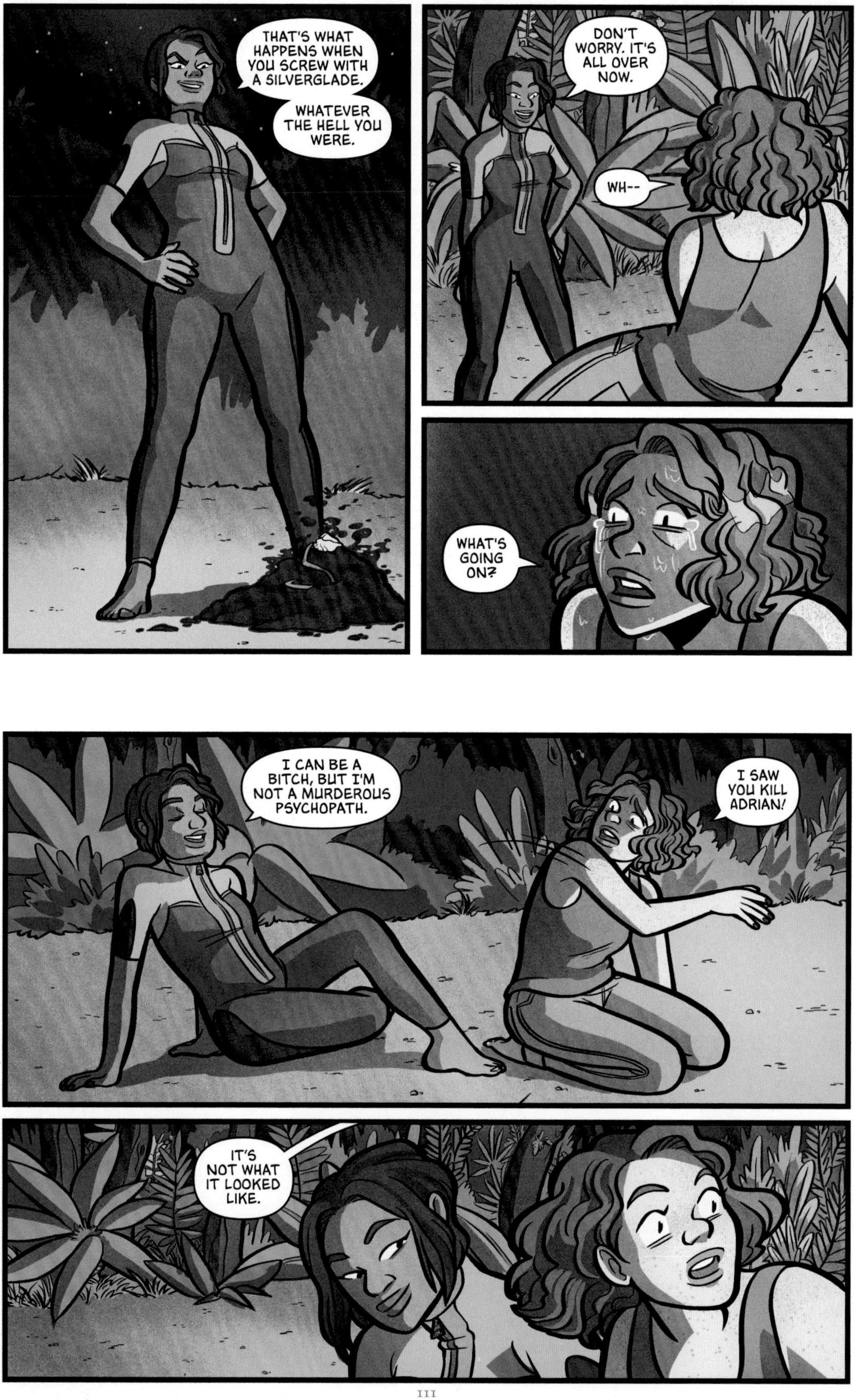
THAT'S WHAT HAPPENS WHEN YOU SCREW WITH A SILVERGLADE.
WHATEVER THE HELL YOU WERE.
DON'T WORRY. IT'S ALL OVER NOW.
WH--
WHAT'S GOING ON?
I CAN BE A BITCH, BUT I'M NOT A MURDEROUS PSYCHOPATH.
I SAW YOU KILL ADRIAN!
IT'S NOT WHAT IT LOOKED LIKE.

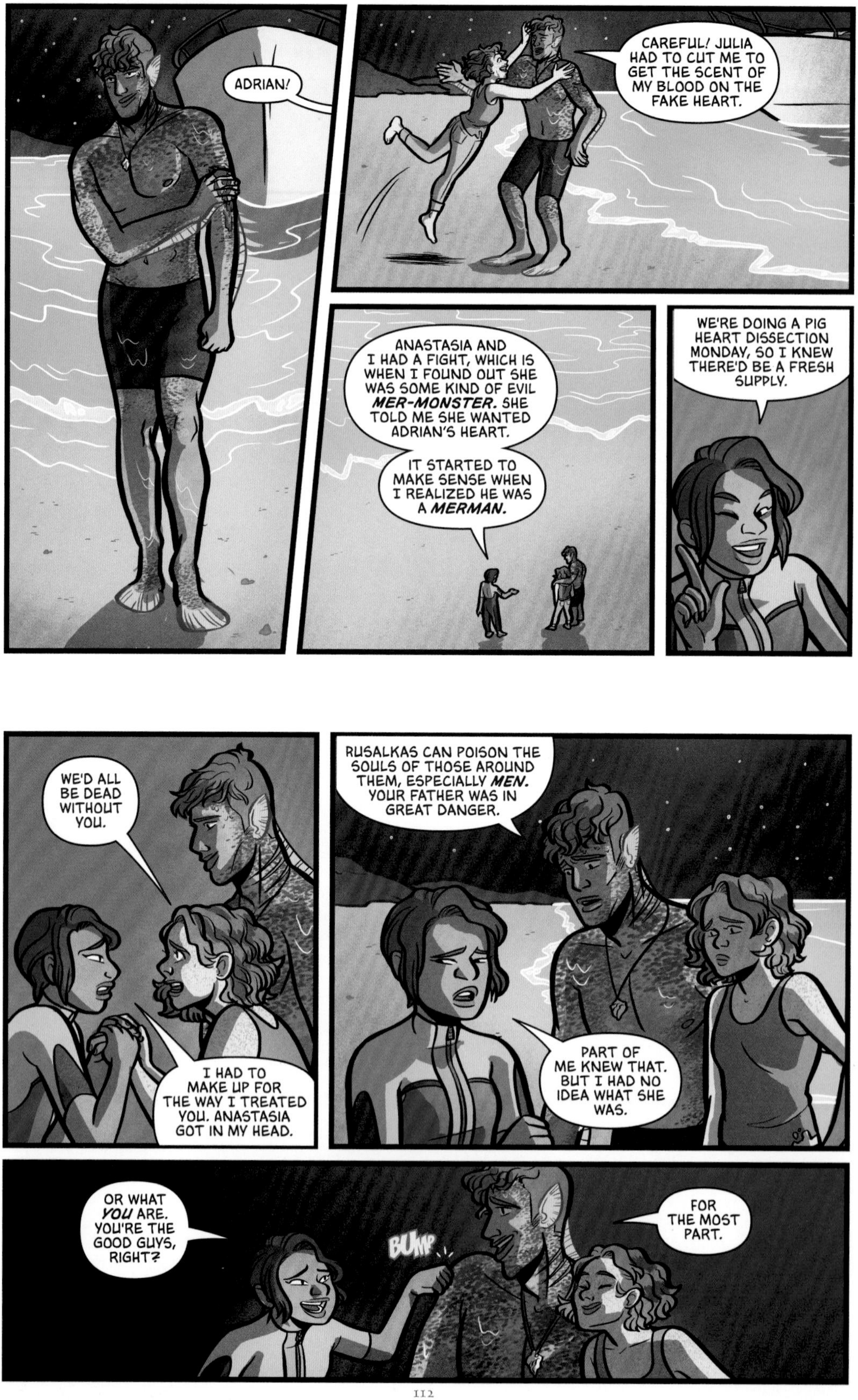
ADRIAN!
CAREFUL! JULIA HAD TO CUT ME TO GET THE SCENT OF MY BLOOD ON THE FAKE HEART.
ANASTASIA AND I HAD A FIGHT, WHICH IS WHEN I FOUND OUT SHE WAS SOME KIND OF EVIL *MER-MONSTER.* SHE TOLD ME SHE WANTED ADRIAN'S HEART.
IT STARTED TO MAKE SENSE WHEN I REALIZED HE WAS A *MERMAN.*
WE'RE DOING A PIG HEART DISSECTION MONDAY, SO I KNEW THERE'D BE A FRESH SUPPLY.
WE'D ALL BE DEAD WITHOUT YOU.
I HAD TO MAKE UP FOR THE WAY I TREATED YOU. ANASTASIA GOT IN MY HEAD.
RUSALKAS CAN POISON THE SOULS OF THOSE AROUND THEM, ESPECIALLY *MEN.* YOUR FATHER WAS IN GREAT DANGER.
PART OF ME KNEW THAT. BUT I HAD NO IDEA WHAT SHE WAS.
OR WHAT *YOU* ARE. YOU'RE THE GOOD GUYS, RIGHT?
BUMP
FOR THE MOST PART.

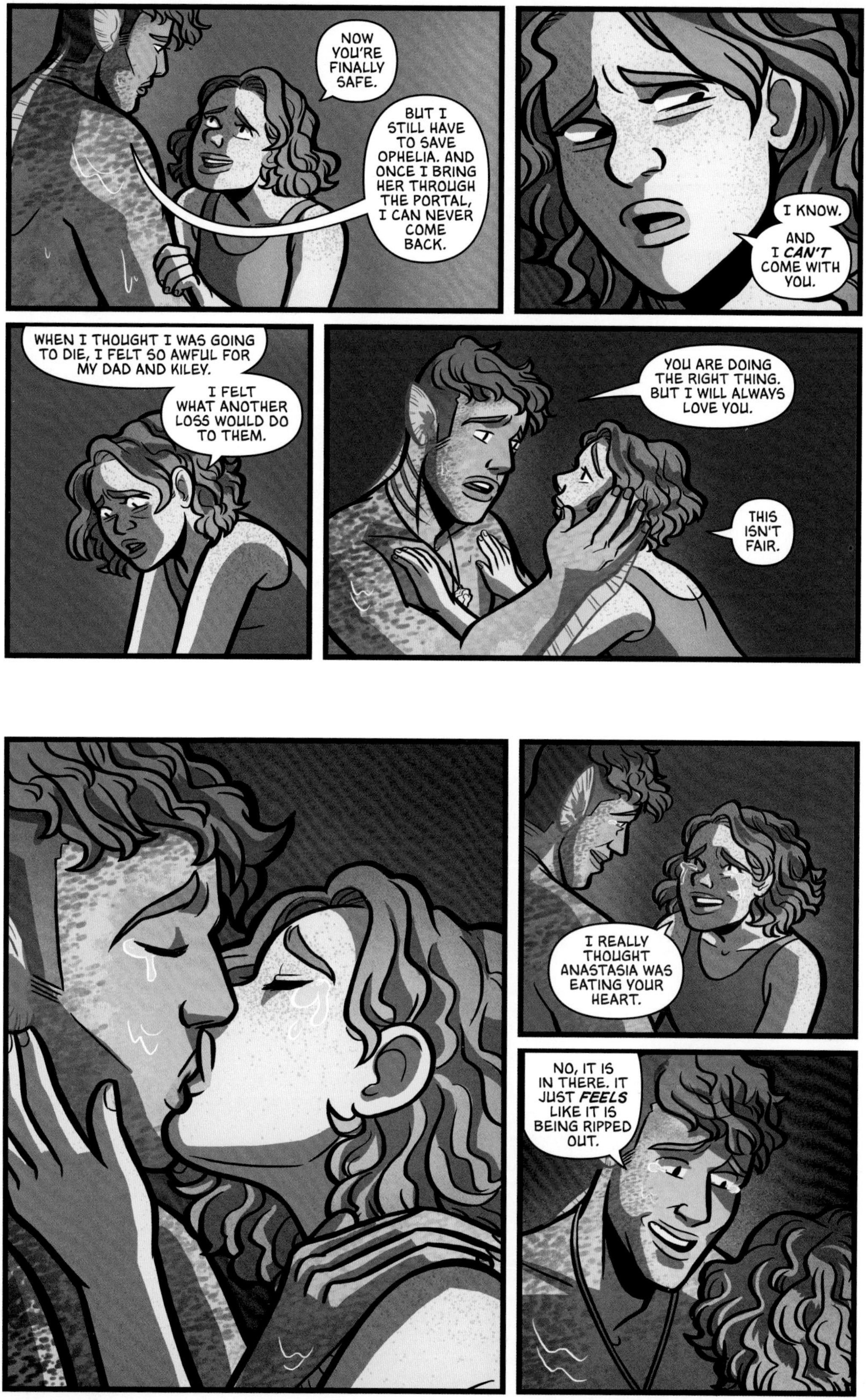
NOW YOU'RE FINALLY SAFE.
BUT I STILL HAVE TO SAVE OPHELIA. AND ONCE I BRING HER THROUGH THE PORTAL, I CAN NEVER COME BACK.
I KNOW.
AND I *CAN'T* COME WITH YOU.
WHEN I THOUGHT I WAS GOING TO DIE, I FELT SO AWFUL FOR MY DAD AND KILEY.
I FELT WHAT ANOTHER LOSS WOULD DO TO THEM.
YOU ARE DOING THE RIGHT THING. BUT I WILL ALWAYS LOVE YOU.
THIS ISN'T FAIR.
I REALLY THOUGHT ANASTASIA WAS EATING YOUR HEART.
NO, IT IS IN THERE. IT JUST *FEELS* LIKE IT IS BEING RIPPED OUT.

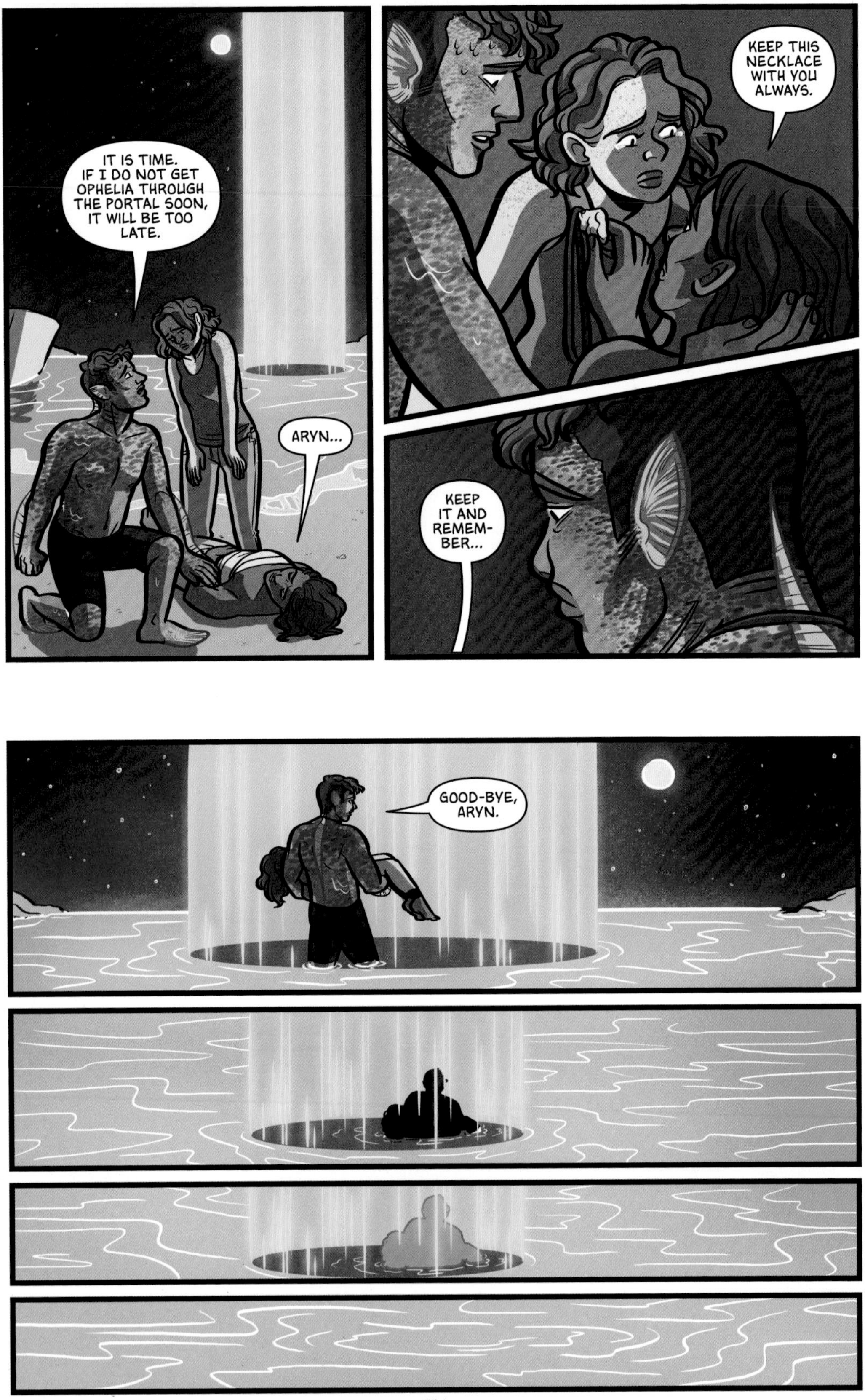
IT IS TIME. IF I DO NOT GET OPHELIA THROUGH THE PORTAL SOON, IT WILL BE TOO LATE.
ARYN...
KEEP THIS NECKLACE WITH YOU ALWAYS.
KEEP IT AND REMEM-BER...
GOOD-BYE, ARYN.

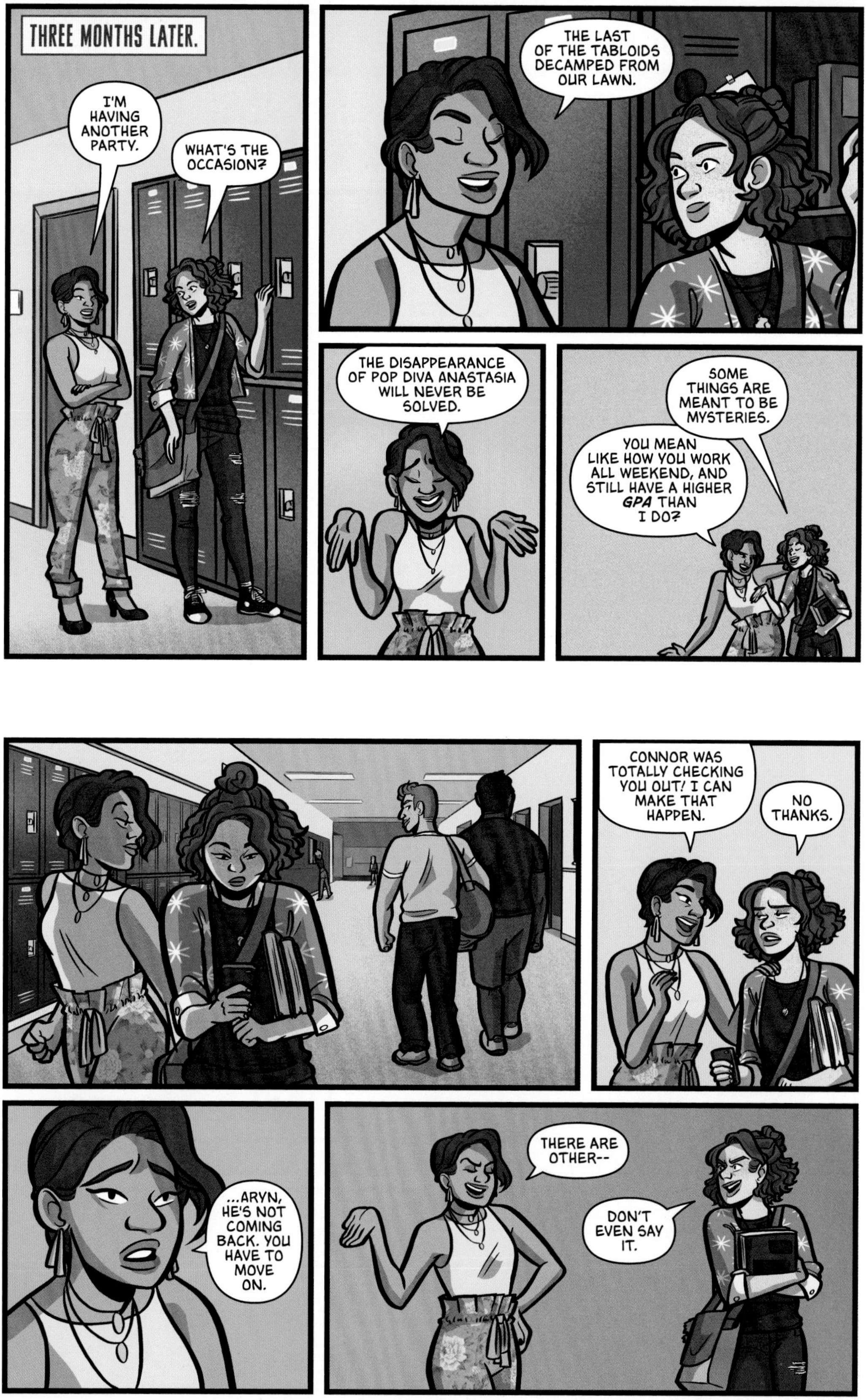
THREE MONTHS LATER.
I'M HAVING ANOTHER PARTY.
WHAT'S THE OCCASION?
THE LAST OF THE TABLOIDS DECAMPED FROM OUR LAWN.
THE DISAPPEARANCE OF POP DIVA ANASTASIA WILL NEVER BE SOLVED.
SOME THINGS ARE MEANT TO BE MYSTERIES.
YOU MEAN LIKE HOW YOU WORK ALL WEEKEND, AND STILL HAVE A HIGHER *GPA* THAN I DO?
CONNOR WAS TOTALLY CHECKING YOU OUT! I CAN MAKE THAT HAPPEN.
NO THANKS.
...ARYN, HE'S NOT COMING BACK. YOU HAVE TO MOVE ON.
THERE ARE OTHER--
DON'T EVEN SAY IT.

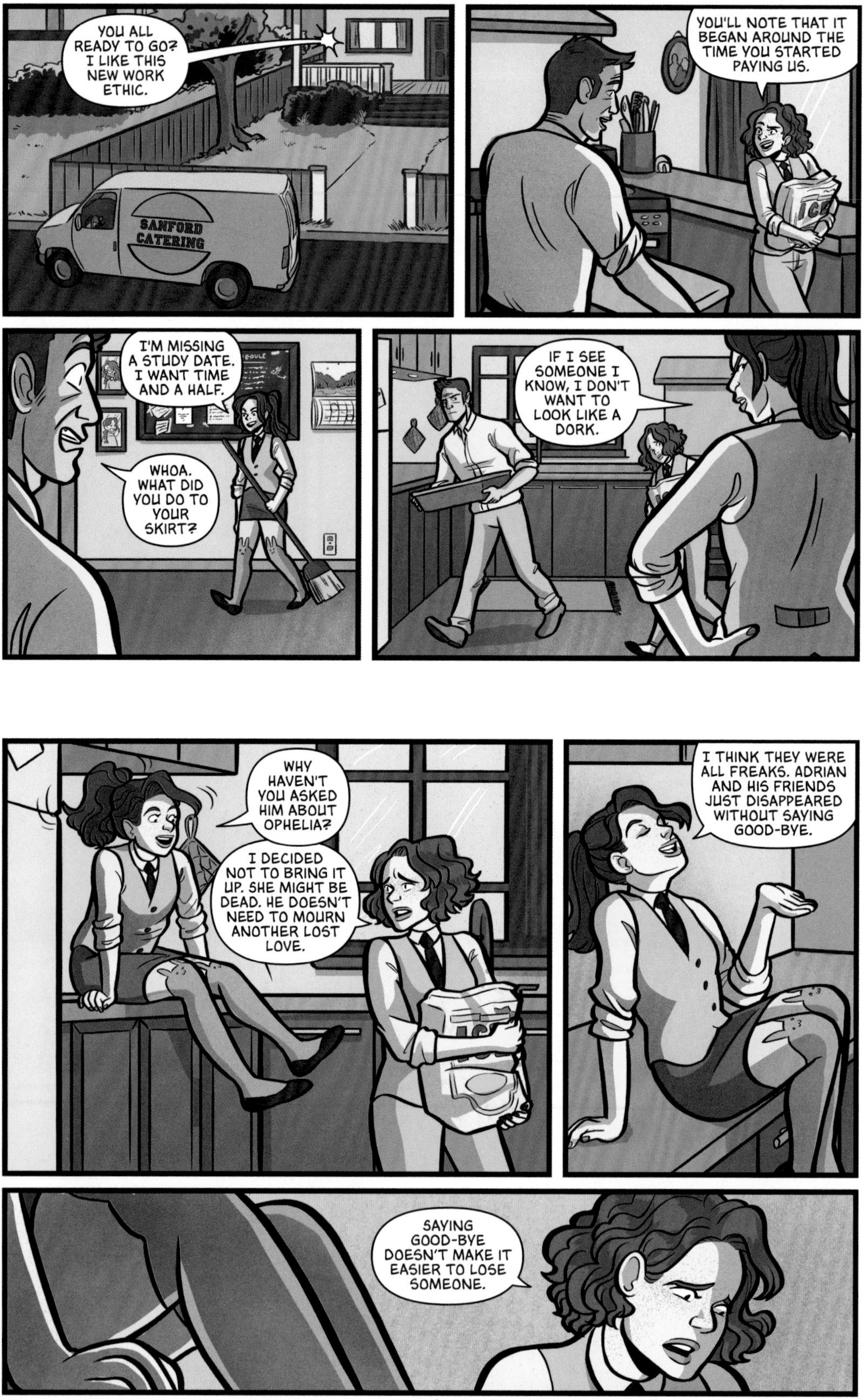
YOU ALL READY TO GO? I LIKE THIS NEW WORK ETHIC.
SANFORD CATERING
YOU'LL NOTE THAT IT BEGAN AROUND THE TIME YOU STARTED PAYING US.
I'M MISSING A STUDY DATE. I WANT TIME AND A HALF.
WHOA. WHAT DID YOU DO TO YOUR SKIRT?
IF I SEE SOMEONE I KNOW, I DON'T WANT TO LOOK LIKE A DORK.
WHY HAVEN'T YOU ASKED HIM ABOUT OPHELIA?
I DECIDED NOT TO BRING IT UP. SHE MIGHT BE DEAD. HE DOESN'T NEED TO MOURN ANOTHER LOST LOVE.
I THINK THEY WERE ALL FREAKS. ADRIAN AND HIS FRIENDS JUST DISAPPEARED WITHOUT SAYING GOOD-BYE.
SAYING GOOD-BYE DOESN'T MAKE IT EASIER TO LOSE SOMEONE.

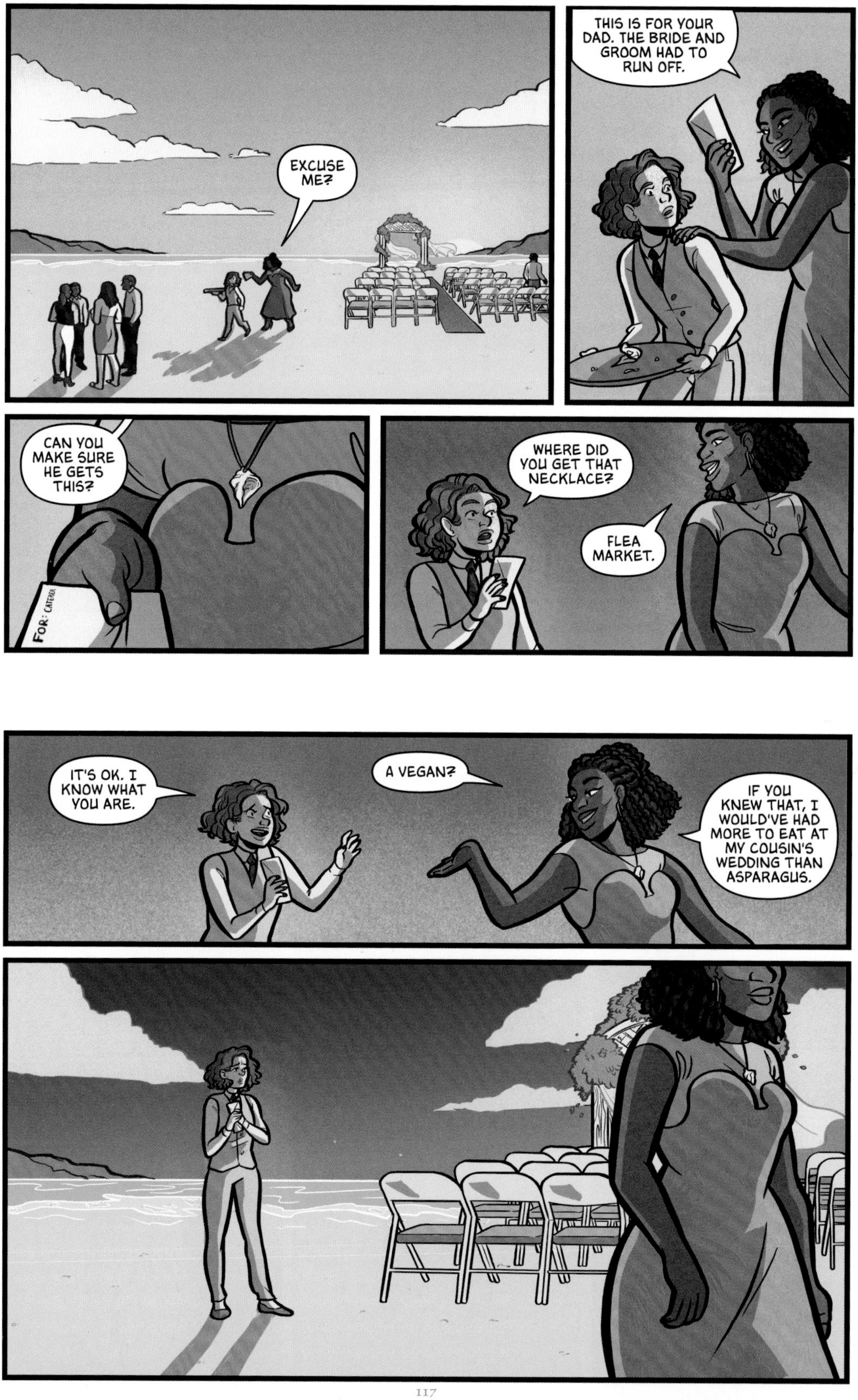
EXCUSE ME?
THIS IS FOR YOUR DAD. THE BRIDE AND GROOM HAD TO RUN OFF.
CAN YOU MAKE SURE HE GETS THIS?
FOR: CATERER
WHERE DID YOU GET THAT NECKLACE?
FLEA MARKET.
IT'S OK. I KNOW WHAT YOU ARE.
A VEGAN?
IF YOU KNEW THAT, I WOULD'VE HAD MORE TO EAT AT MY COUSIN'S WEDDING THAN ASPARAGUS.

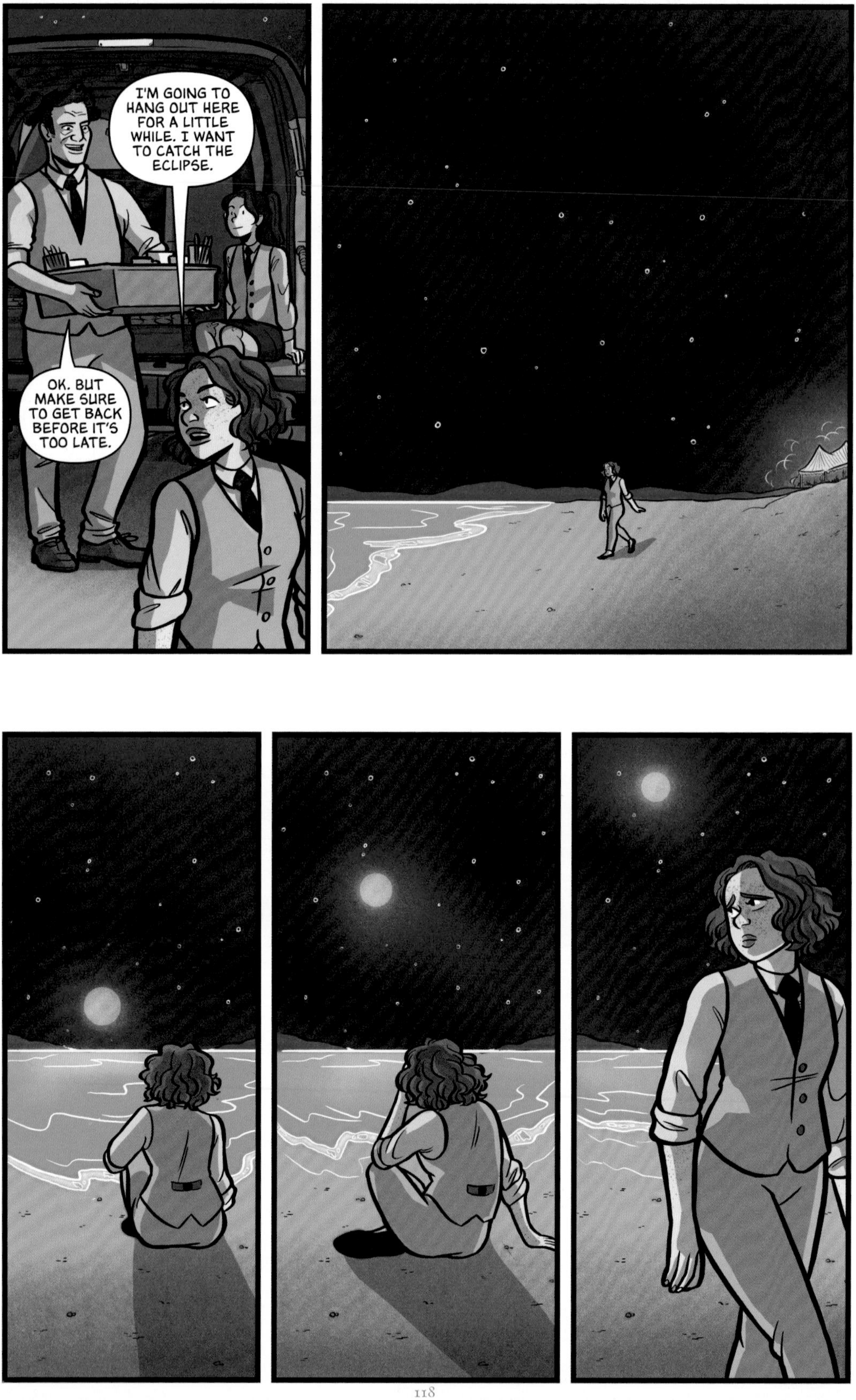
I'M GOING TO HANG OUT HERE FOR A LITTLE WHILE. I WANT TO CATCH THE ECLIPSE.
OK. BUT MAKE SURE TO GET BACK BEFORE IT'S TOO LATE.

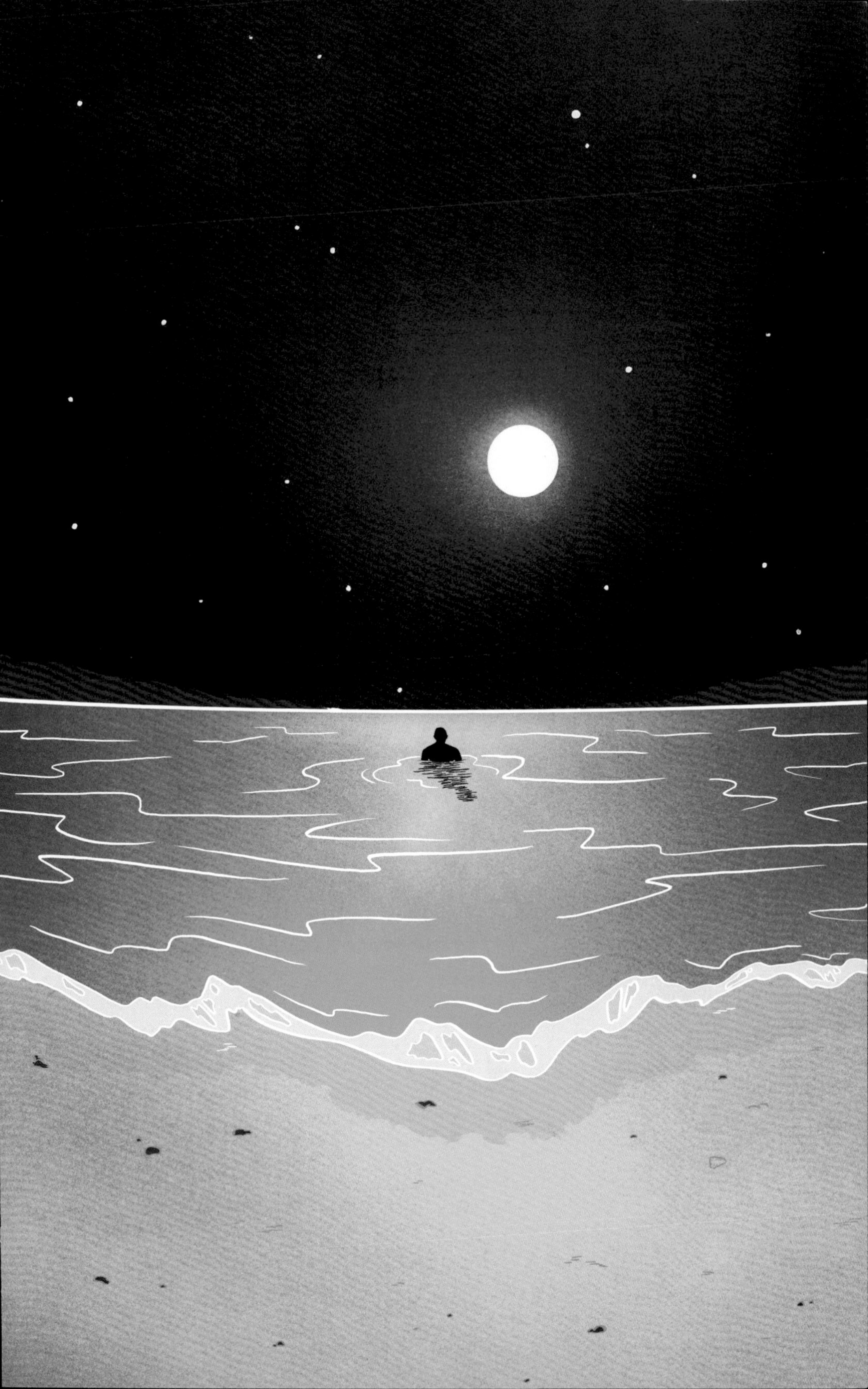

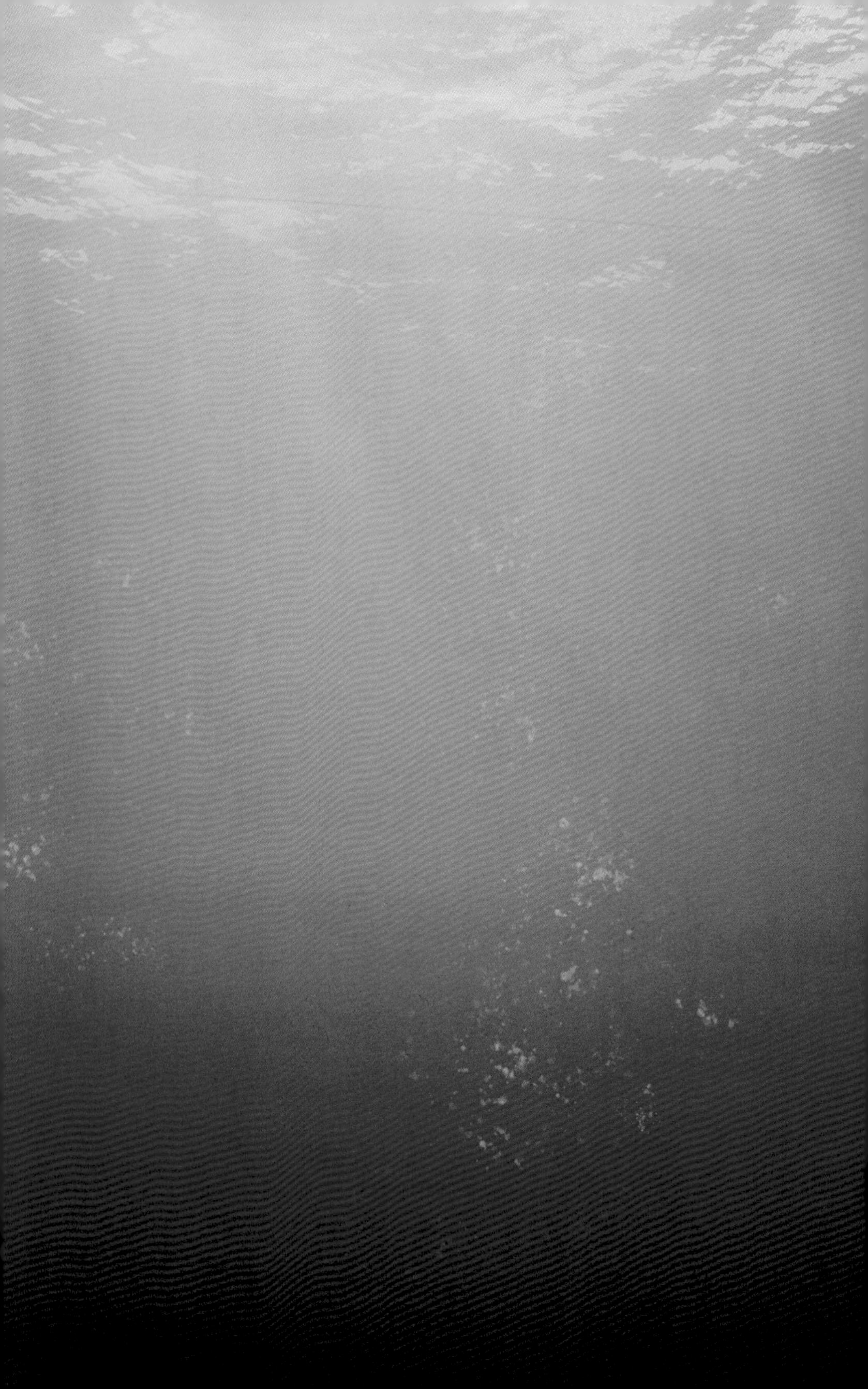

MER

NOTES & DESIGNS

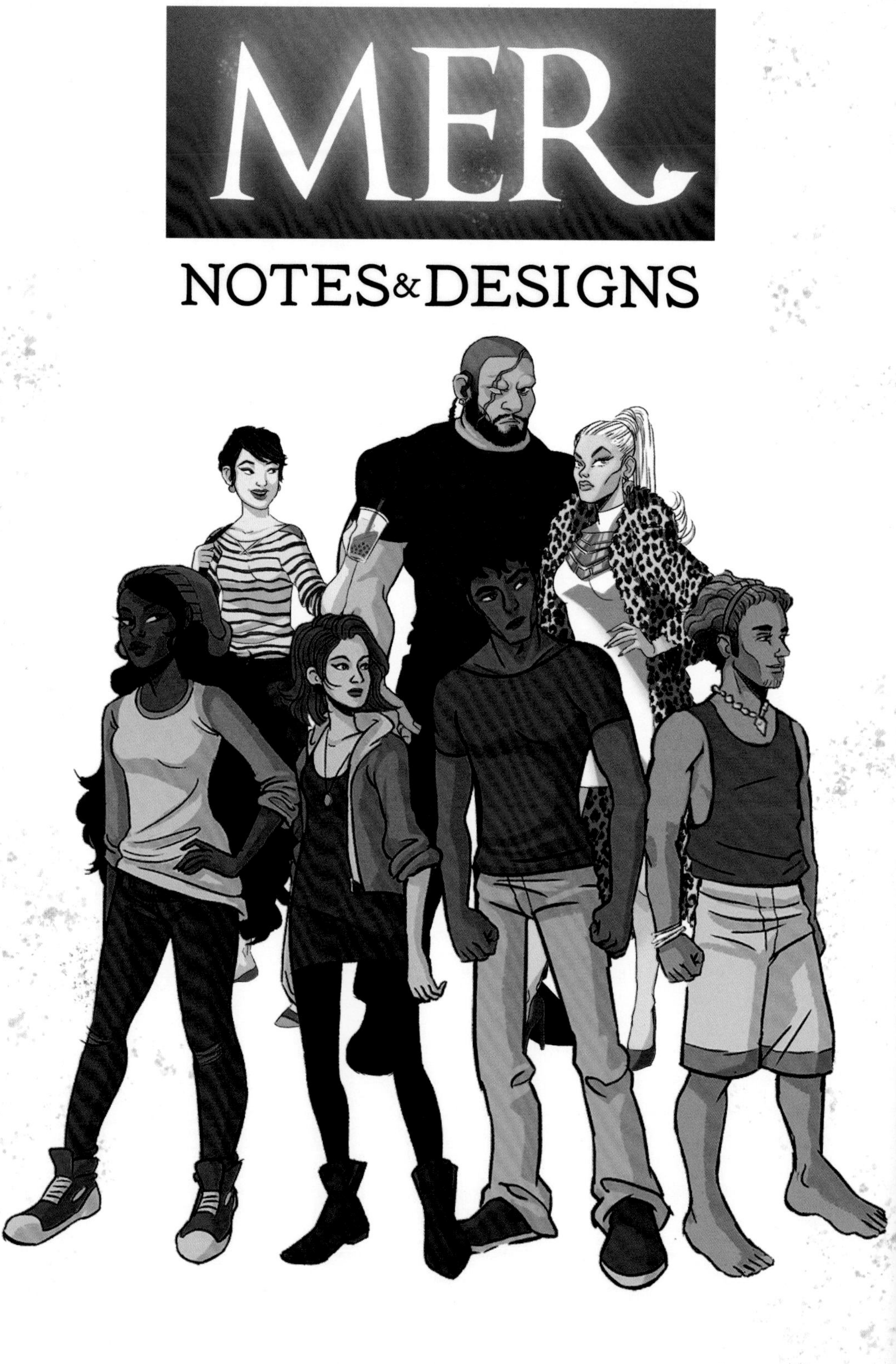

MORE ABOUT CREATURES OF THE SEA

Merfolk have been making waves in legends and folklore for thousands of years. Some of their earliest appearances occurred over 4,000 years ago. Oannes, the Babylonian god of the sea, had the lower body of a fish and a man's upper body. And the ancient Assyrians worshipped Atargatis, a fertility goddess who took the form of a mermaid.

African mythology describes the mermaid Mami Wata as a water spirit, while mermaids also appear in *The Arabian Nights*. Greek and Roman mythology is full of mermaids, mermen, and sirens [the merfolk's half-bird counterparts whose singing lures sailors to their deaths]. Nearly every seafaring culture has some form of merfolk myth.

However, some would argue that they're not all that mythical.

Christopher Columbus recorded mermaid sightings in his ship logs. Explorer Henry Hudson spotted them along the coast of Russia. All over the world, people have reported finding mermaids washed up on shore or caught by local fishermen. One of the most infamous displays was showman P. T. Barnum's Fiji Mermaid exhibit. A documentary film even contained footage purported to be of a submarine's brush with a mysterious mermaid.

Unfortunately, all of these claims either turned out to be hoaxes, or were never proven.

MERFOLK: FRIENDS OR FOES

Mermaids have been described as beautiful maidens who frolic in the waves, as well as hideous creatures who bring death and destruction to unlucky mariners. Centuries ago, it was common for sailors to tell of mermaids swimming alongside their boats. However, these explorers were probably encountering local marine life that was exotic to them, such as manatees or sea cows.

As scientists began to study the oceans, the mer people became more romanticized and less of a fisherman's worst nightmare. Hans Christian Andersen's story "The Little Mermaid"—as well as its more upbeat animated film adaptation—casts the lead character as a sympathetic figure who falls in love with a human. Mermaids in popular culture are often portrayed as being friendly and helpful, or even love interests to human men or women.

OTHER SEA CREATURES

Mermaids aren't the only legendary inhabitants of the sea. The tale of the rusalka began with pagan Slavic tribes who told of supernatural beings that emerged from the water each spring to fertilize crops. By the nineteenth century, these sprites evolved into reanimated drowning victims who haunted rivers and lakes. The rusalkas, described as great beauties, would lure men to their watery deaths—often by using their seductive voices. In Russia, Belarus, and the Ukraine, swimming was once forbidden during Rusalka Week in June, when these creatures were considered most active.

But mermaids and rusalkas have plenty of neighbors in the mythical waters. Selkies are seals who shed their skins to live as humans on land. Nixies are shape-shifting water sprites. And a kelpie is a water horse that can change into a human. If you read the mythology of various cultures, you'll find hundreds more.

ATLANTIS

According to legend, Atlantis was an advanced island civilization that, in a great disaster, was swallowed by the ocean. Nobody's sure where it was located, though theories range from near South America all the way to the North Pole. The ancient Greek philosopher Plato wrote that the people of Atlantis attacked the city of Athens. This angered the gods, who sunk the entire island. Other theories suggest Atlantis could have disappeared after a huge earthquake. Although this lost utopian society has been extensively studied, no archaeologist or oceanographer has found any evidence that Atlantis ever existed.

BIBLIOGRAPHY AND FURTHER READING
Alexander, Skye, *Mermaids: The Myths, Legends, and Lore*, Adams Media, 2012.
Breverton, Terry, *Phantasmagoria: A Compendium of Monsters, Myths and Legends*, Lyons Press, 2011.
Osborne, Mary Pope and Troy Howell (ill.), *Mermaid Tales from Around the World*, Scholastic, 1993.
Ventura, Varla. *Among the Mermaids: Facts, Myths, and Enchantments from the Sirens of the Sea*, Weiser Books, 2013

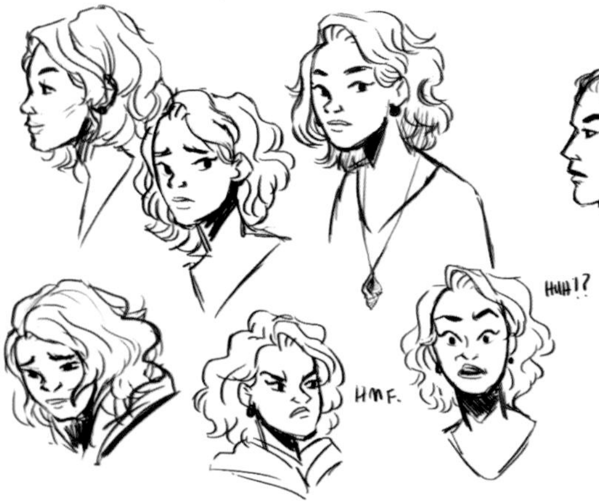
HUH!?
HMF.

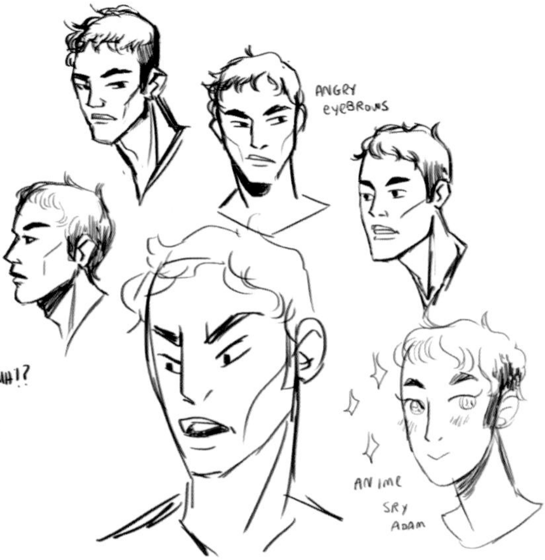
ANGRY eyebrows
ANIME
SRY
ADAM

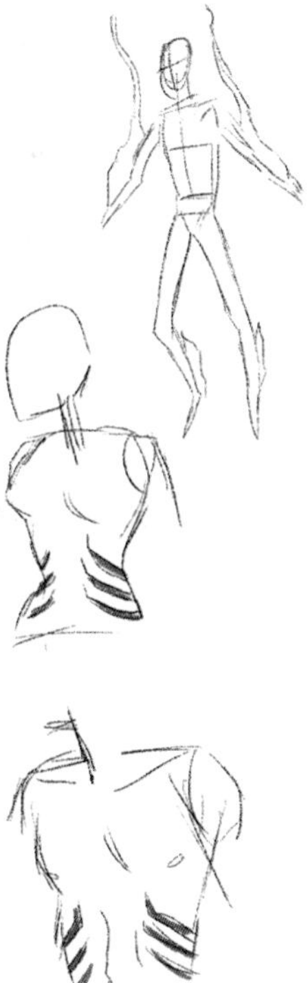

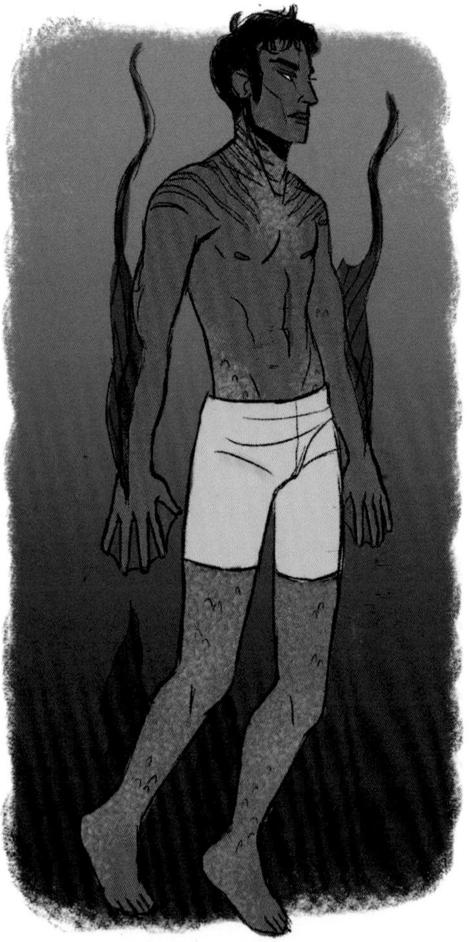

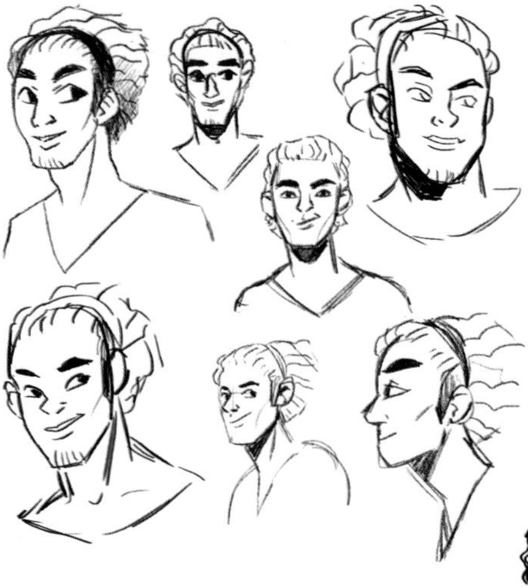

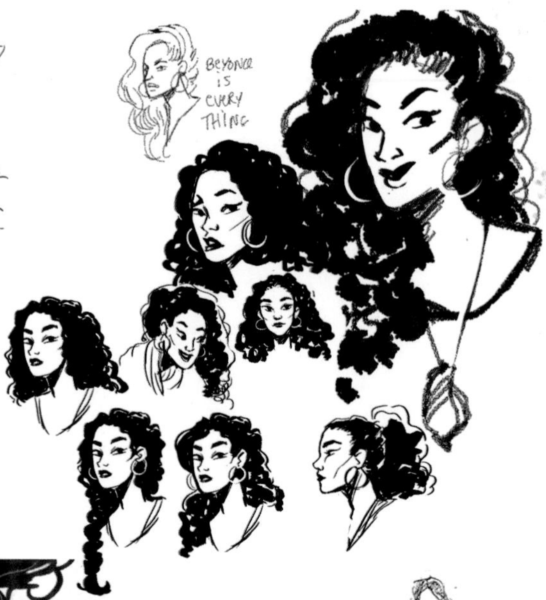
BEYONCE
IS
EVERY
THING

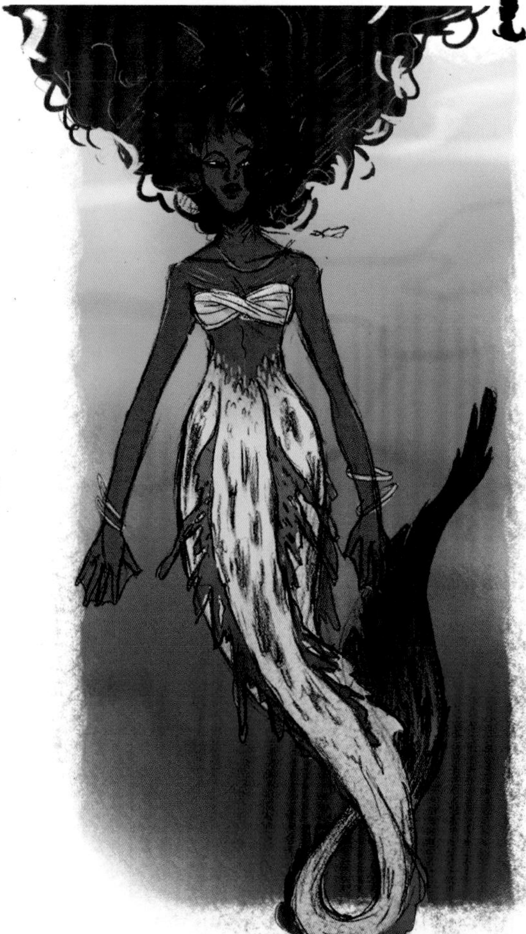

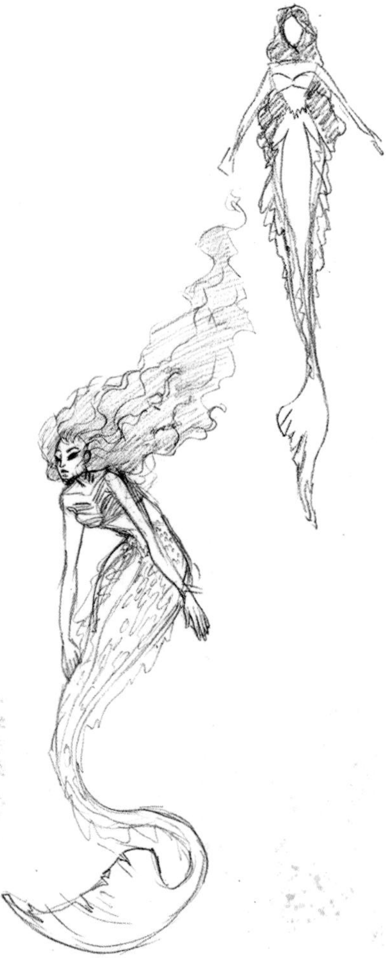

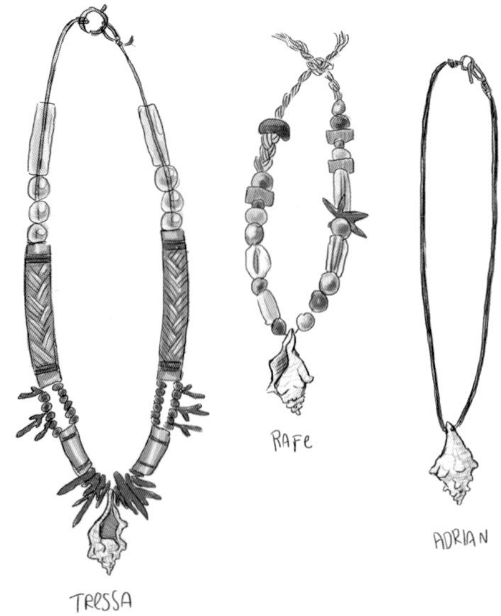
TRESSA
RAFE
ADRIAN

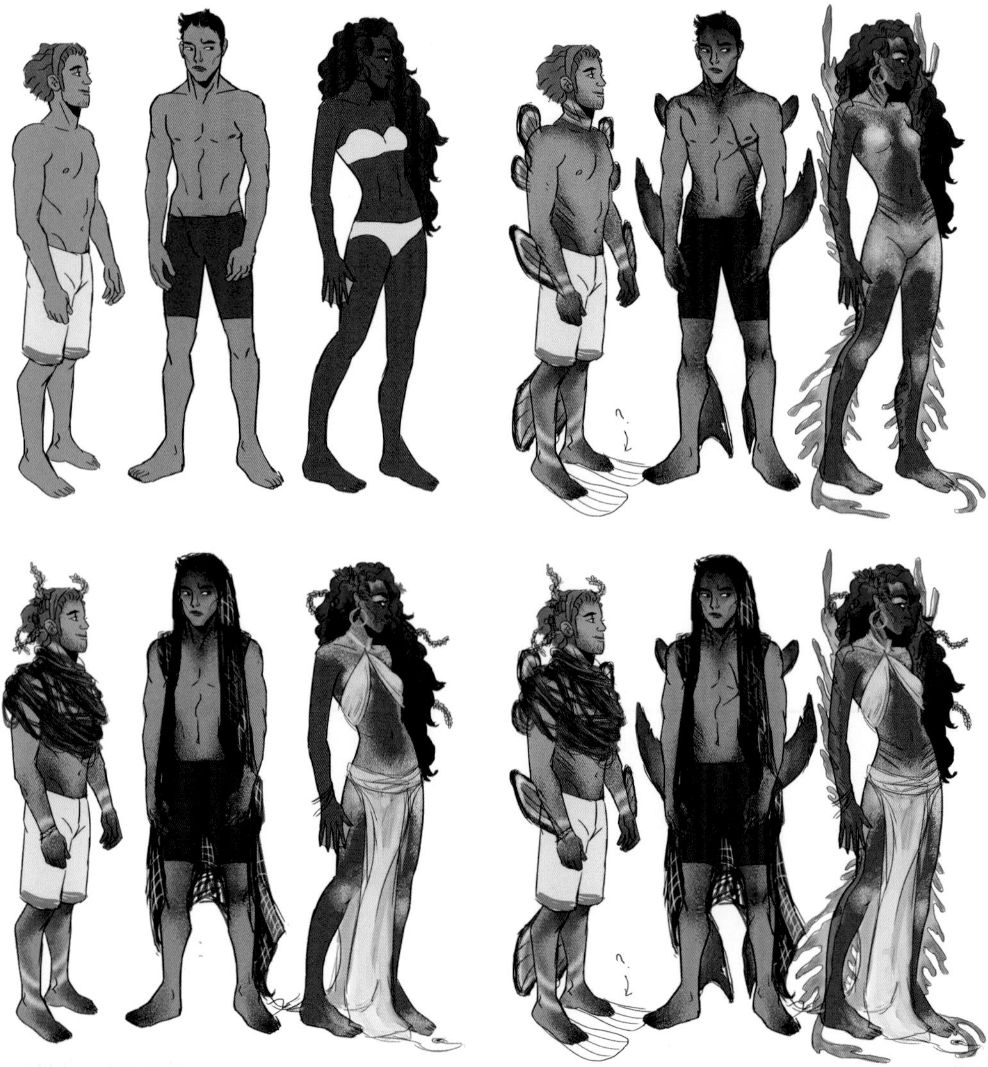

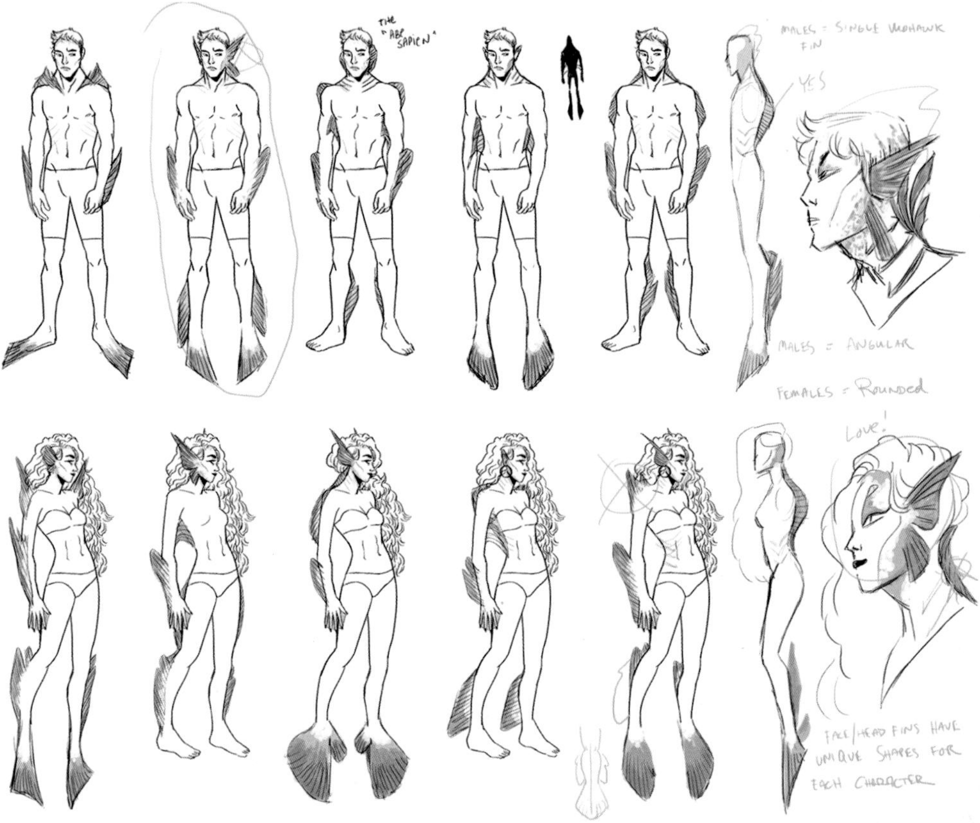
THE "ABE SAPIEN"
MALES = SINGLE MOHAWK FIN
YES
MALES = ANGULAR
FEMALES = Rounded
Love!
FACE/HEAD FINS HAVE UNIQUE SHAPES FOR EACH CHARACTER

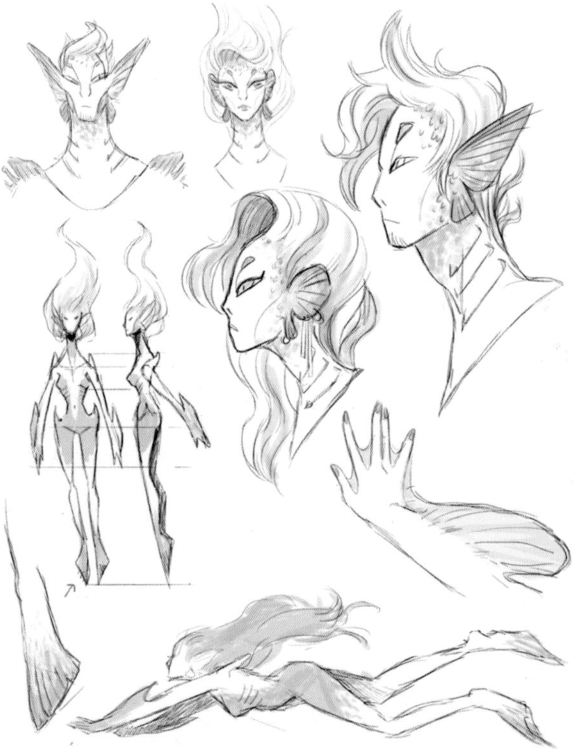